I0604589

COMING HOME

A HAVEN BAY NOVEL

KATIE BECK

Copyright © 2024 by Katie Beck

All rights reserved.

No part of this book may be reproduced in any form or by any electronic or mechanical means, including information storage and retrieval systems, without written permission from the author, except for the use of brief quotations in a book review.

This book is a work of fiction. The character and events in this book are fictitious. Any similarity to real persons, living or dead, is purely coincidental and not intended by the author.

Cover design by StorySpark Creative

Editing by StorySpark Creative

ISBN: 978-1-0688235-0-3 (print)

ISBN: 978-1-0688235-1-0 (ebook)

authorkatiebeck.com

For anyone who has ever lost themselves in a relationship.

I hope the journey to rediscovering who you are is the sweetest, most rewarding gift you give yourself.

You deserve it.

CHAPTER 1

AVERY

The best thing about small towns is that nothing ever changes.

The worst thing about small towns is that nothing ever changes.

A fresh coat of paint on Miss Carla's shop. A new awning on Thompson's Hardware. All minor changes but as a whole, still the same. Inside Miss Carla's display case lies her fat, white cat Audrey (named after Audrey Hepburn), where she has regally laid for as long as I can remember.

I would bet good money that Millie Loffman still comes in once a week, sneezing and red-eyed, to complain about Audrey. Miss Carla would then tell Millie for the umpteenth time that if Millie doesn't want to be near her "precious pussy" (her words, not mine), she could take her business elsewhere. As far as I know, Millie has yet to actually buy something from the store but shows up religiously every week to complain anyway.

A light snore comes from the backseat. Gavin's mouth hangs open with his head thrown back against his car seat. He made it through the first half of the drive on Goldfish crackers and questions about Gram's house before finally giving into sleep a few minutes ago.

I continue down Main Street, exploring the town. I used to know Haven Bay like the back of my hand and, though it's mostly stayed the same, there are some notable changes, too. I tell myself it's nostalgia that causes the lump in my throat.

Glad you're still good at lying to yourself.

A familiar sight springs into view, pulling me from my thoughts. I slow the car in front of my favorite building on the strip.

The Book Nook's light blue sign has seen better days and the once-matching blue and white awning has faded to almost white. But, as it always has, the familiar display of books in the windows causes a calm to wash over me. I breathe easily for the first time since leaving the city.

Turning my attention back to the street, I can't help but marvel at the picturesque view before me. Straight ahead, at the bottom of the hill where the road ends, is a small beach. The bay is calm today so the distant mountains appear mirrored on its clear, glass-like surface. The outline of the towering mountain tops against the pale blue sky make me feel both peaceful and free.

Something I haven't felt in a long time.

To the right of the beach, the old boardwalk stands strong and sturdy. I make a mental note to give Gavin a refresher on water safety before we visit the beach.

There are beautiful sights in the city but nothing beats the breathtaking view of Haven Bay.

It's no wonder tourists swarm to town every summer like bees to wildflowers. With an abundance of trails, cute cottages and unique shops downtown, Haven Bay is a tourist's paradise.

Slowing the car to a stop just before the hill, I drag my attention away from the water. The Main Street Diner's large red sign still hangs proudly on the front of the building. Below it, two older ladies sit at one of the bistro sets on the sidewalk. Maeve Monroe and Dottie Adams have occupied those same spots every day for the last twenty years, gossiping with anyone who stops to chat and ogling any man who passes by.

Luckily, they don't seem to have recognized my car. If they did, I'm sure they wouldn't hesitate to walk right into the middle of the street, traffic be damned. Getting hit by a car would be worth it for even a morsel of gossip. My reappearance after so many years away will have the rumor mill in a tizzy.

Shaking my head in silent laughter, I turn my car onto Maple Street where stores give way to old Victorian houses and modest bungalows. Tall, old trees line the street, towering over both sides while providing shade for the group of speed-walkers passing by. I slow the car as a team of preteens on rollerblades scurry to move hockey nets to either side of the street as I pass.

Finally, my mom's house comes into view. The small one-story is outdated with its plain white siding and simple land-scaping, but the house and yard are meticulously well-kept. I park my car along the curb and stare out the window at the home I grew up in. The combination of relief and regret cause my eyes to fill. Swiping at my face, I take a steadying breath and get out.

Leaving our meager luggage in the car, I slowly unbuckle Gavin from his car seat. Careful not to jostle my sleeping child, I scoop him into my arms and climb the steps of the front porch. The well-loved wooden porch swing sways in the light breeze beside me, as if waving in welcome.

Adjusting Gavin's weight, I pull open the screen door and knock. Through the glass in the door, my mom's slight frame enters the hallway, gingerly making her way to the door. The obvious effects of her sickness weighing on her causes a heaviness in my chest. It hurts my heart that her usual lively energy is nowhere in sight.

"Avery!" she calls as she pulls open the door. I lift a finger to my lips and point at Gavin's sleeping body. "I'm so happy you're here," she says, dropping her voice to a whisper.

As she ushers us in, I take in the dark circles under her eyes and the pallor of her skin. The heaviness in my chest deepens and I'm more sure than ever that I made the right decision coming home.

When I received the call last week from the hospital, I was shocked. Since I was listed as her emergency contact, the doctor called to inform me that my mom had collapsed while working in her bookstore. Luckily, a customer called 911 and she was rushed to the hospital. My mom is usually so vibrant and full of life. She has always seemed invincible, despite being diagnosed with multiple sclerosis when I was young.

The doctor explained that MS can cause something as harmless as a common cold to worsen into pneumonia. I'd known that this was a potential complication with her condition. Growing up, whenever my mom was sick, I would step up to help out around the house and at the shop. I always made sure she took the time to rest.

With me gone, I assumed she had Franny or one of her employees help her when she got sick. Instead, she ignored her symptoms over the last few weeks. Since she refused to rest, her body made the decision for her.

This is your fault. This would've never happened if you had been here.

Laying Gavin down on the couch in the living room, I turn and wrap my arms around my mom.

Well, I'm here now.

AFTER GAVIN WOKE up from his nap, he and my mom read a few of his favorite books on the couch while I made a light dinner. I couldn't help but smile at the sight of them cuddled together, my mom animatedly reading while Gavin giggled beside her. It doesn't seem like so long ago that it was me cuddling up beside her while she read the latest Junie B. Jones book.

When Gavin finally fell asleep, tucked into my old bed, my mom and I went outside to sit on the porch swing, each with a mug of tea and a cozy lap blanket. The late April days are starting to warm up, but the evenings still bring with them a chill.

Late spring in Haven Bay is usually the sweet spot of not too hot and not too cool. Soon, the combination of bugs and heat will make evenings outdoors uncomfortable.

I take a sip of my chamomile tea, letting the warmth slide through me. "So. Now that I'm here, will you please tell me what happened? You might be stubborn, but you're not usually careless. Especially about your health."

She sighs. "I know. Looking back, I should've just closed the shop when Tammy called saying little Jeremy had the flu. And with Franny being gone on her vacation with Pete, it was the perfect storm. I thought I could handle the shop for a few days on my own. Obviously it wasn't the right choice." She covers my hand with hers. "I'm so sorry I worried everyone. I promise to take better care in the future."

"Why didn't you call me? I could've helped you."

She gives me a pointed look that tells me exactly why she hadn't called.

Mitch.

Staring down at my hands, a pregnant silence falls upon us. After a moment, she breaks the tension by changing the subject to local gossip. No matter how hard you try, even the most reserved locals are weak to the allure of a small town rumor mill.

Eventually, our voices fade and the only sound is the swing creaking back and forth. Stars appear in the twilight sky. The dark blanket of night threatens to cover the retreating canvas of light. Even at this time, the amount of stars decorating the sky is more than the clearest night in the city. I gaze in wonder at the beauty, nostalgia washing over me like a warm bath.

Finally, my mom breaks the quiet and asks the dreaded question, "So, how long are you here for?"

I'm honestly surprised that she hasn't asked sooner. But I think she knows there's more to the story than what I've told her. More than what I'm ready to share yet.

I take a moment, choosing my words carefully. I know she would accept any answer I give her, even the full truth. But I'm not ready to get into it.

At least not tonight.

"I'm not sure. I know that's vague but I want to focus on you and getting you better before we dive into my mess."

She slowly nods. "Of course it is. I'm just happy to have the two of you for as long as I'm able."

I give her a shaky smile and then take a cleansing breath. "While I'm here, I'm going to take over for you at the shop." I hold up my hand to stop her protest. "You and I both know that if you don't rest, it's going to take twice as long to get your energy back. I'll bring Gavin with me to the store during the day and I'll coordinate with Tammy so she still keeps her part-time hours now that Jeremy's better."

"Avery, as much as I appreciate your help, I can't ask you to do that. I'm about to start the renovations next door. It's going to be loud and complicated keeping the business running while expanding." Her brow furrows and it's like looking in a mirror. I know that look well since I do the same when I'm worried or upset.

I mimic her gesture from earlier, placing my hand over hers. "Mom, I've got this. You can trust me. I love the shop as much as you do and I am ecstatic that you're finally going through with adding on the cafe. I promise to make sure it's done to the Angie Owens standard."

That makes her smile. "Fine. But as soon as these bags under my eyes are gone, I'll be up there every day pestering both you and the construction crew."

"Deal." I lean back in my seat and take another sip of my tea. "Who's doing the expansion anyway?" Humor flashes in my mom's eyes so fast I'm not sure I actually saw it.

"Taylor Construction."

I have no idea what that was about but I'm sure I'll find out soon enough. For now, I let the breeze caress my cheek and carry my worries away, feeling content for the first time in a really long time.

The next morning, Gavin and I walk hand-in-hand down the sidewalk to the bookshop. He babbles along beside me about how Gram promised they could bake cookies together later and rent the new Spider-Man movie this weekend. I'm not sure who's more excited that we're here—Gavin or my mom.

The light breeze ruffles our hair. The sun warms our skin while the trees glisten with morning dew. Spring is making way for summer and nature is rejoicing in the change.

Convinced that she was feeling well enough to take Gavin during the day, my mom offered to babysit him while I was at the shop. I stuck to my guns and told her at least one more week of rest first. Gavin isn't as busy as he was when he was a toddler but 4-year-olds still have a lot of energy. He wears me out on my best day so I was going to make sure neither of them overdid it. Even if that makes me the bad guy.

Turning onto Main Street, Gavin's rambling slows as he takes in the town. He was asleep when we first drove through, so I turn him away from town to point out the hill that leads down to the beach. His eyes grow as he takes in the glistening water and long, raised boardwalk.

"Can we go see it, Mommy? We've never been to the beach before! Please, Mommy?" He practically vibrates beside me.

"You have so," I laugh. "You were just too little so you don't remember." My laugh fades. It's been so long since we were here last, he doesn't even remember it.

And whose fault is that? my mom guilt asks.

I shake the thought aside and squeeze Gavin's hand. "We can't go right now, buddy. We have to go open the shop. But how about we go after dinner tonight? I'm sure Sushi would love to go, too."

Sushi is my mom's white and tan Shih Tzu and Gavin's new shadow. He declared her his bestest friend ever at bedtime last night when she jumped onto his bed and promptly fell asleep at his feet.

"Sushi would *love* the beach! I bet she's the best swimmer *ever!*" he exclaims. He continues walking, telling me all the things that he and Sushi will do tonight.

We pause for the few cars to pass before we can cross the street. A throat clears behind me, followed by a raspy, "Call my doctor, Maeve. I must be hallucinating. Ain't no way that's little Avery Owens—back from the dead!"

Holding back a sigh, I force a smile and turn to the voice behind me. Dottie and Maeve are perched in their usual spot in front of the diner.

"Mornin' Dottie, Maeve. It's good to see you, too," I say, choosing to ignore the dig about my absence.

"Well, now. Who's this handsome gentleman?" Maeve leans forward in her chair, reaching out to grab Gavin's cheek.

He grimaces at the pinch and scoots closer to me.

"This is my son, Gavin. Can you say hi to Dottie and Maeve, Gav?"

He gives a small wave and a quiet "hi" before turning his face into my leg.

"What an adorable little boy! Looks just like his mama. Not like his uptight, grump of a da–"

"Well, we better get over to the shop," I say loudly, cutting Dottie off so Gavin doesn't hear the rest of her comment. I turn him away and take a couple of steps in the opposite direction. "I'm sure I'll see you two again soon."

We hurry across the street but not before I hear Dottie yell after us. "Be a dear, Avery, and check and see if my *Fifty Shades of Grey* book is in! Harold's back is feeling better and we're—"

Unlocking the door to the bookshop, I guide Gavin inside before quickly closing the door behind us. I sag against the frame, unsure whether to laugh or gag at the thought of Dottie and her boyfriend, Harold, attempting to recreate any of the scenes in the erotic book.

"Mommy, what's *Fifty Shades of Grey*?"

How is it only 9 am?

I SPEND the morning working through the list of tasks that had fallen to the wayside while my mom was sick. I clean the tops of the bookshelves, check inventory, and update the list of authors' release dates.

Before long, it's time to open the shop. I'm pleasantly surprised by the steady stream of customers until quickly realizing that most are locals more interested in prodding me for information on my sudden reappearance than they are in finding their next read.

It shouldn't surprise me. Haven Bay's rumor mill has always been quick and plentiful, though often fantastical.

It seems there are a number of crazy explanations behind my sudden arrival. One is that I lost my house to a gambling addiction (those damn ponies will get ya!). Another is that I'm pregnant with Chris Evans's love child and he paid me off to raise the baby alone in Haven Bay.

Can't say I hate that rumor. At least I hooked up with Captain America in that one.

My personal favorite was when the church's elderly pianist, Mrs. Creevey, pulled me aside while I was working on the window display. Dropping her voice to a conspiring tone, she told me that if I ever needed a place to hide out from "the fuzz", she had a spare bedroom and her husband's old shotgun ready and waiting.

"In case things get messy," she whispered with a wink.

I don't know whether I should be impressed or concerned at the way our town spins tales for their entertainment.

Since she's the third person to imply such a thing, I decided to go with it. "I appreciate it. Do you have a large safe I could borrow, too?"

The look on her face was worth the guilt of lying to such a sweet, old lady.

Around noon, I set Gavin up with another book and his favorite lunch—a peanut butter sandwich with a side of apple slices. Once he's settled on the couch, I turn to see a tall, slim woman with long chestnut hair breezing through the door. She's dressed in a chicly-cropped leather jacket and white skinny jeans. The stylish outfit combined with her confident stride make her seem more likely to be on a runway than in Haven Bay.

"Good morning! Can I help you with anything?" I ask.

"I hope so. Is it true you just escaped a religious cult and you came back to plan your revenge on the leader?" the woman deadpans.

I'm stunned silent for a moment. "Well, that's a new one," I mutter, shaking my head in disbelief. This town should write fiction. "Sorry to disappoint you but no, nothing that exciting.

Angie is my mom and I came back to help her at the store while she recovers from pneumonia."

"Damn. Well, there goes twenty bucks. Though I would've loved to see Lana Murphy's eyes bug out when I told her that it was true." She laughs. "My name's Jolie St. James. I own Amaryllis, the yoga studio next door. When it's nice out, you'll probably hear us in the park behind the shops."

"Avery Owens." For some reason, using my married name doesn't seem right here. In Haven Bay, I've always been Avery Owens. It only seems fitting to go by Owens again now that I'm back.

I reach over and shake her hand. "Sorry, 'hear' you? Isn't yoga usually pretty quiet?"

"Not the way I do it, honey," she replies with a wink.

I have no idea what that means but I'm instantly intrigued. The pull I felt to her earlier strengthens and I can't help but like her already.

"Anyway, so if you weren't in a cult—" she raises an eyebrow at me as if to make sure I haven't changed my mind since she last asked.

I haven't so I shake my head.

She looks almost disappointed when she asks, "Where have you been all this time?"

Coming from anyone else, the question would be intrusive and rude. For some reason, coming from Jolie, it just seems like genuine curiosity.

I surprise myself by answering truthfully. "Edmonton. I moved there for college and have been there ever since."As much as I seem to trust Jolie, I don't know her well enough to go into further detail, so I stick to the basics. "This is my son, Gavin. He's helping me out today while Gram rests."

"As much as a woman like Angie can rest," Jolie chuckles.

I smile back. I was right in my assessment of Jolie. She clearly knows my mom well enough to make that kind of statement. My mom prides herself on being active and independent. She used to joke that the MS will eventually take her mobility, but it would have to take it from her kicking and screaming.

"Well, aren't you a handsome little devil!" Jolie exclaims, looking over to where Gavin is sitting. "And such good taste in comics, too. Spider-Man is the coolest!"

Gavin's eyes go wide. He may be a shy kid when you first meet him, but the fastest way to get to his heart is through dogs and superheroes. "You read Spider-Man, too?"

She nods. "I have an older brother who loved comic books as a kid. Spider-Man and me go way back."

Encouraged, Gavin launches into a lengthy explanation on why Spider-Man is the best superhero to ever live. Jolie plops herself on the couch beside him, holding her own with the superhero lingo. So much so that they hardly notice when I walk away a few minutes later to help a customer.

Eventually, Jolie offers him a fist bump and climbs off the couch. "Well, Gav, as much as I'd love to talk Spidey with you all day, I have a class in twenty minutes I need to go set up for." Turning to me, she says, "You should come to one of my classes sometime. I have my schedule posted on the front window next door and on my website. You'll like it; I promise."

She heads toward the door but stops and turns back suddenly. "Hey, I know this might sound weird, but Haven Bay is a small place and there's only so many local women our age. Would you want to have lunch sometime? I have a class tomorrow at noon but I could come by after."

I bite back the grin that threatens to overtake my face.

Play it cool, Avery.

"That sounds great."

"Awesome. I'll see you both then. Bye Avery, bye Gav!"

I think I just made a friend.

CHAPTER 3

MATT

"So I told that two-bit Millie that if she so much as utters Audrey's name one more time, I'm going to fill her mailbox with kitty litter."

I'll never know what I did to piss Bud off so much that he continues to stick me with Miss Carla's jobs. What I do know is that the punishment definitely does not fit the crime.

I've heard more gossip since I showed up to fix her dressing room door at her shop than I have all week around town. In the last twenty minutes, I've learned that Jerry Jenkins slept on his front porch again last night after his wife kicked him out and that Pastor Dan caught the Franklin twins trying to steal from the collection plate on Sunday. Now, it seems to be time for the latest Millie Loffman drama.

Did I ask for any of this information, you might wonder? Not even the slightest. In fact, I've managed to get in about three words this whole time.

She finally pauses to take a breath.

"Well, if you ever need bail money, you know I've got your back, Miss Carla." I say, giving her a wink.

She giggles. "Oh, Matt Brady, you're always good for a laugh."

The familiar cloud of dread rolls over me.

Yep, that's me. Good ol' Matt Brady. Good for a laugh but not much else.

Shoving the thought aside, I turn back to my work and finish screwing the fixed door back onto its hinges. Miss Carla continues onto the next juicy tidbit but I tune her out.

A small whimper grabs my attention and I look over my shoulder to see my dog, Ham, inching closer to me. He keeps low to the ground, his eyes never leaving the front window where the proud and powerful Audrey sits perched on her ledge.

You'd think that my ninety-pound mutt would be the one glowering at the ten-pound Persian cat instead of the other way around. But Ham is a softy and Audrey is as temperamental as her owner. I don't blame him for cowering into me. If I could do the same right now, I would.

"...Connie said she was on the run from the police but I told her there's no way our sweet Avery could've robbed a whole jewelry store by herself. At least not without a decent getaway car that is. That old Volvo she pulled up in wouldn't be able to take corners well enough for that."

My head jerks up at the mention of that name. Miss Carla keeps talking but I interrupt. "Did you say Avery? As in Avery Owens?"

Miss Carla stops long enough to give me a triumphant look. She knows she has my attention now. I'm sure she's making note of my sudden interest to report back to the rest of the town but I don't give a shit. I need to make sure I heard her right.

"Oh, that's right." She draws out the last word, feigning surprise. "You and Avery grew up next door to each other, didn't you?" She leans onto the counter, knowing she has me on the ropes. She has information she knows I'm desperate for and I can tell she's going to make me work for it.

"I remember you two being quite close." She pauses for dramatic effect. "Well, you must be so happy to hear she's back in town then."

My heartbeat stutters before returning to its regular pace.

Avery? Back in town? Since when?

I know I shouldn't show my interest since Miss Carla has taken much less and spun a tall tale from it but I can't help myself.

"When did she get back? What's she doing here?"

Miss Carla's smile tells me I'm playing with fire asking so many questions but it's not the first time I've been burned by Haven Bay's rumor mill. All I care about is finding out if there's any truth to this one.

"Just yesterday afternoon, I heard. Pulled up outside her mama's house and her car hasn't moved since. I'm surprised you haven't heard." She smiles, loving the fact that she's the one to deliver this news. "As for what she's doing here, we're not sure for certain but, as I was saying, Connie thinks she's on the run from—"

I toss my screwdriver into my toolbox then snap the lid shut. "I should get going, Miss Carla. I have a few more stops to make before calling it a day. Your door is finished, as is the rest of your to-do list. I'll let Bud know to bring your bill over tomorrow." I grab my toolbox and climb to my feet.

Ham jumps up beside me and practically runs me over to get outside, giving Audrey a wide berth as he passes. We're out the door before Miss Carla can finish her sentence. I should feel bad about being rude but I can't stop my mind from spinning.

Avery's back? And she's staying with her mom?

I don't believe a word of the rest of it. Haven Bay's known for their love of fairy tales. While the Avery I knew as a kid was definitely capable of pulling off a jewelry heist, she wasn't dumb enough to get caught.

Growing up, when trouble found us (as it always seemed to around Avery), I was usually the one taking the blame while "sweet Avery" batted her eyes as if to say *Who, me?* No one ever believed me when I would tell them that she was actually the mastermind behind the majority of our pranks.

Like the time when we were twelve and my mom baked fifty of my nonna's famous homemade cannolis for our school's bake sale. Avery convinced me to use my birthday money to buy fifty cannolis from the local bakery, replace the cream filling with spearmint toothpaste, and then switch my mom's cannolis with the toothpaste-filled ones.

I will admit, the look on everyone's face when they bit into the cannolis expecting my mom's deliciously creamy dessert, only to come away with a mouth full of minty paste was hilarious.

My mom didn't seem to agree.

Not even my own mother believed me when I told her that it was Avery's idea. She cuffed me on the back of the head for that one and grounded me for two weeks.

Later that afternoon, I watched Avery snack on the real cannolis through her bedroom window. She shot me a smug, cannoli-filled smile as I pulled weeds from my mother's garden.

I shake my head and chuckle to myself. Only I knew how much of a ball-buster the real Avery was. I didn't realize how much I had missed her until I heard her name again.

She's always been in the back of my mind—you don't spend your entire childhood with someone and not think about them from time to time. But Avery was always different. Even before I knew why.

Miss Carla mentioned she was staying at her mom's. Perfect timing. I need to check in on my mom's house while she's away. Maybe I should stop by after work.

And if I happened to catch a glance of Avery next door, well, that's just a happy coincidence.

Smiling at my plan, I continue to saunter down the side-walk towards The Book Nook. Today is shaping up to be a fine day.

I pull open the door to the bookshop, holding it open for the two ladies leaving. Glancing up, I stop dead in my tracks as I come face-to-face with the wavy honey-brown hair and whisky eyes I'd recognize anywhere.

Avery.

Yes, it's a fine day indeed.

CHAPTER 4

AVERY

My first day at The Book Nook has been a success. Gavin has been in heaven with all of the new picture books he's looked through. I don't think he's left the children's section all day, except for lunch.

Despite a few hiccups with the point-of-sale system, by the second wave of customers, I managed to pick everything back up pretty easily. New technology aside, things haven't changed much in the shop—until the expansion is completed, that is.

A few months ago, my mom finally decided to knock out the adjoining wall between the shop and the building next door. She bought the adjacent storefront years ago in the hopes of one day adding a cafe onto the bookstore. Until now, it had mostly served as an extra storage area.

She called me the day she spoke with the construction company and I could hear the excitement in her voice. I was thrilled for her that she was finally going through with her dream of expanding.

Unfortunately, she got sick not long after finalizing the plan, which pushed back the demolition a few weeks. Now that she is recovering at home, she's green-lit the construction crew to start demolition this week after-hours. After that, they'll be working during the day to bring her cafe to life.

I'm helping the last customer of the day while I wait for the foreman to arrive. He's supposed to be coming by to discuss the demolition process and so that I can give him a key to the store.

I hand the customer her bag then round the counter to start closing up. Just then, the bell above the door jingles and I glance towards the front.

I freeze as my eyes lock with the one man I was hoping to avoid a little longer.

Matt.

It's not that I'm not happy to see my childhood best friend. I am. I guess I was hoping that the first time I saw him, my life might be less of a shit show.

I can't help but stare. In high school, Matt was athletic and lean but the man before me is all wide shoulders and hard muscles. His signature backwards baseball cap rests on top of his shaggy dark brown hair. That look made my stomach flutter as a teenager and it seems to have the same effect on me as a grown woman.

What is it about a guy with a backwards baseball cap that causes every woman's insides to melt?

A wide grin spreads across his face as he spots me. "Avery! You're actually here!" He pulls me towards him for a quick hug. "You never know with this town. Last week Millie swore she saw Elvis slurping oysters over at Sam's Crab Shack." He holds me back at arm's length. "But damn, am I ever glad to see you."

A flutter of butterflies takes flight in my stomach as he runs his gaze over me appreciatively.

Did Matt just check me out? I slam that thought down. *Definitely not.* Guys who look like Matt Brady don't check out girls that look like me.

"Hey, Matt," I try for a casual reply, but my heart races at the sight of him. I take a small step back so I'm no longer in his grasp and my pulse slows slightly. "How have you been?"

"Oh, you know. Living the dream," he shrugs but keeps his eyes on mine. "How about you? What are you doing back home? Connie Sheridan said you were on the run from the cops, which honestly wouldn't surprise me." His eyes sparkle with humor and he shoots me that lopsided grin that I love so much.

I laugh and shake my head. "Actually, I'm here for my mom. She was sick with pneumonia, so I came back to help her with the shop."

Matt's eyes soften. "Yeah, my mom mentioned that. She's gone on a trip with Pete for their anniversary and feels terrible that she isn't around to help."

That sounds just like Franny. When Matt's dad passed away when we were fourteen, our moms went from friendly neighbors to nearly inseparable. They're best friends but they treat each other more like sisters.

According to my mom, after us kids had all moved out, they considered moving in together and living out their days as "old spinster sisters." That was until Franny met Pete a few years ago.

But Franny's new relationship didn't change anything; they were still inseparable. My mom said poor Pete has had to tuck them in a few times after a little too much wine during one of their "sleepovers".

"It's not her fault. You know my mom. She's too proud to say when she needs a little extra help."

And if I was a good daughter, she never would've had to ask.

I change the subject before the guilt can pull me under. "So, how've you been? You look great!"

That's not just me being polite. Matt's always been a good-looking guy and time has only enhanced that fact.

Combine that with his charming personality and witty sense of humor, he's every woman's dream guy.

"You think so? It's my new diet of gummy worms and Pop-Tarts. It's been tough, but it's all about discipline." He smacks his abs and shoots me that adorable smile again.

That's it. The butterflies in my stomach are in full swarm now.

"Anyway, it's great to see you, even if not under the best of circumstances. Are you staying with your mom?" he asks.

I always forget the way Matt looks at people. When he talks to you, he looks you right in the eye, giving you his full attention. I forgot how nice it is to be the center of someone's focus—even for a few minutes.

I nod. "She said that was the only way she would only allow my 'hovering', as she calls it. I mean, she was in the hospital a couple weeks ago, for God's sake. I think that warrants me a little hovering." I roll my eyes, remembering the long, useless argument I had with my mom over this very topic.

Matt laughs. "Stubborn as always, that Ange."

Is it just me or is he leaning toward me? I look up at his face, which seems closer than it was a minute ago. "So, if you're going to be around for a while, maybe you'd want to—"

Whatever he was about to say is cut off by Gavin's excited voice. "Mommy! Are you almost done? You said we could take Sushi down to the beach after work and it's after work now. Pleaseeee, Mommy?" He bounces up and down on his heels, pulling on my hand.

I take a step back, looking down at Gavin's eager face. I pull him to my side. "Soon, buddy. Can you say hi to Matt? He's—" I look back up at Matt in curiosity. "Actually I never asked. Why are you here, Matt?"

Gavin, just realizing someone new is nearby, takes a hesitant step behind me. He eyes Matt warily and it makes me sad for my once outgoing boy. There was a time when Gavin would babble away to anyone who approached him. The mailman, the cashier at the store, the children at the park.

That seems so long ago now.

I put my arm on his shoulder reassuringly then look back at Matt. He's staring down at Gavin, eyes wide with shock. He doesn't seem to realize I've spoken.

"Matt?"

He finally snaps out of his daze, giving his head a slight shake. "Oh, um, I work for Taylor Construction. I'm the foreman handling your mom's expansion."

Ah. Now I understand the look in my mom's eye last night. She knew Matt worked for Taylor Construction and conveniently decided to leave out that fact.

Great.

If I'm not mistaken, Matt was about to ask me out and is now about to have a coronary over the fact that I have a son.

Not that I would ever be embarrassed of Gavin. Or that I would even say yes to a date with Matt. Or with anyone right now. My life is a complete dumpster fire. I don't need to add any more fuel to it.

Matt continues to look back and forth from Gavin to me, so I do what any normal woman would do.

I spew word vomit all over the hot construction guy.

"Oh! Right! Yes!" *Am I yelling?* "Construction. Demolition. Makes sense. I'll just let you get to demolishing then." *Smooth.* "Gavin and I were about to go take Sushi to the beach." *We've already established that.* "The dog, Sushi. Not the food. Though I'm sure the food would be good, too. Is there a sushi place in Haven Bay now?" *Stop talking.* "Anyway, we should go. Gavin, grab your backpack. See you later, Matt!"

I all but drag Gavin to the door before Matt's voice stops me. "Avery, wait. I need a key to lock up." Matt seems to have momentarily pulled himself out of his shock and is reaching towards me.

"Right. The key. Here you go!" I practically it into his outstretched hand. "Okay then. Bye!"

I slam the door closed behind me and hurry down the street. Gavin doesn't seem phased by my temporary lapse in sanity and starts chattering away again about the beach.

I blow out a harsh breath and tip my head skyward.

What the hell was that?

CHAPTER 5

MATT

oly shit balls. What was that?

Avery's a mom? She has a kid—like a full-on child. My head finally stops spinning as it reaches out and latches onto that thought.

Wow.

The fact that she has a kid isn't a surprise. I knew she had a kid. My mom went to her baby shower. She showed me picture after picture that Angie sent her when he was born.

But to see him in person, the spitting image of his mom—the girl that dared me to eat a dirt in kindergarten—was a shock I wasn't prepared for.

I shake my head again and pull out my sledgehammer. Ham saunters over to the rug and with a dramatic sigh, drops to the floor. Laying his head on his paws, he promptly falls asleep. In the three years since I adopted him, he's been on construction sites more often than not, so the noise doesn't bother him anymore.

I already went through the shop last week and marked which parts of the wall we'll knock out and which will stay. So when I launch the steel head of the sledgehammer into the drywall, I let my mind wander a bit.

I can still remember the night I started to see Avery as more than the girl who chased me around the yard with a snake when we were seven.

Back in high school, there was a path hidden behind the old Smith place that wound downhill and into a small portion of beach that only locals knew about. In the summer, teenagers would gather with coolers filled with whatever beer or spirits they could sneak past their unsuspecting parents. A bonfire would rage just large enough to elicit excitement but not big enough to catch the attention of nearby cottages or Sheriff Bolton.

One night, Avery sat by the fire, talking and laughing with a few of her friends. She was well-liked around school and was the star pitcher for the junior girls' softball team.

Avery had a kick-ass fastball that had bruised my hand more times growing up than I could count. I eventually gave up practicing with her after she "accidentally" gave me a softball-sized welt on my shin. It just so happened to be the day after I let it slip to her mom that it had been Avery who broke her mom's favorite vase, not the cat.

I always knew there was something special about Avery, but that night, something changed.

To this day, I'm not sure if it was the way her sun-kissed skin made the adorable freckles on her face stand out or the way her hair fell in careless waves across her shoulders. Maybe it was the way her eyes lit up when she laughed at something her friend had said.

Either way, it was as if the whole world darkened and the only light was coming from Avery's smile. My heart stuttered as I took in the new sight that was my best friend. She started the night as just Avery and ended it as *Avery*.

Unfortunately, Mitch Olsen seemed to have the same idea. Kids from Bakersfield tended to stay away from Haven Bay, claiming it was too "redneck" for them. An opinion they conveniently forgot every summer when Haven Bay was the closest beach to Bakersfield.

I remember watching him strut over and sink himself down into the sand beside Avery. Leaning closely, he whispered something into her ear. Whatever he said made her cheeks flush and brought a small smile to her lips.

My stomach churned and a rush of unexpected rage shot through me. Who did this entitled prick think he was? Just because his dad was one of the richest men in Bakersfield, he thought he could just waltz in with his designer clothes and slimy smile and Avery would just fall in his lap?

I don't think so. My girl would see right through his fake exterior.

Except she didn't.

Mitch's arm settled over Avery's shoulders as he pulled her into his chest. I watched, waiting for Avery to hand him his balls on a silver platter for such a bold move. She'd laugh to me about it later over slushies, mimicking his whiney voice. I smirked to myself but it was quickly wiped away by disbelief when I watched them stand up and walk hand-in-hand into the darkness.

By Monday morning, it was all over school that Mitch had a new girl—Avery.

At first, she tried to get us to all hang out together. I quickly realized that her new friends (aka Mitch's loser buddies and their Regina George girlfriends), were not my crowd.

Even though we all went to high school together, there was a very clear divide between people who lived in Bakersfield and people who lived in Haven Bay. Bakersfield was filled with stuffy, rich people while Haven Bay folks were about as blue-collar as they come.

We didn't mix well.

Once, when we were all hanging out, I told a joke that

made Avery throw her head back laughing. The rest of the group stared at me like I had three heads. Mitch then berated Avery in front of everyone, telling her how unattractive it was for her to snort like that.

His friends all laughed and it took all of my effort not to smash my fist into Mitch's nose when she blushed. I started to tell him off when Avery put her hand on my arm and told me to stop. I could never say no to Avery, but I also couldn't sit by and watch him mistreat her.

So I stopped going around them after that.

Avery tried to bring Mitch around to hang out with Rhett and me but the whole time Mitch kept her glued to his side. If she was more than an arm's length away, he would quickly pull her back to his side. If he thought I was talking to her too much, he'd make up an excuse and they'd leave shortly after.

I tried to push my feelings aside and suck it up for Avery. She had been my best friend since kindergarten and I didn't want to lose her. But the more I saw her be mistreated by Dickless Mitch, the less I could control my temper.

I asked her once why she was with someone who treated her like shit. She got upset and told me that I didn't know the real Mitch so it was unfair for me to judge him. She said it was getting really hard to choose between her best friend and her boyfriend and she wished I'd see things from her perspective. The tears in her eyes just about broke me, so I let it go.

Their relationship left a douchebag-sized hole in our friendship that it never recovered from.

After high school, Mitch and Avery moved to the city for college and, according to my mother, married soon after. I tore up the invite when it came in the mail, then texted her an apology that I couldn't take the time off work.

I have no idea if they're still together, but I'm taking the fact that she's back in town and Dickless Mitch is nowhere to be found as good news.

And she has a kid.

A really cute kid from what I remember from my earlier shocked state. The more I pull myself together, the more I can see Avery as a mom. I don't know why I was so surprised; she'd be an amazing mom. She's funny, empathetic, smart and sassy. I bet her son doesn't get away with anything. Probably because she's already done it all herself as a kid. There's nothing he could do to surprise her.

My small smile turns into a full grin. Her having a kid isn't a dealbreaker. Hell, I love kids. My brother loves to remind me that I still am one. I even want a few of my own.

Eventually.

One day.

The more I think about it, the more into the idea I am. I finish demoing the wall, clean up the mess as best I can, and then pack up my tools. All the while I'm thinking about Avery's sunny smile.

There's still some more of the wall to take down in the morning but I wanted to do the loudest part when there were no customers around.

I guess that's one benefit of being the boss's number two. I keep my own hours for the most part, and as long as the work gets done, Bud doesn't care when I clock in or out.

The odd hours are easy to manage when you're a single, unattached guy.

I close the door behind Ham then turn to lock up. I make my way back toward my apartment, conveniently located on the next block over. I let my mind wander again as I walk, thinking of the way Avery's warm eyes lit up when she looked down at her son. I catch myself smiling.

I sure have been doing that a lot today.

AFTER JUMPING in the shower and pulling on some clean clothes, I cross the street from my apartment above Taylor Construction and walk the short distance to The Dive. Having the only bar in town directly across the street from my apartment definitely has its perks. Especially when I stumble home after a few beers on a Friday night.

My buddy, Rhett, owns the bar as of last spring. He was the managing bartender for the last ten years, so he all but owned the place before that. The previous owner had dragged his feet, claiming he'd sell it to him when Rhett was ready. No one knew what that meant and he never got the chance to explain. He passed away last year from a heart attack. Turns out, ol' Bill had left the bar to Rhett in his will. Rhett has a picture of him hanging up on the wall over the bar in tribute.

Since then, Rhett has turned the dingy, dark bar into a clean and lively pub. He built a stage almost before the ink dried on the deed and started booking local musicians soon after. Now, Rhett has a year-long schedule of gigs, with some bands coming from as far as Vancouver to play at The Dive.

I give Ham a pat on the head and motion for him to lie down on the back patio. Rhett and the rest of the town love Ham, but the tourists can be weird about a dog being in a bar. Complaints get made which means the cops have to come in and give Rhett a warning. Then Ham has to stay home while I'm out and I come home to the cold shoulder from the world's pettiest pooch. It's easier for everyone if Ham stays on the patio during the tourist season.

I pull open the heavy oak door to The Dive and cross the room, waving at a few locals on my way to the bar.

"Hi there, handsome," a seductive voice purrs as I pass by.

I turn and see a blonde woman I don't recognize. She's playing with her straw in a way that leaves little to the imagination of her intent. Usually, I'd take her blatant invitation and flirt back. Tonight though, I give her a polite smile and continue to the bar, where my brother sits on a stool.

"You feeling okay?" Luke asks, cocking his head at the blonde. "Pretty sure she was talking to you."

"I know. I'd just rather spend the night with my favorite big brother," I reply, ruffling his hair.

He scowls and swings a fist toward me. I dodge it and laugh, taking the seat beside him. He smooths his short hair back down and gives me one last shove before turning back to his beer.

Only being a year apart in age, Luke and I look a lot alike, with our dark hair, olive skin and dark eyes. Luke is a police officer for the local department, so while I leave my wavy hair longer and slightly unkempt, his is always short and clean-cut. He's a bit taller than me and, if I'm being honest, a bit more muscular from his training on the force.

But I could still kick his ass. And occasionally still do.

"Now, now, kids. Don't make me separate you two," Rhett drawls as he approaches from behind the bar.

"Sorry, Dad," I joke at the same time that Luke growls, "Shut up, Rhett."

Rhett's been one of my best friends since we were fourteen and he moved to town to live with his grandma. We're practically brothers. He has the whole quiet, broody musician thing going for him that drives all the women wild. That, combined with the tattoos, blonde hair and beard, he looks like a biker Thor. But deep down, he's a goofball like me. He just doesn't show that side of himself to many people.

"How come you're not trying to take the blonde home?" he nods behind me. Rhett's not one for subtlety.

I don't bother turning around. "You know, it's sad how obsessed you two are with my sex life. Don't you have better things to do than watch me score? I can give you some lessons if you're having a hard time on your own."

Luke rolls his eyes and Rhett scoffs. "If you could figure out how to handle your dick, maybe you'd get a couple of repeat offenders instead of one-night stands all the time."

They both laugh and I give a half-hearted chuckle. Truth is, I'm not the player that they think I am. Do I like to have fun? Sure. Who doesn't? But I'm not some creep with a new girl every night.

Don't get me wrong, I had my fair share of fun when I was in my early twenties. In a town filled with pretty tourists looking for a vacation fling, it was hard not to. Sometimes it was a one-time deal and others it was a short-term affair. Either way, we both went into it with the same mindset; it was temporary.

But just because it was temporary, doesn't mean it was purely physical. I didn't just pick the first girl I laid eyes on. We talked, hung out and did more than have sex.

Eventually though, that got boring too. I tried being in a long-term relationship a few years ago, but it ended the way all the others had—easily and amicably.

Lately, if the mood was right, I'd flirt with a pretty girl, buy her a couple of drinks then spin her around the dance floor. At the end of the night, I'd drive her home or to whatever vacation rental she was staying at and walk her to the door.

The guys assume the worst of me so I've given up trying to convince them otherwise.

Rhett twists the top off of my favorite beer and passes it to me. I'm mid-swig when Luke comments, "So, Avery's back."

I choke on my drink at his statement. This town talks too much. Luke side-eyes me with a smirk then takes a drink of his own beer.

"Matt's Avery?" Rhett asks.

I can't quite look him in the eye when I say, "She's not *my* anything." I look back at Luke. "And how'd you know she was back? She's been home less than 24 hours."

"Same way anyone finds anything out in this town," Luke says. "Heard she's got a kid, too. Jared or something like that."

"Gavin," I correct, then regret it immediately.

Luke smirks again and turns to me. "So, you've talked to her then? Interesting."

Shit.

"Not interesting. Not anything. You know we're doing Angie's expansion at the shop. Avery was there helping her mom out while she recovers at home." I hope my voice sounds as nonchalant as I'm trying to act.

"Hmm. Like I said, interesting." Luke gives a pointed look at Rhett.

"Funny how the one night you don't feel like picking up is the first night Avery's back in town," Rhett muses.

Again, subtle as a freight train.

I take a long pull of my beer instead of answering. My first instinct is denial; one has nothing to do with the other. And what if it did? Avery is nothing like these women.

It's been a long week, that's all, and I just want to sit with my friends. Which suddenly doesn't seem very relaxing anymore.

"About the kid," Luke starts.

"What about him?" I ask, narrowing my eyes at him.

"You gotta be careful there, man," Luke points his beer at me. "Kids mean there's no messing around. It's either serious or nothing. You don't just walk away from a kid."

"So, what? You're saying I can't be serious?"

"You haven't been serious for longer than fifteen minutes since I've known you," Rhett answers, mixing a drink and then sliding it across the bar and into the waiting hands of a customer.

Their words eat at me, my excitement from earlier twisting

into something uncomfortable. I liked Avery as a teenager. I'd like to get to know her as an adult. Just because she has a kid doesn't mean that I have to marry her and become a dad overnight.

I set my beer on the bar. "For all I know she's still married." My stomach twists. "So, why don't we talk about something important like how Luke arrested Dottie for public nudity again this week?"

My attempt to change the subject is weak but somehow works. Luke groans and then launches into a story about how he had to explain to eighty-something year old Dottie that Haven Bay's beach was not a nude beach. Again.

I laugh along half-heartedly but my mind is stuck on what they said earlier. Part of me wonders if they're right. But the larger, angrier part of me is offended that my own brother and best friend don't think I'm good enough.

And that's just the thing, isn't it? No one takes me seriously because I never give them a reason to. No one needs a serious Matt.

And that scares me more than anything.

CHAPTER 6

AVERY

The morning after I spewed word vomit all over Matt, I'm feeling more sane. Just in case, I take my time on the short walk from my mom's house to the bookstore to clear my head.

My mom received the all-clear from her doctor yesterday so she asked to take Gavin for a couple hours this morning. I initially said no and that she still needed to rest. All that got me was a lecture from my mom and puppy dog eyes from Gavin.

We finally compromised on Gavin spending a couple of hours with my mom and then she would drop him at the shop after lunch.

Despite my protests, I'm glad they have each other and my son can have fun with his grandma while she's still mobile enough to play. I want Gavin to know the same woman that I knew growing up. The one who danced around the kitchen, singing along to the radio. I used to roll my eyes at her but Matt was always quick to jump in and spin her around our old linoleum floors.

Speaking of Matt...

I sigh. I'm not even sure why I freaked out. Possibly because I'm pretty sure Matt was about to ask me out and I don't think I knew how to answer. Hell, even now, I don't know how I'd answer.

Technically, I'm still married but things haven't been good between us for years. I'd say we've been more like roommates, but even roommates have better a relationship than we did.

At first, I fought hard to keep our family together. I offered to go to counseling or make time to talk through our issues but he brushed off all of my attempts and belittled my concerns. Eventually, when you're the only one left trying, you start to wonder what you're fighting for.

I was tired of the condescending remarks, the endless criticisms. Tired of being on the receiving end of his whirlwind of emotions. Just...tired.

I finally worked up the courage to tell Mitch I wanted a divorce on New Year's Day. But since I didn't have a job, I couldn't afford to move out. Mitch didn't want the scandal of a divorce right before one of his business deals went through, so he agreed to let me stay at the house until I could find something.

Finding a job when you've been out of the workforce for five years isn't easy. Even with my degree in business management, I couldn't get a single call back. Not even from Starbucks.

When I got pregnant with Gavin, Mitch insisted I quit my job to stay home and focus on the baby. I agreed. Though I'll never regret my time with Gavin during these first four years, I missed working. I loved my job, my coworkers and the freedom it brought with it. Now, a part of me wishes I had something to fall back on, something of my own that Mitch couldn't take away.

Long story short, I'm not ready to start dating again. I'm

not sure if I ever will be. Because dating leads to marriage and marriage leads to losing yourself.

I've been with Mitch since I was sixteen years old. We got married when I was twenty-two and I had Gavin less than a year later. My whole identity was being Mitch's girlfriend, then the perfect society wife, then being a mother. I have no friends, only the wives of Mitch's business associates. I don't even remember the last time I did something for myself.

It's exhausting.

When I got the call from the hospital saying my mom was ill, I told Mitch I was going back home. He told me I was being selfish and ignoring my "wifely duties".

What is this? 1950?

After I reminded him that we were separated and I no longer had any "wifely duties", he stormed out of the house.

I tried to leave with the Mercedes but he told me he had paid for the SUV and if I really wanted to go see my mother, I could take my old Volvo.

I'm not sure why I kept my 2012 Volvo when Mitch had started making enough money that we upgraded to nicer vehicles. Looking back, I wonder if, deep down, I knew something like this might happen one day and I might need it again.

Regardless, I packed up the car with Gavin's and my essentials and left for Haven Bay.

So was I still in love with my husband?

Absolutely not. Our marriage died a long time ago.

But I also wasn't ready to lose myself again to a relationship before I even had the chance to rediscover who I was.

Who knows? Maybe I read the situation wrong yesterday and Matt wasn't even interested. He was probably asking because Franny told him to check in on me. Nothing romantic about it.

The tension in my shoulders relaxes as I turn the key to

open the front door to the shop. I switch on the lights and the little bookstore awakens.

The Book Nook has always been my favorite place. My safe space. No matter what age I was or what problem was plaguing me, it was nothing that a few minutes snuggled into the worn velvet couch in the corner couldn't fix.

I spent many days after school curled up with a book about faraway adventures or nail-biting thrillers. As I got older, my interest turned to swoon-worthy heroes, who always knew what to say or do to make their lovers' toes curl.

But some stories were just that—stories.

Happily-ever-after doesn't always happen and sometimes you end up married to the toad instead of the prince.

A loud thud pulls me out of my thoughts. It's then that I notice the clear tarp fastened to where a wall used to be.

Right, the expansion. Yesterday was demo-day and now it's about to get a whole lot louder and a lot more chaotic around here.

Oh, well. The expansion would only take a few weeks. The long-term benefits of adding the small cafe to the shop would outweigh the mayhem in the short-term.

The store will be opening soon, so I pull out my phone and turn on the overhead music. I turn the volume up a bit louder than usual to try and drown out the sound of hammers and saws next door.

I work my way through my checklist for opening the store. As I'm wiping a rag along the ledge of the window display, my phone vibrates.

MITCH

When are you home?

Not a word asking about his son or how my mom's feeling. I wish I could say I was surprised. I doubt he's even noticed our absence other than that I'm no longer around to take care of the house.

That's it. When I get back, I really need to look into getting my own place.

I shove my cell phone into my back pocket and take another angry swipe at the offending dust.

Selfish, controlling, manipulative—

"Avery!"

I jolt at my name. Unfortunately, my shock causes me to jump backward, bumping into the table behind me. I reach out to steady the stack of books perched on top but my hand collides with a large hand instead.

Half a dozen books fall to the ground. With a groan, I squat down to retrieve them. "Sorry about that. I was off in my own little world, I guess."

I look up to see Matt bent over and collecting a couple of paperbacks from under the table.

"Yeah, no kidding. I called your name three times before you snapped out of it," he chuckles, handing me the collected books. "Must've been a pretty crappy daydream. You've got that line between your eyebrows you get when you're upset." He reaches up and softly touches the spot.

"You remember that?" I ask. It's been years since I've seen Matt and even longer since we've been this close.

He smiles softly. "I remember everything when it comes to you, Freckles."

The space between us suddenly seems much smaller and it causes my heart to race. My eyes widen and I hold my breath, afraid to move and break whatever spell his touch has cast on me.

He must feel it too because his smile fades and his eyes darken. He holds my gaze for another second before it drops to my mouth. His hand slowly traces my cheek, following his eyes to my lips.

My breath hitches and I watch his Adam's apple bob as he swallows hard. The air thickens around us and my pulse races.

He's so close. He smells like sawdust and something outdoorsy.

It's strangely intoxicating.

Suddenly, I don't care about my failure of a marriage or all the reasons why kissing Matt would be a bad idea. The only thing I can think of is how his lips would feel against mine, how his hair would feel if I ran my fingers through it, and how his hard chest would feel against mine.

The sudden whir of a distant drill breaks our trance. I pull back at the same time his hand drops and he clears his throat.

Matt stands, then reaches a hand out to me. Giving my head a small shake, I put my hand in his calloused one and let him help me to my feet.

What's wrong with me? This is Matt. The same guy who got kicked out of our school play in the fourth grade for making fart noises with his armpit.

"Thanks," I croak against the sudden dryness in my throat. I turn and busy myself by arranging the paperbacks back on the table. "Did you need something?"

He blinks a couple of times before realization hits him. "Right. I came over to let you know we have to cut the power to that half of the store's grid." He gestures toward the back office. "It shouldn't affect the cash register, but you might want to make sure your computer is turned off."

"Thanks. I'll do that." Since he hasn't mentioned it yet, I decide to bring up the elephant in the room. "I'm sorry about being so weird yesterday. I guess I'm getting used to being back home and seeing everyone again."

"Don't worry about it," he says, leaning against the counter. "I'm sure it's strange coming back after all this time and having everyone know your baggage before you've even unpacked it."

I shoot him a grateful smile. Leave it to Matt to make me feel better without even trying. "Exactly. Half the time I feel like a gorilla being watched in a zoo and the other half it feels like I never left. The other day Dottie asked me if her *Fifty Shades Darker* book was in yet. She's going to put poor Harold in a wheelchair if they keep this up." I shiver at the visual.

Matt throws his head back and laughs. "You think a wheelchair would stop her? Her and Maeve have been banned from half of our construction sites. They used to bring out their lawn chairs, put their hard hats on and catcall the guys all day. Most of us ignore them but some guys got in trouble for strutting around for them shirtless instead of working. When Bud told them they had to leave, Maeve asked if it was because they'd been 'bad girls'. I didn't know Bud's face could turn so red."

By the end of his story, I'm laughing so hard, I have tears in my eyes and I'm scared I might pee a little.

The joys of motherhood.

When I finally pull myself together, Matt's looking at me with a half smile and something else I don't recognize in his eyes. Is that...desire?

That sobers me quickly. I wipe a finger under each eye and clear my throat.

"Wow, I haven't laughed that hard in years," I say. "It felt good."

"Looked good, too," Matt replies, huskily.

There's a tense silence around us as we stare at each other. The heat of my blush creeps up my neck and over my cheeks. Matt's eyes darken but before I can figure out what it means, the jingle from the bell on the front door announces a customer's arrival.

"Well, I should get back to work. Let me know if you need me," I say and start towards the customer.

"Will do, Freckles," he drawls.

I bite my lip to hold back my smile at his use of his childhood nickname for me. I used to hate that nickname, but hearing it in his gravelly voice now makes my insides melt.

I'm in trouble.

CHAPTER 7

MATT

How did I forget how adorable Avery's laugh is? If I could, I'd record her laugh and listen to it every day on repeat.

And it's not just the sound, though it is melodic. It's the way she lets loose, her whole body lost to the moment.

It's how I picture she would be in bed. The image of Avery sprawled out naked on my bed flashes in my mind. Her hair draped across my pillow, head thrown back in ecstasy. Her pretty mouth parted in a silent prayer as I thrust deeper and deeper inside her. The visual has all of my blood rushing south.

I readjust my growing erection. That's not something I should be thinking about right now. To distract myself, I grab my measuring tape and climb the ladder beside me. Grabbing a marker from my tool belt, I measure from the wall to where the pot light will be installed. Then I mark the ceiling at the proper distance.

My mind strays back to her and those damn freckles. I used to tease her about them when we were kids, but I've always loved them. How they're sprinkled across her nose and over her cheeks like toppings on my favorite dessert. And they don't stop there. They're dusted over her shoulders and down her chest. I'd never given much thought to how far they go, but now I can't think of anything else.

I climb down and move the ladder farther along the wall. Before climbing back up, I tip my head to see around the tarp. I can only see the back of Avery's head as she chats with a customer but I can tell her posture has gone back to its rigid stance.

When I walked up to her earlier, I planned to make a joke about her awkwardness from the day before—something the old Avery would've laughed about and retaliated with a joke twice as funny.

But instead of the confident, laidback Avery I once knew, I found her staring out the window, a distressed frown on her face. At that moment, I would've done anything to ease her worries.

Apparently that includes almost kissing her. I don't even know if she's still married and I was ready to say the hell with it and devour her pretty mouth.

I blame her eyes. She's got these big, expressive eyes that have little flecks of gold in them. I could see the worry and hurt reflecting in them and it just about broke me.

It's always been that way with Avery though. Even before I realized my feelings for her in high school, she always had a hold on my heart. I'd rather chew off my arm than see her hurt.

Once, when we were twelve, our teacher had us create a Family Tree. The day we presented them, Jeff Wiens announced to the whole class that Avery's tree was so bare because her dad had left her and her mom. He declared that even her own dad didn't want her.

Avery fought back tears then mumbled something about not feeling well and went home sick.

Jeff ended up with eight stitches that day after I "accidentally" clocked him in the face at recess.

When I went to see if Avery was okay after school, word had already gotten back to her about Jeff's face. She had rolled her eyes, shoved my shoulder and called me an idiot. She must've told her mom about it, too, because though she never mentioned it, my mom let me have an extra helping of dessert that night.

Otherwise, Avery was a tough, take-no-shit type of girl. So to see this new awkward, polite, watered-down version of herself felt wrong.

I want to know what happened the last ten years that she felt she had to change so much. I could probably take a guess at what the cause was. Or rather *who* the cause was.

I hate the fact all the same. One of the best parts about Avery was her spunk. Why would anyone ever want to dull that?

Folding the ladder a little too roughly, I shove it aside with a loud thud. The other two guys on my crew jerk their heads up in surprise. They've never seen me anything but happy and joking around.

"Just making sure you're all awake," I say, forcing a smile.

They chuckle and go back to work. I take a long steadying breath. I can't change the past, but I wouldn't mind making Avery laugh like that again soon. Real soon.

Just then, I catch a glimpse of honey-hair flying through the front door of the shop. I turn to see Gavin launching himself at Avery. He excitedly chatters away to his mom while Angie steps into the shop behind him.

I'm glad to see Angie up and around. She gave us quite the scare when she collapsed at the shop a few weeks ago. My mom was a mess when I called to tell her Angie had been taken to the hospital. Luckily, it wasn't anything that rest and some strong antibiotics couldn't fix.

I start to walk over to the trio, then look back at Ham, who's lounging nearby with the guys. "You comin'?" He hops to his feet and prances over to me. I give his ears a quick scratch then lead the way.

When I get close enough, I pull Angie into a big bear hug. "Hey, Ange. You better be taking care of yourself." She squeezes me back. "You're not allowed to scare me like that again, okay? Who's going to protect me from my mother's wrath if you're not around?"

I force another tight smile but the reality is, Angie was as much of a mom to me growing up as my own. I don't even want to think about a world where she's not in it. I squeeze her a little tighter, a sudden lump forming in my throat.

Lifting onto her toes, Angie whispers just quiet enough for me to hear, "You don't have to worry about that, Matty. I'm not going anywhere any time soon."

I hold on for a second longer, and when I'm sure she won't disappear, I straighten. I try to clear the sudden raw ache from my throat.

I notice Gavin standing below me and grin down at him. "Hey, big guy. Do you remember me? I'm Matt. I'm a friend of your mom's. We sort of met the other day before you and your mom had to leave so suddenly." I shoot Avery a wink, causing her cheeks to pink.

Gavin's eyes drop to his feet and he steps behind Avery.

"He's a little shy," Avery explains.

I crouch down so I'm at eye level with him. "That's okay. I was a little shy growing up, too. There's nothing wrong with that. Besides, the ladies love a sensitive guy." I bounce my eyebrows at him playfully.

He covers his mouth with his tiny hand and giggles.

"You know who else used to be real shy? My buddy Ham here. When I adopted him, he was pretty scared of people. He didn't have the best life before I met him. His other people were kind of mean to him and left him outside all the time. But eventually, he realized most people are alright and started to trust me. So, if you ever want someone to talk to, ol' Hammy is the best listener around."

Gavin takes a hesitant step out from behind his mom then another toward Ham. I motion for Ham to lay down and he flips onto his back, arms in the air and a goofy smile on his face.

Gavin lets out a big laugh this time and bends over to rub Ham's belly. "Mommy! Ham loves belly rubs just like Sushi! I bet Ham and Sushi would be bestest buddies!" His excitement grows with every pat on Ham's belly.

Ham is loving the attention, his tail thumping on the hardwood, but the rest of him remains still. It's as if he knows that Gavin needs to go slow and gain some confidence first.

I stand back up and notice a soft-eyed Avery and a delighted Angie watching me. For some reason, their stares make me uncomfortable. I take a step back, looking anywhere but their faces. Before I can excuse myself though, I'm saved by Jolie waltzing through the front door.

"There's my favorite guy!" Jolie says, walking towards us with her arms wide.

My eyebrows shoot up in surprise at the welcome and brace myself for her embrace. When she walks past me instead, understanding dawns on me. I watch her scoop Gavin off of the floor. She makes an elaborate show of squeezing him tightly, and to all of our surprise, Gavin wraps his tiny arms around her neck.

Jolie drops him back to his feet and ruffles his thick curls with her hand. "What's happening, my dude?"

If possible, Gavin's grin grows even wider. "Gram and I just got done bakin' cookies and Gram said we have to let them cool first or else we'll burn our mouths. We came to see Mommy at the store and then later Gram said we could bring

Sushi to the beach!" By the end of his speech, he's bouncing up and down with excitement.

I can't help thinking how much he reminds me of Avery as a kid. They have an energy about them that's contagious. I can't help but smile watching his confidence grow.

"Lucky guy! Sounds like an awesome day." Jolie turns and puts her arms around Angie. "And you, my friend, are looking fantastic. I'm so happy you're feeling better. I've missed our lunch dates." She smiles at Avery. "Though I think I've found an excellent replacement. Until you're feeling up to joining us, of course."

"Absolutely. I can't wait. But for now, I'm going to head back home and cuddle up with Sushi and my new book. Gram had a busy morning." She pulls Gavin in to kiss the top of his head then starts toward the door.

"Mom, should you be walking so far by yourself? Why don't you wait and I'll walk with you," Avery pleads after her.

"Goodbye, my overprotective daughter!" Angie calls, not bothering to turn around. Instead, she waves over her head and hurries out the door.

"On that note, I should get back to work. I'll see you later, Gavin. See ya, Jolie." I motion for Ham to follow.

"Bye, Freckles," I drawl.

Then, just to see her blush once more, I toss her a wink over my shoulder. As I expected, an adorable blush darkens her cheeks.

Yep, worth it.

"Holy shit! What was that?" Jolie grabs my arm and spins me toward her after Gavin wanders over to the kids' section. Her blue eyes are wide and imploring. "You've been holding out on me, Owens. I need all the details. Now."

She pulls me down to the couch, tucking her legs beneath her and eagerly leans toward me.

I laugh at her ridiculous antics. "I don't know what you're talking about. There's nothing to tell."

She shoves my arm playfully. "Bull puckey! I saw that wink he gave you. Not to mention the way you looked like you wanted to jump his bones when I walked in. Now spill it."

Gavin hurries over and saves me from having to answer. "Mommy! Can we go to the park?"

I look up as Tammy Jacobs, my mom's part-time employee walks through the door. "Let me just go check in with Tammy and make sure she's okay if we leave for a bit."

I climb off the couch and hurry over to the counter where Tammy is putting away her purse. I swear I'm not avoiding Jolie's questions, but if this happens to change the subject, it's a happy coincidence in my opinion.

After Tammy reassures me she can handle the lunch hour on her own, I pack up Gavin's lunch from my office mini fridge. Bag in hand, I studiously avoid Jolie's questioning gaze as Gavin races ahead to the park behind our building.

We're lucky that our building backs onto Greenwood Park. A short walk takes you to the children's playground, complete with monkey bars, a jungle gym and a row of swing sets.

A few benches encircle the playground, where a couple of moms are sitting with strollers and wagons. They chat over their coffee cups, occasionally calling out warnings when a kid gets a little too brave on the jungle gym. One scoops up a sleepy baby from the stroller and stands to sway the infant, never breaking the conversation.

Behind the playground is six-kilometres of thick forest filled with trails that walkers, bikers and runners come from all over the county to enjoy. The entrance to the private beach that locals keep secret is tucked inside, far enough off the path that tourists won't find it.

In high school, on warm summer nights, it was overrun with teens. We always thought no one else knew about the area, only to later find out as adults that our parents had known about it all along. Most of them had gone there as teens themselves. They let us have the illusion of rebellion, as long as things didn't get too rowdy.

I turn my head to the sky and let the sun warm my face. Soon, we'll have to worry about the heat and crowds of tourists, but for now, it's nice to enjoy the calm.

I take a seat on one of the nearby picnic tables, keeping Gavin in my view on the playground. I'll let him play for a bit before I attempt to wrangle some food in him.

Jolie walks over and takes a seat across the table from me. She unzips her light blue running jacket and inhales deeply. "Nothing better than some spring sunshine after a long winter, is there? Cool enough for a light jacket but warm enough for sneakers. Perfect."

Jolie points a finger to me. "Don't think this little field trip gets you out of answering my questions. Now I want the dirt, woman. And make it juicy. It's been a boring spring." She crosses her arms on the table and leans forward. "Alright. Matt Brady. Avery Owens. What's the story there?"

I relent, huffing out a breath. "Fine. But I'm warning you. It's not that exciting." I lean back in my seat. "My mom and I moved in next door to Matt and his family when I was six. My mom had been diagnosed with MS the year before and it didn't take long for my dad to decide he was too much of a chicken shit to stick around."

The ache at the mention of my dad has lessened over the years but it's still there, like a broken ankle that never healed right.

"After he left, my mom tried to make ends meet for a while but life is expensive in the city as a single mom with medical bills. So when she found out her new specialist's office was over in Bakersfield, she jumped on the phone to her realtor. We sold our apartment in the city and a month later, we moved to Haven Bay."

Jolie smiles. "Your mom is such a badass and I love it."

"I know, right? She really is. So, our first day in Haven Bay, my mom and I are unpacking in the kitchen when we hear a knock on the door. It's Matt, with a plate full of cannolis that his mom had given him to bring over. My mom invited him inside and we ate our weight in cannolis over our little aluminum kitchen table. Eventually, we ended up playing a board game of some kind. When I started losing, I yelled out, "You're killing me, Smalls!" Turns out, Matt is a huge fan of the movie *Sandlot*." I shrug. "We were best friends from that day on.

"Our families had been close but when Matt's dad got

sick, our moms became like sisters, co-parenting and leaning on each other. After his dad passed, Matt changed. He'd always been a goofball, but after, it seemed like he took on the role of the jokester to ease some of his family's grief. Especially his mom."

Jolie sits up straighter. "Okay, so you were friends growing up. What happened between then and now? Did you ever hook up? What's with the 'do me' looks you were giving each other?"

I loudly shush her and pointedly look around to make sure no one heard. "Geez. A little louder next time. I'm not sure Pastor Dan heard you from the church," I whisper.

She waves me off. "No one's listening. Now stop stalling."

I should feel weird about spilling my guts to someone who is essentially still a stranger. But something about Jolie makes me trust her. It also helps that she comes highly recommended from my mom.

"For starters, no, we never hooked up."

Jolie groans and I bite back a laugh. "When high school started, we had to go to Bakersfield since Haven Bay doesn't have a high school. So with the bigger school, we made new friends. Matt met Rhett and we all hung out together but not as much. If I'm being honest, I guess it all changed when my husband, Mitch and I got together." My head tilts in thought. "Or soon-to-be ex-husband, I guess."

Mitch was your typical rich boy. His dad owned a wealth management company in Bakersfield and invested in a ton of real estate in town. Which meant if he didn't own it, he probably financed it.

"I knew you were married but I didn't realize you were high school sweethearts," Jolie comments.

I snort. "I don't think anyone would ever refer to Mitch as a sweetheart. He was charming, definitely. He knew how to suck you in and make you feel needed. Which, as a teenage girl with daddy issues, I ate right up."

When we first started dating, Mitch was attentive and showered me in affection and gifts. For a girl with limited experience, our relationship was everything I thought romance was supposed to be—exciting, flashy and overwhelming.

Not long after, things started to change.

Looking back now, I can see the red flags that my younger self thought was normal. The backhanded compliments, the subtle digs disguised as jokes. Eventually, he stopped disguising them and said them flat out. By that point, he had me questioning my own judgment and the validity of my feelings so I didn't realize I should've been running for the hills.

"If it makes you feel any better, we've all been young, dumb and in love before," Jolie reassures me.

"True, but most people don't marry the guy."

Gavin calls out for me to watch him on the monkey bars. There's a few other kids at the playground but he mostly sticks to himself. I hope being in Haven Bay will bring him out of his shell a bit.

He was outgoing as a toddler, but Mitch's indifference toward him quickly diminished that. The only thing worse than his indifference was his criticism. Just like with me, Mitch was always finding fault in Gavin. He didn't walk early enough or he played with his toys too loud. When he got older, he wasn't athletic enough—not that Mitch ever spent enough time with him to teach him anything about sports.

The saddest part was, I don't think Gavin even noticed the loss anymore. It was to the point that when I sat him down to explain our separation to him a few months ago, he hardly batted an eye.

Of course, I had planned to tell him with his father, but Mitch could never be bothered to show up. After multiple attempts, I ended up telling Gavin myself. After which, Gavin accepted my hug and then asked if we could go watch Spider-Man.

I truly think Gavin is happier being away from his father and that breaks my heart.

"Anyway. Mitch and Matt didn't get along, which should've been another red flag. So we started to drift apart. Our moms were still super close, so we hung out on occasion, but usually Mitch would get upset and stop talking to me when he heard I was hanging out with Matt. It was easier to make an excuse why I couldn't join and avoid the argument. After high school, Mitch and I moved to the city for school and Matt and I lost touch completely."

Jolie lets out a low whistle. "Man, this Mitch guy is a piece of work. Normally I wouldn't say something like that if you were still married...well, I might but I wouldn't be as blunt. But since you're no longer with him, I'm allowed to call him a douchenozzle."

I smirk. "You can. We've been separated for months. I haven't officially served him the divorce papers yet but that's the next step. There were some reasons why, but I'm starting to think they were just my bullshit way of avoiding change." I shake my head. "He texted me today asking when I would be home. I honestly feel like he thinks the separation means he can just mess around without consequences, while I still cook and clean. Meanwhile, he gets to keep the image of the perfect family."

Jolie gives me a sympathetic look. "That's awful. You deserve so much better than that. Let me know if you need anything." She sits up a little straighter. "You know, I have a friend in the city who's a lawyer. He's in corporate law but I'm sure he knows someone that could help you out. I can give you his number, if you want."

Before I can respond, Gavin comes running over and plops down beside me on the picnic table. "Mommy, I'm hungry."

I turn to him, smiling. "I bet you are. You were running so fast out there. Do you want your sandwich?" He nods and I start to unpack his lunch bag. To Jolie, I say, "Thanks. I might take you up on that."

Jolie doesn't say anything, only nods and then steals one of Gavin's carrots from his plate. She takes an exaggerated bite and he giggles. "Eh...what's up, Doc?" she drawls.

Gavin laughs louder this time. "That's Bugs! Like from Space Jam!"

I hug Gavin because he's just so sweet. Before long, it won't be cool to hug his mom anymore so I take any chance I get to wrap my arms around him.

Any time I think about how much of a mess my life is, I look into his warm brown eyes and toothy smile and remind myself that I must have done something right to have such a great kid.

In all the ways that being with Mitch changed me, I can honestly say becoming Gavin's mom was my greatest transformation. And even though I have a lot of baggage to unpack from our marriage, I could never regret a second of it because it brought me my greatest gift–Gavin.

He deserves the best life and the best version of me. Which is why I make a decision right there in the park.

"Actually, Jolie, I will take that phone number."

I haven't talked to Avery in a few days and it's starting to bother me. She's only been back a week and I already crave her presence more than I care to think about.

It's weird that I went so many years without talking to her and after only a few conversations, I'm hooked like an addict craving their next hit. Except in this case, it's the sound of her laugh I'm itching for.

Instead of following her around, begging for attention like a lovesick puppy, I throw myself into my work.

The expansion is going well, though we ran into a couple of problems with the electrical not being up to code. It seems that the previous contractor liked to cut corners. We've rewired the space, installed the pot lights and spaced the outlets correctly. Next on my list are the counter and display case where the staff will serve beverages and baked goods from. I'm excited about this part of the project since I'll be designing and building the display case completely on my own. When I asked Angie what she had in mind, she told me she trusted me to design something beautiful.

I'm afraid her faith in me might be misplaced, but I'm looking forward to trying to prove her right. Life has dealt her a shitty hand but she never complains. It only makes me want to work that much harder to make it perfect for her.

Usually, when it's a custom piece like this, I would do most of the work over at the workshop and then transport it back to the cafe to be installed. The shop has everything I need and I can be as loud as I want without worrying about disrupting the customers. But even though I know I should stop acting like a damn teenager, I can't stay away.

I try to tell myself it's because I need to check up on the guys and make sure everything is going smoothly. It's complete bullshit though. I hand-picked this crew because they're efficient and skilled enough to not need constant supervision. I wanted Angie to have the best that we had.

Now, I'm seriously regretting it. Every time I've tried to get a minute alone with Avery, a customer needs help finding a book or Bud calls to talk about a job. I'm pretty sure the guys think I'm losing it. Either that or they realize the real reason for my unnecessary drop-ins. I know one or two of them have caught me trying to catch a glimpse of her from behind the construction tarp. It should embarrass me, but I can't seem to bring myself to care anymore.

The universe must take pity on me because when I walk in today, I notice the bookstore is mostly empty. Avery is sitting at one of the small tables near the back, clacking away on her laptop. She doesn't see me enter. Tammy is at the front counter, sorting through a box of what looks like a new shipment of books.

Tammy, Avery and I all went to school together. Tammy was a few grades behind us but, like it is in most small towns, we've known each other forever. Her husband, Keith is the same age as Luke and plays on my beer-league softball team. We've become good buddies since he joined the team a few years back.

"Hey, Tam. How's it going? Jer feeling better?"

Their little guy, Jeremy, had a bad case of the flu a few weeks back and Keith missed a few games so he could stay home with him. When I texted him to see how Jeremy was, Keith said they were taking him to the doctor to get checked out.

"Much better," she says, sighing in relief. "He had us worried for a bit there when he didn't want to eat or drink. The doctor was concerned about dehydration, so that was scary." She puts down the book she was holding. "It was awful seeing him so sick when he's too young to understand why. I'm glad he's back to his usual wild self again."

She stacks a handful of paperbacks on top of each other then carries them over to a shelf.

"Avery's doing some research in the back if you wanted to say hi." She nods her head in Avery's direction and gives me a knowing smile.

I act like I'm considering it before I shrug. "Sure. Since I'm here anyway." I try to act casual but I'm sure she sees right through it.

I walk over to where Avery's sitting. She hasn't noticed me, she's so lost in thought. I take advantage of the moment to check her out.

She's definitely changed over the years; it would be weird if she hadn't. She used to be a thin, gangly teenager, but now she's got curves in all the best places. She's never been tall, measuring in at 5'5 on her best day. There was a time when we were young that she had been taller than me, but once high school hit, I towered over her. It didn't matter though. Her little legs could still skate circles around half the guys I knew during hockey season, and easily ate up the field on the baseball diamonds.

Teenage Avery might've been the girl of my dreams, but the Avery before me was all woman. My hands itched to touch her, to run them over her curves and squeeze her firm ass.

Avery looks up and smiles. It's like a kick in the gut and it takes me a second to recover.

"Hey, Matt. I didn't see you come in. How's the cafe coming?"

"Good. I started on the display case this morning. Your mom gave me the green light to be creative with it, so we'll see how that goes." I shove my hands in my pockets, suddenly self-conscious. "Hopefully I don't completely mess it up."

Where did that come from? I never let anyone see my insecurities. They'd never understand. Which was exactly why I've never told anyone about my true passion.

Avery's eyes soften. "You'll make it beautiful, Matt. I'm so excited to see what you design."

I should feel pressure from her words but instead her confidence sparks my own.

"Thanks, Freckles." I smile then point to her laptop. "What're you working on? What could possibly keep you so focused that you didn't notice when a fine male specimen like myself walks in?" I slide in behind Avery to see what's on her screen, but she quickly snaps it shut.

My eyebrows shoot up in surprise. "Well, well, well. Now I'm even more intrigued. What could Avery Owens be looking at that she wouldn't want anyone to see? It's pretty risky to watch your adult movies in public. I didn't take you for the kinky type, Freckles," I tease. Her cheeks turn that adorable shade of pink that I can't get enough of.

"Shut up, Matt. It's not porn, you perv." She gives my shoulder a small push. "Besides, I read my porn. Like a lady." I snort. She puts a hand protectively over her closed laptop. "It's nothing. Really."

"Come on, Ave. Tell me. No, wait. Let me guess." I stroke my chin in mock deep thought. "You're an international spy commissioned by Miss Carla to find out whether Millie is actually allergic to cats." I wave my hand in front of my face, dismissing the idea. "Nah, too obvious. Hmm." I snap my fingers. "I've got it! You've been hiding your identity this whole time and you're actually the incredibly talented yet highly underrated popstar, Hannah Montana."

My sense of humor confuses most people, but Avery doesn't miss a beat when she responds. "Close. I'm a jewel thief hired by the King of Spain to steal back the priceless Phalange Diamond. We believe it's hidden in Dottie's underwear drawer, but no one's been brave enough to venture inside. The last guy who tried locked himself in a psychiatric hospital. The things he saw in there," she shudders. "The poor guy will probably never be the same again."

I throw my head back laughing and Avery smiles triumphantly.

Damn, I like this girl. She's always gotten me in a way that no one else has. The more I'm around her, the more I'm seeing the old Avery shine through. But there's a new side to her that I would like to get to know, too.

"Alright, Catwoman. Don't tell me then. I'll just keep bugging you about it until you do. Every day. From now until I'm old and gray. Even as a ghost, I'll come back and haunt you. Every night, before you go to sleep, you'll hear me," I shakily moan like a ghost from a bad horror movie. "Avery. Tell me. Tell me," I whisper.

Avery rolls her eyes. "Fine. If it'll shut you up, look." She opens the laptop and spins it toward me.

I lean closer to the screen to make out the print. Across the website header reads the line *How to start a bookmobile.*

"Bookmobile? What's that?"

The drop of her chin is subtle but I notice it right away. "It's just an idea I had. In the winter, there's a lot of older people who don't want to risk driving in the snow. Or residents of retirement and long-term care facilities. So instead of them going without books for half of the year, I figured they could order their books through us and we could deliver them." She looks down at her hands in her lap. "I'm not even sure how it would work or if anyone would be interested. It's probably stupid."

My back straightens, taken aback. Not from the idea. The idea is great. It's exactly what a small, rural area like ours needs. The winters in Haven Bay can be long and harsh. Even though we try to keep up with the snow plows, the wind off the bay can cause drifts to build. Visibility can be minimal on the back roads, making it hard for even the best drivers to maneuver.

What has me so shocked is the tone of self-deprecation in Avery's voice. The Avery I knew wasn't conceited but she definitely wasn't what you'd call humble. If she had an idea, she was following through on it and damn anyone who didn't like it.

I have to keep reminding myself that the woman before me isn't the same girl I knew in high school.

There's nothing wrong with changing but this part of Avery doesn't sit right with me. Mostly because I know the cause and I want nothing more than to ring his stupid neck for it.

Tamping down my anger, I gently place my hand on her shoulder. "I think it's a great idea, Freckles. You shouldn't doubt yourself. You know this town better than anyone. If you figure out the logistics of the program, your mom would be crazy not to implement it."

She bites her lip, trying to hold back a smile.

"Thanks, Matt. I appreciate that."

My eyes pull to the plump lip between her teeth. *Man, this woman gets to me.* I mentally push aside the erotic thoughts those lips conjure and focus on her.

"So, I don't think you ever said. How long are you in town for? Is Mitch going to be joining you guys soon?" I try to keep my voice light but I need to know the answer. If I have to push aside my feelings for her again, I might as well start distancing myself now. I don't know if I can watch her be his emotional punching bag again.

"Mitch and I are separated. We have been for quite a few months now. Jolie actually gave me the number the other day for her friend who's going to help me find a divorce lawyer."

Inside, I'm pulling a "Michael Scott when he finds out Holly's not engaged" worthy celebration, complete with noise makers and Kelly Clarkson songs. I want to shout from the rooftops that I might finally have a chance with my best friend.

I don't care how long it's been; Avery will always be my best friend.

Instead, I say, "I'm so sorry, Avery. That's really rough. Are you okay?" As much as I'm celebrating inside, ending a marriage must be an emotional and painful time. Especially when a kid is involved. I'm sure this hasn't been easy on her.

She nods solemnly. "Yeah. It needed to happen. I'm more worried about Gavin than anything. He and Mitch weren't close by any means, but a kid should have their dad, y'know?" Her eyes wander over my shoulder, lost in thought.

Guessing she's thinking about her dad, I nod. Avery's dad was a piece of shit, in my opinion. Who just ditches their family like that? Especially after receiving such life-altering news, like Angie's MS diagnosis.

I can't even imagine having a dad like that. My dad was the best. He taught me how to fish, play hockey, throw a ball. But out of all the things he taught me, woodworking was my favorite. I remember the first time he let me use the table saw. He held it and did most of the work, but to an eight-year-old, it was the coolest thing I'd ever done. By the end of the weekend, I had a wooden car that I had made with my own two hands.

He once told me that it took a special eye to be able to look at a stump of wood and see it not for what it was, but what it had the potential to be.

Which was probably what I loved most about woodworking—taking something as mundane and ordinary as wood and creating something beautiful. Every time I pick up a chisel or sander, it makes me feel closer to my dad.

So yeah, I know how much a dad's presence, or lack of, can affect a kid.

"So this ended up being good timing for me." She winces. "That sounds awful, doesn't it? I mean, I would've dropped everything to come here and help my mom, no matter what I had going on. And I don't mean to say I'm glad my mom got sick—"

"Avery." I put my hand on her shoulder and it quiets her instantly. "I know. You don't have to explain to me."

She looks up at me then blows out a breath. "Long story short, I'm not sure what my next move is. I'm not sure where the future will take us, whether it's Haven Bay or Edmonton, so I'm trying to live in the moment for now."

I nod, smiling again. "Good for you. You deserve to be happy. I'm proud of you for realizing that."

She treats me to a small smile before her phone lights up with a silent alarm.

"Oh, I better get going. Gavin's been with my mom for three hours now and I'm trying not to let her get too tired. Though neither of them seem to want to listen to me," she half-heartedly complains. I'd say that Angie and Gavin playing together too long is a good problem to have, all things considered. She packs her laptop into her light blue bag with a big smiley face and the words "Have the day you deserve!" in script writing on it.

"See you later, Matt." She slings the strap over her shoulder and starts to walk to the front door.

"Avery," I call out and she looks at me over her shoulder. "You should tell your mom about your bookmobile idea."

She smiles. "Yeah. I think I will." She waves to me and then calls out a goodbye to Tammy.

Tammy shoots me another knowing grin but I ignore her. Then I walk to the construction zone, whistling the tune to "Wrecking Ball".

I open the screen door to the sounds of music and laughter. Hanging up my jacket, I follow the melodic sound into the kitchen. Gavin sits perched on a stool beside my mom at the kitchen counter. They're singing along to Disney's *Coco* while Gavin presses a fork into the tops of the peanut butter cookies that line the sheet pan.

"Was anyone going to invite me to the sing-along? I love a good peanut butter cookie as much as the next guy," I say, grabbing a cooling cookie from the first batch's tray.

"Mommy!" Gavin jumps down from the chair and launches himself into my arms.

I hoist him up and settle him on my hip. He's almost too big for me to carry but I'll do it for as long as I'm able. One day, I'll pick him up for the last time. But today's not that day, so I snuggle him closer.

It's hard to believe that he'll be starting school in the fall. It feels like just yesterday, he was cuddled up in my arms as a newborn while I rocked him back to sleep. Those late nights, when it seemed like we were the only two people awake in the world, were some of the hardest and best times. Looking back,

I treasure those moments because all too soon, they're gone and all I'm left with are the memories.

Giving him one last squeeze, I pull back to look him in the eye. "Hi, handsome. Did you have fun with Gram since I dropped you off?"

He nods his head eagerly. "Yeah! We played fire trucks outside and builded a city but Sushi crashed into the bridge when a bunny ran by. But then Gram said that it was actually an earthquake that knocked over the bridge so the firefighters had to use their special 'copter to save the people instead." He waves his hand in the air, mimicking a helicopter flying. "Then we came back inside and Gram said that peanut butter cookies were your favorite so we should make some for you to eat when you got home. Then I told the 'Lexa to play Disney songs and I told Gram I can sing louder than her. Then Gram let me push the forks on the cookies before they go in the oven."

God, I love him.

I know that's a ridiculous thing to say because of course I love my kid. But he is just so cute and funny and kind. I give his side a tickle and revel in his delighted squeal.

"Oh boy! You had a busy day. I guess you wouldn't be interested in playing Snakes and Ladders tonight then? And maybe after we can watch the new Disney movie. I figured we could have popcorn but if you made cookies, maybe we could eat those instead. What'd you think?"

His eyes widen. He places a hand on either side of my face, making sure I'm looking directly into his eyes. "Mommy," he says, expression serious, "that is the bestest idea you ever had."

I laugh and put him back on the floor. "Then go help Gram finish up those cookies while I call Niro's and order a pizza. We can't have a movie night without pizza."

Gavin jumps up and lets out a loud whoop in celebration. "Gram! Did you hear that? We're having pizza, cookies

AND movies! This is the best day EVER!" He stops suddenly. "I'm going to go grab Spider-Man so he can help, too." He races away to his room to grab his favorite stuffed toy.

"I can't believe you're still standing, Mom. I'm tired just listening to your day. Maybe you shouldn't have him so long next time. I don't want you to get worn down."

My mom wipes her hands on her apron and walks over to me. She mimics Gavin's earlier gesture and holds my face in her hands.

"Avery. Listen to me closely. I mean this with all the love in the world: quit nagging me. I'm fine. I know I pushed it too hard this spring but I know better now. I promise you I won't ignore my health again. But that little boy and I have not spent nearly enough time together over the years."

My smile falls and she holds up a hand to cut off my response. "I'm not blaming you. I should've tried harder, too. We'll get into that more another time since Gav will be back soon. But, please, let me get to know him again. Let us spend as much time together as we can. I promise I will rest when I'm tired but right now, I want to run around with him and ride bikes down the street. Because I'm not sure how much longer I'll be able to do that with him and I want to savor every second of the time I do have."

She wipes away the tear I hadn't realized had fallen with her thumb.

"I'm sorry." I sniffle. "I just don't want to lose you. I know one day I'll have to live without you, but I'm not ready for it yet. I'm not strong enough for that."

My mom clucks her tongue at me in that familiar, disapproving way of hers. "Avery Marjorie Owens."

Her "mom" voice still makes my back straighten, even at twenty-seven.

"You are a strong, smart and beautiful woman. You're the

best mom and daughter out there. Don't ever talk that way about yourself again, you hear me?"

"Yes ma'am," I choke out. I wrap my arms around her, pressing my head into her shoulder.

"Well, that's enough of that. Gav's going to be out here soon, so wipe your face and have a peanut butter cookie. They're some of my best." She gives me a squeeze, then walks over to the oven and pops in the last tray of cookies.

"Hey, Mom? After Gav's asleep, do you think we could talk about something?" She crooks an eyebrow at me skeptically from over her shoulder. "It's nothing bad, just something I want to discuss about the store." I pick up another cookie and bite off a chunk. I softly moan as the moist confection hits my mouth.

"Well, you've definitely piqued my interest. Meet you on the porch swing after bedtime? I'll bring the wine."

"Deal."

Gavin charges into the kitchen, stuffed Spider-Man in hand. "Spidey and I are ready, Mommy! Can I have a cookie now?"

I ruffle his hair and grab my phone. "After dinner, buddy. I'm going to go call Niro's now. Why don't you go grab Snakes and Ladders and get the couch set up?"

I walk out of the room, only to hear a quiet gasp and a loudly whispered, "Thanks, Gram!" from behind me.

I shake my head at my mom's spoiling, then dial the pizzeria.

"Hey, Niro, it's Avery Ols–uh, Owens. Thanks it's good to be back— No, I'm not in witness protection. Yes, I'm sure. I don't think I would've told you my name if I was—" I let out an exasperated sigh. "Can I place an order now, please?"

This frickin' town.

I'M IN A FANTASTIC MOOD. We had so much fun last night playing board games and watching movies. I'm glad that Gavin and my mom have this time together. I'm not sure how long we'll be here but one thing I know for certain, no matter where we are after this summer, we'll be visiting a lot more often. Or maybe my mom will come visit us.

After Gavin went to bed, my mom and I sat on the porch swing and I told her all about my idea for the bookmobile program. She asked logical questions, which I had prepared for. I laid out my plan—initial costs, potential routes, projected profits, etc.

The fact that she hadn't immediately agreed and instead listened unbiasedly to all the pros and cons of the program made her approval that much sweeter. I knew she hadn't just agreed because she was my mom; she was a businesswoman investing in an idea.

After that, I couldn't contain my excitement and the ideas started pouring out of me. By the end of the conversation, we had a list of programs and promotions that we were going to start rolling out over the next couple of months.

The bookmobile will probably take the longest to get up and running. We'll need to gather a list of potential customers and reach out to local long-term care facilities. Then we'll need to arrange prepayments and schedule drop-offs with customers. The town may be small but our surrounding county is large with many back roads, making drop-offs more time-consuming.

The start-up costs will be minimal if we use my mom's SUV in the meantime, but eventually, if the program takes off, we might have to consider something bigger. For now, we've decided to start small. We're hoping to have the program up and running for the winter months.

The first new program we're going to start is a monthly book club. I'm planning to get in touch with Hank Jones from the butcher shop down the road to see if we can work out a deal on some charcuterie boards. Then I'm hoping Alana Fox from Silver Fox Winery will be interested in supplying the wine and spirits. Once the cafe is open, we'll be able to offer coffee, tea and some of our baked goods as well.

I can hardly contain my excitement, so I've been working on a to-do list whenever there's a lull at the shop this morning. The easiest part will be spreading the word. I could probably let half the town know by lunch if I told the next three customers that walked through the door about it—one of the few bonuses of living in a town filled with busy bodies.

I'm immersed in spreadsheets and quotes when Jolie strolls through the front door. She spots me at my usual back table and switches directions toward me.

"Avery! What's shaking? Actually. Don't answer that. I'll tell you what's shaking. Me, you and our fine asses at The Dive tonight." She wiggles her hips and I laugh. "I'm in dire need of a girls' night and I can bet you are, too. Call your mama and see if she can put your sweet boy to bed tonight."

She must sense my hesitation because she clasps her hands together under her chin, sticks out her bottom lip and widens her baby blues into puppy-dog eyes that could rival Gavin's.

"Please," she begs, dragging out the last syllable. "Pretty, pretty, pretty please with a cherry on top? First round's on me."

I try not to smile but she's being so ridiculous, I can't help it. And, okay, it feels good to have a friend again who wants to hang out and do fun, normal things.

"Let me call my mom to make sure she's okay babysitting. But if she's okay with it, then sure. That sounds like fun."

I barely finish my sentence before Jolie launches herself into my arms, pulling me up and rocking me back and forth. "Yay! I'm so excited! You should come by first and we'll get ready together. I've been dying to get my hands on your beautiful hair. And I have a jacket that would look kick ass on you. Ah! I can't wait!"

Her phone beeps and she looks down at the screen. "Oh, shit. I have to go but let me know what your mom says, okay? See you tonight."

She rushes out the door but pauses in front of the window to shake her hips at me again. I laugh and wave her away.

Looks like I have my first girls' night tonight.

CHAPTER 11

MATT

It's been a long week. The granite countertop I ordered for a custom job came in on Monday and was the wrong color. I had to spend a day and a half going back and forth with the supplier trying to find the right one.

Bud has been known to be a little (a lot) hotheaded so it's easier if I fix the problem myself and wait to tell him about it until after it's resolved.

While I was primarily working on Angie's expansion, I still had my hands in some other projects that needed custom work. Bud might be a gasket waiting to blow, but he knows I'm the best he has when it comes to custom jobs.

Then one of our guys had a family emergency and had to fly home. Bud told him to not worry about work and to take care of his family. That's one of the reasons I've continued working with the old grump all these years—he takes good care of his crew.

While I felt for the guy, being down a laborer during our busy season meant longer hours and everyone pulling double the weight.

Which means by the time Friday afternoon rolls around, I'm sweaty, tired and in no mood to be around people. All I want to do is sit on my couch with a cold beer and my goofy dog and watch baseball in silence.

Instead, I'm at The Dive with Luke while Rhett works the bar. When Luke texted me asking if I wanted to go out, I almost said no. But I never say no to a night out and I knew Luke would ask questions, so it was just easier to go. I figure I'll stay for a couple of beers, listen to the band play a few songs and then call it an early night.

That was until Avery walked through the door. It's honestly a little embarrassing how quickly my mood lifts at the sight of her.

She's wearing ripped jeans that look like they're painted over her lush hips and curvy legs. Her hair falls in waves at her shoulders and a pale pink jacket covers a lacy white top underneath. She always looks beautiful but tonight she's turning heads. If I could form a sentence right now, I'd have a few words with some of those heads about keeping their eyes to themselves.

Did I mention how well those jeans hug her ass?

They walk over to the opposite end of the bar, grab a couple of drinks then head to a high-top table. Luke is still talking beside me, about what I have no idea anymore.

I lift my beer to my lips and take a long drink, never taking my eyes off of her.

After Avery mentioned that she and Mitch were separated, I wanted to ask her out on the spot. But even I know that's a tactless move. So I've been waiting (not so) patiently until the right time.

I think I just heard my resolve snap in half.

AVERY

My eyes take a second to adjust to the suddenly dim lighting as we walk through the doors of The Dive. I wasn't old enough to get in before I moved away to college so I've never been inside the old bar.

Then, it was a dark and dingy place where you could get a cheap beer and a view of the bay but not much else.

From what Jolie's told me, the previous owner left Rhett the bar a year ago after which he turned it into a respected pub known for its live music. I look around, noting the already crowded bar and dance floor. The band is playing a Bruce Springsteen cover and the lively beat vibrates within my chest.

I haven't been to a bar since college and never as a single woman. I'm glad Jolie's here because I'm suddenly feeling like a fish out of water. Since I became a mom, I haven't dressed for anything other than functionality.

Even when Mitch hosted a business dinner, I wore dark colors in case Gavin woke up and needed snuggling back to sleep. Black hid the drool or spills well enough that I could seamlessly shift from host to mom and back again without much fuss.

Jolie coached me through picking out an outfit for our night out. It was fun to dress up and I felt fantastic twisting and turning in front of her full-length mirror.

Until I looked at the tag and noticed the dusty pink suede jacket Jolie let me borrow is dry clean only. *Um, pardon?* Does Haven Bay even have a dry cleaner? Then the white top. Is she nuts? White is a magnet for juice spills and grubby kid fingers. I guess when you're kid-free, you can dress without having to worry about those things.

Before we left, I tossed a stain remover pen into my clutch. Just in case.

Perched at a high-top table near the dance floor, I twirl the straw in my vodka soda. No way was I risking the bright pink of my usual vodka cranberry with this outfit.

"So, since you're a busy single mom running a business, I'll give you a small break on the fact that you've been here almost a month and haven't come to a single one of my classes yet." Jolie arches a perfectly manicured eyebrow in my direction.

"You still haven't told me what types of classes you offer," I counter, mirroring the look back at her. "For all I know, I could be signing up for a nude yoga class. I wouldn't put it past you or this town."

Jolie throws her head back laughing, unaware or unbothered by the stares she receives. "That's true. Don't give me any ideas because I can be easily persuaded. Especially since it'll probably give Officer Grouchy Pants a coronary." She snorts, tipping her drink toward the bar where Luke is sitting. "As for what kind of classes they are, you'll just have to come to one and find out."

I laugh at her nickname for Luke Brady. For some reason that I haven't figured out yet, they have a bit of a tense relationship. When I asked her about it, she just shrugged and said something about Luke's ass being too nice to have a stick lodged so far up it.

"Speaking of nudity," she says, lifting her rye and Coke to her lips. "Matt Brady has not stopped eye-fucking you since we walked in."

I choke on my drink. After I pull myself together, I hazard a look in the direction Jolie is staring. At the end of the bar are Luke and Matt. Luke looks like he's in the middle of telling a story but Matt doesn't seem to be listening. Instead, he stares back at me, his eyes dark and unwavering. The corner of his lips turn up in a half smile. He leans over and says something to Luke, his gaze never leaving mine as he stands.

Luke seems to grumble something back but he stands to

follow. They round the bar and make their way toward our table.

"Holy shit. What do I do?" My eyes widen as I spin to Jolie.

"Relax and enjoy a hot guy's attention." Jolie smiles like a cat to a canary. "Matt, Officer Grouchy Pants. What brings you two over to a couple of hot ass women like us?"

Luke rolls his eyes. "Jolie. I almost didn't recognize you without the group of screaming octogenarians following you."

My eyebrows shoot into my hairline but Jolie just waves me off.

Matt leans closer and smiles pointedly at me. "We were hoping you'd take pity on two pathetic guys and let us have a drink with you beautiful ladies."

"Good answer. Pull up some chairs, Bradys." Jolie leans back and gestures to the seats across from us.

Matt sits in the chair beside me. "Hey, Freckles. You look gorgeous. Though your usual messy bun really does something to me." He wags his eyebrows at me and a giggle escapes my lips.

Really? A giggle? Pull it together, Avery.

"Thanks. It's nice to dress up but can I tell you a secret?" He nods and I lean in conspiringly. "I'm dreaming about my pjs right now. Fuzzy slippers, big socks–the whole nine-yards."

He chuckles. "I don't imagine you still have those unicorn pjs, do you?"

"I'll have you know, Matt Brady, that those pjs were the comfiest pair I've ever owned. The material was perfectly worn and stretchy and I'll never find anything as good ever again." I sigh dramatically.

"They were so stretchy because you'd had them since you were twelve and wore them until you were seventeen. I'm surprised they didn't disintegrate." He wrinkles his nose in mock revulsion.

I swat his arm and hold in a laugh. "I didn't realize you were so preoccupied with my bedtime attire, Matt Brady."

"I was preoccupied with everything involving you, Freckles. I still am." His voice drops to a low, gravelly tone and his eyes darken. "Especially what you wear to bed."

The combination of his voice and those words cause my head to spin faster than when we used to ride the Tilt-a-Whirl at the town festival. Matt liked me? Since when?

Before I can respond—with what, I have no clue—the band starts to play a slow, sensual Chris Stapleton song.

Matt puts his drink down and stands, offering a hand to me. "Come on, Freckles. I believe you owe me a dance."

My body moves on instinct and I place my hand in his. He pulls me to my feet and keeps my hand in his as we make our way to the dance floor.

We weave through the crowded bar until Matt finds the spot he's looking for and stops. He pulls me to him, then wraps an arm around my back. He takes the hand he's still holding and brings it to his chest, pressing it right over his heart. I lift my free arm to his shoulder and we start to sway.

"Did I mention how beautiful you look tonight? Not just the clothes, which are," Matt closes his eyes and lifts his pinched fingers to his lips, "chef's kiss." I roll my eyes but I can't stop my smile or the blush creeping up my chest. "But you seem lighter. More relaxed. It's nice to see."

I think about it for a second. "I feel lighter. Lighter than I have in a long time."

The corner of his lips draw down but I don't want his sympathy. I don't want to bring *him* here so I change the subject. "Hey, what's all this about me owing you a dance? I just got back to town. I don't remember any deals being made since then."

The song ends but another slow one starts in its place. Matt makes no move to stop so we continue to sway.

"I'm a little hurt you don't remember." I give him a confused look. "Seventh grade. The Valentine's Day dance. Every other guy had danced with a girl that day but me. I asked you to save poor lonely me a dance so I wouldn't seem so pathetic but you spent the whole night holding hands with Jake Fender." He grumbles and I try not to laugh. "I never recovered from the humiliation. Jake still stops me to gloat whenever I see him at the grocery store with his three kids."

My face is starting to hurt from how much I've smiled and laughed tonight. "He does not, you big baby. If only you could get over such an awful, embarrassing moment from *fourteen years ago*. I'm sure the ladies really eat it up when you tell them that sob story."

We both know I meant it jokingly but something in the air shifts. I don't want to think about Matt with other women but I'm not stupid. I know there's been women. Probably a lot by the looks of how well he filled out since high school.

And what right do I have to get upset? I was married for the last five years and in a relationship for six years before that. I've been with exactly one man in my life and his idea of foreplay had been a few misplaced strokes at my crotch.

Matt pulls me out of my thoughts by tracing his finger down the line on my brow. "I'm not thinking about any other girls, Freckles. Not since you came back to town."

I bite my lip to stop the small smile that threatens to overtake my face.

"I know you haven't been separated very long and you've got a lot on your plate. But I missed you, Avery. I missed laughing with you. I missed talking about life and our dreams on the old swing set. I even missed those stupid pranks you'd pull and I'd end up taking the blame for." His finger slides along my jawline to the edge of my bottom lip. "I miss my best friend. I know a lot has changed but I want to get to know the new Avery. Because she seems pretty kick ass, too." He looks down at me with hopeful eyes and a crooked smile that shows just a hint of vulnerability.

My heart does Olympic-worthy backflips then promptly melts into the floor.

All the reasons for saying no that I've been reciting since the first time he almost asked me out go flying out the window.

Right now, with the music low and his dark eyes focused intently on mine, every part of me is screaming *hell yes!*

"Matt, I—"

"Matt? Is that you?" A silky voice behind us asks, bursting our bubble of intimacy.

We both turn to see a tall, slim brunette standing before us. She's wearing a black tank with "Stacey's Last Fling Before The Ring!" in glitter across it. Behind her, a group of girls with matching shirts cheer as the apparent bride throws back a shot.

"Oh. Hey, Dana. How's it going?" Matt lets his hand drop from around my waist and gives Dana a quick one-armed hug but keeps my hand locked in his.

"Good! We're just here for my friend Stacey's bachelorette weekend. I told her all about my trip here last year and how," she looks him up and down with an obvious smile, "hospitable the men are here. We had a good time, didn't we?"

My stomach plummets and a sudden rush of nausea slams into me. Avoiding Matt's eyes, I take a step back, pulling my hand free. "Well, I don't mean to interrupt but I told my mom I wouldn't be late so I should get going. Do you mind letting Jolie know I'm heading out?"

Before either of them can respond, I spin on my heel and search desperately for an exit. I'm in luck and find a back door propped open nearby. I nod politely at the two guys having a smoke outside as I push past them and into the parking lot.

What was I thinking? I almost made a big mistake.

If I were to say yes to Matt, there's no way I could be casual. The connection we've shared so far is proof of that. If I were to date him, I could see myself not just falling but face planting into love with him. As much as I care about Matt, he doesn't seem like the serious relationship type. I know he cares about me, too, but I'm a package deal. I can't let Gavin get hurt.

Even if protecting him means hurting myself in the process.

I quicken my pace when I hear someone calling my name. Seconds later, I'm being spun around by the elbow to face Matt. We're outside the bar, just past the parking lot so there's no one around to hear us.

"Avery. It's not what you think," Matt pleads.

"So, she's not an ex or past hook up or whatever you want to call her?"

"Look, Dana's—"

I place my hand on his arm to stop him. "Matt. I'm not mad or judging you for your past. You're single and you have no responsibilities; you should be having fun and doing what you want. I just can't do that. I don't have the luxury to have fun. I can't screw around because a little boy who depends on me."

I sigh. "I don't think this is a good idea, Matt. You and me." I let out a humorless laugh. "Hell, I'm still legally married. My life is all kinds of complicated. I don't need to drag anyone into it, especially someone just looking to have fun."

Matt's face hasn't moved a muscle since I started talking. A hard and determined look replaces his normally carefree demeanor when he finally responds.

"Avery, you better listen good when I tell you this because I'm not saying it twice," he says slowly, his voice as hard as his eyes. "I am not giving up on us. I've been waiting most of my life for a chance with you. So unless you tell me right now that you're not interested, I'm not giving up." He pauses, waiting for me to deny it but I can't.

"That guy that Dana knew?" He jerks a thumb over his shoulder toward the bar. "I'm not that guy anymore. I haven't been for a while now. And I'll do whatever it takes for you to see me as the guy you can rely on. The guy who shows up and continues to show up every day. Who treats you and that little boy of yours exactly the way you should be treated. I may not deserve you both yet, but I'll do everything in my power to get there. Because you deserve the world, Avery. You just have to ask for it."

He reaches into his pocket and pulls out his keys. "Here. Take my truck home. It's the black Dodge behind Taylor Construction. I don't like the idea of you walking home alone this late at night." I start to refuse but he pushes them into my hand. "Please. I know it's Haven Bay and nothing bad ever happens, but I'd feel better if I knew you got home okay. Just leave the keys under the mat and I'll get the truck in the morning."

I'm not sure what to say, so I take his keys. He nods then turns and walks back into the bar, leaving me standing on the sidewalk, stunned with my heart at my feet.

After Matt's proclamation, I stand on the sidewalk in shock before eventually picking my jaw up off the ground.

Taking out my phone, I shoot off a text to Jolie telling her my mom called saying Gavin wasn't feeling well and I was heading home. Lying to her sucks, but I can't handle a conversation right now. I'm too thrown off by what Matt said.

I cross the street toward Taylor Construction and easily find Matt's truck in the otherwise empty parking lot. I pull open the door and climb onto the worn leather seat.

Swinging the truck out onto the street, I head toward my mom's house. I turn up the music, trying to drown out my thoughts and the feeling of being Matt's arms earlier. I can't get the look of hurt in his eyes out of my head when I told him I couldn't date him. When I first came back, I had a feeling that he wanted to ask me out but to hear him say he'd been thinking about it since high school floored me.

It's not that I never thought of Matt that way. In fact, he was my first crush.

When we were twelve, Jeff Wiens had made some asshole comment about my dad leaving my mom and I. Usually I could brush off stupid comments like that, but for some reason, that day I couldn't get past it. I just about lost it in class before I faked sick to go home and cry into my pillow. Usually I didn't let my dad leaving us bother me; it was his loss. But every once in a while, my insecurities would pop up and I'd ask myself: why was it so easy for him to leave me?

When I heard that Matt punched Jeff in the face for what he said, my heart made a weird squeezing feeling I'd never felt before. When he came by to check on me, it squeezed again. The next day at school, Jeff approached me, face battered and bruised. He looked warily at a fierce-eyed Matt behind me before grumbling out an apology. While he scurried away, Matt put his hand in mine in silent understanding and I softened more.

Matt stole a piece of my heart that day.

The Valentine's Day dance was the following week and was the night I was going to tell him I liked him. I was so nervous all week that he teased me about acting weird. He tried so hard to get me to tell him why, even trying to tickle my feet which he knew were super sensitive. I ended up giving him a black-eye from his face being a little too close when he tickled a reflex move out of me.

He never dared to try that move again and I never told him how I felt.

Even though I'm home earlier than expected, I hardly sleep that night. I toss and turn until the morning light starts to peek through my blinds. When I finally do fall asleep, I'm startled awake moments later by the sound of my phone's alarm.

I check the time and bolt upright. With only ten minutes until I'm supposed to leave for the store, I rush through my morning routine. I pull on dark yoga pants and a t-shirt that may or may not have a stain on the chest; I don't have time to check.

Luckily, my mom is hanging out with Gavin today so I don't have to wake either of them before I fly out the door. The shop is pretty close but I'll be late if I walk like usual, so I head to the shed to grab my old bike, noticing that Matt's truck is already gone.

Pushing all thoughts of last night out of my head, I pull my bright red bike out from the shed and take off down the driveway. I make it to The Book Nook with three minutes to spare. I pull my bike up around the back, not bothering to lock it up.

Like Matt said, nothing bad ever happens in Haven Bay.

I hurry through the shop to the front door and unlock the deadbolt from the inside.

Before I can turn, Dottie barges through the front door with Maeve right behind her. "I thought you weren't going to make it. I bet Maeve that you finally got laid last night and were too busy going for round two to open." Dottie cackles. "Damn, I guess the drinks are on me tonight."

"I had faith in you, honey." Maeve pats my hand. "I knew you were too responsible to go back for seconds and leave us waiting. But if you want to call Tammy in, I'm sure your handsome man will still be waiting for you."

For the love of—

I'm way too sleep deprived for this. The worst part is, since I was late this morning, I didn't have a chance to stop for my usual caramel latte from the diner. I've been drinking them since high school and they've been essential to my morning routine.

I silently count to three before responding.

"Sorry, ladies, the only man in my bed these days is the one with nightmares and needs his mom to cuddle him back to sleep."

I see Dottie's eyes light up mischievously so I stop her before she scars me for life. "Gavin, Dottie. I'm talking about my son. It's too early to hear about whatever weird kinks you're thinking of."

"Weird kinks, eh?" A deep, raspy voice says from behind me. "Does that mean my suggestion for expanding the erotica section to include dinosaur smut has been approved?"

My heart jumps into my throat at the sound of Matt's voice. He walks through the front door with a to-go cup in each hand. The crew isn't in on weekends, so I didn't expect to see him today. Especially not so soon after our—whatever that was—last night.

Despite his speech the night before, I expected him to go home and realize that I wasn't worth the effort. I figured we'd avoid each other for a few days, then we'd engage in meaningless small talk on Monday until eventually things were back to normal.

Instead, he's in my mom's bookstore, joking with me about dinosaur smut like nothing happened.

Did I imagine last night?

Dottie throws her head back and laughs. "Oh, Matt Brady, you always know how to test an old lady's bladder, don't you?"

Matt's nose wrinkles but he forces a smile. "And you always know how to test a man's stomach, Dottie."

His comment sparks another round of cackling from the older women.

Shaking his head with an exasperated smile, he turns to me. "Mornin', Freckles. I figured you might need a little extra caffeine this morning." He passes me one of the to-go cups in his hand.

I accept it gingerly. "Thanks, Matt." I bring the cup to my nose and inhale the mouthwatering aroma of caramel and coffee.

He remembered my order.

My heart does that ridiculous dance that it seems to save

just for Matt. I glance over at Dottie and Maeve, who seem to have wandered over to the romance section. Even with the distance, their bloodhound ears might be able to hear me so I lean toward him and whisper, "Listen. About last night—"

He takes a step closer, his height causing him to tower over me. My stomach clenches at his close proximity. I try not to breathe him in but God, he smells like forbidden sex in a forest.

Jeez. Down, girl.

"Look, we can talk about last night all you want, but nothing's changed. You're not ready to date. I get that and I respect it. But I'm also not going to just roll over and let you slip away. So, I'll wait for you until you are. As long as that takes." He lifts his hand up to gently cup my cheek. I allow myself a small moment of weakness and lean into his palm.

"You're worth the wait, Freckles." There's an intensity in his eyes I've never seen before. Then something crazy happens.

I believe him.

IT'S BEEN twelve days since the morning after The Dive. Twelve days since Matt first brought me that first caramel latte. Every morning since, without fail, Matt comes walking into the shop with a cup in each hand—a caramel latte for me and a dark roast coffee for him.

It's gotten to the point where I've stopped buying my own in the morning or else I'll be wired by lunch. The second day, I drank both lattes and ended up rearranging the front window display five times, ordered all of our Thanksgiving and Christmas stock and picked out our next five "Book of the Week" books. All before lunch. Then I went into the back office and crashed at my desk until Tammy came in with a gigantic bottle of water and told me to hydrate.

Apparently two sugary lattes in under an hour exceeds my caffeine limit for the day.

But it wasn't just coffee. Every day, Matt has made sure to come over to the shop side and chat, whether it's random small talk or giving his input on the design for the Book Club posters.

Probably the most thoughtful thing of all, was when he came in with a poster for the local summer camp at the recreation center. He said he had looked into some activities to entertain young kids locally and the summer camp came highly recommended.

I was so touched that he had thought not only of me, but of Gavin, that I could barely manage a "thank you" through the lump of emotion in my throat.

The best part? Matt said that his mom's boyfriend, Pete, has grandchildren that go to the same camp. Matt asked if Gavin would want to meet them so he would know someone if he decided to go. He knew how hard it is for Gavin to make friends and, instead of just letting him fend for himself, he wanted to help Gavin feel comfortable.

All of this attention was starting to feel a little overwhelming. It's how I imagine Dottie would feel if she ever saw a Magic Mike show in person. It's amazing and wonderful but I also feel like my heart is going to leap out of my chest at any second.

If I'm not mistaken, he's been making every excuse to touch me. A brush on the arm while he told me a story, a hand on my lower back when he passed by. All of it meant to deliberately drive me crazy. I was sure of it.

The other day, I excitedly told him about all of the new programs and projects my mom and I would be implementing over the next few months. After I finished explaining, he wrapped his arms around me and told me how proud of me he was. "I knew you had it in you, Avery. You just have to believe in yourself as much as the rest of us do."

But the icing on the swoon-worthy cake was how hard he worked to get Gavin to open up.

A few days ago, Gavin asked what the screwdriver Matt was using was for. Instead of brushing off the question, Matt bent down and patiently explained what the name of the screwdriver was and showed him how to use it properly. When Gavin's eyes lit up after successfully driving the screw into a piece of wood, Matt grabbed a handful of tools to let him try, too. Gavin was in heaven and I'm pretty sure I had cartoon heart eyes popping out of my head watching them together.

The rest of the day, through dinner, and even during bedtime, Gavin talked about the different types of screwdrivers and the proper way to hold a hammer. It was the most excited I've seen him since he met Spider-Man at the mall last year.

But just when I thought my weak heart couldn't take any more, Matt came in the next morning with a kids' tool belt, exactly like his. He had filled it with a couple of screwdrivers, a small hammer and a measuring tape. Gavin was so excited when Matt gave it to him, that he jumped up and gave him a big hug. Matt looked at me wide-eyed over Gavin's shoulder but quickly recovered and wrapped an arm around his back.

It was my allergies that caused my eyes to water. I swear.

So to say that by the twelfth day my resolve was wavering was the understatement of the year.

Luckily, Matt had been pulled away to work on another site and left not long after dropping off my latte. The time alone gave me some time to think. Or argue with myself, depending on who you ask.

I can't deny that I have feelings for Matt. I'd be stupid to even try. But was it enough? I've been burned so many times by thinking that love could fix everything when, in reality, it caused me to lose it all instead.

My independence.

My self-confidence.

My family and friends.

My home.

Only, I didn't feel that when I thought of Matt. Not that I was anywhere near ready to be in love again, but the thought suddenly didn't seem as scary as it once did.

I know these past few weeks don't guarantee that Matt's serious about the future and to be honest, I'm not even sure where I'll be by the end of the summer. I have an appointment with the lawyer Jolie's friend recommended in a few weeks. Hopefully I'll have more answers on the divorce and custody arrangements then.

For now, all I know for sure is that I want Matt. Maybe there's a small part of me that always has.

Matt's the type of guy to give you the shirt off his back. In fact, once at a school dance, he gave me his dress shirt after I spilled a drink all over my new dress.

My mom has mentioned that before Pete, Matt used to mow his mom's lawn in the summer and shoveled her driveway in the winter.

When his younger sister, Tori, decided to live out her dream of being an event planner in Toronto, Matt took the week off work to move her across the country and help her get settled.

And he might love to give Luke shit, but I know he would drop everything in an instant to help him without a second thought. He's always willing to lend a hand and quick to defend when he senses trouble.

Probably best of all, Matt makes me feel safe. Seen. He makes me feel protected and confident. Like even if I make the wrong decision, it doesn't change my self-worth.

Maybe love doesn't make you lose yourself. Not the right kind of love anyway. Maybe that's what I've missing all these years.

The bell at the front door chimes. I glance up to find the smiling face I've been waiting to see since I came home.

"Avery, honey! It's so good to see you." Matt's mom pulls me in for a hug. There are few things as calming as a mother's hug. Even if she's not my mom by blood, Francesca Brady has never treated me as anything other than one of her's.

I squeeze her back. "It's so good to see you, too. I missed you. How was your trip?"

Now that Franny and Pete are both retired, they take frequent trips all around North America. Her most recent trip was a month-long Alaskan cruise, which was where she had been when my mom got sick. She tried to cancel the cruise until my mom threatened to not drink wine with her for a year if she did.

"When did you get home?" I gesture for her to sit at one of the small tables.

"Late last night. I was so excited to see you, I wanted to come over right away. But Pete convinced me to wait until you were all awake before I went running over." She scrunches her nose at the idea of having to wait until morning and I bite back a laugh.

"Anyway, I can't stay long. I'm meeting your mom and Gavin at the park. I can't wait to see how big he is now! But I wanted to see you first and personally invite you to our house on Saturday afternoon. We're having a barbecue with some family and friends. Tori said she couldn't get the time off work, so she won't be there but everyone else I've talked to is coming. Pete's daughters are coming with their families, so there will be lots of kids for Gavin to play with."

Before I can respond, she lightly smacks her legs and stands. "So, it's settled then. You'll be there. Anytime after three. Can't wait to catch up!" She waves over her shoulder and takes off out the door.

Typical, Franny. She has a heart of gold and means well; she really does. But when her "old-world Italian side" comes out, as Matt used to call it, she tends to steamroll over people. She tries to hold back when it comes to serious matters, so we let her get away with it on trivial things like this.

Used to her overbearing nature, I take out my phone and start scrolling Pinterest for appetizer ideas to bring to a barbecue. As I scroll past recipe after recipe, I let my mind wander. I swear I only think about Matt's jean-clad butt about about 60% of the time.

Okay, no more than 70%. Max.

CHAPTER 13

MATT

"You don't sign a guy that's 32 years old to an eight-year contract. The only thing Elsher has done for the Jays is hit that homerun to move them into the conference finals. The rest of the time the guy's a whiney diva," Rhett remarks.

He takes a sip of his Coke and leans against the railing on my mom's porch. His face is straight but I can see the glint of humor in his eye as he riles Luke up. Sometimes I think the only reason Rhett is a Mariners' fan is to piss off Luke, a die-hard Blue Jays fan.

We're sitting on my mom's back porch, enjoying the sunshine at her "welcome home" barbecue. Kids are running around the backyard, kicking balls and laughing. Groups of my mom's friends and family sit around chatting. Luke's manning the barbecue while Rhett and I "supervise"—otherwise known as drinking beer and ribbing Luke about the meat being cooked wrong.

"Are you fucking serious?" Luke turns to Rhett, shooting him an incredulous look. "He was top ten in the league last year in at-bats. The guy has never been injured. He's an iron horse and a stud on third base. He's a future Hall of Famer. Why the hell wouldn't they sign him?"

Luke's voice raises with every argument. I have no idea how Rhett's keeping a straight face because the look on Luke's face is priceless. "Dude, he's thirty-two. He's in his back nine and he's not getting any younger."

Luke throws his hands up. "Yeah, he's thirty-two and still playing at that caliber! He's not slowing down any time soon. Worst case, in a couple years we move him to first base or DH. I bet he'll still be kicking ass when he's pushing forty." He shoves the spatula under a hamburger and flips it angrily. He turns and points the utensil at me. "Would you talk some sense into this guy?"

I shrug, biting back a grin. "I don't know. Rhett might have a point. Elsher might be about as far past done as your hamburgers." Luke swats me with his spatula and I finally let loose the laugh I've been holding in.

"At least I'm not sitting around making googly eyes at the neighbor. Should I be worried about stalking?" he says then grins wickedly. "I'm sure I could make a few late-night calls to check in on our little Avery." He wags his eyebrows at me. "Out of the goodness of my heart, of course."

He hardly finishes his sentence before I jump out of my chair and launch myself at him. I know he's joking. He would never make a move on Avery; they're practically siblings. But the thought of Avery with him, or anyone else for that matter, doesn't sit well with me. He's still my brother, though, so I take it easy on him.

Shoving my shoulder into his gut and wrapping my arms around his waist, I knock him off the porch and onto the lawn below.

You'd think he'd see it coming after all these years of us roughhousing. Luke struggles to get out of my hold but I tighten my grip to keep him in place. He delivers a quick jab to my kidney, causing me to falter long enough for him to slip out of my grip. He wrestles me to the ground and we grapple on the grass.

There's no malice in the fight and it feels good to get out some of this pent up energy.

A sudden sharp pain in my ear halts my next move. Luke and I spring apart, yelping at the same time. Sitting in the grass, I look up to see my five-foot-nothing mother looking down at us with an ear in each hand.

"Oh, good. I have your attention now." She looks down at us as if she's swatted a bothersome fly. "Well, if you're done acting like idiots, I think I'll have another glass of wine." She releases our ears and strolls up the porch steps and into the kitchen.

Rhett walks over with his Coke in hand, not even trying to contain his laughter. "Francesca Brady is a goddess. What a woman. Do you think she'd double as a bouncer for me on weekends? Rowdy drunks would be no match against her ear-pinching." Luke reaches up and punches him in the thigh, which only makes Rhett laugh harder.

I scan the yard. Most people have gone back to their conversations, laughing off our antics. Avery is standing with Pete's oldest daughter, Robyn, and Jolie. Avery arches a brow at me and I offer her a sheepish shrug from my seat on the ground. She rolls her eyes, but as she turns her attention back to the other women, I catch the hint of a smile on her lips.

Just the sight of her smile has me grinning.

I usually don't need a reason to wrestle with my brother. Sometimes I do it just to show him I still can. Assert your dominance and all that. But the truth is, Luke's right; I have been watching Avery all day.

Whether she was laughing with my mom or helping set out plates and cutlery, wherever she went, my eyes followed. It was like she had a magnetic hold on me, pulling me to her no matter the distance. Then when she sneakily handed Ham a hotdog when she thought no one was looking, I officially fell a little harder for the wonder that is Avery Owens.

Now if only she'd give me a chance.

But I promised I wouldn't push her. I plan to stick to that promise. So instead, I push myself up off the ground, offering a hand to my brother and helping him to his feet. I give him a friendly clap on the shoulder then go off in search of another beer.

If I can't have my hands on Avery, I guess a cold beer will have to be the next best thing.

***

AVERY

This afternoon at Francesca's has been great.

Gavin was a little hesitant when we first arrived. Five or six other kids were playing in the backyard, of varying ages. There's a couple of kids around the same age as Gavin who were chasing each other with water guns. He watched them longingly but stuck to my side. Even when Pete's daughter, Robyn, offered to introduce him to the kids, Gavin shook his head shyly.

He's currently sitting on the porch steps with my mom, talking to Franny. Gavin quickly took to her when she brought out Matt and Luke's old Pokémon cards and correctly named Gavin's favorite character.

I'm standing with Jolie and Robyn, trying to focus on the conversation but, as it has all day, my skin prickles with the awareness of Matt's eyes on me. Every time I catch him staring, his eyes warm but he has yet to come over and talk to me. His dark hair curls under his worn baseball cap and he's wearing a white t-shirt that shows off his tanned, muscular arms. He lifts the beer in his hand to his lips and my eyes follow the move, admiring the way his large hands wrap around the bottle.

Out of the corner of my eye, one of the boys chases after a soccer ball that lands at Gavin's feet. He looks to be about Gavin's age. I watch as Franny says something to Gavin, who shyly shakes his head and inches closer to my mom. The boy runs off to rejoin the other kids.

My heart sinks for my little boy. I wish I knew how to help him come out of his shell. He's such a happy, funny kid once he opens up. He deserves to have fun with kids his age. Instead, his insecurities overpower him. Another issue courtesy of his critical dad.

I'm about to excuse myself and go talk to him when Matt walks over to the porch. He sits on one of the steps below Gavin, his large frame now closer to eye level with my little boy. I can't hear what Matt says to him, but Gavin's eyes slowly lift to meet his. Matt leans closer and Gavin copies the move as if sharing a secret.

A sudden smile lights up Gavin's face and he nods eagerly. They both stand and walk over to the group of kids. Matt waves toward the porch and soon Luke and Rhett join them. Teams are then chosen and a game of soccer begins.

I watch, anxiously following the ball as the other kids run around the yard. Gavin follows behind, always a little bit farther behind than the rest, but still included. Suddenly, the ball is kicked toward him. I hold my breath as he hesitates, not wanting to make a mistake. Matt is nearby, though, and calls out encouragement. Gavin kicks the ball hard and two kids chase after it.

Gavin's smile is instant and unabashed. Matt jogs over and gives him a dramatic high-five. Luke calls out his name and throws him a thumbs up, while Rhett starts to chant his name. You'd think he'd just scored the game-winning goal by their reaction. My eyes mist up, watching Gavin join the rest of the kids laughing and playing without a hint of insecurity.

All thanks to Matt.

Jolie and Robyn must've been watching the interaction as well because Jolie whistles low. "Damn, that was adorable. Why are you holding out on him again?"

Lately, I've been wondering the same thing.

Matt never needed to prove himself to me. He's always been good enough, more than worth my time. I know the boy he was and he's shown me the man he is today. The problem is me. I'm the one who's scared. Scared of the uncertainty of my future and what opening myself to someone again could do to my new-found identity.

But I'm tired of being afraid. I don't know where I'll be three months from now but I know for sure where I want to be at this moment.

Excusing myself, I cross the lawn, coming up behind Matt. He turns to me and his eyebrows shoot up in surprise.

"Avery—"

I cut him off, afraid I'll lose my nerve. I've never asked someone out before and suddenly, the idea is daunting. "Matt, would you like to go on a date with me?"

He frowns. He looks over to where Gavin plays then back at me. "Avery, I didn't do that for you. I would never use Gavin to get to you."

I smile because it's such a "Matt" thing to say. Instead of jumping at the offer of a date, he wants to make sure he's not taking advantage of me.

"I know you wouldn't. Which is exactly why I'm asking you. And for a lot of other reasons. But mostly because I really like you." I take a step closer. "It doesn't hurt that the way you're filling out that shirt is driving me crazy." I run my finger over his bicep and down his arm. "So, what'd you think?"

His lopsided grin is slow and genuine as he stares down at me. "I'll pick you up tomorrow at six."

I smile back. "It's a date."

What the hell was I thinking?

I'm standing in the doorframe of my small closet, staring in dismay at my meager wardrobe. I let my head fall back against the wood frame in frustration.

When I asked Matt out, I was flying high after watching him help Gavin overcome his fears and, if I'm being completely honest with myself, the sight of him running around in those damn Levi's of his. Now that the high has faded, I'm regretting it.

Not because I don't want to go out with Matt. Now that I've accepted my feelings for him, I'm giddy with the idea of spending more time with him one-on-one.

What I am regretting is the idea of a date. I haven't been on a first date since I was 16 years old. Somehow, I don't think we'll be going to a movie with eight of our closest friends that our moms drove us to.

What does an adult date even look like? Should I be wearing something fancy? I don't own any formalwear. I left whatever nice clothes I had in the city with Mitch since I didn't think I'd be needing any of it in Haven Bay.

I put my hands over my face and groan. What am I doing? Matt's going to be here in an hour.

Men have it so easy. He could throw on a paper bag and I'd still want to jump him.

Me? I'm average. I've always been average.

From my mousey brown hair to my average height, I've never been one to stand out in a crowd. After Gavin, I was more focused on being the best mom and wife I could be than what was hanging in my closet. The baby weight that I never bothered to lose still clings to my stomach, hips and thighs. The extra ten (okay, fifteen) pounds I carry with me that never bothered me before suddenly stare accusingly back at me in the mirror.

A knock at my door pulls me out of my thoughts.

"Hey, honey. Can we come in?"

"Sure," I call back, stepping out of the closet as my bedroom door swings open.

My mom, Gavin and Jolie pile into my small room.

"We thought you might like a little company getting ready for your dinner tonight," my mom explains.

I decided that instead of telling Gavin about my date, it would be best to tell him I was going for dinner with a friend. Though he knows Mitch and I are getting a divorce, I'm not sure he's fully grasped what that means yet. I don't want to push him too fast, especially since it's only one date.

Who knows if it'll lead to more?

Gavin and my mom climb onto my bed while Jolie heads straight for my closet. She immediately starts pulling out hangers, handing me an array of dresses, shirts and shorts. An armload of clothes later, she seems satisfied with her haul and shoves me toward my bathroom door.

"Try these. Then come back out and show us." She claps her hands decisively. "We'll have a fashion show. Gav, what do you say we help Mommy pick out something beautiful to wear tonight?"

"Yes!" He bounces up on his knees in agreement.

I feel a bit silly coming out of the bathroom in the first outfit. My shyness is quickly replaced with laughter when I see the three of them holding up pieces of paper with numbers scribbled on them.

"I feel like Carrie Ann on *Dancing with the Stars!*" My mom squeals.

The first outfit only earns two 7s and a 6.

"It's cute, but you kind of look like you're going to do his taxes," Jolie comments.

Three more outfits later and I'm feeling deflated again.

"Try on the blue floral dress with the cap sleeves," Jolie coaches from outside the bathroom door. I pull the dress over my head and pull up the hidden zipper along my side. I hazard a glance in the mirror, pleasantly surprised by my reflection. Not only do I look cute, but the dress is comfortable and hugs all the right places.

The best part? It has pockets.

Pulling open the door, I walk out and spin in place. Three 10s go shooting up in the air and I smile, striking another pose.

"You look beautiful, honey." My mom stands and then leans over to hug me.

"Screw that. You look *hot,* girl! You're going to stop that man's heart when he sees you." Jolie runs into my closet. "Now time for shoes."

"Mommy, you look like a princess!" Gavin wraps his little arms around my waist.

Fuck losing the baby weight. I love this body, in all its shapes and forms because it brought me my sensitive, caring baby boy.

And in his eyes, I'm the most beautiful woman alive.

MATT

I'm nervous.

I haven't been this nervous for a date since I was fourteen and took Krista Jackson out for mini golfing and pizza. That date ended with me spilling my root beer all over her lap, staining her brand new white shirt. She bought it with her babysitting money and it was her first time wearing it. She cried and ended up calling her mom to pick her up early.

So, yeah. I don't do well with nerves.

Then to layer on more nerves, it's my first date with Avery. The girl I've been thinking about since I was a kid. If I mess this up, it could be my only date with her ever.

No pressure.

I'm standing on Angie's front porch, psyching myself up to knock on the door. I take a deep breath and roll my shoulders.

You can do this.

But before I can lift my hand to knock, the front door opens.

Gavin stands in front of me, looking confused. "How come you didn't knock? If you don't knock, we won't know you're here."

My shoulders relax. "I guess you're right. How did you know I was here then?"

He shrugs. "I was watching the squirrels with Sushi," he says simply.

He doesn't look like the shy kid I first met a couple months ago. Or even the insecure one from yesterday. He looks relaxed and at ease. I'm honored that he feels comfortable enough to be himself with me.

"How come you have flowers?" he asks, eyeing the bouquet in my hand.

"They're for your mom," I answer. His brow furrows, the mirror image of Avery as a kid.

"But it's not her birthday."

I kneel so I'm at eye level with him. "You don't only buy girls flowers on their birthdays. The best flowers are the ones that she's not expecting. I bring my mom flowers all the time and it always makes her smile."

Gavin seems to consider this. "Do you think Mommy would like it if I got her flowers, too?"

This kid is too sweet. "Tell you what, buddy. Why don't you give your mom these flowers? They're daisies, which I happen to know are her favorite. We can tell her you bought them."

Gavin's smile is immediate but falls just as quickly. He shakes his head. "I'm not s'posed to lie."

I pretend to think about it. "What's in your pockets right now?" He sticks a chubby hand in his front pocket and pulls out a few rocks and a piece of lint. "Perfect. That's exactly how much these cost. You can buy these from me and then it won't be a lie."

His wide smile returns. "For real?"

I nod as he hands over the rocks. I pass over the flowers, making sure he has a good grip on the heavy bouquet before letting go.

"Now, let's go see if your mom's ready to go."

I follow Gavin into the kitchen where Avery is perched on a stool, watching her mom stir a pot on the stove. Hearing our footsteps, she spins in her seat to look at us.

"Matt! I didn't hear you knock. When did you get here?" She catches Gavin as he rushes over to her.

"Mommy! I got you flowers!" He proudly thrusts the bouquet into her hands.

"You did?" She looks down at him confused before glancing up at me with soft eyes. She smiles down at Gavin.

"That was so nice of you, buddy. I love them. Let me put them in a vase."

Angie walks over and takes the bouquet from Avery's hands. She admires the flowers while shooing us away. "I'll take care of that. You two go on ahead. Don't worry about us, we're going to have boatloads of fun." She reaches into the cupboard above her head and pulls out a vase. "Gavin, hug your mom goodbye and then come help me sprinkle the cheese on your noodles."

After a quick hug from Gavin, we're on our way out the door.

Avery closes the front door behind her and gives me a small smile. "That was really nice of you, Matt."

I shrug off the compliment. "Every guy should give their mom flowers. When he starts making his own money, he can buy you some himself. Until then, I'm happy to foot the bill." I pause on the front step, taking a minute to drink her in.

I take my time, letting my eyes rake greedily over her body from her strappy sandals to her bright eyes. She's wearing a blue dress with tiny white daisies sprinkled over it. The neckline plunges into a deep V, accentuating her cleavage. I don't want to seem like a total creep, so I make sure not to let my gaze linger too long but damn, it's hard to pull my eyes away. Her hair falls in soft waves on her shoulders and it makes me want to run my fingers through it. My eyes finish their journey at her pretty smile.

"You look beautiful, Freckles. That dress is a killer. But the real kick to the heart is this." Holding her chin, I rub my thumb over her bottom lip. "I love your smile."

She looks up, eyes searching mine as if looking for any hint of insincerity. Finding none, she smiles down at her feet.

The blush I've come to adore slowly creeps up to her cheeks. She's wearing a floral scent that's making my blood hum. I could lean down and kiss her. I can tell by the way she's leaning toward me, her eyes on my mouth that she's thinking the same.

But that kiss would be for the kids we once were. Before her marriage. Before Gavin. When I kiss Avery for the first time, I want it to be for who we are right now.

I take her hand in mine. "Come on, Freckles. I've got plans for us."

"I can't believe this is what you chose for our first date."

The arcade's lights flash above us. Eddy's Arcade is down the street from our old high school in Bakersfield. Before Mitch, Matt and I would spend hours at here, competing for the title that Matt had named Emperor of Awesome.

When Matt's dad got sick, we spent a lot more time at the arcade, distracting ourselves from the uncertainty and emotions of his home life. I think that was when Matt started using humor to deflect real life. I didn't blame him either. Dealing with a parent's illness is difficult at any age, but especially at a time when a boy needs his dad most.

"I promise the whole date won't be a trip down memory lane," Matt says. "But every time I tried to come up with an idea for a date, I kept coming back to our old stomping grounds." He slips a twenty dollar bill into the token machine. "Besides, I believe at last count, you were ahead of me in the standings for Emperor of Awesome. I know you thought you'd graduate and leave town so you'd win by default, but I don't play with quitters."

I glance around the arcade, awash in a flood of nostalgia.

The familiar clatter of tokens and ringing of the games transport me back to simpler times. Despite the addition of numerous modern games, Eddy kept all of the classics.

The whirring and banging from the games make it hard to hear so I lean a little closer to him. "Fine. Game on. But since I'm ahead, I get to decide the first game." I fill the yellow plastic cup Matt hands me with tokens and start walking away.

He groans, following close behind me. "Oh, come on. Not Skee-Ball. That stupid game is rigged."

I smile mischievously at him over my shoulder as we approach the game. "Funny, it seems to work just fine for me." To prove my point, I insert my tokens and wait as the balls roll down the chute. I pick up one of the plastic balls and send it flying down the ramp. It shoots up to the right and sinks into the 100-point cup.

Matt groans again. "Definitely rigged."

I line up my next shot and send another ball flying, this time hitting the left 100-point cup.

"Quit your whining, Brady. Either put up or shut up." I send another ball flying, this time dropping easily into the 50-point cup then turn to him, smiling triumphantly.

Matt laughs and slips his tokens into the machine beside me, waiting for the balls to roll down the end of the chute. Meanwhile, I've racked up another 250 points.

"Geez, Freckles. Take pity on a guy."

I sink my last shot in the 50-point cup then brush a speck of invisible lint off my shoulder. "Can't. I'm just *that* good."

Matt leans closer, smirking wickedly. "Alright. If you're going to kick my ass in Skee-Ball, it's only fair that I wipe the floor with you in basketball next." He winks and the shot of electricity it causes goes straight between my legs. I feel the blush spread over my cheeks but I'm too busy biting back a grin to feel embarrassed by it.

Over the next couple of hours, Matt beats me in some

games while I crush him in others. Eventually, we make our way to the air hockey table. It was one of our favorites growing up since we were equally matched in skill.

We slide our tokens in and the low buzz of the air blower kicks in. Matt holds the thin orange disc above the plastic rink. "You ready for this, Freckles?"

I shoot him a cocky grin. "Bring it on, Brady."

He grins back and drops the puck. He shoots the disc toward my net but I slap it back toward him. Minutes tick by and we meet each other goal for goal until finally, there are forty-five seconds left in the game. We're tied 3-3. If Matt wins air hockey, he'll pull ahead in our bid for Emperor of Awesome.

I refuse to go down without a fight.

When Matt gets ahold of the plastic disc, it looks like it might be game over for me. He watches as the seconds tick down on the overhead neon timer.

"Oh, Freckles. You were so close," he says, toying with the disc as he slides it back and forth in front of him. "You thought you had me, but when will you learn? I'm destined to be the Emperor of Awesome. You might as well give up now and save yourself the embarrassment of your defeat."

I bend my knees in a ready stance. "Just shoot, Brady," I call out.

He grins back wickedly. He thinks he's about to win.

Well, we can't have that, can we?

"Okay, but you asked for it," he replies, placating me. Just as he's about to take his shot, I whip out a move I haven't used since my college days playing beer-pong. As he lines up his shot, I bend over and push my boobs together right in his line of sight.

The second his gaze meets my cleavage, his eyes glaze over and his paddle fumbles the puck. Instead, it clumsily slides down to me where I smack it back to his end. The puck slides past his stunned hand and, before he realizes what's happening, slides effortlessly into the net.

The buzzer sounds to signal my goal as the timer hits zero.

I throw my hands up in victory and dance around the table. "Take that, Brady. Wait, so who's the Empress of Awesome? Oh, right. It's me!"

He rounds the table, smiling at my goofy dance moves. I moonwalk over to him but before I reach him, I stumble over a nearby cord. He reaches out to steady me. I look up at his face, sobering the second I notice his eyes are dark with unexpected heat. He clears his throat and all traces of darkness clear, making me question if it was ever there to begin with.

He smiles down at me playfully. "Careful, Freckles. Let's get you out of here before you break an ankle. We've got reservations at Tony's in half an hour." He puts an arm around my waist and guides me through the winding maze of games and people. I lean into him, loving the feel of his arm wrapped around me.

"Oh, I love Tony's. I haven't been there in forever," I comment as we walk outside toward his truck. Matt follows me to the passenger door then opens it for me. He waits for me to hop inside before leaning in close enough that it causes my breath to hitch.

"Avery?"

"Hmm?" I've lost all train of thought at his closeness.

"Flash those pretty tits at me again and I'll show you what happens when you tease me. I've only got so much restraint when it comes to you."

With that, he closes the door, leaving me sitting with my jaw dropped open and my wide eyes staring straight ahead. For the first time in longer than I can remember, I'm really turned on.

What did I get myself into?

CHAPTER 16

MATT

Okay, so I probably shouldn't have said that.

I told myself I would take it slow with Avery. I know she'd only been with Mitch in high school and they got married right after college. I don't want to rush her into anything she's not comfortable with.

But when she bent over that table to distract me with her boobs, I just about swallowed my tongue. I figured if I had to drive with a hard-on, the least I could do was return the favor.

After a quiet, sexually charged drive to the restaurant, we both start to relax once we're settled at our table. Wanting to take advantage of my time alone with her, I called ahead and asked for a quiet table in the corner.

Bakersfield is far enough away from Haven Bay that the likelihood of running into anyone we know is slim, but I'm not taking any chances. I finally have Avery all to myself and I don't want any interruptions.

After placing our drink orders with the waiter, I put my menu down. "So, I heard your first book club is this week. Are you excited?"

Avery's eyes light up. "I can't wait. Hank gave me a really great deal on some meats and cheeses and Alana told me she'd offer me a frequency discount on the wine since we'll be ordering once a month. We've already had eleven people sign up and I'm hoping once word spreads after the first one, we'll have more."

I can't help but grin watching her enthusiasm. Gone is the timid Avery from a few days ago. This Avery is passionate and confident. It makes me so proud to watch her push past her insecurities and go after what she wants. It takes balls to be unsure of yourself and follow your heart anyway.

So I tell her exactly that.

"That's awesome, Avery. I'm so proud of you. You're working hard and bringing your ideas to reality. I know a lot of older folks are already talking about how great of an idea the bookmobile is. My mom is going to sign my nonna up when the program starts."

She beams. "Thanks, Matt. That means a lot."

Her eyes hold mine, but the moment is cut short when the waiter arrives with our drinks and to take our orders.

The rest of the dinner passes too quickly. We spend half of the night talking about our lives over the past decade and the other half reminiscing about our childhood.

Avery talks about college and being pregnant with Gavin. I tell her about how I started with Bud and how I moved up the line to be his number two.

She tells me about her pregnancy cravings for macaroni and cheese with Cheetos and pickles. I tell her about my trip to San Francisco with Luke and Rhett when we turned 21 and how Rhett got so drunk he tried to race a cable car on foot.

She talks about how Gavin got sick as a toddler and had to stay overnight in the hospital. Luckily it was nothing serious but my heart broke for her, wishing I could've been there with her.

The only thing we don't talk about is Mitch. I'm not sure

if it's on purpose or a happy accident but I'm glad. He doesn't deserve to occupy her thoughts a minute longer.

Conversation with Avery has always been easy. Even after my dad passed away, she was the only person I never had to worry about putting on a happy front with. I could be real with her. Even now, as an adult, I never have to worry if I'm coming off as too pessimistic or serious. The laughs we share don't feel forced or fake.

The waiter eventually comes over to clear our plates. He gestures to the rest of Avery's meal and asks, "Do you wanna box for your leftovers?"

Without missing a beat, she replies, "No, but I'll arm wrestle you for it." The waiter smiles politely at her corny joke but all I can do is stare at her.

I'm half-convinced I made her up in a dream. A woman who kicks my ass at Skee-Ball *and* tells Dad jokes?

I swear I'm going to marry this girl.

On the drive home, we fall into a comfortable silence. Tonight has been fun and refreshing. I don't want it to end. The sun has already set but, as we turn onto Main Street, the trail to the beach is lit with solar lights. I slow the truck as we approach the main intersection and I decide to test my luck.

"Y'know, usually after I've been gone for this long, I like to take Ham for a walk down to the beach. Let him stretch his legs after being cooped up inside. It's not that late yet. Would you wanna join us?" I keep my eyes trained forward, hoping to disguise my nerves.

She looks at her phone, I assume looking for messages from her mom. Finding none, she looks over at me. "That sounds nice. I've never seen your place before."

Instead of turning onto her mom's road, I take a left toward home. "I rent the apartment above Bud's workshop. It's nothing fancy, but it's convenient for work and Bud lets me use the shop after hours if I want." I pull my truck around the back of the building and swing into my parking space. We climb out of the truck and walk over to the building. I unlock the back entrance, flipping the overhead light on as we enter.

We take the stairs on the left that leads to my apartment. I try to quickly remember what state I left my apartment in. Deciding there's nothing I can do at this point anyway, I push open the heavy metal door and motion for Avery to step in first.

A loud howl comes from the bedroom and seconds later Ham comes barreling around the corner. I start to reach for Avery, trying to shield her from his overzealous welcome. He tends to forget how big he is and has taken me out at the knees once or twice in the past. Before I can intercept him, Ham stops abruptly, plopping his butt down on the floor before her.

Avery drops to a crouch, massaging his jowls. "Such a good boy, Hammy. And so handsome, too," she croons. "Did you miss me, buddy?" She showers his large head with kisses.

Never thought I'd be jealous of a dog.

Ham flops onto his back and she switches to rubbing his belly. "He was a rescue dog when you got him, right? Did he come with the name Ham?" Avery asks, looking up at me from her place on the floor.

I shake my head. "No, they're not sure what his name was before I adopted him. His owner left him outside all the time and didn't care much for him. The neighbor reported his owner so many times for neglect that the guy finally let Animal Control take him. Brenna took him into Doyle's Safe Haven to help him get over his anxiety. A week after he was deemed adoptable, I happened to be doing some work on the outdoor kennels. I walked past Ham's kennel and saw a droopy set of brown eyes staring up at me. I knew he was meant to be with me."

Avery's eyes soften and she hugs Ham's head to her chest.

"That's so sweet. I'm so happy you found him." Her eyes suddenly harden. "I hope his old owner gets hit by a truck for what he did to Hammy."

I can't help but smile at her rage. Trust me, it's nothing I haven't thought about before. It took all of my control not to drive over to the prick's house and leave him in a cage with no water in the summer heat, like he did to Ham.

She gives him another kiss on the head. "Why the name Ham?"

I widen my eyes incredulously. "Only after the greatest baseball player turned wrestler of all time, of course."

She raises an eyebrow at me questioningly.

"The Great Hambino," I inform her.

Avery rolls her eyes. "Of course it's a *Sandlot* reference. Why didn't I think of that?"

I smile, shrugging. "I can't help it if it's the best movie ever made." I grab Ham's leash off the hook and whistle. He jumps to his feet. "Let's go, Hammy. So many trees to pee on, so little time."

We make our way down the hill that leads to the beach. Ham stops every few feet to sniff a bush or lift a leg. When we reach the beach, Matt unhooks Ham's leash so he can gallop along in front of us. He never gets too far ahead but enough to enjoy his freedom. Whenever he does happen to stray, Matt is quick to call him back.

Matt and I walk side-by-side in silence for a little while. The only sounds in the otherwise silent night are the tide washing over the sand and the distant music from The Dive.

When Matt first picked me up, looking all kinds of hot in his dark pants and pale green button-up, my nerves were shot. It was my first date in over a decade. Matt has probably been on more dates in a week than I've been on in my entire life.

To say I was out of my element was an understatement.

But once we got in his truck, conversation flowed naturally. The arcade had been the perfect spot—casual, fun and laid back. Leave it to Matt to make me forget my nerves and worries and just have fun. Then dinner at Tony's, my favorite restaurant. I wasn't sure if it was a coincidence or if Matt had remembered. Regardless, the food was amazing and the atmosphere was relaxed and intimate.

It was the perfect first date.

But the part of the night that I can't get out of my head was Matt's statement in the parking lot. Every time I think of his low, raspy voice whispering such dirty threats in my ear, a deep ache throbs between my legs. Part of me is still in shock that the goofy Matt I know had said such panty-melting things. The other part of me wants nothing more than to find the closest bed and take him up on his threats.

We walk along the water's edge, close enough that our hands brush occasionally. He doesn't make the first move, so neither do I.

Is holding hands even a thing anymore? Is that something only teenagers do? Or does he not want to hold my hand?

Ugh, I already hate dating.

I try to distract myself instead. "Did you ever think about leaving Haven Bay? After graduation, I mean."

Matt picks up a stray stick and tosses it into the water. Ham bounds after it, splashing clumsily. "Honestly? Not really. I traveled a bit across the country and into the States after college but mostly, I'm content where I am. My family's here, my friends are here. I know everyone and everyone knows me." He shrugs. "It's home."

A simple statement but it causes me to pause. *It's home.* Did I ever feel that way about Edmonton? Sure, it was where I lived. It's where my husband was and where Gavin was born. I had warm memories there from college and watching Gavin grow up.

But was it home?

I don't think I'm ready to dive too deeply into that yet.

Besides, my home is wherever Gavin is. We don't need anything other than each other to make a home. There's a possibility that next week the lawyer will tell me I have to go back to the city. As much as I don't want that to happen, I would work to make that feel like home, too.

As long as Gavin is with me.

Real great first date etiquette, Avery. You're supposed to be having fun and flirting with a cute guy, not thinking about your divorce.

If Matt notices the change in my demeanor, he doesn't mention it. Instead, he continues. "I might not have known what I was going to do with my life when I was five like Luke, but I'm good at what I do. Bud is a good boss, I have a lot of flexibility, and, as his number two, he lets me do my own thing. More and more clients are asking for me specifically on custom jobs. My name might not be on the building, but I've created a pretty solid reputation for myself in the wood-working business."

I listen as he talks about his job. There's a hint of defensiveness in his tone as if he has to prove himself to me. As if his success isn't as significant because it doesn't come with the keys to a Mercedes.

"That's amazing, Matt. You should be really proud of yourself." I bump his shoulder with mine. "I know I am."

Matt looks down at me and smiles softly. "Thanks, Freckles."

We walk along the beach a little longer. "Does being Bud's number two mean you'll eventually own the business some-day? Is that something you'd want?"

He looks out into the water. The silence stretches as if he's internally debating his answer. He tosses the stick to Ham again. "It's what Bud wants. Even though he's years off from retirement, he's been grooming me for the position for a few years now." He says it in the same tone that someone might state the weather.

I tip my head, looking up at him closely. "But is it what you want?"

Again, he pauses before answering. When he does, I barely hear his quiet "no".

I'm a little surprised by his answer, but if there's anything I've learned recently, it's that life's too short to waste time being unhappy.

"Then don't do it," I say.

He scoffs, looking out at the bay. "It's not that easy,"

I stop as I'm struck with an idea. He turns and faces me.

"Close your eyes," I demand.

Matt smirks. "Are you trying to have your way with me, Freckles?"

I roll my eyes. "Just do it."

Still smirking, he closes his eyes.

"Pretend I have a magic wand. If I could wave it right now and make your career dreams come true, what would you want to do?"

His smirk disappears. He pauses so long that I think he's not going to answer until he finally whispers more to himself than to me, "to create".

I watch as his eyes slowly open. I don't push for him to elaborate. He smiles softly and reaches out to clasp my hand in his. His calloused hand feels rough against my skin. I can't help but think how perfectly our hands fit together.

"Come on, Freckles. I should take you home before you turn into a pumpkin."

I scrunch my nose and Matt laughs. "I don't think that's how the story went."

We turn and Matt whistles to Ham as we make our way back up the beach to the road. He doesn't let go of my hand until we reach the truck. Even then, once we're seated with Ham in the backseat, he has one hand on the steering wheel and the other reclaiming the hand in my lap. The butterflies in my stomach flutter wildly now.

A short drive later, we pull up outside my mom's house.

I'm about to thank him for the date when Matt cuts the engine, releases my hand and slides out of his truck. Apparently, he's walking me to the door. Suddenly the delicate butterflies in my stomach have turned into a swarm of anxious birds.

Oh my god. What's the protocol here? Do we kiss? Do I hug him? A crisp high-five?

No, even I know that's weird. I wonder if I can text Jolie without him noticing.

Too quickly, we reach the front door. Internally, I'm freaking out. Is he going to kiss me? Is it old-fashioned of me to wait for him to make a move? Should I kiss him first? Would he be freaked out if I threw myself into his arms? Because he's suddenly really close and all I can think about are his lips on mine. Or on other parts of me.

"I had a lot of fun tonight. Thanks for taking me out," I say, twisting my house key in my hand nervously.

"Me too."

His warm, chocolatey eyes latch on mine. His head inches lower and my breath catches.

This is it.

I tip my chin slightly as my eyes fall closed. His arms circle my waist and he pulls me against his chest. Then I feel a light brush of his lips on my forehead before he pulls back.

What the hell?

"Goodnight, Avery." And with that, he turns and walks down the steps toward his truck.

I stand there dumbstruck for a few seconds before unlocking the door and stepping inside. I close the door quietly behind me, trying not to wake the rest of the house. I lay my head against the wood door in defeat.

Well, that was embarrassing.

I spent the whole night thinking that there was this attraction, this chemistry between us. Have I been reading the signals wrong this whole time? Did he decide that he's not into me that way?

Oh, God.

Now I'd have to deal with the humiliation of him breaking it to me gently that we're better off as friends. I let my head fall back against the door again. The hollow thud resembles the dread in my gut.

Ugh. I'm so stupid. Why would a guy like Matt want to be with a girl like—

A soft knock behind my head startles me out of my thoughts. What is he still doing here? Did he want to rip the Band-Aid off and tell me tonight instead? I shakily turn the handle and pull the door open. Matt stands on the other side, jaw set and eyes staring intently into mine.

"Look, Matt. You don't have to—"

My next words are cut off as Matt rushes through the doorway toward me, his hands reaching out to pull my face to his. His mouth crashes against mine, knocking me back a few steps with such force that my back hits the wall behind me. I hardly have time to comprehend what's happening before Matt tilts my head, deepening the kiss. One hand slides up from my jaw and into my hair, holding me in place.

Thankfully, my instincts kick in and I kiss him back. His teeth nip my bottom lip and a soft whimper escapes my throat. I've never made that noise before in my life but Matt seems to like it. He groans in response and his hand in my hair tightens. The sharp hint of pain mixes with pleasure, thrilling me.

Nerves long gone, I fist his shirt, pulling him closer to me until we're touching everywhere. I tip my hips toward his, then gasp at the feel of his hard erection pressing into my stomach.

That seems to pull Matt back to reality, as he slows the kiss. He brushes his lips lazily over mine once, twice more before untangling himself. I pry my hooded eyes open to see the heat in his. He smiles, taking a step back. His hands slide down my arms to my hands. He brings one hand up to his lips, giving me one last soft kiss. It's as if he can't convince himself to stop touching me.

My heart flutters and at this point, I'm a puddle on the floor.

He raises his head and smiles up at me, suddenly shy. "I wanted to take it slow. I tried to. You deserve to take things slow. But I couldn't convince myself to leave. I tried. I got as far as my truck but I couldn't convince myself to turn the key. I couldn't stand the thought of leaving without kissing you."

Good, God. This man is adorable.

He runs his thumb over his bottom lip, still grinning as he slowly walks backward down the steps. "I guess I should go now. For real this time."

Just when I think he's about to turn away, he takes the steps two at a time to give me another quick kiss. Pulling away far too soon for my liking, he leans his forehead against mine.

"Sweet dreams, Freckles."

Then he turns and jogs down the steps to his truck. He opens the door and gives me one last smile before sliding in.

In a daze, I give him a small wave and close the door. I slump against the wall. I can't stop the smile that overtakes my face.

Wow.

Best. Date. Ever.

"What's got you grinning like an idiot this morning?" Johnny, one of the laborers, calls after me.

I turn and shoot him a wink. "Maybe I'm just happy to see you, Johnny. Ever think of that?"

He rolls his eyes at me but he's right. I've been grinning so wide all morning that my cheeks are starting to hurt. I've caught myself whistling more than once but I'm so deliriously happy, I couldn't care less.

All the cheesy lines from those chick flicks are true. The sun is shining brighter, the sky is a little bluer and the spring in my step is a little lighter.

All because of her.

Last night was hands down the best date I've ever been on. Not because we did anything different or exciting. Exactly the opposite actually. The arcade was a bit out of the ordinary but then it was a typical dinner followed by a walk on the beach.

Nothing fancy.

What made the night special was Avery. She brings out a side of me that I've long since hidden away from the rest of the world—the real me. The guy who doesn't have to think about every response out of his mouth in cause it comes off as too serious or sad.

It was refreshing to not have to worry if someone would judge or dislike me if I show any emotion other than humor. It was the first time in a long time I could just relax and enjoy myself.

I'm working at the cafe this morning. The expansion is almost done. We have to finish the flooring, then we'll be installing the display case I built. It's weird to think I won't be seeing Avery every day anymore after we're finished.

Guess I'll have to think of another reason to stop in.

The jingle of the bell above the door catches my attention. In walks Avery wearing cutoffs and an oversized t-shirt that falls off one shoulder. Her hair is pulled up into a casual ponytail that swings with every step she takes.

My grin somehow widens at the sight of her. I start toward her but the second she sees me, she trips over her feet. I bite back a laugh as she catches herself, thanking the nearby customer who asks her if she's okay.

Well, that's one way to boost a guy's ego.

I saunter over to her. "Hey, you," I drawl.

I wanted to bring her usual latte again this morning, but we didn't talk about what time her shift started last night. Seeing her now makes me wish I had thought to ask yesterday.

She spins around at the sound of my voice, almost losing her balance again. "Matt! Hi! Didn't see you there. What's new?" She cringes. "I mean, I know I saw you like, twelve hours ago so probably not much has changed. Well, actually a lot can change in twelve hours. Not that anything's changed for me. I mean—"

Tammy calls her name and Avery's shoulders drop in relief. She excuses herself then scurries away. I watch her half-amused and half-bewildered.

What happened to the sassy, confident Avery from last night?

Something obviously changed since I saw her. The last thing I remember is watching her walk inside with a very satisfied look on her face, if I do say so myself. Obviously, I wasn't the only one affected by that kiss.

But what changed between now and then?

I go back to working on the flooring but I can't help watching as she makes a point of avoiding this side of the shop, looking anywhere but in my direction. The more I watch her, the more confused I get. We had a great time together, but now she's pulling away.

Did last night not mean anything to her?

After a few hours of avoiding me, Avery takes advantage of the lull in customers by heading to her office in the back of the store. She finally allows herself a peek in my direction. When she finds me staring back, she ducks into the office and closes the door swiftly behind her.

I toss my pull bar aside and stalk over to the office door. I don't bother knocking before pushing my way through the door and into the small room.

There's a small wooden desk with an old desktop computer and an antique stained glass lamp perched on it. A few filing cabinets line the wall to my left. Avery sits in a worn leather chair behind the desk, her head in her hands. Her head snaps up at my abrupt entrance and for a second, she looks like she's about to bolt.

"What's going on, Avery? Why are you avoiding me?"

She arches a brow at me. "I'm in my office, Matt. I'm working. How is that avoiding you?"

I tamp down my growing annoyance, taking a slow breath before I respond. "You know exactly what I mean. You're acting like I'm a door-to-door salesman that you're trying to shake off. You haven't looked anywhere near me since you got pulled away from me earlier. You hardly ever use this back office if there's an open table out front. So, what gives?" I swallow hard at the thought of her answer to my next question. "Are you regretting last night?"

"No!" She shakes her head vehemently. "Absolutely not."

I try not to show my relief, but I can feel the tension leave my body.

"Then what's going on?" She hesitates so I gently place my hand over hers. "You can tell me anything, Freckles."

Staring at our hands, she responds so quietly I almost don't hear her. "I wasn't sure if you'd changed your mind."

My heart tugs at her honesty but she keeps going, so I stay quiet.

"I haven't been on a first date since I was sixteen and I wasn't sure what to expect after. I spent all night reliving that kiss but somewhere between last night and this morning, I got scared. I wasn't sure what it meant to you, if anything. For all I know that's how you end every date and it was all just casual fun."

She shrugs, still avoiding my eyes. "When I saw you, I didn't know what I should say or do. I guess trying to act casual didn't work out like I planned." She finally looks up at me from under her lashes with a shy smile.

God, this girl.

I round the desk and turn her so she's facing me. I grip the arms of her chair, caging her in. Her eyes grow wide as I bend until my face is a whisper away from hers. I can see her pulse skipping in her neck and her breathing has quickened.

I hold her gaze, trying to portray to her how serious I am. "How many times do I have to tell you, Freckles? I'm in this. I want to be with you. I want to get to know you again and get to know your cute-as-hell kid, too." I watch her eyes soften. "What will it take to convince you that I want you? All of you. Every part."

My gaze dips to her parted lips. "What if I told you that I couldn't keep the stupid grin off my face this morning? Johnny even called me out on it. Or that it took all of my control not to pull you into my arms this morning and kiss you all over again?"

My voice thickens as I trace a finger down the column of her neck. She swallows hard and I take a shot, hoping my next words don't scare her off again.

"What if I told you that I get hard every time I think about last night? How the taste of you haunted my dreams. How badly I wished I would've slid my hand up your thigh to feel if you were as turned on by that kiss as I was."

My finger slides over her pulse and it quickens. "What would I have found, Freckles? Would you have been wet for me?" My finger continues its path down her throat, over her collarbone then dips below the neckline of her shirt.

Her eyes flutter closed and her head falls back but not before I catch her small nod. I dip my head but instead of her lips, I place a small kiss below her ear. Her eyes burst open with a sharp intake of breath. I place another small kiss on the side of her neck, feeling her pulse dance under my lips.

I'm glad I'm not the only one affected.

I place my lips on her again, this time on her collarbone. Her head falls back further, weighed down by lust. Finally, I brush my lips against hers, then give her plump bottom lip a small nip between my teeth. She lets out a tiny whimper and my cock pushes against my jeans at the sound.

Something inside me snaps. One minute, I'm in control, teasing us both before I planned to pull away. The next, my insides are ablaze with desire, the animal inside me desperately clawing to get out. My hand reaches around to grip her hair, pulling her ponytail back to lift her jaw, deepening the kiss. My tongue hungrily slides over hers and she matches my energy, eagerly welcoming me in.

Just like that, our kiss turns feral—tongues chasing, teeth biting. A low groan rumbles in my chest when she reaches up to thread her fingers through my hair, holding me in place.

As if there's any chance of me leaving her any time soon.

Last night, the thought of her mouth had tortured me. No matter what I did, no matter how many times I told myself I couldn't have her yet, I couldn't end the night not knowing what she tasted like.

Now I know. And knowing is an exquisite torture. Because now that I know how addictive her taste is, how consuming she is, I don't know how I'll be able to be around her without wanting to devour her completely.

I lean into her, grinding my aching cock against the seam of her shorts. Her throaty moan encourages me as I push myself against her again, wishing our clothes would disappear. I want nothing more than to feel her bare against me. I can tell by the tilt of her hips and the short, quick pants of her breath that she's right there with me.

"Avery? Are you back here?" Tammy calls from behind the office door.

We spring apart. Avery stares up at me, wide-eyed. Her eyes never leave mine when she answers breathlessly. "Yeah! What's up, Tam?"

"The register is acting up again. Do you mind giving me a hand rebooting it? I tried but it doesn't want to work for me," Tammy asks, oblivious to the moment she's interrupting.

"Sure. I'll be out in a minute." We listen as Tammy's footsteps retreat. "Um, I should get out there. Are you coming?" I smirk at her choice of words and she blushes, rolling her eyes. "You know what I mean, perv."

"I think I might need a minute. I don't want to give Dottie any ideas." I gesture at my very visible erection.

She blushes harder, biting back a smile. "Right. Yeah. She might fake a fall to get a better view."

I laugh while helping her to her feet. Only Avery could make me laugh with a hard-on.

"So I guess I'll see you out there," she says and I love how easily she smiles now, her earlier self-consciousness long forgotten.

It's why I can't resist tipping her chin and taking her mouth once more. I allow myself a few moments to pour myself into the kiss before begrudgingly pulling away. I smirk at her heavy-lidded, dazed expression, then turn her so her back is to my chest.

I dip my mouth to her ear. "Get going, Freckles, before you get us both in trouble." I give her a small push and she floats toward the door before looking back at me one last time. I shoot her a wink, earning another smile from her.

When she closes the door behind her, I try to focus on naming the Mariners' last ten Hall of Famers then listing my nonna's cannoli recipe. Anything to will away the bulge in my jeans.

I must've lost my mind. I just made out with Matt in the back office—if you can call that making out. Making out makes me think of high school and awkward, sloppy kissing and groping in the backseat of your mom's car. There was nothing awkward or sloppy about what we did.

Or almost did.

Matt kisses like a starving man given his first meal.

I'll be honest, if Tammy hadn't interrupted us when she did, I can't tell you what I might've done. Actually, I could but we all know it would've involved a lot less clothes. The only thing separating us from a store full of customers was a very old, very thin wooden door. The rumor mill would've had a heyday over that one.

The only logical explanation is that I must have lost my mind in the last 24 hours. Either that or I'm so sex-deprived that I've actually lost the ability to think when there's even the slightest chance at an orgasm.

Not that I'd know what that's like.

By the time I asked for the divorce, Mitch and I hadn't been intimate in over a year. I like sex, but I get in my head too much and have a hard time letting go. Mitch often complained that I would take too long. The few times we tried foreplay, I often found myself faking it when I could tell he was getting bored.

When we had sex, it usually consisted of a few minutes of missionary until he'd collapse on top of me. Then he'd give me a quick kiss, roll over and fall asleep.

Riveting stuff, really.

So while I'm beyond thrilled that a few kisses from Matt have caused more of a reaction than I've had in years, I have to admit that I'm scared. What if it's the same with Matt?

Logically, I know Matt is different than Mitch. I know he would never make me feel bad about my insufficiency, but the thought of having to explain myself is mortifying.

Which is why I go out of my way to find Matt after the crew is packing up for the day. "Hey, do you mind if we talk quickly?" I motion for him to follow me toward the back of the shop.

When we're out of sight, he pulls me to him by the hips.

"Why, Miss Avery, are you looking to finish what we started earlier?" He wags his eyebrows at me suggestively.

I laugh but put my hand on his chest, stopping his forward movement. "Talk about a one-track mind." I shake my head at him, smiling. "But I actually did want to talk to you about that."

He studies me closely, his tone instantly changing to serious. "Are you okay? I didn't hurt you, did I?"

I shake my head again, pulling in a shaky breath to build my nerve. "No, nothing like that. I—"

Matt covers my hands to stop my fidgeting.

"I think that maybe we got a little too carried away in there. And maybe we should, you know, take it slow." I glance up nervously at his serious expression.

The line between his brows deepens. "Avery, I'm so sorry. I never meant to–"

I put my hand up to stop his unnecessary, and quite frankly, ridiculous apology. "Please don't apologize. I know exactly what you're thinking and you didn't take advantage of me. I know you would never hurt me and I was just as willing a participant as you were. An *extremely* willing participant, I might add." I try to lighten the mood but Matt barely smiles at the comment. "Seriously. It was nothing you did. I just want to do this right and take it slow."

He eyes me for a second before wrapping his arms around me, and tucking my head under his chin. "We'll go as slow as you want. It's like I said before; I want every piece of you. But only the pieces you're ready to give. So, baby, the ball is in your court. You decide what you're comfortable with and let me know."

He leans down to gently kiss my forehead. I squeeze back the emotion at both his words and his actions.

"Thanks, Matt."

"Anything for you, Freckles."

I used to consider myself an optimist. When bad things happen, especially when you're young, people will tell you to "look on the bright side" or to "find the silver lining". But as you get older and bad things seem to outweigh the good, those silver linings start to tarnish.

So, when things go too well for too long, it makes me anxious. I'm always waiting for the other shoe to drop. Some people call this being a pessimist, but I like to think of it as being a realist.

Which is why I'm not at all surprised when two days after my date with Matt, I get a text from Mitch.

MITCH

When are you coming home?

This tantrum of yours has gone on long enough.

My knuckles go white from the effort it takes to refrain from throwing my phone. *Tantrum?* Only Mitch would think a separation is my way of seeking attention.

I knew continuing to live together after the separation would complicate things, but I honestly thought he understood. I thought he would cooperate as long as I agreed to keep it quiet until after his business deal.

Apparently, I gave him too much credit.

AVERY

It's not a tantrum, Mitch. I told you months ago. I'm done.

MITCH

We're still married, Avery. You think I'm going to let you leave me? I let you have your little adventure.

Come home.

AVERY

We're separated.

Gavin and I are not leaving Haven Bay, at least not yet. I'm not sure if I'll be living in Haven Bay or in Edmonton, but either way, we're not getting back together.

I'm not coming back to that house.

Or you.

I shove my phone into the back pocket of my shorts. I pick

up a hardcover from the shipment of new releases that came in this morning and shove it a little harder than necessary onto the bookshelf.

Again, no mention or concern for Gavin. Mitch hasn't once asked about him since we got to Haven Bay. I'm not sure why it shocks me. He wasn't involved when they were under the same roof; why I thought that would change when they were in different towns, I have no idea. But it's not right. A father should care about his son. Mitch should care that he hasn't seen Gavin in months.

And calling our separation a tantrum? As if I'm an emotionally incompetent toddler who was given the wrong color cup with her lunch. Not a grown woman who—heaven forbid—fell out of love with her husband. I left to help my sick mother, not go partying in Miami.

Jackass.

I take a deep breath, trying to calm my anger. My phone vibrates in my pocket. I take a minute to gather myself before pulling it out and checking the screen.

MITCH

We'll see about that.

This time I do throw my phone. It's only at the pillow on the nearby couch but it's still satisfying.

"Arrogant prick!"

"I prefer Ms. Arrogant Prick, actually."

I spin to see Jolie leaning against the counter. It's early. The shop hasn't even opened, yet I'm not surprised to see her. She seems to get around things like closed signs and locked doors, so I don't even question how she got in.

"Sorry. I didn't think anyone was here. My stupid soon-to-be-ex-husband is being a jerk." I pick up my phone and pocket it again. I don't bother dignifying Mitch's last text with a response.

I wish I could say I don't let his words get to me but his messages bring back all the reasons why I left him in the first place. The gaslighting, the manipulation, the condescension. Every comment, every look chipped away at my self-esteem until I no longer recognized the timid and obedient woman in the mirror.

My face must give away my thoughts because Jolie's humor fades and she crosses to me. "Hey, are you okay? Did he hurt you? Give me a picture of the guy and I swear they'll never find the body." She pulls me in for a tight hug.

The fact that she can threaten a man's life while offering affection is pure Jolie. She's the perfect combination of soft and hard. She's a fiercely loyal friend and I'm lucky she's now one of mine.

I squeeze her back, thankful for the distraction. "No, nothing like that. He's just confirming what a piece of shit he is. That appointment with the lawyer can't come soon enough."

"Well, you let me know if anything changes. My dad's been teaching me self-defense since I was five. After a while, the line between defense and offense starts to blur." She winks and I laugh. "I've used a few moves on some drunken assholes when I was bartending in Vancouver and they got too handsy with the waitresses."

She puts her hands on my shoulders and looks me in the eyes, surveying my face. "Are you sure you're okay?"

I shrug. "I will be. I'm just mad. At him for ignoring his kid. At myself for letting his treatment of us go on for so long. At the whole situation, really."

Jolie smiles ominously, looking like the Cheshire Cat. "Oh, girl, do I have the perfect thing for you. Cancel your lunch plans today and come over to the studio at one. Don't worry, I've got extra mats." And with that, she struts out the door.

I'm not sure I'm in the mood for peaceful gongs and calming music but I'll give it a shot for Jolie.

"**M**otherfucking piece of shit twat gremlin."

Did I say peaceful? I don't think anyone in their right mind could describe this yoga class as peaceful.

Apparently Jolie teaches a different style of yoga than your run-of-the-mill kind. She called it "rage yoga", which essentially means that instead of slow, purposeful breaths and calming melodies, we're listening to punk music and yelling curse words.

That particular gem of a line came from Maeve beside me. I swear she and Dottie are trying to outdo each other for Most Off-The-Wall Comment this class. I should've known something was amiss when Dottie insisted I place my mat between the two of them.

Always a fan of the dramatics, Jolie gave me no warning on what I was walking into so when the first member yelled out "FUCK" from behind me, I just about jumped off my mat. I spun to look at Jolie, who was walking around the group, calling out encouragement as if nothing happened. She didn't look at me but I caught the slightest smirk twisting at her lips as she ambled past my mat.

We're outside in a small clearing behind Jolie's studio, far enough away from the park that no innocent ears can hear our calls. Jolie said she likes to have as many outdoor classes as possible during the summer since our winters tend to be so long.

We're about forty minutes into the class and I've got to say, I get why it's so sought after. It's therapeutic being able to relax and stretch your body into new positions while tossing out curse words that would make a sailor blush. Sometimes I don't even know what I'm saying and just let out unintelligible shouts.

I'm on my knees with my arms above my head, staring up at the sky while Jolie walks us through our next move from the front.

"Before you descend into Shavasana, I want you to hold the pose you're in but close your eyes. Now think about something that has been bothering you. Whether it's a conflict at work, worries in your personal life or frustration that the diner was out of blueberry scones this morning," A few people chuckle. "Whatever it is. I want you to think about it for a few moments. Let it fester within you. Let it sit low in your gut. Feel the weight of it pulling you down."

I think about Mitch's texts this morning. How after so many years together, he still doesn't respect me enough to take my feelings seriously. How he expects me to come crawling back to him because he told me to. How he hasn't once asked about his son.

The worst of it is, Gavin hasn't asked about him either. I think about their non-existent relationship. How I've lost myself over the last number of years, turning into someone I don't even recognize.

How I haven't felt this at home in the decade I spent in the city as I have these past few months in Haven Bay.

"Then when the weight feels immovable like it's starting

to fill you up with no way out, I want you to tell that weight to fuck off!" Jolie yells the last word. "Shoot all the middle fingers at it! Punch that weight out through your arms and into the sky. Let the universe take that stupid fucking worry and shove it up its ass!" Jolie's voice grows louder until she's shouting along with us.

I punch the sky, roaring out a slur of curses with every purposeful thrust of my arms. I picture Mitch's face. I picture my own insecurities. I picture the good little society wife I once was. I picture all of my forgotten goals and dreams from long ago.

Then I give one last shout for the woman I lost and can hopefully find again.

"Amazing. You guys are all amazing!" I open my eyes and see Jolie smiling proudly at me from her place in front of the group. I smile back, the weight of this morning lifted and replaced with a sense of peace.

"Now, let's all get down on our backs and close our eyes. Legs and arms are going to lie weightlessly on your mat as we relax into Shavasana." The music switches to the punk ballad *It Ends Tonight* as I follow the rest of the group to the ground.

A few minutes later, the song ends and everyone starts climbing to their feet. I stand and walk over to Jolie. She's pulling out her cooler of post-yoga beverages for the class, both alcoholic and non.

Oh yeah, did I mention rage yoga comes with booze?

Truly revolutionary.

"So," Jolie says, drawing out the last syllable. She hands me a wine cooler and we step aside from the rest of the group. "What did you think? Pretty kick ass, right?"

I take a sip of my drink and nod. "Pretty kick ass," I agree. "It was surprisingly cathartic. I feel like a whole new woman." I tip my drink to hers in cheers. "Thanks. I really needed that."

She bumps her can against mine. "Any time, sugar plum."

Just then, a tall figure rounds the corner, stalking toward our group.

"Uh oh. Here comes the fun police," Jolie mutters to me. She lifts her head and smiles sweetly at Luke. "Officer Grumpy Pants. You're right on time. We're celebrating the end of another successful class. Want a beer?"

Luke stops before her, scowling down at the drink in her hand. "How many times do I have to tell you: you can't drink alcohol in a public place. Beside a playground, no less." He jerks a thumb over his shoulder to the playground behind him.

"Relax, Captain America. No children were corrupted today. The playground is about a football field away from us, and there's only a couple of toddlers there. The worst they could hear was some garbled shouting. As for the drinking," she opens the cooler to show off the inside. "I brought enough for one drink each. After that, people will have to head to The Dive to get their drink on."

Luke mutters something that sounds like "insufferable woman", then points a finger at the cooler. "It's still open alcohol in a public place."

"Oh, lighten up, Luke. No one's getting plastered here. Isn't there a kitty stuck in a tree somewhere for you to save?" Jolie tilts her head to the side and smirks.

"That's a firefighter, not a police officer," Luke snaps. "Trust me, I'd like nothing more than to be anywhere but here. But we received a noise complaint. Again."

"That grumpy, old coot tattled on us again?" Dottie says as she and Maeve walk up, beer bottles in hand. "I'm telling you, Doug needs to get laid. He wouldn't be whining about a few curse words after our Maevey got done with him."

"He might be shouting a few of his own instead," Maeve says, taking a long, casual drink of her beer.

Jolie and I erupt into laughter while Luke looks like he might be sick.

"It doesn't matter who called it in." Luke shakes his head, probably trying to erase the image of Maeve and 80 year old Doug Feldman from his head. "Would it kill you to keep it in the studio?"

"Well, I can't say for sure but I figure I shouldn't risk it. Just in case. This butt is too cute for a coffin," Jolie says, winking at Luke.

He narrows his eyes. "Cut the shit, woman. I'm serious. Keep it inside or I'm writing you a fine." With that, he turns and stomps off.

"Wow. Luke hasn't lightened up much over the years, has he?" I comment.

"And here I thought he saved it for me." Jolie takes one last swig of her drink before tossing it in a nearby recycle bin.

Now that the excitement of Luke's warning has worn off, the crowd starts to disperse. Jolie collects her cooler, mat and speaker and I follow her inside.

"Aren't you worried about being fined? I can't imagine that's cheap."

"Nah," Jolie waves away my concern. "He's been threatening to fine me since I started this class years ago. Until I see the paperwork, I'll keep calling his bluff." She tosses her mat into a nearby cubby. "Anyway, are you done for the day? Want to grab lunch?" I glance down at my smartwatch. I don't have to pick up Gavin from summer camp until four and with everything that happened with Mitch earlier, I forgot to eat.

"Lunch sounds great. Let me check in with Tammy and make sure she's okay on her own."

Jolie links her arm through mine. "Perfect. Let's go, chickadee!"

AFTER CHECKING in at the store, I grab my purse and Jolie and I head to the diner. Maeve and Dottie have already returned to their usual seats out front.

"See any cute butts out there, ladies?" Jolie asks.

"Nothing better than tourist season in the summer," Dottie muses. "New men every day. My only complaint is that swim shorts are too long these days. We need to bring those European-style thong suits to Canada. I want to see more buns and thighs!"

Jolie and I laugh, then wave and head inside. If left to it, Dottie would ramble on for hours about the male body. It's better to take your exit when you see it.

We head to the corner booth and slide in, grabbing menus from the napkin holder. Brandy Loffman, Millie's daughter, comes walking over to fill our glasses with water. After the mandatory small talk, Brandy takes our orders and then wanders away to the next table.

"So, are you feeling better after the class?" Jolie leans back against the booth and sips her water.

"Much. I'm really impressed with the class, by the way. I wasn't sure what to expect when Sue Franklin screeched out that first time but it was really relaxing. It was exactly what I needed."

"Yeah, Sue's one of my regulars. I think those twins of hers keep her on her toes. She comes in at least twice a week and lets it all out. She joked to me once that my class was the only thing keeping her sane," Jolie says and I laugh.

The Franklin twins are Hell on wheels. I could only imagine the patience it takes to be home with them all summer long.

"How'd you get into rage yoga, anyway? I've never heard of it before today," I ask her.

"Well, I've had a lot of different jobs. Like, a lot. I've been a bartender, a dog walker, a masseuse, a mechanic's apprentice, a web developer and a legal assistant. I still do a bit of web development on the side. But none of those things ever felt right, you know? I've never been the girl who knows my next step until I'm in it. So, I kept trying new things. It was when I was working for a spa in Kelowna that I found yoga. But it was too tame for me, too restrictive. I loved the power and strength that came with yoga, but the environment wasn't my thing. I'm a talker, in case you didn't notice." She smiles at Brandy's approach and thanks her when she places our meals in front of us.

"So, I was talking to the yoga instructor at the spa about this and she told me about rage yoga. I tried a class at a local studio and was hooked. I got certified that year and have been teaching ever since. It wasn't until I came to Haven Bay though that I had my own place."

"That's really cool, J. Good for you. Do you teach traditional yoga, too?" I take a bite of my B.L.T sandwich and moan. Nothing beats a Main Street Diner B.L.T.

Jolie takes a bite of her chicken wrap before answering. "I do. It's not that I don't like the traditional side of yoga. I just think that it might not be for everyone. I teach a few traditional classes a week and usually increase classes during the tourist season. But I find in the off-season, the locals like rage yoga better and request it more often."

"That's very cool. Good for you. Finding what you love and doing it your own way." I admire her ability to stand up for herself and do what works for her instead of what others expect of her. "I wish I was like that."

Jolie puts her wrap down and looks me in the eye. "Avery, you are like that. You're strong and resilient. Just because life hasn't been what you expected, doesn't mean you can't still go after what you want. You have a beautiful son, a mom who loves you and some pretty awesome friends, if I do say so myself." She reaches out and squeezes my hand. "Give yourself some credit, girl. You're still figuring it out. Do you know how long it took me to find my path? It doesn't happen overnight."

Jolie isn't what I expected. She's strong and outgoing. She seems like an open book but I've noticed there are parts of her story that she keeps hidden. She doesn't trust people easily, she's told me so herself. But it's times like these when I'm honored she's decided to open up to me.

"Now, enough of that. Tell me how your date with Matt went. Your texts were not detailed enough and I need the dirt." She leans over the table conspiringly. "Was it amazing? What'd you do? How big is his dick?"

I choke on my sandwich at the last question. This girl's going to kill me one day with her bluntness. Coughing, I take a large gulp of water to help wash the bite down. Jolie waits, unconcerned by her inappropriate question. I finally get a hold of myself.

"I'm not sure I'll ever get used to your uh, straightforwardness."

She waves me away. "Of course you will. Now, answer."

I put down my drink. "I wouldn't know because we didn't have sex. It was our first date and we've known each other for over twenty years, for God's sake."

She throws her hands up. "Exactly. That's twenty years of pent-up sexual tension begging to be let out. It's screaming 'Do him, Avery! Do him!'"

I toss my napkin at her but she just laughs back at me.

"Okay, fine. If you didn't jump his bones, then what did you do?"

I tell her all about our date, the arcade, his comment on my teasing, the walk along the beach and the heart-stopping kiss afterward.

"I knew it. You two are pure heat when you're together. Something that hot, it's only a matter of time before you combust."

"I haven't even told you about the next day yet," I tell her, then laugh when she smacks both palms on the table.

The napkin holder rattles but she doesn't even notice.

"There's more?! Sweet Jesus, you've been holding out on me, woman! We'll talk about your lack of prompt sharing after." She leans forward eagerly.

I tell her about the awkward day after and how he called me out on it. Then I tell her about the "almost" moment in my office.

Jolie fans herself with her menu. "Okay, why are you wasting a single second here with me when you should be locked in a bedroom somewhere with Matt?"

I take a bite of my sandwich, taking longer than necessary to chew while I think over my answer. "It's not that I don't want to. I do. A lot. But I was with Mitch for eleven years. The only other date I've been on before that was in the seventh grade. Besides being absolutely terrified at the thought of a new guy seeing my post-baby body, I'm worried it's too soon. Shouldn't I be working on myself before jumping straight into a new relationship?"

What if I lose myself again?

The thought has been bouncing around in my head since our first date. Once I picked my jaw up off of the floor after that amazing kiss, of course.

Jolie's expression turns soft. "I know you're going through a lot and you shouldn't discount that. I'm not saying you have to jump into a relationship. You shouldn't do anything you're not comfortable with. But don't forget to have fun, whatever that looks like to you. Be cautious if that's what you want to do. All I'm saying is don't let what happened in the past rule your future." She smiles at me reassuringly. "Only you know what's best for you."

I smile back and, luckily, the subject changes but I'm still thinking about her comment hours later.

Only you know what's best for you.

With Mitch, he made most of the decisions for us. When I did make a decision, he would tell me how it was wrong or that I should've done things differently. The first decision I made for myself in years was to ask for a divorce. Even that took me months of second-guessing before I finally followed through.

But Jolie's right. Only I know how to make myself happy. Only I can decide what's right for Gavin and me.

I might not be used to making decisions but it's about time I start practicing.

MATT

The display case for the cafe is finally finished. To be honest, it's been done for a few days now but I haven't had the balls to admit it. I've spent the last week going over every detail, making sure it's perfect.

I don't know why I'm so nervous. I make custom pieces for customers all the time and, while it's always nerve-wracking, I don't usually care this much.

Maybe it's because of the intricate details I carved along the edges. The main design is abstract, made up of swirls and fine lines. But I've also carved some subtle nods to Angie and her family into the design. If you look carefully, there are book spines for Angie, spiders for Gavin's love of Spider-Man, and daisies for Avery. That last one is also a nod to our first date.

It's the closest thing to my art that I've done for Taylor Construction and the idea of showing people this part of my life, even in a small capacity, both excites me and scares the shit out of me.

Will they like it? Will they laugh and tell me to stick to construction?

The unknown is killing me. But it's killing me more to stare at the display case, day after day, wondering.

So I'm delivering it today. Which means our end of the expansion is complete. The rest is up to Angie and Avery to decorate and make the space their own. I know they're both excited to get their hands on it and I can't wait to see what they do.

Even if I'm a little disappointed that I won't be seeing Avery every day anymore, I'm happy for them.

Just thinking about her makes me smile. It's been over a week since our date and I still can't stop thinking about her. We haven't had a chance to go on another date since we've both been busy with work and family, so we've settled for stolen moments during the work day or phone calls at night instead.

I can't help hoping that the more invested Avery gets into the bookshop and now, the cafe, the better chance she'll want to stick around Haven Bay. She hasn't decided what her plan is after the summer, but she has an appointment with her lawyer tomorrow that she's hoping will give her a better idea of her options.

Johnny and a few of the guys from the crew arrive with the flatbed trailer to deliver the display case. It takes all five of us to load the display case onto the trailer. We're only going a block up the road, but we make sure to securely strap it down. Finally satisfied, I give the strap one last pull before hopping into the truck with the guys.

On the way over, I'm so focused on making sure nothing happens to the display case that I don't notice the small crowd waiting in front of the shop. As Johnny slowly pulls up, I lean my head out the window from the backseat of the truck.

There's got to be around twenty people standing on the sidewalk. Dottie and Maeve are seated in the road in lawn chairs, blocking off the two parking spaces directly in front of the cafe. They slowly stand and move their chairs to the sidewalk as we approach.

"Saved a spot for ya, Matty!" Dottie calls out, waving at the parking spaces in front of the cafe. Johnny puts on his hazard lights and we all pile out of the truck. I spot Avery and Angie on the sidewalk, so I walk over to them.

"What's going on?" I ask, confused.

Avery shrugs. "I guess word got out that the display case is being installed today. A bunch of people wanted to see the big reveal." She smiles as if to say, *what can you do?*

"Only in Haven Bay," I force a smile and Avery laughs.

Inside, I'm freaking out. I was nervous enough about Angie, Avery and the crew seeing my work. I mean, I knew eventually others would see it but at least I wouldn't be around to witness their reaction. Now, a crowd of people are watching as we "unveil" the case, which will spark conversations all around town about the either success or failure of my work.

A bead of sweat rolls down my back that has nothing to do with the summer heat.

"Hey, Matt. You gonna stand there all day looking pretty or are you gonna help us unload this bad boy?" Johnny calls from the trailer.

I take a deep breath. *Here we go.* I walk over to the trailer, forcing myself to put on a happy face.

I dramatically bat my eyelashes at him and cup a hand under my chin. "You really think I'm pretty?" I ask him.

Johnny rolls his eyes and shoves me away, making the rest of the guys laugh.

Together, we unload the display case and walk it toward the doorless entrance. It takes a bit of finagling but we get it through without a scratch. We finally get it in place and carefully lower it to the floor.

"Oh, Matt. It's beautiful!" Angie croons, tracing a hand along the edge. She suddenly inhales sharply. "Avery! Come look at the details."

I'm sweating, watching the two of them inspect the case. After what seems like hours, Avery looks up at me with misty eyes. "You did this?" I nod.

She strides over to me, then stands on her toes to give me a gentle kiss. She pulls back and smiles. I try to keep my face neutral but fail.

Avery hasn't shown any PDA or given any indication of interest other than when we're alone. I've been wanting to shout it from the rooftops, but I was letting her set the tone. I didn't want to rush her or make her feel uncomfortable. Technically, we haven't even had "the talk" yet to establish what our relationship is.

For her to kiss me in front of her mom, the crew and a handful of the town is a big deal. I'm ecstatic but I try to keep both the happiness and surprise off my face. I give her a questioning look and she subtly nods in response.

Well, okay then.

"Thank you for this. It means so much to Mom and I. It's absolutely perfect."

I'm at a loss for words. She doesn't know but her reaction to my work is more than I could've ever hoped for. The tornado of emotions threatens to run me over, so I pull her to me, wrapping my arms around her.

I wonder how it would feel to bring the artistic side of myself to the light. To allow everyone to see the real me, not only what I choose to show them.

Avery's reaction gives me hope that maybe they might accept me.

All of me.

"GOOD MORNING, BEAUTIFUL LADY," I lean across the shop's counter to give Avery a quick kiss. Her public show of affection yesterday has given me the confidence to touch her in all the ways I've been wanting to since that first day after our date.

She seems to like it, too. She's biting back a smile while she looks up at me through her lashes. It takes all my effort not to pull her into the back room and take my time with her.

"What time is your meeting with the lawyer?" I ask instead, sliding over the caramel latte I brought her.

"It's at 10:30 in Bakersfield, so I'm leaving in fifteen minutes to make sure I give myself enough time to find it."

Hmm, I can do a lot in fifteen minutes.

Her phone rings, pulling me out of my thoughts.

"Hello? Yes, this is Avery." Her smile falls. "Oh, no. Okay. Yes, I'll be right there." She ends the call. "Shit. Shit, shit, shit. Of all days."

I set down my coffee, concerned. "What's wrong?"

Avery shoves her hands through her hair in frustration. "That was Gavin's summer camp. Their counselor went home with the stomach flu that's been going around and they don't have anyone to cover for him. So they're closing the camp today. Which would be fine but my mom has a doctor's appointment that she can't miss so she can't watch him. I'd ask Jolie but she's busy, too." She lets out a groan. "I'll have to bring him with me to the meeting. I was really hoping to leave him out of anything to do with the divorce."

Before I can think it through, I hear myself saying, "I can watch him."

She pauses, watching me skeptically. "You want to watch Gavin?"

I shrug. "Sure. Why not? The guys are in good shape, so they don't need me here anyways. I can take the afternoon off. We'll hang out until you get back."

The more I think about it, the more I like the idea. If I'm

going to be dating Avery, things like this are bound to happen. Besides, I like Gavin. He's a good kid. Not that I know much about kids, other than I once was one.

She chews her lip, hesitating.

I reach out and tuck a stray strand of hair behind her ear. "Come on, Freckles. You can trust me. Worst case, my mom's home today as backup."

She slowly nods and I try not to dwell too much on her only agreeing after I mention my mom helping.

"Okay. Thanks, Matt. I really appreciate it. I shouldn't be gone long." She smiles in relief, then quickly goes into Mom-mode. "He has his lunch I packed for camp so you won't have to worry about cooking for him. He's picky but he has everything he'll need in his backpack. I'll run out and pick him up quickly before I go."

She frantically searches her purse for her keys then checks her watch again. "Shit," she mutters.

I put a reassuring hand on her wrist. "You're going to be late. Go. I'll get him."

She pulls out her keys just as Tammy walks in. "You'll need his car seat. It's in my car." I follow her out of the store to where her car sits out front. She unhooks the seat from her car then walks over to install it in my truck. Satisfied that it's securely in place, she stands and turns to me. "Thank you again. Call me if you need anything. I can be back in half an hour if anything happens."

I walk her back to her car then open the door. "We'll be fine. Stop worrying. If we get bored, we'll watch T.V. He's seen *Family Guy*, right?" Her mouth drops open and I laugh. "I'm kidding. Now, go."

She rolls her eyes, smiling. Then she slides into her car and pulls away. Jumping in my truck, I swing by my apartment to pick up Ham then make our way to the rec center where the summer camp is held. Swinging into a parking space, I open my door when a thought hits me.

How the hell do you entertain a 4-year-old?

CHAPTER 22

AVERY

The ticking of the clock on the wall is taunting me. I'm sitting in the lawyer's office in one of those stylish accent chairs designed for aesthetics, not for comfort. I readjust my position for the fifth time since I sat down.

The receptionist and I are the only ones in the waiting room. She seemed nice enough when I came in but I instantly felt self-conscious when she greeted me in her designer clothes and perfectly-styled hair. I tug at the shirt I borrowed from Jolie and force myself to stop comparing myself to someone I know nothing about.

I check the clock on the wall again, noticing it's only been two minutes since the last time I looked. I can't sit still, my leg bouncing anxiously.

The large mahogany door beside me finally swings open and a well-dressed woman in her fifties walks out. She's wearing a dark green pantsuit with tall red-soled heels. Her hair is cut in a short bob, with silver streaks fashionably accenting her dark hair. She's wearing bright red glasses that I'd bet are designer and are probably worth more than my car.

She passes a file to the receptionist then approaches me.

"Mrs. Olsen? I'm Margot Sanders." She reaches out and shakes my hand. "Please, come in." She gestures toward her office, so I step inside.

She follows me in and closes the door behind her. She sits in a large white leather chair. I take a second to survey the room before taking a seat across from her. The walls are white with black decor accents. There are a few plants tucked into corners but otherwise, it's clean and tasteful.

My leg starts to bounce again.

Margot slips off her glasses and leans toward me. The motion brings attention to her piercing blue eyes, staring almost unsettlingly into mine. "So, Mrs. Olsen. You're here to discuss your options for filing for divorce, correct?"

I shift my attention from her jewelry to her face. "Call me Avery. But yes. I officially asked my husband for a divorce in January but we didn't file as I was unemployed and couldn't afford to move out." I fill her in on the details up until this point while she continues to stare, expressionless other than the occasional purse of her thin, brightly painted lips.

When I finish, she sits back in her large chair. "Now, what are your plans for the future? Are you working now? Where are you planning to reside full-time?" She places her glasses back on the edge of her nose, then leans forward again. She picks up a pen, pausing with it hovering over her notebook, then looks up at me over the rim of her glasses.

I readjust in my seat. "I'm working at my mother's bookstore. As far as our living situation, I'm not sure where we'll be permanently yet. I guess that depends on what answers you can give me today." I swallow hard. "Do I have to move back to Edmonton?" I try to slow my bouncing knee but I'm too anxious.

A lot of my future depends on this moment. Gavin's future school, the friendships he's made at camp, my position at the store and our future in Haven Bay.

Matt.

She delicately crosses one leg over the other, sitting regally in her throne-like chair. "That answer depends on a few answers from you. First being whether we are going after sole custody." Again, she peers over her glasses at me in question.

I shake my head, not bothering to think about it. "I can't do that to either of them. Whether or not he wants to start acting like a father is on him. But I won't stand in the way of their relationship. If he wants to share custody, I'm very open to it."

This was one decision I was adamant on. I knew what it was like to grow up without a father and I didn't want that life for Gavin. Luckily, Matt's dad made sure I had a father figure to look up to growing up. But I won't keep my son from his father, unless Gavin specifically asks me to.

Margot gives me a slight nod before making a note on her notepad. "Very well. Second is whether you plan to work with your ex-husband to arrange pick-up and drop-offs of your son. Do you have reliable transportation, Avery?"

I nod. My Volvo might be old but it runs and has been well-maintained over the years, despite Mitch's protests.

"Good." Another note. "The last part will depend on your ex-husband. Since you left without giving written notice sixty days prior to your departure, Mitchell may decide to contest the move. We can assert that you haven't officially had a change of address as your departure was due to your mother's health concerns. A judge may decide to take this into account or they may take your departure as violation of this. Since you are not officially divorced, it becomes a gray area that will depend on the judge's ruling in the hearing. In the instance that the judge rules against you, you may have to move back to Edmonton, at least temporarily while custody arrangements are made."

My head is spinning. A hearing? A judge? I thought it

would be a matter of signing some papers, splitting our assets and arranging a custody agreement. All of that seemed daunting enough. Who knows how long all this might take now.

Margot must sense my unease. Suddenly, she's standing in front of me, leaning against her desk and pushing a bottle of water into my hands. I take a long drink, trying to calm my nerves.

"It's going to be fine. We're going to take this in steps and we're not going to worry until we have a reason to. Even then, we're going to be prepared so we know what to do, should Mitchell contest it." She pats my hand and I can feel the color in my face returning. She stands and returns to her seat behind the desk.

"The first thing we're going to do is file for divorce. We will request joint custody with negotiations as to what that schedule will look like. Your alimony and child support will—"

She continues explaining the terms we will put forth for the divorce agreement but my mind is reeling. I knew this process would be complicated but I think I underestimated it all.

When she asks if there are any assets I'd like to go after, I shake my head. I just want to be done. To be in charge of my own life. I'm thankful for our time together because it brought me Gavin but I'm not looking to make a fortune off of him.

I want to be free.

By the end of the meeting, I feel a bit better than when I went in. Mitch is going to be served later this week and we'll have to wait and see what his response is. The easiest thing for all of us would be if he just signed the papers. But I know Mitch and he is not going to be happy about this.

I decide my best option is to hunker down and brace myself for the storm.

MATT

"Then you put the arm buckle in the bottom buckle."

Yeah, you're reading that right. A 4-year-old is teaching me how to buckle him into his own car seat.

I'll take *Things I Never Thought Would Happen* for 200, Alex.

Once I finally have Gavin secured in the car seat, I round the truck and slide into the driver's seat.

"How come you picked me up today 'stead of Mommy?" Gavin asks.

I pull out of the camp's parking lot and onto Main Street. "Your mom had an appointment she had to go to and Gram was busy. So I thought you and I could hang out today. We'll have a guys' day. Is that okay with you?"

Gavin thinks it over for a minute before shouting his response. "YES! Guys' day! Can Hammy come, too?"

"Heck yeah, buddy. I think Ham would be sad if we didn't bring him along."

As if he knows we're talking about him, Ham drops his head to my shoulder from the backseat beside Gavin. I reach back and scratch his chin.

"So, what do you think we should do today?" I glance back in the rearview mirror at Gavin. He's bouncing his tiny legs while petting Ham's large flank.

"Donno," Gavin replies.

"Well, what do you like to do with your mom and Gram?"

"Sometimes we take Sushi to the beach or we go to the playground or we read Spider-Man. Sushi *loves* Spider-Man. But Sushi and me can't read so we let Mommy read it out loud and we just look at the pictures. Gram bakes the best rainbow cookies and we take them to Miss Franny's house and eat them on her swing." He hardly takes a breath, chattering away excitedly. Then he looks at me knowingly. "Miss Franny's your mom," he says.

He says it more like a statement than a question but I answer him anyway. "She sure is," I say, trying to keep up with his train of thought.

I think back to what I liked to do as a kid his age. Images of digging up worms in the garden and pretending to eat them to make Avery squirm flash in my head.

Suddenly, an idea hits me. "What'd you say we swing by Miss Franny's house then we head down to the boardwalk? I've got an idea I think you'll like."

"'Kay, Matt." Gavin says cheerily, looking out the window. "Look! A tractor!"

After making a quick stop at my mom's then over to Chuck's Gas and Tackle, I pull into the parking lot in front of the beach. I let Ham out the back door, unhook Gavin from his car seat, then round the truck to pull open the tailgate. I grab my dad's and my old rods from the bed of the truck, balancing my dad's old tackle box in my other hand.

"What's that?" Gavin eyes the fishing gear.

"Fishing rods and bait." He looks at me blankly. "Have you never been fishing before, Gav?" He shakes his head.

I gasp and clutch my chest. Gavin giggles. "Well, we can't have that, buddy. Every kid should go fishing at least once. It's like a right of passage in Haven Bay."

"What's that mean?" Gavin asks.

Right. Clearly I'm not used to talking to kids.

"It means something you should do before you grow up," I explain and he accepts that answer with a nod.

We start towards the walkway that leads across the beach

and to the boardwalk. Before we can cross, Gavin stops suddenly.

"What's wrong?"

He wordlessly reaches out a hand to me. There are definitely going to be some learning curves today. I reach back and grab his tiny hand in mine. Together, we cross the parking lot.

As we walk, Gavin chatters along beside me, telling me about his summer camp and his new friends—one of them being one of Pete's grandsons. I listen intently and can't help but feel proud of the change in this little boy.

A few short months ago, he was a timid kid, scared of anything or anyone new. Afraid to make too much noise or take up too much space. Now, he doesn't hesitate to wave at a young family and the little girl about his age with them as they walk by us.

When we finally arrive at the boardwalk, we put our things down on an open bench and I start to prepare the rods. Once the rods are set up, I pull the container of worms from the tackle box.

"What're those for?" Gavin sits down on the bench between Ham and I, watching me carefully.

"The worms go on the end of the hook so when the fish tries to eat the worm, they get stuck on the hook. Then we can reel the fish in, weigh him and then let him go," I explain.

Gavin goes quiet. Staring at the ground, he chews his bottom lip nervously. I pull out a worm and hold it steady, lining it up to the hook. Just before I push the hook into the worm, Gavin whimpers. I spin to see the cause of his distress. He slinks onto the bench, casting his eyes downward but not before I notice the tears filling them.

I drop to my knees before him. "Hey, buddy. What's wrong? What happened?" I ask, concern lacing my voice.

He remains silent but I notice his quick glance at the worm in my hand. Realization dawns on me.

"Gav, does it bother you to use worms on the hook?" I ask gently.

He hesitates before nodding shyly.

"That's okay. We don't have to use worms. My dad kept lots of other types of bait in his tackle box that will work." I pull the tackle box toward me and dig through it. "How about these rubber minnows?" I take out a small plastic bag and show him the artificial bait.

Gavin nods and I let out a small sigh of relief. I bait the hook on his fishing pole then pass it over to him. He takes it hesitantly, still watching his feet more than the pole. I watch him for a moment before bending to eye level again.

"Gav, buddy. You can tell me if something's bothering you. I won't get mad," I tell him.

He puts a hand on Ham's side, petting him slowly. He doesn't lift his head, staring at Ham's fur. Then he whispers, "Does it hurt the fish when we catch 'em?"

His question stuns me, knocking me from a kneeled position to my ass. *Man, could I have fucked this up any more?*

To be honest, I've never given any thought to either the fish or the worms. I thought about taking Gavin fishing because it was something my dad used to do with Luke, Tori and I as kids. We always had a great time, so I figured it was something all kids would like.

I should've known that not all kids are the same. Just because I liked something as a kid, doesn't mean Gavin has to. He's a thoughtful, caring kid who has big emotions and there's nothing wrong with that. Something I'm sure Dickless Mitch would disagree with and might even condemn him for.

I mentally kick myself. Of course he was scared to tell me. He probably thinks all men act like his worthless dad. I wish I could have ten minutes alone with that asshole. I'd show him exactly what I thought of how he treats his kid.

Instead, I place my hand gently on Gavin's shoulder.

"Honestly, Gav, I'm not sure. I've never thought about it. But I think it's really cool that you did. You're a great kid and you should never feel embarrassed about thinking about other people's feelings." I take my hand from his shoulder to stroke Ham's neck. "Especially animals. They can't talk to us so we have to make sure we talk for them."

Gavin smiles shyly, then wraps his arms around Ham's middle.

"Alright. How about this? If you're interested, I've got an idea of something we can do instead of fishing. What'd you think about hitting up the arcade? I'm going to text your mom and see if she wants to meet us there." Gavin lets out a whoop, jumping to his feet. I throw my head back and laugh. "I'll take that as a yes. Let's go, big guy. I feel like kicking some butt at Whac-A-Mole."

I push open the doors to the arcade and the flashing lights and ringing music from the games instantly overload my senses.

When Matt texted telling me about the fishing incident, I felt bad for him. I didn't even think that it might be something that would upset Gavin. When Matt described how he dealt with it, I was pleasantly surprised at how well he handled the situation. He didn't push Gavin to do something he wasn't comfortable with or make him feel bad about his feelings. When he asked if it was okay if he took Gavin to the arcade instead, I happily agreed.

I'm feeling drained after my meeting with the lawyer and I'm sure both Matt and Gavin could use a distraction from their earlier incident. What better way to forget your problems than some good old-fashioned fun?

I search the crowd, eventually spotting them at the Whac-A-Mole. I walk toward them and can't help but notice how natural the two of them look together. They're focused on the game and don't notice my approach. Gavin swings the rubber mallet down on the colorful moles while Matt helps him by hitting them with his hands. Gavin's laugh rings out as I get closer and the melodic sound instantly lifts my mood.

"Holy, look at you go! Those poor moles don't stand a chance."

Gavin spins at the sound of my voice. His face lights up when he sees me and he rushes toward me. "Mommy! Look at all my tickets!" He lifts up the plastic cup filled with prize tickets. "I got so many and Matt said I'll prob'ly have enough for the Spider-Man mask."

"Wow! Good work, buddy," I praise, giving his little cheek a kiss before he runs back to the game.

Matt gives him a high-five then slips another few tokens in the machine. With Gavin busy playing, Matt saunters over to me.

"Do I get one of those, too?" he teases, pointing a finger to his cheek.

Smiling, I lift myself onto my toes to kiss his cheek.

"Hmm, now what about one here?" He smiles mischievously and taps a finger to his mouth. I look over his shoulder at Gavin who's still whacking the rubber mallet.

Matt grows serious, noticing my hesitation. "You don't have to in front of Gavin if you'd rather not."

I reach up on my toes and give him a quick peck on the lips. "I'm not hiding it, I promise. I'm fine with Gavin knowing. I just haven't had a chance to talk to him about it yet."

"When you do, can we ask him together?"

I nod, touched by his question. The simple way he phrased it shows me he's not only considering Gavin's opinion on us dating, he's taking his answer seriously.

He gives my hand a quick squeeze before walking back over to where Gavin stands. His game has finished and he bounces up and down, unable to contain so much excitement in his little body.

"Can we play the race car game again, Matt?" he asks.

"Let's do it. I'm not taking it easy on you this time, though." He jokingly wags a finger at Gavin. "Maybe your mom wants to play, too. Then I can kick both of your butts!" Together, they run toward the racing game, Gavin laughing while trying to keep up.

"Nuh-uh. I'm gonna kick your butt!" Gavin exclaims, hopping into the seat and turning the steering wheel back and forth enthusiastically.

"We'll see about that. I used to beat Matt all the time at this game when we were kids," I tell Gavin. "He's a sore loser."

Matt raises his eyebrows at me and I smirk over Gavin's head at him.

"You think so, eh? We'll see who's the sore loser in a few minutes."

Three games later, Gavin's jumping out of the driver's seat in victory. "Woohoo! I win again!" He dances beside the machine. "Winner, winner, chicken dinner!"

Matt groans while I laugh. "Kid definitely got his competitive streak from you."

"I know. I love it," I joke.

He watches me, his gaze turning tender. "Me too."

My heart trips and we share a look of longing. It's times like this where he reminds me so much of the boy I grew up with. The boy I laughed with, cried with, rode bikes with. And when he looks at me the way he is right now, I wonder if he's thinking about that, too.

I can feel my walls start to crumble and, for once, the thought of letting someone new in doesn't scare me. Gavin calls out, snapping us out of the moment. He turns and takes off toward the next game.

Slowly, Matt and I follow behind him. When he's sure Gavin is distracted, Matt slips his pinky finger around mine and my walls crumble to dust.

Is THERE anything hotter than watching the guy you're dating teach your kid how to play Skee-Ball?

I'm here to tell you that no, there is not.

Matt is currently showing Gavin how to swing his arm so that the ball has enough momentum to shoot up the ramp. Gavin's brow furrows and his tongue sticks out in concentration as he eyes up the ramp. Matt whispers something to him and he nods slightly. Then he swings his arm back before thrusting it forward, sending the ball flying down the ramp. The ball rockets upward and sinks into the 25-point cup.

Gavin's arms shoot above his head and he's wearing the widest grin I've ever seen. He turns to Matt, jumping up and down victoriously. Matt lets out a whoop, mirroring Gavin's stance. Then he scoops Gavin up, throwing him over his shoulder and runs around the game.

Okay, I stand corrected. That's pretty damn hot. I don't know how much more of this my mama heart can take.

Matt stops and places a laughing Gavin on his feet before me. I can't count the number of times I've heard Gavin laugh today. He's never laughed this much with his dad and that devastates me.

I decide not to dwell on it, mentally shaking the thought away. I lift my hand up and Gavin slaps it in celebration. "Way to go, Gav! That was awesome!"

Matt gives him a high five, too. "No kidding! You're on your way to being named Emperor of Awesome. You might even be better at Skee-Ball than your mom." He winks at me.

I scoff. "Oh, Gav. I love you, kiddo, but no one is better than me at Skee-Ball." I toss some tokens in the slot and the balls roll toward me. I toss all nine balls up the ramp consecutively, earning a sweet 410 points. I pump my fist in victory then turn and bow at Matt's applause.

"Nicely done," he says. "But I think your form could use some work."

"You think so, eh?" I reply, arching a brow, knowing exactly where he's going with that cheesy comment. He steps up to the game, sliding more tokens into the slot. The balls roll down and I pick one up. He slides in behind me, his body molding to my back. His hand slides slowly down my arm to cup my hand that holds the plastic ball. Goosebumps cover my arms and it takes all my effort not to drop the ball when his breath tickles my ear.

"Am I making you nervous, Freckles?" he whispers, his lips grazing the outer shell of my ear.

My heart thunders in my chest. I take a quick look behind me to make sure Gavin can't see us, but to my relief, he's busy a few games over on the ring toss.

Realistically, what we're doing is very PG. To anyone else, it would look like two people playing a friendly game of Skee-Ball. But the way my heart is tripping over itself and the way my body temperature has risen at least 10 degrees, it feels anything but friendly.

His other hand is lightly holding my hip, keeping my butt pressed against his groin. I'm nearly panting and he's not even touching me anywhere exciting.

"Keep grinding that sweet ass of yours against me and you're going to get me kicked out of here." Matt's husky voice in my ear causes a shiver to run down my spine.

My spine straightens and I still my hips instantly. I didn't even realize I was moving against him. He lifts my arm, swings it back then thrusts it forward. The ball leaves my hand, shooting up the ramp and into the 100-point cup.

"Perfect," he rasps, sending another shiver through me. He steps back and clears his throat as if suddenly remembering where we are.

Gavin looks up from his place behind me at the ring toss.

"Wow, Mommy! Good job!" He shoots me a thumbs up then goes back to his game.

I'm off balance and grateful that no one seemed to notice the innocent looking but sensual moment between Matt and I. I hazard a look at him, my mouth suddenly dry when I see the heat in his eyes. They're clouded with desire and something dangerous.

I have to look away before they consume me.

"Hey, Gav. Last game then we should head home. What do you want to play?" I ask, hoping the change of subject will give us a chance to cool down.

Gavin's eyes scan the room before landing on a target. "That one!" He points at the air hockey table.

Of course.

I'm immediately brought back to the last time Matt and I had played that game and his statement that followed. Matt's heated stare tells me he's thinking about the same thing.

"Let's go, kiddo." Matt calls as Gavin follows behind eagerly.

A few minutes later, Matt is beating Gavin 2-1. I like that Matt doesn't openly let Gavin win but also doesn't try his hardest. It's a fine line to walk, not wanting to raise a sore winner nor a sore loser. It surprises me that I don't have to explain this to him either. He instinctively knows. Like he did with the fishing incident. Matt might not have known fishing would upset Gavin, but he knew not to push him or make him feel bad about his feelings.

Matt keeps surprising me in all the best ways and I don't even think he knows it.

I'm pulled from my thoughts by the clanging of the plastic puck slamming into the metal slot. Gavin cheers, pumping his fist.

"All tied up. You ready for sudden death, big guy?" Matt teases.

"Oh yeah!" Gavin calls.

Back and forth, they meet each other shot for shot, neither giving an inch as the seconds tick down on the overhead timer.

Déjà vu.

I can tell Matt's focused on the game. I think about the events of the day. The way Matt helped me out when I was in a lurch with Gavin. The way he dealt with Gavin and how seamlessly he's integrated himself into our lives.

The way he teased me at the Skee-Ball machine, his touch igniting that uncontrollable fire within me.

I know that my next move will come with consequences; ones that Matt made me fully aware of last time.

"Flash those pretty tits at me again and I'll show you what happens when you tease me."

But the thrill of knowing how I affect him is too much to ignore. For the first time, I feel powerful. I feel craved.

"I've only got so much restraint when it comes to you."

So I take a step back, shielding myself from Gavin's view and lean forward. I watch as Matt's eyes flash to my cleavage, then shoot up to mine. If I thought his look from earlier was dangerous, the one he shoots me now is lethal.

I give him a suggestive smile then press my arms to either side of my breasts, squeezing them higher. Matt's eyes turn black. Gavin smacks the plastic puck past him and into the net.

"GOAL!" Gavin shouts and I stand up straight before he turns to me. "Mommy, I won!"

I catch him as he jumps into my arms, oblivious to the thick tension surrounding him.

"I saw! Awesome job, buddy!" I put him back down on his feet. I smile devilishly back at Matt, who is still standing behind the table, stunned. "Why don't we go see if you have enough tickets for the Spider-Man mask?"

I collect our plastic cups and guide Gavin toward the prize

counter. Matt sneaks up beside me, leaning down to whisper just loud enough for me to hear. "Careful, Freckles. You're playing with fire."

I keep my head unturned, face neutral. "What if I want to get burned?" The only answer is Matt's low groan and I can't keep the smile off my face as I bounce away.

Oh, yeah. I don't want to get burned.

I want to be incinerated.

MATT

oly fuck.

I don't know what happened to Avery or where this sexual goddess came from, but she's driving me insane.

And she knows it.

After our last encounter in her office, I've been trying to take it slow. It's been killing me, seeing her all the time and holding back. But I know I can't rush her. I want her to feel comfortable with me, build trust and work our way from there. I figured she would let me know when she was ready.

She sure knows how to send a message.

Together, the three of us walk back to her car and I try to focus on baseball stats, work or the words to my favorite song. Anything other than the way her pants cup her ass perfectly or the sway of her full hips.

She opens the door and takes the car seat from my hands. Shoving it inside, she leans over to install it. I bite back a groan when her shirt rides up, giving me a glimpse of her soft, smooth skin and a front row view of her perfect ass.

She buckles Gavin in then turns to me. "Thanks again for today. I really appreciate you stepping in with Gavin. I think I can speak for both of us when I say we had the best time." She smiles sweetly, the sultry woman from before tucked back away. She turns to Gavin. "What do you say to Matt, Gav?"

"Thanks, Matt. I had SO much fun!" His tiny voice is muffled from beneath his Spider-Man mask, but I can hear the grin in his voice.

I lean my forearm on the roof of the car and bend my neck to look in. The position cages Avery's body between mine and the car and I watch her swallow hard.

"Any time, kiddo," I say to Gavin. "I had a blast."

I linger a minute longer than necessary, basking in the sweet smell of mangos from her shampoo. *Who knew fruit could be such a turn on?*

Finally, I step back and she closes the car door. I reach around her to pull open the driver's side door. Her eyes widen as she looks up at me.

"Drive safe, Freckles."

She nods, eyes still wide. Then she turns on her heel and slips into her car. Closing the door behind her, I lift a hand in goodbye as she pulls away.

Fuck. It's going to be a long night.

I need a cold beer and an even colder shower. I climb into my truck and spend the rest of the drive home getting my head on straight.

One thing I know for sure is that Avery was every bit as attracted to me as I was her today. Which should be a relief but the problem is I don't know what that means for us. Does she want to take our relationship to the next level? Is she waiting for me to make the first move? Was that her way of making the first move and I missed the hint?

I'm usually smooth when it comes to women but Avery has me out of my mind. I'm terrified of making the wrong move and screwing this whole thing up before it's even started.

Twenty minutes later, I swing my truck into one of the

parking spaces behind my apartment building and shut off the lights. I debate going straight into the shop to work off some of this pent up energy but decide to shower first.

After the coldest shower known to man, I throw on a pair of sweatpants and an old t-shirt then make my way back downstairs, Ham in tow. I'm about to flip the switch to the workshop when I hear a car door shut outside.

My heart leaps. There's only a few people who would be at my door this late on a weekday. If it's either Rhett or Luke, I'm going to kick their asses for getting my hopes up. I walk toward the back door, anticipation propelling me across the short distance. I pull open the heavy metal door to find Avery approaching.

"Hey. I wasn't expecting to see you again tonight. Everything okay?" I ask, backing up to let her in. She steps inside, remaining oddly quiet. I look down at her in concern. "Avery?"

"Do you want me, Matt?"

Her blunt question takes me by surprise. It takes my mind a second to catch up, finally deciding to respond honestly.

"Yeah. I want you, Avery."

She closes her eyes, her face expressionless. Moments pass and I'm wondering if I said the wrong thing when the tiniest corner of her lips tilt upward. She opens her eyes and I see temptation reflecting back in them.

"Then take me."

I'M PRETTY sure I've stopped breathing. I know I'm taking too long to respond but it's like a record scratched and with it, all of my brain power screeched to a halt at her words. I can't seem to form a coherent thought. This seems like a test, one I'm terrified to fail.

The stakes are too high.

Finally, my brain spins back to life. "Avery, if this is because of earlier, I wasn't trying to pressure you. I don't expect—" She steps closer, putting a finger to my parted lips. I fight the urge to slip my tongue out to taste her smooth skin.

"Matt, I know you. You'd never pressure me into anything. Which is exactly why I'm here." She looks up at me from under her lashes. "I want you. I want *us.*"

I've definitely stopped breathing now.

Avery takes another step and her breasts flatten against my chest. The V of her shirt dips, revealing the black lace of her bra. *Holy shit.* Somehow, I tear my eyes away from her cleavage and meet her gaze.

"Are you sure? I know you wanted to wait, to take things slow. I don't want you to do anything you're going to regret tomorrow."

I'm trying to be a gentleman, I swear. But the way her hand is running down my chest and her eyes are screaming *fuck me,* I don't know how much more restraint I've got in me. But I have to be sure. This is too important to be rushed into the wrong way.

She's too important.

Her hand slides back up my chest and my eyes follow the movement.

"I like you, Matt. Not because we grew up together and not because you're good with Gavin. Not even because you're the first guy I've dated in over a decade," she slides her hand up the back of my neck, playing with a curl at the base. "But because you're kind, funny, and loyal. You're so many things. But most importantly, you make me feel like me again. The real me. Not the girl from high school or the obedient wife and mom. *Me.*"

My heart squeezes at the break in her voice. I tuck a stray hair behind her ear, searching her face for any sign of hesitation. Instead, I find eyes set with determination. The way she chews on her bottom lip gives away her vulnerability and it just about takes me to my knees.

"I like you, too, Freckles. A lot." She smiles up at that. "So if at any time you change your mind, if we're moving too fast, you have to tell me." I hold her gaze. "I don't want to mess this up with you. I can't."

She nods, suddenly serious. For a moment, neither of us move. Then, torturing us both, I slowly lower my head. Even though she's essentially given me the green light, I'm giving her time to change her mind.

But instead of backing away, she tips her chin to meet me and the small move is all the answer I need. I close the distance, slowly brushing my lips across hers. I reach up to cradle her face in my hands.

I don't think I'll ever tire of kissing Avery. She's soft and pliant in my hands, melting into my touch. I touch my tongue to her bottom lip and she parts her mouth in invitation. Leisurely, I change angles, diving deeper into the sweet bliss that is her mouth.

At the first brush of her tongue against mine, a small whimper escapes her and I'm instantly hard at the sound. Her fingers tighten around the fabric of my shirt as she pulls me closer.

Suddenly, the kiss changes. What started as gentle and indulgent quickly becomes feral and desperate. It's like I can't get close enough to her. Yanking her hips toward me, I let her feel exactly what she's doing to me. She moans as I rock my hips against hers, driving us both crazy.

God, I want nothing more than our clothes to dissolve and feel her bare skin against mine.

My hand in her hair tightens, pulling her head back to give me better access to her neck. I hungrily explore the sensitive area below her ear to the base of her throat and back up again.

She tastes so good, it's killing me. The smell of her shampoo is making my head spin and I have to fight to control the need that is threatening to break me.

I want her with a desperation that surprises me. But I don't want to scare her, so I hold back.

I kiss along her jawline, teasing myself as much as her. I pull away slightly, taking in the sight before me. Her eyes are closed with her head thrown back, lips swollen. There's a slight redness across her cheeks from the stubble of my beard. My cock pulses at the sight of her. She looks like a goddess.

She opens her eyes and her half-lidded gaze stares back at me, beckoning and pulling me under like a siren's song. We reach for each other hungrily, mouths crashing, hands roaming. I can't get enough of her. She's everywhere all at the same time, surrounding me completely. Drowning me in her essence.

I hope I never resurface.

I back her up a few steps until her back meets the exposed brick wall behind her. I lift her slightly, pressing against her hips to hold her in place. I settle a leg between her thighs and I return my attention to her neck, devouring every inch of her skin. She lets out a throaty moan that shoots right to my cock. Encouraged by her reaction, I slip my hand under her shirt to palm her breast. She lets out another moan, rocking herself against my thigh.

The feel of her pleasuring herself against my leg has me losing my mind. I lift my knee to press my thigh harder against her, playing with her nipple through the thin lace of her bra.

She throws her head back against the wall. "Matt," she whimpers, "I need you."

Holy fucking shit.

I'm seconds away from blowing my load and we haven't even taken our clothes off. The sounds coming out of her mouth are turning me into a horny teenager.

I rotate my hips at the same time as I nip on the sensitive spot on her neck and she gasps. My vision tunnels. All I can focus on is the feel of her heat on my leg and the breathy sounds she's making. Her flimsy shorts and the thin fabric of my sweatpants offer little barrier between us. I push my leg higher, rubbing against her center as her breath quickens into short pants.

"Yes. More."

I'm willing to give her anything and everything she could ever ask for when the flash of a headlight from the front window causes us both to freeze. The windows are tinted enough that no one would be able to see inside, but the light still snaps us back to reality.

I glance down at her, both of our chests heaving, the heat between us still palpable.

"Want to take this upstairs?" I ask her.

"Definitely."

*W*ow.

My head is spinning as I follow Matt up the stairs to his apartment. I'm starting to come down from the intense...moment downstairs. I've never been so overwhelmed with passion. A second longer and I would've ripped my clothes off and begged him to take me right then and there. Thankfully, the reminder of where we were brought us to our senses before our first time was up against a wall.

Not that I would've minded at the time.

During the drive home from Bakersfield, I couldn't stop thinking about Matt. How he was so much more than I had ever expected. How my feelings for him were growing by the day.

How badly I wanted him.

Why was I still holding back? I knew I was attracted to him and after today, there was no doubt in my mind that he feels it, too. So what was I waiting for?

I knew in my heart that Matt was different from Mitch. He's shown me that countless times over the past few months. I've already had more of a reaction to Matt's flirting and kissing than I ever had when I was with Mitch.

When I pulled into my mom's driveway, I asked her if she would mind putting Gavin to bed and told her I would be home late. I ignored the smug look in her eye when she agreed then drove to Matt's apartment before I changed my mind.

Now that the adrenaline has worn off, I've lost my nerve. My show of bravado from earlier is long forgotten and I am suddenly hyper-aware of what I'm about to do.

Sex has always been, well...okay. I've read enough romance novels to know how it's supposed to feel. I've gotten close a few times but I've never felt that all consuming feeling that people describe during orgasm. Maybe I'm broken. My body can't do the things that most women claim they can.

With Matt, I had high hopes that this could be something more. But I'm once again slapped in the face by the *what-ifs*.

What if this time is no different than the rest? What if I've built up Matt's expectations only to let him down by my inadequacies?

What if he decides I'm not worth it?

By the time Matt opens the door to his apartment, I'm practically shaking from the nerves. I let Ham inside ahead of me then step into his apartment, looking anywhere but at Matt. Then he's in front of me, lifting my chin to meet his confused gaze.

"Hey, what's up? Are you okay?" His eyes search mine. "You looked like you were a million miles away."

I try for what I hope is a convincing smile. "I'm fine. Just cold, I think."

He searches my face. "Are you sure? If you've changed your mind, we don't have to do anything. We can watch a movie or something."

My heart squeezes. *Could he be any sweeter?* My confidence from earlier starts to bloom back inside me. I might be feeling nervous but more than anything, I want this. And I want it with Matt.

I step toward him, running a hand down his hard chest. His sharp inhale causes my confidence to soar and I drag my finger along the top of his waistband. "I'm sure."

His eyes darken, tracking my hand's path. As I dip the tip of my finger below his waistband, he snaps and pulls me to him sharply. Our mouths meet and this is no slow, teasing kiss from earlier. The heat between us from earlier rekindles, searing me from the inside out as he brands me with this kiss.

At the first brush of his tongue against mine, I lose myself to the moment, letting myself be swept away by his touch. His fingers tangle in my hair, holding my mouth to his. I can't escape his assault but there's nowhere I'd rather be than in his arms right now. My hands roam over his chest, his back, finally touching him in all the ways I've dreamed of.

Somehow, we end up in his bedroom. It's my first time inside it, but my mind hardly registers anything more than the dark wood bed frame. Tugging my shirt over my head, I toss it aside. I shove at my shorts, leaving me in only my bra and panties.

His mouth only leaves mine long enough to add his shirt and sweatpants to the growing pile of clothing on his floor. He pauses, letting his eyes roam over my body while I do the same to him.

I knew he was lean and muscular from years of physical labor. I've felt his hard body under his shirt but nothing prepared me for seeing him bared just for me. I want to drag my tongue across the subtle ridge of his abs. *Is that weird?* At this point I'm so overwhelmed with desire, I don't even care.

My eyes dip lower, following the trail of dark hair that disappears beneath his boxers. I swallow hard at the outline of his erection. Feeling him pressed up against me is one thing, but seeing the clear evidence of his arousal causes my belly to twist in anticipation.

I lift my gaze to meet his. He stares back at me with the

hungry appreciation of a predator stalking its prey. He takes a step closer, then closer still until our bodies are melded against each other. My breasts feel heavy against my bra and my nipples beg for attention. He gently lowers me down onto his bed until I'm lying on my back, our eyes never breaking contact.

The air around us is thick and I have to force in a breath when he lowers his head to place a light kiss on my breast. I'm practically panting now, as he follows the outline of my bra with his mouth toward the valley between my breasts.

He continues his journey to my other breast, licking and teasing my skin. I inhale sharply when he dips his tongue beneath my bra to circle my nipple, sending a jolt of arousal straight between my legs. Eager for him to continue, I lift myself up just long enough to unhook my bra, leaving my chest bared to him. I toss it onto the floor beside me.

"Feeling a little impatient, Freckles?" He chuckles at my quick nod. "Good. Me too."

Without warning, he closes his mouth around my nipple, lavishing it with attention while using his hand to tease the other to a stiff point. The juxtaposition of him alternating between pinching then kneading, biting then licking has me shaking beneath him. It feels so good, I can't focus.

His mouth suddenly releases my nipple. He works his way down my stomach, stopping to nibble the sensitive spot below my hip. I squirm in response, but I can feel myself tense as he works his way lower.

I tug on his hair softly to get his attention. He looks up at me, confused. "What's wrong, baby?"

I chew on my bottom lip hesitantly. "You don't have to do that."

His frown deepens. "I don't have to do anything. I want to."

I avoid his questioning stare, looking anywhere else. "It's okay. It's not worth it."

I can tell by the way he continues to stare down at me that he's not satisfied with my roundabout answers.

He lifts himself up, sitting back on his heels. His brow is furrowed but he places a gentle hand on my calf reassuringly. "I told you before, Avery. You can tell me anything. What's going on?"

I close my eyes and take a shaky breath. *This is it.* I take the coward's way out and stare at the ceiling while I hurriedly explain.

"I can't orgasm. I never have. It was a bone of contention between Mitch and I." I can feel my eyes welling with emotion at the memories. The blame, the accusations. The hurt. "I'm not sure what's wrong with me. Everything leading up to it feels great but when it comes down to the final event..." I shrug.

I hazard a look at Matt but his face is expressionless. He's probably thinking of a way to let me down easily. Who wouldn't be looking for an exit? I basically told him that sex with me is one big disappointment. I don't blame him for wanting out.

I brush aside a stray tear that escapes down my cheek. "So, yeah. Now you know."

He still hasn't said anything.

I start to sit up. "I think I should go."

Matt leans forward, blocking my exit. His hands settle on the bed on either side of my waist, caging me in as he did earlier. I don't move, unsure of what he's about to do or say next.

"Avery, your ex-husband is a worthless piece of shit."

I huff out a laugh. Well, that was definitely the last thing I expected him to say.

His face remains serious. "I've tried to hold back from

trash-talking him because he's Gavin's dad. But if you're telling me you spent over a decade with a guy who not only didn't make you orgasm, but made you feel bad about it, I can't keep quiet anymore. He's a spineless, insecure little prick for making you feel anything other than worshipped."

He cups my cheek with his hand and strokes his thumb over my skin.

"There's nothing wrong with you, Avery. Lots of women have a hard time orgasming. There's things we can try to do to get you there. Let me help you figure out what works for you. But please, baby, don't ever let anyone tell you you're not worth the effort. Because you're worth all of it, Avery. You're worth everything."

The tears are openly flowing now. I don't even bother brushing them away as Matt leans down to kiss them. He slowly kisses his way down my cheeks until his lips meet mine. Every insecurity, every condescending comment, every negative thought melts away as he continues to kiss me. I'm still a little nervous but I'm feeling more confident about trying than ever before.

I might not be able to make it over the peak, but, for the first time, I'm excited for the climb.

Again, our kiss deepens, Matt leaning into me until I'm lying on my back again. He lifts his head, his expression serious. "I'm going to try again and I want you to tell me not only what feels good but what doesn't, too. Do you trust me?"

I'm touched by his words and his effort even though it may be for nothing. My voice comes out softer than I anticipated when I answer him.

"Yes."

He moves down my body, taking my nipple into his mouth again. Instantly, the pleasure engulfs me. Every movement from his skilled mouth and hand brings me higher. His hand disappears, until I feel his calloused fingers between my legs. My hips buck when he finds my clit.

"You like that, pretty girl?" His head lifts and he watches my face. "You like it when I play with you?" I nod quickly, unable to respond. "Use your words, Avery."

"Yes."

"Good girl."

My insides clench at his praise. *That's new.* It's like his words have a direct link to my core and I can't get enough.

His hand continues to drive me crazy until he shifts so that his head is between my thighs. His finger plays with my slick slit, then he looks up at me for permission. I nod, unable to tear my eyes away from his. He pulls my panties down my legs, then he slips a finger inside me, curving it upward. I cry out as he hits that special spot.

This part has never been a problem for me, though. The build up always feels amazing.

Until it doesn't.

No. Not thinking about that.

Trying to distract myself, I grind myself against his hand. He follows my lead, pressing against my clit while pumping his finger in and out.

As it always does, the pressure begins to build, climbing higher and higher but never quite reaching the peak. My thoughts push their way through the haze, soon overtaking me until I can feel myself pulling away.

Frustrated, I throw a hand over my face.

"I'm sorry," I whimper from under my hand. "I can't."

"Avery, look at me." I hazard a glance at him. "Don't you dare apologize again, you hear me? You talk like that again and I'll bend you over my knee."

He's uncharacteristically serious, his finger still buried inside me. He's glaring down at me like a teacher scolding his pupil.

It's hot as hell.

His face softens at my nod. "Now hold on, baby. I want to try something."

He dips his head, his mouth a whisper from my entrance while he holds my stare.

"It's not going to work," I say, blowing out a frustrated sigh.

"It's okay if you don't orgasm, Avery. I promise," Matt tells me.

I bite my lip, still unsure.

"I've been thinking about tasting this pretty pussy since you first flashed your tits at me all those weeks ago. I'm dying to know what you taste like. Why would you want to deprive me of your sweet taste?" Before I can answer him, he adds a second finger with the first, slowly fucking me with his hand.

"Will you let me try? Please?"

For the umpteenth time tonight, he's rendered me speechless. Who knew sweet, goofy Matt had such a dirty mouth on him?

I love it. "Yes."

He smiles wickedly up at me before retaking his place.

"Eyes on me, pretty girl."

That's all the warning I get before he drops his head between my legs, licking me from slit to clit. I let out what can only be described as a squeak. Under any other circumstance, the sound would embarrass me, but I can't focus on anything other than the feel of his tongue driving me upward, his fingers still pumping into me, taking me under. The combination of sensations is intoxicating and overwhelming at the same time.

I close my eyes to sink further into the moment when a sharp smack of pain against my ass rips my attention back to Matt.

"I said eyes on me, Freckles. Don't make me tell you again."

Holy shit.

Regular Matt makes my heart flutter. Dominating Matt makes my pussy weep with tears of joy.

He gives me no time to recover, continuing to pump into me while ravishing me with his mouth, setting a merciless pace. It takes all of my effort to keep my eyes open and focused on him. I can feel myself getting closer. To what, I'm not sure but I can feel its impending arrival. It's building in a way that's both familiar and brand-new.

I suddenly realize why he was so intent on keeping my eyes open. Watching him overpower my body, my pleasure in his complete control is its own kind of aphrodisiac. Combine that visual with the friction of his tongue against my clit, the fullness of his fingers inside me and I'm a goner.

My orgasm is no longer improbable but inevitable. The peak that has always been just out of reach is so close I can practically feel it.

"Come for me, Avery," Matt growls against my clit right before he sucks it into his mouth. Hard.

I'm launched over the peak and into a free fall. My body bows off of the bed and his name is ripped from my throat. Matt never stops, dragging every ounce of pleasure from me until I finally relax against him.

Weightlessly, I float back to reality, drained from the strength of my first, real orgasm.

H *oly fucking shit.*

I lift myself from between Avery's legs and sit back on my feet, staring down at her in wonder. Her eyes are closed, head thrown back with her hair splayed across my pillow. Her chest rises and falls in quick succession like my own. She looks relaxed, sated.

She's a vision. I could sit here watching her exactly like this for the rest of my life.

I lean over her flushed body, my mouth claiming hers. She lazily kisses me back. I take my time, exploring her mouth, giving her time to come down from her orgasm, despite my protesting cock pushing against my boxers.

Finally, I pull back and a sleepy smile tugs at her lips, eyes still closed. "How you feelin', Freckles?" I manage, my voice hoarse with desire.

"Perfect," she practically purrs and my cock flexes at the sound.

I drop one last quick kiss on her lips, before dropping to my side beside her. I curl my arm around her waist, pulling her body so she's flush against my chest.

"Matt?"

"Hmm?"

Avery lifts herself up onto her elbow beside me and looks down at me, brow furrowed. "What're you doing?"

"Cuddling," I reply simply.

She frowns, confused. "Well, I thought... we were... " She gestures between us. "What about..." She nods toward the outline of my very obvious erection.

I brush a stray wave from her adorably mussed head behind her ear. "You just had your first orgasm. I don't want to rush you into anything. Don't worry about me," I look down to where my cock is still pressed against her leg. "Or him. It's fine."

Her eyes search mine for a minute before a slow, mischievous smile spreads across her face. She traces a finger over my chest, the sight mesmerizing us both. "Has anyone ever told you that you're too good of a guy sometimes?" she teases.

"Can't say that they have," I answer hoarsely, watching in fascination as her hand trails lower and lower until she reaches the hem of my boxers.

Slowly, she dips her finger below the waistband until she brushes against the head of my cock. My hips involuntarily jerk as if chasing her hand.

I notice a triumphant glint in her eye as she repeats the movement, my hips jerking upward again. I should do something, say anything, but I'm helpless watching her hand tease me. On her third pass, she tucks her hand beneath the waistband and takes me into her small hand.

I barely bite back a groan.

She's turning me into a desperate mess. I feel like a horny teenager again, ready to blow my load at the first touch of a pretty girl's hand around my cock.

Hesitantly, her hand works my shaft up and down. When she reaches the tip, she uses her thumb to spread the small drop of precum over the head and I hiss out a breath. She smiles and her confidence must grow because her grip tightens as she continues her exploration.

My breathing is coming in short, labored pants. I can't tell if it's her growing confidence or Avery herself, but I can't look away. I know I should be making this about her, making her feel new and exciting things, but I'm lost under her spell.

She scrambles to her knees, shoving my boxers down. She starts to dip her head but the spell breaks and I intercept her descent. Grabbing the back of her head, I pull her mouth to mine. I'm desperate for her. I can't put it into words so I try to show her instead with every touch of my hands, every stroke of my tongue against hers.

I pull my boxers the rest of the way down, kicking them off when they reach my feet. Her mouth is still fused to mine as I turn her so that she's underneath me, my body looming over hers.

My hand reaches between us, searching for that magic spot between her legs. A sharp inhale against my lips tells me I've found it, so I circle it, applying enough pressure to make her breath quicken.

I slip a finger inside her, arching up to hit the other spot she loves so much. She cries out, still sensitive from her recent orgasm. I add a second finger, plunging in and out, driving her higher.

"Matt," she chokes out. "I want you inside me."

Fuck. I drop my head into her neck and groan, trying to hold onto what little control I have left. "Are you sure?"

"God, yes," she answers, her walls clenching hard around my fingers.

I reach across her to my nightstand drawer, praying that there's a stray condom in there. I haven't had sex with anyone in a while, even longer since I brought anyone back to my apartment. Searching through the drawer, my hand comes up empty and I drop my head again, this time in frustration.

"Shit. I don't have a condom," I tell her.

I blow out a breath in disappointment, trying to calm my raging hard on.

"What if we don't use one?" she asks. "I have an IUD and I've only ever been with Mitch."

Her implication shocks me so it takes me a second before I answer. "I'm clean," I tell her. "But you don't have to–"

She silences me by grinding herself against my very hard, very willing erection. I just about go blind by the white hot rush of desire shooting straight to my dick.

"Stop talking and fuck me."

Yes, ma'am.

Again, Avery shocks me with her sudden confidence but I'm loving it. I love that she feels comfortable enough with me to let this side of herself out.

Only with me.

I'm not usually the possessive type but Avery is bringing out a new side of me, too.

I notch my head against her entrance, pausing to take her in. Her teeth nibble anxiously at her bottom lip and I take it into my mouth to soothe the sting. She's trusting me to make this good for her and I can't disappoint.

"I've got you, Freckles."

She gives me a small nod. I ease into her, her tight warmth surrounding me. A sharp intake from Avery pulls me out of my head, but when I look down at her glazed eyes, I know it's not from pain.

"Fuck. You're so tight." I groan. Slowly, I sink deeper until I'm seated fully inside her. "Relax, baby."

After a few moments, the tight grip on my cock starts to ease. "That's my girl," I praise and she clenches around me.

So, my girl likes praise, eh? I can work with that.

I start to move slowly, rocking my hips against her to form a rhythm. A few moments later, I can feel her start to retreat into her head. To bring her back to me, I slip a hand between us, circling her clit. She arches off the bed with a cry.

"That's it, baby. Show me what you like."

I adjust our position, tilting her upward so that I'm leaning into her pressing myself against her clit. I rock against her and she moans in appreciation. I pull a leg up over my shoulder to get a better angle.

She throws her head back with a moan, hands pulling at the sheets below. "Yes! Oh, god. Right there."

Encouraged, I rock against her clit again, still thrusting inside her.

Harder.

Deeper.

I can't resist bending my head to pull one of her hard nipples into my mouth.

Her hand automatically goes to my head, holding me to her. "More," she demands and I couldn't be happier to oblige. Sucking her nipple further into my mouth, I give it a sharp tug and she cries out, her fingers scraping against my scalp. The bite of her nails should hurt but it only pushes me closer to the edge.

Chasing her release, she rocks her hips against mine. She's close, I can feel it. I slip a hand between us once more, this time pinching her clit between my fingers and plunging my cock into her as deep as I can go. All the while, I'm sucking her nipple hard.

When I feel her start to clench again, I lift my head to her neck. "Come all over my cock, baby," I growl into her ear.

A few thrusts later, she cries out my name. Her legs tremble with the force of her orgasm. I try to hold off my own release. I want to prolong this feeling of nirvana for as long as possible but her walls grip me almost painfully. She pulses around me over and over until I have no choice but to follow her. I spill myself inside her with a long, low groan.

I topple onto her then quickly move to the side, not wanting to squash her under my weight. We're both panting hard, unable to speak. Eventually, I lift myself up to kiss her forehead. Moments ago, I was physically unable to talk and now that I'm able, no words seem profound enough to describe how I'm feeling.

I'm overcome with an emotion I'm not quite ready to name yet. Instead, I wrap my arm around her and tuck her into my chest, listening as her breaths grow slow and steady.

When I finally close my eyes, it isn't the stars I dream of but a beautiful constellation of freckles beneath powerful whisky eyes.

I'm trying my best to act normal this morning—cool, calm, collected. As if I hadn't experienced not one, not two but three earth shattering orgasms since last night. Seriously, I think my legs are still shaking.

I think I'm doing okay. The only mishap was when I nearly had a heart attack when Miss Carla came in asking for a book on how to keep "her pussy stimulated." Apparently, Audrey has been feeling a little blue lately and Miss Carla wanted to make sure she was "satisfied".

There's no way she didn't do that one on purpose.

But I kept it together and directed her to a couple of books on enriching your cat's life and brain-stimulating games for cats. If she noticed the crimson shade of my cheeks, she was polite enough not to mention it.

You know the feeling when you have a secret and it seems like the whole world is watching you? That's how I feel today. Every greeting, every customer, every wave on the street makes me feel like everyone is staring at me, knowing all the dirty things that I did the night before.

It's not that Matt and I are keeping our relationship a secret—there's no such thing as a secret in Haven Bay. But I also don't need the whole town asking me what positions we tried or how big Matt is. This town doesn't know the meaning of the word boundaries.

Around lunch, I've managed to calm my paranoia to a solid six on the panic scale and am no longer blushing at every unintentional euphemism.

We've hired a few extra employees for the cafe side and I'll be training them over the next couple of days. This time next week, the cafe side will be bustling. But for now, it's quiet.

It's story-time with Mrs. Bunn—one of my favorite new programs we've added to the shop. Mrs. Bunn was my grade two teacher and was always such a warm and welcoming person. She's long since retired, but when I approached her about coming in once a week to read stories to some of the local kids, she eagerly agreed. It's been a hit. I've already had parents asking to add another day throughout the week.

I lean against the counter and listen to Mrs. Bunn's animated voice. She's reading a story about a curious tiger and his adventures in the jungle to a group of preschoolers and their parents. The children are all laughing at a particularly funny part of the story when the bell jingles above the door.

Jolie walks in. I press a finger to my lips, pointing at the group seated on the carpet in the corner. She nods and quietly walks over to where I'm standing. She stops suddenly, mouth gaping and eyes wide.

"OH MY GOD!" she yells, right before I practically tackle her to slap a hand over her mouth.

I mouth my apology to Mrs. Bunn as I shove Jolie toward my office. The second I shut the door behind me, Jolie grabs me by the shoulders. "You had sex!"

I debate denying it but I can't hold back the sudden grin at the memory of last night. Apparently that's answer enough for Jolie.

She whoops in excitement, giving my arm a playful slap.

"That's my girl! How was it? Was it amazing? Those Brady boys look way too good to not be studs in the bedroom." I arch a brow at her comment and she waves me off. "You know what I mean. We're not talking about Officer Grouchy Pants." She throws herself into my desk chair then props her chin in her hands like a teenager at a sleepover. "Tell me everything. Don't skip any details. Start at the beginning."

"Well, some scientists believe that there was a big bang—" I laugh, ducking the highlighter Jolie tosses at me. "Okay, fine. Well, yesterday Matt offered to watch Gavin for me when the summer camp canceled on me." I continue to tell Jolie about the fishing incident, the arcade, the tense moment in the parking lot and then my decision to go back to Matt's house afterward.

"Oh, I feel like a proud mom," Jolie says after I've finished, wiping away an imaginary tear. "I'm so proud of you. You deserve amazing sex. You deserve all the happiness and orgasms and I'm so happy you're making it happen." She hugs me tightly.

"I have to know. How big are we talking?" She lifts her hands in front of her face, palms facing each other with about three inches of space between them. She slowly moves her hands farther apart. "Stop me when I'm getting close."

A knock at the door interrupts any further conversation. I pull open the door to find Matt standing in the hallway, holding an iced coffee and a white paper bag with the diner's logo on it.

"Hi, beautiful," he drawls, shooting me a sultry smile. His gaze roams over me, devouring every inch of my body as if it's been months since he last saw me instead of mere hours ago. I can tell he's picturing all the obscene things we did last night. And this morning.

Well, now so am I.

"Hi," I manage to croak out over my suddenly dry throat.

"Woo wee, did it get hot in here or is it just you two?" Jolie steps past me, fanning herself. "I'll leave you two lovebirds alone before I get a very awkward, though definitely interesting, show." She steps around Matt, then holds her hands up behind his back, this time about eight inches apart. She raises her brow in question.

I pull Matt inside, shutting the door behind him to Jolie's laughter. I haven't seen him since this morning. We woke up to his alarm, which luckily was early enough that I could get home before Gavin woke up. I hadn't planned on staying the night and I didn't want him wondering why I wasn't home.

But not before Matt rolled me over and worked me with his mouth and fingers until he ripped another orgasm from me.

I will say, the guy is thorough.

I don't make the mistake of thinking it will be like this every time. I know my body is complicated and unpredictable. But the fact that Matt is willing to try new things and work with my body's signals instead of in spite of them, makes every experience with him that much more special.

Around five a.m, I tried to sneak back inside my mom's house unnoticed, but always the early riser, she was sitting at the kitchen island, coffee in hand and a smirk on her face. Lucky for me, she managed to keep her questions to herself— at least for now. I'm sure she'll have plenty when I get home.

"I didn't get to bring you your latte this morning since someone made me late for work," He gives me a pointed look but the smile on his lips tells me he didn't mind it at all. "So I opted for an iced coffee with caramel drizzle instead," he says, handing me over the cup.

I take a long drink. Closing my eyes, I moan softly as the caffeine and sugar overtake my tastebuds. It's delicious.

A low groan pulls my attention away from the iced drink and I look up to see Matt's dark, lustful expression.

"You're killing me, Freckles," he groans, watching me pull the straw between my lips.

I'm not sure if it's the three orgasms in the last 24 hours that are making me brave, but I decide to have some fun with him. Holding his gaze, I slowly pull the straw out from its place in the drink, keeping my finger over one end to trap the coffee inside. Then I wrap my tongue around the other end, letting the liquid roll down my tongue and into my mouth.

He groans again, taking a step toward me but the sound of clapping pulls us from our trance. Mrs. Bunn must have finished her story. I know Tammy has it under control but I take a deep breath and step back, putting some much needed distance between us.

It's far too sexually charged in here for the middle of a workday.

Matt takes the hint and clears his throat. "I swear I didn't come here to jump you, as tempting as it may be." He offers me the paper bag.

I open it to find a blueberry scone inside.

"I wasn't sure if you'd eaten lunch yet but I figured if you had, you could eat it later for an afternoon pick-me-up."

God, why is he so great? Sexy *and* thoughtful.

I don't think in the whole time we were together Mitch ever brought me home a snack or made sure I ate.

I lift myself on my toes to plant a short but firm kiss on his lips. "Thank you. That was really sweet of you."

He gestures for me to sit in the chair Jolie just vacated and he takes the seat opposite of me. He leans forward with his forearms on his thighs. "With everything that happened yesterday, we didn't have a chance to talk about your meeting with the lawyer. How did it go?"

"It was okay. I'll be officially filing for divorce this week once the paperwork is complete. I'm going for shared custody, which hopefully he will agree to. It complicates things a bit but I think it's best for Gavin to spend some time with his dad. Maybe they can reconcile their relationship."

Matt nods solemnly. I know he wants to say more. He's never been a big fan of Mitch, even as teenagers. But I appreciate that he doesn't bash him. Despite everything, he's still Gavin's dad and half of Gavin's DNA.

"Since I didn't give Mitch written notice sixty days before leaving the city, he could contest my being here with Gavin and we might have to go back. Margot said she would argue that no official address change has been made and that I'm here helping my sick mother, but it depends on the judge." I take a bite of the scone and chew it thoughtfully. "So we'll have to wait until Mitch is served this week to see what our next move is."

Matt nods again, leaning back in his chair. He's uncharacteristically silent, absorbing my words. Then he leans forward again and takes my hand in his. "I'm going to be here for you every step, okay? Don't worry." He squeezes my hand. "We've got this."

More times than I can count, Matt has left me speechless. This is another one of those times. I simply nod, touched by his comment.

We've got this. Despite his goofy exterior, Matt is a protector of the ones he cares about. No matter the fight–literal or figurative–he's there through it all.

Some might be surprised by this serious side of Matt but this side of him is my favorite. It's the side he always kept hidden from the world—except from me.

"Do you have any plans tonight?" he asks as his thumb caresses my knuckles.

I nod. "Tomorrow's our first book club meeting. I have a bunch of things to do here to prepare."

"What about after? If it's not too late, can I take you and Gavin for ice cream?"

"The arcade *and* ice cream? You're going to be his favorite." I laugh. "We'd love to."

"Perfect. Text me when you're done and I'll pick you up." He bends his head to give me a long, slow kiss. By the time he pulls away, my head is spinning.

"See you soon, Freckles."

As MOST AVID READERS KNOW, there are a lot of different types of book clubs.

There's virtual and there's in-person. There are single title clubs where everyone reads the same book. There's multi-title clubs where everyone reads a new book each week but the same group of books work their way around to each member. Some are hosted by libraries, online or broadcast over the radio.

But the most important thing that almost all book club-bers know is that the first half of book club is about the book; the second half is about socializing.

Which is why a group of twelve women and six men, ages 19 to 83, are sitting in a circle at The Book Nook. We're currently discussing if Haven Bay's mayor decided to run a *Hunger Games*-esque tournament, who would win and what weapon they would use to kill off the rest of the town.

"A machete is only useful for close fighting," 23 year old Jessie Chapman explains to old Mrs. Creevy. "If you're going to kill Mrs. Drouillard for beating you in the bake-off, you'll need something you can use from far away. She's old but I've seen her in the seniors' kickboxing class at the gym and she could definitely take you."

"Perhaps a crossbow would work," Doug Feldman replies. "That way you could use it for revenge and for hunting food."

"The only hunting I'd be doing is for some ass," Dottie howls from across the circle.

"Speaking of, I heard Helen and Rainer Dutton got caught having sex in the church parking lot again last Friday," Miss Carla says salaciously. "Poor Pastor Dan had to break it up and send them home. Word has it Pastor Dan was knocking on the window for ten minutes before either of them noticed he was there."

"Oh, I heard it was at the drive-in theater and it was one of the teenage employees who caught them," Millie Loffman corrects her.

Miss Carla shoots Millie a glare that would make a lion cower.

"Okay," I interrupt whatever inevitably rude response Miss Carla is about to fire back. "I think we've gotten a bit off-topic again. Can we go back to discussing the book?"

"Absolutely," Miss Carla answers almost too cheerily. "The only weapon I would need to take out my enemies would be my cat." Her tone directly contradicts the scowl she launches at Millie.

I find Jolie's eyes a few seats to my right and give her an exasperated look. She raises her wine glass to cover her snicker.

"While we're on the subject of inappropriate places for a cat to be—" Mille starts and I stand quickly, nearly knocking over my chair in the process.

"Alright, everyone. Great first meeting." The group claps in agreement. "Since Jessie was our first draw winner, next month's book will be chosen by..." I pull a piece of paper from one of Gavin's baseball hats. "Mrs. Creevy. Same rules apply as last time. Nothing with any of the triggers from our list and within the price range we've agreed upon. Other than that, have fun with it!"

I point to the cafe where Tammy and I have set up baked goods, finger foods and various drink stations. Many items are off of our menu, so we're considering this our "soft-soft" opening.

"There's lots of refreshments, so feel free to mingle or browse the shelves. Tammy and I will be around to ring up any purchases. Enjoy!"

Chairs scrape and music begins to play softly in the background. Tammy must've turned on the overhead speaker. The noise level starts to rise as people begin talking and wandering into the cafe.

As I make my rounds, I accept a few compliments and well wishes on the grand opening of the cafe that's set to take place next week. Mom, Tammy and I have been spending every bit of down time cleaning, organizing and triple-checking every piece of equipment. We're ready; I know we are. But the closer we get to the grand opening, the more the *what-ifs* begin to plague me.

Eventually, Jolie walks over to me, passing me a glass of wine. I accept it eagerly and take a long drink. I didn't let myself drink before the meeting because I wanted to make sure my first book club ran smoothly. Now that it's over, I'm happy to let the wine soothe the last of my nerves away.

"Well, that went about exactly as a book club in Haven Bay was bound to go," Jolie says, giggling.

I roll my eyes, giggling along with her. "My God. You'd think they'd be able to behave for an hour. A group of children would've been easier to rein in."

"I nearly lost it when Maeve suggested that Katniss, Peeta and Gale should've had a threesome." Jolie says and it throws us into another round of giggles.

"I hope I'm not interrupting anything, ladies," Maeve comments as she approaches us.

I swallow back a laugh. "Not at all. Are you enjoying yourself tonight, Maeve?"

Jolie snorts from behind me and I reach behind me to pinch her arm. She yelps, rubbing a hand over the sting.

Maeve either doesn't notice or is undeterred. "Oh, definitely. This was such a great idea, Avery. Dottie and I have been looking forward to it all month." She smiles at me warmly.

Where Dottie dresses in bright colors and shirts with funny sayings on them, Maeve has always looked like an innocent, grandmotherly type with her neutral twin sets and slacks. Until you hear the vulgar comments that come out of her mouth, that is.

"Thank you, Maeve. I'm so happy you joined." If I'm not mistaken, it seems that there's a reason for her coming over apart from idle chit-chat.

She lifts her wine glass to her lips. "So, Avery. Are you planning on moving to Haven Bay permanently?"

I'm a little shocked by her blunt question but I recover quickly. "Um, I'm not sure. It depends on a few things."

Impervious to my awkwardness, Maeve presses on. "Well, as you know, Dottie and I own quite a bit of property around town. It's a bit of a hobby for us, really. We have the most charming apartment over on Ridgeway coming available next month. If you were planning on staying, Dottie and I would love to rent it to you."

If I was shocked before, I'm flabbergasted now. "Oh, Maeve... I'm... that's very kind of you but..."

She waves me away. "You don't need to answer now. I just thought I should put the bug in your ear. We're in no rush to fill the vacancy as we want to wait for the right tenant." She pats my hand reassuringly. "Let us know once you figure it out."

She turns to go, then stops to add, "I assumed you'd be staying around since you and Matt Brady are playing hide the sausage now." My jaw drops. "Oh, don't worry, no one told me anything. They didn't have to. You've been walking around the last couple days like someone boinked every bone from your body. Now close your mouth, honey. You've got to conserve that jaw strength."

And with that, she rejoins the crowd while I attempt to pick said jaw up off of the floor.

It's been over a week since our first night together and I have yet to get Avery alone again, though we see each other almost daily. I took her and Gavin out for ice cream and then again to the movie theater. I bring her lattes every day while she's working and we text constantly.

It's no one's fault. We've both been busy—her with the grand opening of the cafe and me with work. But I miss her. I miss being able to touch her whenever I want and have her do the same to me. I miss the sounds she makes when I kiss her neck and the greedy way she says my name when she's begging for release.

I need my girl.

Technically, we haven't had that conversation yet. It's not that I don't want her to be my girlfriend. In fact, there's nothing I want more than to call her mine. I think we're both waiting to hear how Mitch reacts to the news of the divorce. Avery says he was served a few days ago, but he's been eerily quiet.

Another reason why I want to get Avery alone. I can tell the anticipation is getting to her, though she hides it well. But

I can see it in her eyes, in the way she jumps every time her phone rings as if it's a snake ready to strike.

I'm in the workshop today working on another custom job. Bud received an influx in calls for custom jobs after the display case at The Book Nook was installed. I've been almost exclusively working on custom jobs ever since.

It builds my confidence to know people enjoy my craftsmanship, but not enough to show anyone my art. I'm not quite there yet. If I was, I know Avery would be the first person I'd show. If there's anyone who I think would understand that side of me, it would be her.

My phone vibrates and I pull it from my back pocket.

AVERY

Hi, handsome.

Speak of the beautiful devil. It shows how far gone I am for this girl that a text from her instantly makes me smile.

MATT

Hi yourself. What're you up to?

AVERY

Missing you.

How fucking cute is she? That settles it. I'm taking her out on a date, just the two of us. Preferably within the next couple of days. I don't care if I have to kidnap her to make it happen.

MATT

I miss you, too, Freckles.

AVERY

My pussy misses you, too. Your hands. Your mouth. Your cock.

Does your cock miss me, too?

Holy shit. My dick hardens at that last message. I quickly look around the workshop, even though I know I'm alone. Is this real? Avery and I text constantly, often flirting and teasing each other but we've never crossed over into sexting territory.

I'm here for it.

MATT

You have no idea. You're killing me right now.

AVERY

Are you picturing it? Picturing how well you fit inside me?

Jesus, fuck. Now I am. I didn't take her as a dirty talker but damn, I'm harder than steel from only a few texts.

MATT

I can't think of anything else but you taking my cock so perfectly, baby. Your tight pussy taking every inch of me.

If I was to reach inside your panties right now, would you be wet for me?

A few moments go by and I wonder if I've pushed her too far. Until she finally responds and I just about swallow my tongue.

AVERY

The thing is... I'm not wearing any panties right now.

I take off like a bat out of hell, practically running down the street to the bookshop. When I finally throw open the door, my heart is racing and I'm panting, only in part from the run.

Avery glances up at my abrupt entrance, smiling wickedly

when she sees it's me. The shop is empty, which isn't uncommon for a Tuesday morning. It's only Avery inside, wearing a flowy yellow dress with thin straps, highlighting her tan lines. I imagine licking my way down her chest to see just how far those tan lines go.

"Can I help you?" Avery teases but her humor disappears when I flick the lock on the door.

Slowly, I stalk towards her like a lion to an antelope. Her eyes grow wide but I can see the lust clouding them just as much as the shock.

Good. I'm done playing around.

"Unless you want me to bend you over this counter and give everyone outside that window a show, you better get your ass in your office in the next two minutes." I pull her against me, causing her to squeak in surprise.

The sound goes straight to my cock.

She makes no effort to move, frozen in place. Her doe-eyes are causing my erection to push painfully against the metal teeth of my zipper.

"Now, Freckles."

This snaps her out of her trance. She stops to turn the "Be Back in 10" sign on the door. I mentally scoff at that. *Ten minutes? Don't count on it.*

She then rushes past me and I can't resist slapping her ass as she passes. Reaching the back office, she throws a sultry look over her shoulder and crooks a finger at me before disappearing behind the door.

Game on.

I follow behind her but stop dead in my tracks when I round the corner to the office. She's perched on the edge of the desk, one leg crossed seductively over the other. The hem of her dress lifts dangerously high on her shapely thigh.

I take in the sight before me, willing her skirt to lift a little higher so I can see if she was telling the truth. A flicker of nerves crosses her face but she uncrosses her legs despite it. Her bravado despite her vulnerability nearly takes me to my knees. It's then that I notice what's under her dress; or should I say what's *not* there.

She wasn't lying.

My hands twitch at the need to touch her, to feel her soft heat squeeze my fingers. To spread her open for me to lick and use at my whim.

But first I need to show her what happens when she teases me.

I saunter over to her, loving the way her expression changes to heated anticipation. To her credit, she maintains her pose, tipping her chin up to hold my gaze defiantly. I lean into her, placing both of my hands just above her knees. I lazily slide them higher, bringing the soft material of her dress with them until they reach the apex of her thighs. My thumbs slide inward, grazing the lips between her legs and she inhales sharply.

"Have you been walking around like this all morning? Did it give you a thrill to know you're going about your day, working and talking with customers, meanwhile you're revelling in a secret only you know about?"

My thumbs are tracing her lips, up and down spreading her slick heat, but never applying enough pressure to ease the ache. She moans when my thumb barely brushes her clit, but I pull away and her moan turns into a frustrated groan.

"Answer me," I growl.

"Yes," she answers breathily.

I dip my head, brushing an open-mouth kiss below her ear, where I know it drives her crazy. "Did you do that to tease me, Freckles?"

She hesitates, unsure of how to respond. Finally, she nods.

"Remember what I told you would happen if you teased

me again?" I nip the spot on her neck, her gasp driving me wild.

Her wide eyes tell me she does. The hungry glint in them tells me she knows exactly what I'm asking. I pull back so that I'm no longer touching her. I straighten, looming over her seated position at my full height.

"On your knees, Freckles."

If she's surprised by my demand, she doesn't show it. Achingly slowly, she lowers herself off of the wooden desk and drops to the floor before me on her knees.

I can see her pulse thrumming; out of excitement or nerves, I'm not sure. I don't want to push her too far out of her comfort zone. I'd rather cut off my own arm with a butter knife than cause her any pain. If I saw any hint of doubt on her face, I'd stop.

But all I see is white, hot desire.

"You look so beautiful on your knees for me, baby." I croon, caressing her jawline. "You're going to look even better with my cock in your mouth."

She squirms from her place below me. My girl loves when I talk dirty to her. When she told me that she'd never had an orgasm, it took everything inside me not to react. I know that some women have a hard time coming from penetration alone, so it wasn't like it was such a crazy revelation.

The thing that killed me was that she honestly thought I wouldn't be interested in her anymore because of it. That douchebag ex-husband of her's had probably never bothered to try anything to help her and was only concerned with getting himself off.

The other night, after she confided in me, I looked up some articles online about different positions and techniques for women who need more stimulation to orgasm. The fact that this bare minimum effort had never occurred to her ex just proves what a piece of shit he is.

I want to tell her how much of an absolute prick he was for ever letting her think that she was anything other than incredible.

Instead, I show her.

"Take me out of my jeans, baby." My voice is low and encouraging, hoping to ease her nerves.

She lifts her small hands to undo my belt, then slides my zipper down. She looks up at me and I nod my approval. She shimmies my boxers down, releasing my erection from its confinement. She wraps her lithe hand around my dick and it pulses against her palm. She looks up at me with those irresistible doe-eyes.

"Tell me if I'm doing this wrong, okay?"

Between the look of determination on her face and the vulnerability in her words, I'm already halfway to embarrassing myself. I caress her cheek with my thumb.

"Anything you do will feel incredible. Do what feels best for you. I promise I'll love it."

Encouraged, she bends her neck and slides her tongue along the underside of my cock then up and over my tip. She circles the head a few times before closing her mouth around it, careful to use only her lips. I know she's trying to make this good for me but I meant what I said before. Everything she does drives me crazy. The fact that I haven't already blown my load can only be chalked up to sheer luck.

She inches her way down my shaft, bringing me deeper into the heaven of her mouth. My head falls back. It's too good, too much. When she's hit her limit, she slowly retreats only to bring her mouth back down on me. She takes me a little too far and gags on my size. I pull my hips back to give her room to breathe but she tightens her grip on my base, bringing me back in. She adjusts and regains her rhythm. I groan at the sight of sweet Avery choking on my cock.

Her confidence builds and she starts to pick up speed. It's

taking all my effort not to close my eyes to the pleasure but I want to soak up every second of this moment, so my gaze remains on her.

I can tell she's enjoying herself, too. Her hips are subtly rocking and she's rubbing her legs together, trying to ease the pressure between them.

I run my hand along her jaw. "Play with yourself, Freckles." Her eyes widen in surprise but she hardly hesitates before she slips a hand between her legs. Her fingers circle her clit, applying pressure where she needs it most. She easily slides a finger inside, then another when she hears my groan in response.

"That's it, baby. Ride your fingers for me."

Together, we pick up our paces; me thrusting into her eager mouth, her pumping her fingers in and out of her slick heat while her palm rubs against her clit. Harder, deeper we take each other, both chasing our own release.

Avery looks up at me with those whisky doe-eyes and I lose it.

"Baby, I'm going to come," I warn, starting to pull myself from her mouth but she chases after me, doubling down. I groan, unable to stop myself from spilling down the back of her throat.

She takes every last drop.

I pull myself from her mouth and then scoop her into my arms. Carrying her to the desk, I set her down on top. Quickly pulling off her dress and tossing it aside, I lay her down onto the desk. Her back arches when she makes contact with the cool surface and I take advantage of the movement to take her nipple into my mouth. I move her hand aside to replace it with mine, thrusting my fingers deep inside her while sucking her nipple hard. The onslaught of sensation has her crying out. I use my other hand to strum her clit and before long, she's falling over the edge into her release.

Her legs fall open as the waves of pleasure course through her. Bit by bit, she slowly relaxes. I let my head fall against her chest. We're both breathing heavy, the sound of it harsh in the otherwise silent room.

"Wow," she finally whispers and I chuckle into her skin.

"I'll say. That was amazing. Better than amazing. Sublime. Top-notch."

This time it's her turn to laugh.

I kiss her lips softly. "I missed this. I missed you."

"I missed you, too."

I don't want to let her go, but we both need to get back to work. I stand then help her to her feet. Finding her dress on the floor across the room, I help her slip it over her head then tuck myself back into my jeans. I can't resist giving her another long kiss. Seeing the wide grin on her face when I pull away, I bend my head for another before pushes me away.

"You're trouble," she comments, smiling.

"You love it." I wag my eyebrows and reach for her again but she backs away laughing.

I follow her to the front of the shop, pausing at the door while she flips lock on the door.

"Hey, do you want to come to my baseball game tonight?" I ask. "Half the town usually ends up there. There's snacks, beer and no one takes it too seriously but it can be a lot of fun." I lean over the counter on my forearms. "You could be my good luck charm. You and Gav."

I've never invited a girl to watch me play baseball. It seemed like too much of a "girlfriend" thing to do, since a good portion of my family would be there either playing or watching. But the more I think about it, the more I really want Avery and Gavin there, cheering me on.

Thankfully, she smiles that slow smile I love so much. "Sounds like fun. We'll be there." A trio of tourists walk in behind me and I know that's my cue to leave. But before I go, I lift myself up on the counter and give her one last kiss, lingering only slightly longer than appropriate.

Then I nod at the group of customers who are now smiling at us and make my way out the door and down the sidewalk to my workshop.

I'm falling for that girl harder every day. And I think it's about time that I tell her that.

The call from my lawyer comes minutes after Matt leaves. Even though I knew it was a possibility, the news that Mitch is contesting me being in Haven Bay still guts me. It's exactly like Mitch to ruin my fantastic morning with Matt, even if it was unknowingly.

Margot assures me that this isn't the end. Her plan is to appeal to the judge stating that no official address change has been made, so there's no need for me to return yet.

I'm quiet for a moment. "What if there was? What would happen if I officially moved to Haven Bay?" I hold my breath. The weight of her response and, ultimately, my future causes the pit in my stomach to grow.

"An official change in address would complicate things but it would not be the nail in the coffin," Margot answers. "Have you decided to stay then?"

I chew on my bottom lip. *Have I?* "I'm not sure yet," I tell her honestly.

There's an unintelligible voice in the background and I hear Margot's muffled response. To me, she says, "I have to let you go. My next appointment is here. Listen, the second you decide, call my office and I'll submit the paperwork. And Avery? The sooner you decide, the better."

I agree then end the call. Looks like I have some thinking to do.

AFTER DINNER, Gavin, my mom and I drive to the baseball diamonds outside of town. We pull into the parking lot and wrestle our lawn chairs out from the back of my Volvo. Matt was right. Half the town must be here, along with food trucks and other vendors. Walking to the diamond takes twice as long as usual since we're constantly being stopped by other spectators to chat.

Finally, we reach the small patch of grass that Franny and Pete have commandeered for us along the third baseline. Franny waves us over, helping to unload our gear and then hugs each of us.

"Mom, look! It's Matt and Officer Brady!" Gavin pulls on my pant leg, pointing toward the infield where Matt and Luke are tossing a ball back and forth. "Hi, Matt!" Gavin calls, waving erratically at them.

Matt spots him and waves back. He says something to Luke then jogs over to the fence. Gavin hurries over to him, practically vibrating with excitement as we approach the fence.

"Wow, your shirt is so cool! Are you gonna score lots of goals, Matt? Mommy said you used to be a really good baseball player when you were little. Can you hit the ball super far? Could you hit it way over the trees if you wanted?" Gavin pauses to catch his breath and Matt takes the opportunity to cut in.

"Thanks, buddy! My friend Rhett designed our shirts. Heck yeah, I could hit those trees. I choose not to because I wouldn't want to show up my poor brother and his weak swing." He laughs when Luke throws his glove at Matt's legs. "Did you know that points in baseball are called runs, not goals? You have to make it all the way around the bases to get a run. Maybe after the game I could show you how to swing the bat so the ball goes really far. Or maybe your mom can show you. She used to be the best softball player in the whole school when we were kids."

Gavin's eyes grow comically wide. "You were, Mommy?"

I ruffle his hair and smile down at him. "Darn tootin', I was."

"My hand still hurts from her fastball," Matt jokes, clutching his hand in mock pain.

Gavin laughs. "So, can we play with Matt later, Mommy?"

"Sure."

"Yes!" Gavin pumps his fist. "I'm going to go tell Gram. Bye, Matt!" He hurries over to where my mom is sitting.

"Well, so much for giving me a good luck fist bump before the game," Matt chuckles as he watches Gavin chatter away excitedly to our moms.

"Good luck fist bump? Is that a real thing?"

He shrugs. "It should be. I guess I'll have to make do with a good luck kiss from his mom instead," he challenges mischievously.

I turn quickly to make sure Gavin's not looking. He's busy throwing a stick for Ham, who was lying on the ground beside Franny. With the craziness of the past few weeks, we haven't told him about our relationship yet. I know Matt probably thinks it's on purpose, which is why he hasn't mentioned it again.

I press a kiss to his lips through the gap in the chain link fence.

"Ah, metallicky. Just the way I like it," he jokes.

Pastor Dan, the league's umpire, hollers out a five minute warning and Matt starts toward the dugout.

"Hey, Matt," I call after him. He turns back. "Let's tell Gavin about us after the game."

The sudden grin he shoots me is appreciative and completely adorable. He whoops out his agreement and I laugh, shaking my head at his dramatics.

"You're already the best good luck charm I've ever had, Freckles," he calls back.

<hr>

MATT

I'm playing my best game ever. Nothing has gotten past me at shortstop and I'm batting a thousand. It might be because of the 4-year-old jumping and cheering loudly from the fence any time I make a play. Or it could be his sexy mom watching my every move. Either way, I'm loving having them here, even if it is only a beer league baseball game. My mom and Pete come out most weeks to watch Luke and I, but I've never had anyone come just for me.

It's nice.

I'm not the only one who notices either. "So, when should I expect uncle duties to start?" Luke jeers.

We're in the dugout, Luke leaning against the fence, drinking his beer while I'm outside on-deck. I take a few practice swings with the bat, letting his comments roll off of me like the beads of sweat currently dripping down my back.

"I heard there's a sale on white Reebok running shoes over at Moe's this week. Might want to stock up, Daddy Matt," Rhett quips. He's lounging on the bench, munching on sunflower seeds.

"How long have you been wanting to call me Daddy, Rhett?" I wag my eyebrows at him then laugh when he scowls and shoots me the finger.

I don't give a shit about their jokes. I can't remember the last time I was this happy. And not only happy but content. Like everything is finally clicking into place.

The crowd roars as Keith Jacobs hits a low ground ball that the second baseman easily snags. Keith races toward first and hits the base seconds before the ball is launched into the first baseman's glove. Bases are now loaded in the bottom of the ninth inning and we're down by two runs. I'm up to bat.

Of course. No pressure.

I walk up to the plate then twist my cleats into the dirt to plant my feet. My dentist, Doc Ridder, is on the pitcher's mound, tossing the ball around waiting for me. The atmosphere is tense. It might just be beer league, but we take our bragging rights seriously in this town.

To break the tension, I take a step away from the plate. I lift my arm to point at the sky above center field, calling my shot like the legendary Hamilton 'Ham' Porter (okay, and Babe Ruth). The crowd erupts into laughter while my brother groans from the dugout.

I step back up to the plate and take a few practice swings before getting into my batting stance. Doc Ridder eyes me up then throws his arm back before whipping it forward. The little white ball launches toward me. It's a hanging curveball that's left over the middle of the plate.

My favorite.

I swing my bat hard and it connects with a satisfying *ping*. The ball goes sailing over center field, right where I called it. The crowd starts losing it. I can tell they're shocked that I actually pulled it off and, to be honest, so am I.

Our dugout clears to get a better look. I race toward first base, watching as the ball starts to drop while the outfielder tries to get ahead of it. It finally drops on the other side of the fence and the crowd explodes. I slow my pace, rounding the bases until I'm bombarded by my teammates at home plate.

A little dramatic? Sure. You'd think we'd won the World Series instead of a regular season beer league game. But I soak up the glory all the same.

A tiny body launches himself at me, hugging my leg. "That was AMAZING! You hit the trees just like you said!" Gavin cries out.

Acting on impulse, I lower myself to a knee then hoist him up until he's seated on my shoulders. I hold his legs steady with both hands then take off along the fence line, cheering and waving to our adoring fans. Gavin's head is thrown back, laughing and waving along with me. We stop before the area where Avery is standing at the fence, our moms and Pete behind her. Ham jumps at the fence, barking along to the unknown cause of our celebration.

"Mommy! Matt won!"

"I saw!"

I lower Gavin over the fence into her arms. He jumps to the ground, bouncing around with Ham.

"Nice hit, hotshot," she teases.

I know the guys will probably give me shit for this, but I couldn't care less. I pull myself up and over the fence then jump down in front of her. She opens her mouth to say something but I stop her by wrapping her up in my arms. I dip her at the waist then bend my head to claim her mouth.

She reacts to me immediately, kissing me back with all the fervor that a public setting will allow. After a few seconds, I lift my head, laughing at the sounds of catcalls and whistles from the diamond behind me. Avery hides her face in my chest, blushing but I can feel her shoulders shaking with laughter, too.

"Eww!" Gavin groans, throwing one hand over his eyes and his other over Ham's eyes.

Oh, shit. I panic, looking down at Avery. "I'm so sorry, I wasn't thinking—"

She puts a hand on my lips, then turns to Gavin and pulls his hand away from his eyes.

"Hey, Gav. What would you think if Matt and I started dating?"

He tips his head to the side. "What's that mean?"

Following her lead, I bend my knee so I'm eye level with him. "It means I'll be hanging out with you and your mom more. Sometimes the three of us will hang out and sometimes it'll be just your mom and me." Gavin scrunches his nose and for a minute my heart drops.

"Don't you already do that?" he asks and I can't help but laugh as I feel my heart kickstart back to life.

Avery chuckles. "Yeah, I guess you're right."

"Well, there would be one difference. I'd really like to hold your mom's hand, give her hugs and kiss her sometimes." I look at Avery, a smile growing on my face before turning back to Gavin. "Do you think that'd be okay?"

"Only if Ham gets to come on dates, too," he tells me, expression serious.

I stick my hand out and he slips his chubby hand in mine. "Deal."

He hugs Ham who licks his cheek in response. "Can you show me how to hit the ball as far as you, now?"

"Sure, buddy."

He takes off toward the diamond, Ham prancing along behind him. Avery slips her arm around my waist and I pull her to me. "How about we go out Friday, just me and you?"

"Can't wait." She's looking at me with an emotion I think I recognize but am scared to hope for.

It looks a hell of a lot like the one I've been seeing in the mirror lately.

CHAPTER 30

AVERY

"You looked like you were enjoying yourself tonight," my mom comments, peering at me from over her mug.

We're out front on the porch swing after the baseball game sipping our nightly teas before bed. The lap blankets are long gone since the summer heat made its appearance. Too soon, the nights will cool again, so we soak up the warm nights while we can.

I roll my eyes but smile. Subtlety has never been my mother's strong suit.

"It was a lot of fun," I reply, intentionally ignoring her implication. "I didn't realize so many people went to them. I swear I saw most of the town out there tonight. You'd think people would have better things to do than watch beer league baseball games."

She snorts. "You know we take our beer leagues very seriously around here. You should see how packed the rec center gets during the darts league tournaments." She points a finger accusingly at me. "I also know you know exactly what I meant. I wasn't talking about the game."

She sets her mug down on the window ledge beside her

and faces me, tucking her legs under her like a little girl. I laugh at her excited expression but she ignores me.

"Now, tell me. How's everything going with you and Matt?"

I think about keeping her hanging for a minute to watch her squirm but I can't help but smile at the mention of his name. "Really great."

I barely get the words out before she squeals so loud, Sushi jumps up from her spot below us and grumpily slinks away to the opposite side of the porch. Undeterred by her protest, my mom grabs my hands and bounces in her seat. I throw my head back laughing at her ridiculous reaction.

"This is so exciting! I knew this would happen. I told Franny exactly that back when you kids were in middle school and went to your first dance." She pulls me to her in a hard hug then shoves me back to arms length, her eyes wide. "Oh my god, this is too perfect! Does this mean you're moving back?"

"I want to," I start slowly. "Not only for Matt but for Gavin and I, too. I feel more at peace here than I ever did in the city. Gavin's opened up and is a completely different kid than he was a few months ago." I pull the corner of my lip into my mouth thoughtfully. "I still have to work out all the details."

My mom waves me off. "Details, shmeetails. If it's what you want then do it."

I arch a brow at her. "It's a little more complicated than that and you know it. I'll have to get a new job, find an apartment—though I might have a lead on that already. Then I'll have to report my official address change to the court and that in itself could complicate things. If Mitch isn't willing to meet me halfway on this custody thing, it could get messy. It's not a decision that I can make lightly."

She takes my hand in hers and covers it with her other.

"I'm not making light of your situation, Avery. I promise. What I'm saying is if you want something enough, you'll make it happen. You've never been the type to back down from a challenge—even as a little girl. You're as determined as they come. Now is moving back to Haven Bay what you want?"

I nod solemnly.

"Then we'll make it happen," she says decisively.

She sits back on the swing, reaching for her mug. "As for your list, I think I can help you with that." She takes a sip of her tea, then rests the mug in her lap. "I've been meaning to talk to you about something but I was waiting for the right time or for some insight into where your heart was leading you." She takes a deep breath, then looks me earnestly in the eye.

"Avery, I want you to run The Book Nook and eventually, when this mess of a divorce is final, I want you to buy me out."

My mouth drops open but no sound comes out. There's a faint buzz in my ears as her declaration echoes in my head.

Me? Own a business?

Ignoring my shocked expression, she continues. "We can work out all the details of payment options and loans later. But the thing is, I'm getting older and, with my condition, I don't know how many good years I have left."

The slice to my heart is swift and instantaneous. The reality of my mom's condition has always seemed like something that was in the distant future. To hear her talk about a life without her in it so casually makes it hard for me to breathe. I refuse to let her think that way. I start to tell her so but she lifts her hand to halt my protest.

"I'm not being pessimistic, I'm being realistic. I could have fifteen good years left, I could have three. That's the problem with this pesky condition; no one knows what tomorrow will bring. But that's life. I want to spend what good time I have left doing what I love with the people I love. I want to spend time with Gavin while I have the energy to keep up with him. I want to go on girls' trips with Franny and the women from town. Who knows? Maybe I'd even like to try dating again."

My mouth drops open in shock. In all the years since my dad left, I've never once heard her talk about dating. I figured she wasn't interested. Not that I'm against the idea. My mom is a great person and deserves to live her life fully and on her own terms.

"The details don't matter now," she continues. "I love that little shop with all of my heart. It has given me so many wonderful friends and memories. It gave me purpose and, though it wasn't always easy, it gave me financial security after your dad left. I will always be grateful to the shop and all it gave me."

Her eyes mist a little and I swipe at the tears that fall down my face at her candour. I knew that things had been tough for the first little bit when we moved here, but to hear my mom talk about her struggles, especially now being a single mom myself in a similar situation, hits a little harder. I'm so proud of her and everything she's accomplished, despite all the shit that life has thrown at her.

She smiles tearfully. "I'm ready now to let that part of my life go. But I won't sell the shop to just anyone. I've been waiting for the right person to come along." She gives my hand a squeeze. "Avery, you're so smart and strong; stronger than you realize. I'm not offering you this because you're my daughter or because you're in a tight spot. I'm offering you this because it's what you were meant to do. The programs you've implemented over the last few months have increased profits, expanded our reach and brought us out of the slump we were settled in. You love that shop as much as I do. You belong there. You belong here."

The tears are streaming down my face now and I've given up trying to stop them. "And if you think I'm letting you live anywhere but right here with me, you're insane. Don't make me pull my 'sick mom' card. I'm not above using it to get my way." Her face is so serious, I choke out a laugh through the tears.

"Mom, I don't even know what to say. This is too much. This is..." My head is spinning, trying desperately to hold on to a single thought.

Across from me, my mom remains silent, sensing I need a moment to process such a huge revelation.

I can't say it's a complete surprise that she wants to cut back her hours at the shop. Since I've been here, she's had more good days than bad. She's healthier. Happier. But I know that won't always be the case and I understand her wanting to enjoy the good days while they last.

I'd be lying if I said I didn't want to continue running the store. Working there has been eye-opening for me. For once, I'm needed for more than nose wiping, laundry folding or bath-giving. I'm more than a mom there.

Of course, I love being Gavin's mom. Nothing has been more meaningful or fulfilling than becoming a mom. It's the most amazing, stressful, wonderful, terrifying and exhausting time and I wouldn't change a second of it. But it's so easy to lose yourself in the day-to-day responsibilities, the constant demand to meet everyone else's needs before your own.

Working at the shop has allowed me to be something more than just a mom or a wife. It allows me to feed my creative flame—one I didn't even know I had until now.

The more I think about it, the more I realize how much I want this. To work in the shop, to live in Haven Bay. I want late-night talks with my mom, stolen mid-day moments with Matt and lunches with Jolie at the diner. I want Gavin to grow up in a town where everyone knows him, watches out for him and loves him like their own.

I want it all.

I finally look up at my mom. "I swear I won't let you down."

"I know you won't, honey. I have no doubt that you're going to accomplish everything great in this life. And I can't wait to see it all."

CHAPTER 31

MATT

Friday afternoon, I manage to knock off early from work so I decide to swing by Blooms, the flower shop in town. I want to pick up a bouquet for Avery before our date. The look of shock and delight she gave me when I brought them last time made me realize she hasn't experienced little surprises nearly enough.

The owner, Shae, made up a fancy arrangement with bright pink, yellow and orange flowers and some green thing she calls silver dollar. I have no idea what any of them are, but it's cheery so I decide to get another for my mom.

I'm too early to pick up Avery yet and I haven't been by to see my mom in a while—a fact I'm sure she'll be happy to guilt me with. The flowers will sweeten her up so her guilt trip will only last half of the visit instead of the whole time like it usually does.

I knock on her door then listen for her voice before walking in. There was a time when I wouldn't even bother knocking before entering my childhood home as an adult.

Then my mom started dating Pete.

Luke and I decided that to prevent any deep, long-lasting

trauma of seeing parts of our mom that no son should ever see, knocking was necessary.

I follow the sound of music into the kitchen to find my mom baking. She's slipping a pan into the oven, shaking her hips to the upbeat Taylor Swift song that plays through her speaker.

My mom's a big time Swiftie but she sings about as well as a seagull. But her lack of musical ability has never stopped her from belting out a tune. Especially the high notes. Growing up, she would sing in the car with our friends to embarrass my siblings and me, but Avery, Rhett and I would usually end up joining in by the end of the drive.

She turns and spots me. She makes her way toward me, shimming along to the music. Her arm thrusts out to me and I take her hand, spinning her in circles then dipping her dramatically. She laughs as I pull her upright.

"You've got some moves, honey!" She gives me a warm hug, then holds me at arms length to look at me. "Is that where you've been lately? Out dancing with Avery instead of visiting your poor, lonely mother who carried you for nine long months then birthed your giant ten-pound ass. It's a wonder I didn't tear myself in two pushing you out."

Less than two minutes I've been here. That's a new guilt trip record; even for my Italian mother.

I roll my eyes. "It's been a little over a week. I've been busy at the shop and, yes, hanging out with Gavin and Avery." I fetch the bouquet from the entryway, pass it over to her then plop myself down on a stool. "I brought these for you. I saw them and thought how pretty they were but they're not nearly as beautiful as you are, Ma."

When she's mid-guilt trip, it's always best to lay it on extra thick.

"They're gorgeous. Thank you, honey. Shae did a great

job." She turns to fill a vase with water. "So, what brings you by today?"

"I'm picking Avery up for a date in about twenty minutes. Thought I'd visit my favorite mother while I was in the neighborhood." The oven buzzes and while her back is turned to remove the tray, I snag a cookie from the cooling rack.

"I saw that," she comments, her back still to me.

The woman has had eyes in the back of her head since we were kids. I see her skills are still honed, despite being an empty-nester for over five years now. I guess that's what happens when you raise three rambunctious kids.

I wonder how many kids Avery wants.

As if she can read my mind, my mom turns off the oven and turns back to me. "So things are good with you and Avery, then?" She leans her elbow on the island propping her chin in her hand, wiggling her eyebrows at me.

I roll my eyes. And she wonders where I get my dramatics from.

"Yes, Ma. Things are good." I point an accusatory finger at her. "Don't you go pestering her and messing that up. You're too pushy for your own good."

She lifts her hands up in a show of innocence. "I haven't said a word. But I'm not getting any younger, Matty. And I refuse to be one of those creaky, old grandmas who can barely remember their grandkids' names." She points a finger back at me. "So, any time you want to get on that—" She sputters out a laugh. "Pun intended."

I groan at her cheesy joke. Yeah, no doubt about it. She's definitely my mother. Though that line was not only cheesy, but pitiful. Is this how Luke feels with me?

Nah, screw that. I'm hilarious.

"Anyway…" I shake my head at her. "When's your next big adventure?"

For the last couple of years, my mom and Pete have been

taking trips around North America—sometimes nearby, sometimes as far as Florida.

"We're thinking we might go somewhere a bit more southern this time. We've both never been to Mexico, so we're thinking Cabo in January." She steps away from the island and starts to dance the mambo to *Blank Space*.

I jokingly cringe at her dance. "Maybe you should stick to baking, Ma. T-Swift, you are not."

She throws a dish towel at me, giving me a stern look but I mimic it back to her and she throws her head back laughing.

"That's why I love you, Matt. You always make me laugh."

There it is again.

That's why I love you.

I know she means well but when my own mother unknowingly reinforces the fear I've always kept hidden, it hurts. The fear that if I show my family and friends the other parts of me—not only the fun part—they might love me less.

I force a small laugh and stand. "Well, I should go pick up Avery. I'll talk to you later, Ma." I bend my head to kiss her cheek and she gives me a hard squeeze.

"See you soon, Matty. Enjoy your night with Avery. I'd say don't enjoy it too much, but who am I kidding? I want a grandchild." She exaggerates her wink and I groan.

"Goodbye, Ma."

She's cackling to herself as she closes the door behind me. I walk the short distance to Avery's mom's house, shaking my head at her theatrics.

But I can't seem to shake the uneasiness her words leave in my chest.

AVERY

Matt seems off today. I can't quite put my finger on it but something's not right. I can feel the invisible wall he's built between us. His posture is tense and every smile seems forced. When he picked me up, he chatted with my mom and goofed around with Gavin. But even then, it seemed like he was holding back.

We're in his truck driving into town. He still hasn't told me where we're going for dinner so when he pulls up behind his apartment, I'm confused.

"Did you forget something at home?" I ask.

Matt turns to me with an almost embarrassed smile. "I figured we could stay in tonight. I'll cook for you while you relax with a glass of wine and tell me about your day." He shrugs self-consciously. "We haven't been alone together in so long, I didn't want to share you with anyone else tonight—not even the waiter."

He looks shy, so unsure of himself that I don't have the heart to tease him about it. He's too cute. Instead, I lean over the center console to kiss him. I linger a little longer than necessary, pouring into it all the feelings I'm not quite ready to say yet.

Eventually, I pull away, both of us dazed and smiling.

"So, I take it you like that idea?" Matt asks as we climb out of the truck and head toward the building.

"Well, I guess that depends on how good of a cook you are," I tease. "What're we having anyway—macaroni and cheese with hot dogs mixed in?" That was his favorite meal as a kid and funnily enough, it's Gavin's favorite, too. I still don't understand the appeal, but it was a staple in my house as a kid and now again as an adult.

"I thought about it," he jokes. "But I figured we could do a little better than that. I'm making chicken piccata over creamy garlic pasta with roasted parmesan asparagus." He looks over at the expression of genuine shock on my face and throws his head back laughing. "What?"

I shake my head incredulously. "Nothing. I guess I'm a little surprised you can cook. Your mom tried for years to get you interested in cooking, but you could still barely boil water by the time we graduated," I say as Matt unlocks the shop door and we climb the stairs to his apartment.

"Yeah, well. Once I moved out, I realized that living off take-out was not good for my wallet and microwave dinners get old real fast. I started watching some cooking shows and now my Pinterest is overflowing with recipes." He shrugs again, this time in modesty.

I bump my shoulder against him playfully. "Pinterest, eh? Just when I think I know everything about you, you somehow manage to surprise me with something new."

He drops his head and I can't quite decipher his expression but by the time we've reached the top of the stairwell, it's gone. Before I can question it, he opens his front door and gestures for me to go in.

I barely make it inside before Ham barrels into my legs. I rub his flank, kissing his wide head and whispering loving praise into his droopy ears.

"What's a guy gotta do to get a greeting like that?" Matt chuckles as he gives Ham an affectionate pat on the butt.

"Look as cute as him and then we'll talk," I tease. I give Ham's ears one last rub before I look up and stop mid-stroke.

Matt's apartment is very industrial chic. The exposed brick, the wood accents and sparing decor—it's definitely a man's apartment. Tonight, though, there are a few scented candles lit and placed around the apartment and fresh flowers in a simple, clear vase on the coffee table. Matt picks up his phone and taps the screen. A soft, country song fills the air.

I slowly stand and take in the dining table. The large, dark wood table is gorgeous on its own. But again, Matt's added a few touches tonight. In the middle of the table is a small vase with blooming flowers to match the ones in the living room. Two place settings are made up with wine glasses and water glasses beside them. I amble over to the table, touched by the sweet gesture. Again, Matt is checking off boxes on a list I didn't even know I had.

Romantic night-in where I don't have to cook?

Check.

Having a man show his affection for me through little things like candles, flowers and wine?

Check.

I run my fingers over the bewitching detail carved into the back of the dining room chair. I notice an identical carving along the frame that wraps around the underside of the table. I examine it closer. You can tell a significant amount of time and attention was put into intricately designing the art.

I know right away that Matt designed and built this magnificent piece. Even if I hadn't seen the work he did on the display case, I would still know it was Matt's design.

I've never told him this, but I found one of his sketch-books when we were fourteen. I was in his bedroom looking for a textbook I had lent him and needed for an assignment. He wasn't home so Franny had told me to go up and have a look. I opened a desk drawer and there was a black sketchbook with a piece of paper hanging out over the edge. I opened it, thinking it would be some more of the hilarious caricatures he always used to draw.

Instead, I found the most stunning sketches. Landscapes, abstract, wildlife—all black and white but overwhelmingly beautiful. I was in awe. I had a hard time believing that my goofy best friend could draw something so intense and meaningful.

I put the sketchbook away and never spoke to him about it.

We were best friends; we told each other everything. I knew he watched (and cried during) *My Girl* with his mom every time it was on TV. He knew my favorite snack to eat while I was on my period was a Hershey's Cookies and Cream chocolate bar.

If drawing was something he wanted me to know about, he would've told me. He hadn't, so I never brought it up.

After that, I would sometimes see him outside on his back porch, poring over his sketchbook, pencil flying. I noticed he'd spend more time drawing when he was stressed or trying to work his way through something.

The most I saw him draw was when his dad was sick.

It always shocked me that I had no idea of his talent before finding that sketchbook. What kind of person doesn't notice what was clearly such an integral part of their friend's life? Obviously it was important to him since he turned to it in times of distress.

If I wasn't able to vocalize my support, I decided I'd show it by keeping his secret.

A part of me is relieved that he continued his art. When we started hanging out less, I was nervous he would get in his head too much without someone to talk through the hard times with. Like he used to do with me. To know that all this time, he had an outlet to work his emotions through, selfishly eases some of my guilt over leaving.

Despite already knowing the answer, I still ask him. "Did you make this?"

He's in the kitchen, putting the marinated chicken into the oven. He reaches over to stir the sauce on the stovetop then looks up at me, wooden spoon in hand. My insides turn to mush at this big, masculine man looking domesticated just for me.

"Make what?" he asks. I gesture towards the table and chairs.

"Oh." He turns his attention back to the saucepan, though I doubt the sauce needs that much stirring. "Yeah, I did. Bud lets me use the workshop as long as I reimburse him for my materials."

I walk over to him, taking the spoon from his hand and placing it on the counter behind me. I wait until his eyes finally lift to mine, uncertainty clearly written all over his face.

"It's absolutely stunning," I tell him softly, wrapping my arms around his waist.

He shrugs. It's his default defensive move. "It's only a table."

I shake my head, squeezing my arms tightly around him. "It's not. It's a piece of art. Furniture or not, it's a piece of art. It's a piece of you."

He's quiet, his eyes searching mine. I can tell he's having a hard time believing me but he also seems like he's trying to decide something. Every time Matt shows me his vulnerable side, I can feel myself falling a little harder for him.

Finally, he smiles. He reaches behind him, unwrapping my arms from around his waist and holds my hands in his between us.

"Can I show you something?" he asks me, tentatively.

"Of course."

He reaches behind me and turns the heat down to a low simmer under the sauce. He sets the timer on the oven, then smiles down at me again. Wordlessly, hand still holding mine, he guides me out of the apartment and down to the workshop below.

Once downstairs, he flicks a switch and the shop lights up. Last time I was here, I was a bit distracted by the irresistible man before me, so I didn't get a chance to look around. Which is why I take a moment now to do exactly that.

There's an exposed red brick wall, identical to the one in Matt's apartment. The ceiling is also exposed, the metal pipes and ductwork creating an industrial feel to the shop. Wood surrounds the rest of the room; from the deep brown hardwood floors to the large wooden beams that reach from the floor to the ceiling. It's masculine, almost industrial.

To our left, a long, slick workbench takes up most of the space. Beside it, almost hidden away from the rest of the room, is a smaller bench with a white cloth covering it. I'm not familiar with woodworking, but something about the area is different from the rest of the shop. It's more secluded, the cloth offering privacy from the rest of the shop.

As I expected, Matt guides me toward the smaller bench. Matt pulls back the cloth and I gasp. There are dozens of wood carvings, varying in shapes and sizes displayed on and around the workbench.

A large wooden sculpture of an eagle in flight sits on the ground. A circular design that's about the size of a dinner plate leans against the wall. A tall maple tree has been whittled into it and is stained to show a sunset behind it.

Sculptures, clocks, figurines, wall decorations, bowls. Everywhere I look, my eyes catch on another piece. I knew Matt was capable of great things—his work on the display case was evidence of that—but this is beyond anything that I could've expected.

The dining table in the overhead apartment and the display case in the cafe pale in comparison to these pieces. Those were custom projects meant to make mundane furnishings more aesthetically pleasing. These pieces are alive with wonder and passion. They tell stories and create feelings with every slice of his chisel.

"These are beautiful," I tell him. I'm in awe, trying to take in every detail from every piece all at once.

"Whittling is a hobby of mine. It has been for a while now.

The custom jobs that come from Taylor Construction are what pay the bills. But this—" he says, looking down as he runs his hand over the curve of an unfinished piece. "This is where my heart lies. This is where my soul opens up and every piece of me bursts out. Where I can be truly myself–every somber, pensive, genuine part."

His eyes lift to mine and I can feel the weight of his gaze. It's heavy with a staggering intensity that lets me know his next words will be momentous.

"No one knows about this side of me. No one but you."

CHAPTER 32

MATT

The reality of my statement sinks in. No one else in the world knows about my art. Not my family, not Rhett. Not even Bud knows what I do in my little corner of the workshop. As long as I keep it clean and complete my work on time, I could be making wooden dildos back here and he wouldn't care.

But Avery is looking at me like she truly, genuinely cares. Like she sees the real me.

The mix of awe and elation splayed across her face makes me want to believe she's impressed; that she sees the pieces of myself I've poured into every creation.

But until I hear the words aloud, my stomach twists like a fitted sheet in the closet.

"I'm beyond honored that you chose to show me this side of you, Matt." She steps closer to me, wrapping her arms around my neck. "You're extremely talented. Your passion and your creativity shine through in every design. I'm so proud of you. It's amazing." She plays with the curl at the nape of my neck and goosebumps break out down my back. "Can I ask you a question, though?"

My answer is immediate. "Of course."

"Why haven't you told anyone about this? I could see your mom buying up your entire stock and displaying it all over her house. Same with Tori and Rhett. Even Luke. They'd be so proud of you."

My smile falters, my mom's earlier words replaying in my head. After leaving her house, they played on repeat through my mind, echoing my worst fear back to me.

That's why I love you, Matt. You always make me laugh.

Because that's all I'm good for; a laugh. And if the people I love found out about my somber designs—that there's more to me than being the goofy guy with a quick joke—they won't want me anymore.

They won't need me anymore.

I rest my cheek on top of her head then rub my hands along her arms, trying to gather my courage. I've never told anyone how I feel about this but for some reason, I want to share it with Avery. The thought of being this vulnerable with someone scares the shit out of me, but I don't want there to be any secrets anymore.

Not with her.

"People expect me to be a certain way. The goofy guy who doesn't take life too seriously. The guy who's guaranteed to make you laugh. The guy who always has a smile on his face." My stomach turns sour but I force myself to continue. "After my dad got sick, things were really dark in our house for a while. My mom went through a really rough patch. She wasn't herself for a long time. Who would be after losing their husband?"

I take a deep breath and feel Avery gives my hand a reassuring squeeze. She was around when all of this happened as a teenager but there were certain things I hid from everyone—even her.

"I found that, when things were really dark, the only time my mom would smile was when I would crack jokes or do something goofy. Eventually, she started smiling more and the darkness didn't seem so bleak. But I was always worried that if I wasn't there to make her laugh, she might slip back into the darkness again. That I might lose her, too."

"Oh, Matt." Her voice cracks with emotion. She holds my hand tightly, seeming to know I need a minute before continuing.

After a few moments, I figure I might as well lay myself bare to her.

"So, I guess after a while, I started to hide the heavy parts of myself. I tamped down the grief, the anger, the solemnness until all that was left was this goofball whose main purpose in life was to make other people laugh." I take a slow breath, lifting my head to look her in the eyes. "All this time, I've kept up the act because deep down I'm scared that if I stop being the funny guy, what good am I?"

My eyes catch on one of my first designs from years ago—the crying clown. I read an article once about the sad clown paradox after my favorite comedian, Robin Williams, passed away. It inspired me to try my own hand at the concept. I told myself I was so interested in it because of the juxtaposition of emotions but I think even then, I saw myself in the concept.

I watch as a single tear escapes and rolls down her cheek. I brush it away with my thumb.

"Matt, you have to know that's not true. Your family loves you. Not because you make them laugh, but because of who you are." She gives me a small shake when I start to protest. "You're loving, patient and thoughtful. You bring your mom flowers because your dad used to bring her them 'just because'. You pitch in at the bar whenever Rhett's short-staffed or has a busy night. You might tease Luke mercilessly but everyone knows that you shovel his driveway whenever he's out on a late night call so he doesn't have to worry about it when he gets home."

She grabs my face with both hands, eyes intent on mine. She waits until I'm completely focused on her before continuing. "None of those things have to do with you making them laugh and everything to do with you being you."

My chest constricts and I have to fight to breathe past it. Her words create a small ember of hope deep within me. One I'm terrified to fan, though I desperately ache to.

But the thing is, Avery knows about my designs and she's looking at me like I've hung the moon. She looks at my work like it's more than part of an old tree. She sees the beauty in it, the magic of taking something so ordinary and bringing it to life.

The best part is she's not backing away after seeing this side of me. If anything, she's happy I've shared this part of me with her. Maybe others will be, too.

Something to think about later.

Right now, all I can think about is showing Avery how much her acceptance means to me. Every part of me feels alive and free for the first time in my life and I want to share that feeling with her.

Our first time was desperate and hurried—a lifetime's worth of built up tension and yearning finally released upon each other.

This time, I'm determined to take my time with her. I want to worship every irresistible curve, every inch of her smooth skin until she's lost to the feeling of us. Until she starts to feel even an ounce of what I'm feeling for her.

I reach up and take her hands from where they rest on my face and lower them to her sides. I raise my own to cup her cheek gently, then slowly dip my head, keeping my eyes focused on hers the whole time. She's watching me, her resolute expression from moments ago melting with desire.

My lips are a breath away from hers. "Thank you," I whisper against them.

It's not nearly enough but it's all I can muster to fully encompass how much her words mean to me. Everything she does, everything she says is a testament to how spectacular she is.

Before she can respond, I close the distance between us, sealing myself to her in more ways than one. The way she just accepts me, every vulnerable, messy part without hesitation is something I didn't even allow myself to hope for when I brought her down to the shop. I don't know what I expected but this wasn't even close. It feels like the last piece of the puzzle finally falling into place.

And with it, my heart is fully and completely hers.

There's no doubt in my mind that I am hopelessly and irretrievably hers from this moment on. Whatever comes next in life, a piece of me will always be with her—no matter where she is.

I don't want to ruin this moment with thoughts about our uncertain future and her looming divorce. So instead, I pour myself into the kiss, hoping to show her all the love and peace in my heart.

All because of her.

Her throaty moan pulls me out of my thoughts and I bend down to wrap my arms around the back of her knees to scoop her into my arms. Never breaking the kiss, I walk with her to my workbench before gently placing her on top. I finally tear my mouth away from hers to glide it along her jaw, placing open-mouth kisses down to her collarbone. She drops her head back in response and intuitively opens her legs wider. I instantly step between them, pressing myself against where I need her most.

My cock is painfully pressing against my zipper as I rock against her. Her unabashed groan begs me to tear off our clothes and plunge inside her but I hold myself back.

I told myself I'd savor her and that's exactly what I plan to do.

My hands roam over her soft, bare thighs, teasing the edge of her tight shorts. I try to slip my hand under them but the snug fabric restricts any further movement.

When I first saw her in this pale pink one-piece outfit, I could hardly take my eyes off her. The silky material hugged her curves perfectly and my hands itched to touch them. I could hardly drive straight, imagining her legs wrapped around my head, the pale pink accentuating that blush that I know dips low on her chest.

Now, I want to rip the damn thing in two so I can feel her bare skin against mine. I'm not usually the aggressive type but Avery is bringing out sides of me I didn't even know I had.

"There's a button at my neck," she says breathily. She's staring down at me through hooded eyes and I fight to maintain my control.

I'll never understand how this girl has such an effect on me. I'm not even sure I care.

All I know is I need her naked. Now.

I reach around her to find the small button at the base of her neck. Unhooking it, I lower the silky material down each of her arms, past her chest until she's bare to her waist. I flick the clasp on her strapless bra, tossing it to the floor behind me.

She squirms impatiently on the countertop, trying to shove at the rest of the material but I'm too close for her to push it the rest of the way off. Instead of helping her, I lower my head to nuzzle her bare chest. My stubble scrapes against her nipple and her back straightens with a sharp breath. I smile against her skin before doing it again, this time taking her nipple inside my mouth at the same time I pinch the other between my forefinger and thumb.

Her moan urges me on, sucking, pulling and pinching. I don't stop until she's a writhing mess. She grinds herself against me, searching desperately for the pressure she craves. When I pull back, she groans in frustration.

Lifting her by the hips, I yank the clothing from under her and toss it haphazardly behind me. I sit her back down on the countertop, watching her nipples harden as her skin touches the cool surface.

I drink her in, memorizing the sight of her laid bare to me on my workbench. The place I feel most at peace, where so much of my heart has been laid open. I can already tell I'll remember this night for the rest of my life as the night everything changed for me.

For us.

I start toward her then stop short when my eyes catch on the place between her legs. She's not wearing any panties.

Again.

I groan, unable to tear my eyes away from the sweet heaven that beckons to me.

"Jesus, Freckles. You're killing me."

She widens her legs, giving me a full view of her and I think I've forgotten my own name. Then she reaches out, hooks her fingers into my belt loops and pulls me to her. "Please fuck me," she whispers.

Holy fuck.

There's no hotter sight than Avery, naked and spread out on my workbench, begging me to fuck her.

Until she reaches down, a single finger dipping to circle her clit. "I'm so wet for you, Matt. Please."

I stand corrected.

I inhale slowly, trying not to let him see my hands shake. I'm new to this whole "sex-confident" thing. I've never felt sexy before. There have been times where I've felt wanted. But sexy?

Desired?

Craved?

Only Matt has been able to stir these feelings within me.

It's exciting and new and I can't wait to explore my sexuality further. But I'm also not naive enough to think that a couple of hot rolls in the hay will make me some kind of sexual goddess. So while I'm thrilled at the idea of trying new things, it still takes a shit ton of courage to actually act on them.

Yet when Matt looks at me the way he is right now, eyes nearly black with lust, I can feel my confidence building.

His clear reaction makes me braver and I lift my chin to look him in the eye as I sink one finger inside my slit. I know he was trying to take it slow with me earlier but, while I appreciate his thoughtfulness, I want him to be as desperate and out of control as I feel.

His earlier confession broke my heart. To think that such a selfless, compassionate man could think so little of himself makes my chest ache. I'm not even sure he knows how instrumental he's been in my journey to finding myself again. Even when I don't see it myself, he's the first one shining the spotlight on all of my strengths.

It's about time someone did the same for him.

He still hasn't said anything, his jaw tense, hands clenched at his sides in indecision. He's watching me carefully as he tries to tamp down his desire.

It only fuels mine.

I sink another finger further inside myself, arching my back as I try to reach that magic spot deep inside. Matt leans in, framing me. His knuckles whiten from his grip on the counter.

"You know, Matt, there's a lot of things I love about you—your honesty, your courage." My hand starts a steady rhythm, slowly pumping into myself. "You worry that you're too funny to be taken seriously." In. Out. "But there's nothing funny about the way I touch myself when I think about you late at night in my bed."

He swallows hard, staring down at where my fingers disappear. "You do that often, Freckles? Fuck your fingers while you think about me?"

He's looking at me with such intensity that it makes it hard to form a response.

"Yes," I manage against my suddenly dry mouth.

He lets out a low groan, seeming to like my answer. I'm thrilled by the sound, especially since my show of bravado is starting to wane. As scary as it is to step so far out of my comfort zone, I want to do this. Tonight, Matt has been vulnerable with me in a way he's never been with anyone else; he told me so himself moments ago. He deserves to have that vulnerability reciprocated.

He leans in closer, his hands laid flat against the bench. "What do you think about when you're riding your hand for me, baby?" His thumbs brush the skin on my outer thighs.

I continue to lay myself bare for him—both literally and figuratively.

Swallowing my reservations, I look him right in the eye as I answer him truthfully. "Your arms. Your hands. The way you fucked my mouth in my office." To drive my point home, I push another finger inside. My breath hitches at the extra pressure.

"That's it, baby. Stretch yourself for me." His hands lift to spread my thighs wider until there's no hiding from him.

I moan, overcome by the intensity of the moment. Months ago, the thought of another person watching me masterbate would've mortified me. Now, I'm fingering myself eagerly while Matt hungrily watches and I'm ready to come from his words alone.

I love it.

The last few times, my orgasm has felt like a hurried climb, taking me higher and higher until I'm thrown over the edge. This time, it feels more like a steady plunge, falling deeper into the abyss of pleasure.

It seems like I'm not the only one affected because Matt's fingers suddenly dig into my skin and his voice is a gravelly drawl. "You like that, don't you, baby? You like the thought of me stretching you wide with my fat cock. You want me to give it to you? Do you need me to fuck you, Freckles?"

I'm practically panting when I let out a breathy "yes".

"That's my girl. Fuck that pretty pussy until you cum all over your fingers." He leans closer, lifting one hand to wrap my hair tightly around his fist. He gives it a small tug and I swear the move goes straight to my core.

My walls clench greedily around my fingers.

My pace quickens and I'm so close. I need more but I'm unsure of what.

"Come, Avery," he growls before pulling my nipple into his mouth, giving it a sharp nip. Then with his other hand, he circles my clit, applying the perfect amount of pleasure to bring me right to the edge.

It's like my body is an instrument that only he knows the chords to.

My back arches forward. My head drops back and I'm immersed in pleasure. The waves crash over me, each one more powerful than the last until finally they subside.

A muttered curse pulls me from my dreamy state, as I watch Matt struggle to shove his pants off. It's like he can't get to me fast enough. "Jesus, Avery. I almost came just from watching you. How am I supposed to keep it together when you come like that, with *my* name on your lips, *my* designs behind you, your aching pussy dripping onto *my* workbench?"

He finally pushes his pants away and yanks me toward the edge of the bench.

"I wanted this to be soft and slow for you but there's no fucking way I can go slow now. Not after that." Even so, he looks at me, waiting for permission before taking me.

I answer him by wrapping my hand around his length, lining him up to where we both need it most.

That's all the answer he needs. He squeezes my ass tightly, yanking me to him then thrusts into me hard. I'm already a dripping mess so there's nothing but pleasure when he pushes into me. My mouth drops open as my body accommodates him, feeling deliciously full. Yet I need the pressure of him thrusting into me. I crave it.

He must feel the same way because there's nothing gentle about the way he takes me. Deeper and deeper he pumps into me. Then, as if remembering I need more, he tilts my hips so that every thrust delivers sweet friction against my clit.

My body begs for its release again, as if I didn't come mere moments ago.

"Harder," I demand and to my delight, he obliges until the workbench is slamming against the wall behind us.

The tools that are hung neatly on the wall above me are clanging loudly.

I'm so close, my orgasm within reach. Feeling empowered, I slip my hand between us and circle my clit until my orgasm takes me over again. Matt follows soon after, growling my name while claiming my body.

Claiming my heart.

MY HEART HAS FINALLY SLOWED to its normal rate, but it feels as though it's been profoundly changed.

After the hottest sex I've ever had, I'm lying naked on the workbench with Matt's head buried in my neck. He's trying to steady his breathing, his arms wrapped protectively around my waist. I drop a hand to his head to play with the dark curls I adore so much. The silence is comfortable, a testament to how at peace I am with him.

Matt's art surrounds us. To my right, there's a piece of dark wood, probably a couple of feet tall. It's only about a third of the way finished while the rest is still covered in bark. The part that's carved has long, fluid strokes that lead into what looks like a tail.

For some reason, the design causes a tug in my chest. I'm pulled to the piece, which intrigues me since I can't even tell what it is. I tap him and when he lifts his head, I gesture to the piece.

"What's that one going to be?" I ask.

The corner of his mouth lifts. "Just something I've been

inspired by. It's not quite ready yet, but when it is, I feel like it's going to be stunning." Before I can ask what he means by "ready", he drops his lips to mine in a kiss that makes my head spin but is over too quickly.

"Come on, Freckles. I promised you dinner. Although, it might be charcoal by now." He bends and retrieves the clothes we tossed wildly moments ago. He helps me redress then lifts me off the workbench. "I'm not sure how I'll ever look at this bench again without picturing you spread out on it for me."

Feeling thoroughly pleased with that thought, I give him a saucy wink. "Good."

"Keep looking at me like that, you little flirt, and I'll bend you back over it." My thighs clench at the thought but he slaps my ass playfully. "Get upstairs, Freckles."

God, I love it when he calls me that.

I practically skip up the stairs, my mood so light I could float away at any second. When I open the door, Ham looks up at us from the couch. He gives me an unimpressed look, then goes back to napping.

"Is it just me or does Ham look like he knows exactly what we did down there?" I laugh.

"Oh, yeah. He looks absolutely scandalized by it, too." Matt jokes back, taking the chicken out of the oven.

There's no smoke so that's a good sign. I look back at Ham, who's lounging on his back, legs sprawled open and a goofy smile on his face as his jowls dangle upside down. I laugh again.

"Well, it's not going to be my best but it's edible," Matt says, plating our meals.

I take the opportunity to ogle him while I pour my wine. He pulled back on his jeans downstairs but didn't bother with socks. His hair is a mess from when I wrapped his curls around my fingers during the height of my orgasm. That brings back the memory of his mouth on my chest and I can feel myself getting flushed again.

Jeez, where did this sex-obsessed woman come from? After twenty-seven years of going without, am I under some kind of orgasm-induced spell?

Matt places my plate on the place setting before me, dropping a kiss on the top of my head. He rounds the table and takes his seat across from me. Pulling a lighter from his pocket, he lights the candle in the middle of the table.

No, this definitely isn't only from sex. Great sex, mind you, but it has nothing to do with the orgasms and everything to do with the man in front of me.

I was serious about what I said to my mom yesterday. Moving back to Haven Bay isn't only about being closer to Matt. If we weren't together, I would probably still end up here because of my mom and Gavin. But I have to admit, I'm excited to see where this relationship will go. Because if I'm being honest with myself, this means more to me than just having fun.

A lot more.

I'm about to tell him exactly that, along with the good news about moving back, when he clears his throat. "Avery, there's something I want to talk to you about." I'm not sure how long I've been lost in thought for but when I look at him, I realize he must've been as lost as I was. The laughter from earlier is gone and he's fiddling with the label on his beer.

"I know this might seem sudden...well, maybe it doesn't since we've known each other our whole lives... but we've barely started dating so maybe that time before doesn't count..." He huffs out a nervous breath and I can't help but smile.

I secretly love when he gets all flustered around me. It's nice to know I'm not the only one affected by our chemistry. I take pity on him and reach over to stop his anxious hand from its destruction on the label.

"Hey."

He looks up.

I smile reassuringly. "Whatever it is, you can tell me."

That seems to calm him and he squeezes my hand before beginning again.

"What I mean to say is...I'm falling for you, Avery." He shakes his head. "No, that's not right either." He looks me fully in the eye, his rough thumb brushing over my knuckles. "Avery, I'm in love with you. I think a little part of me has always been loved you. But this? What I feel for you now? It's so much more than anything I ever could've imagined back then." He smiles softly. "You're so much more. You're everything."

For the second time tonight, my eyes well up with tears. Only this time, they feel like the slow rise of the sun, giving way bit by bit until the burst of light finally settles over the horizon. It feels just as beautiful, just as inevitable.

"I know you can't commit to anything right now," he continues, "with the whole custody issue and not knowing where you're going to live. I hate that you're going through this. I hate that you're feeling even an ounce of pain or hurt over that piece of shit. If I could, I'd take you and Gavin away from all of it. "

I smile at the fierce way he defends us. His protective nature is another way he shows his heart to those he loves.

He moves from his seat across from me to the seat beside me, our meals now cold and forgotten. He leans forward, hands on my thighs and his eyes searching mine. "I love you, Avery, and I love Gavin. I love that kid like he's my own. He's not baggage or a consolation prize. You two are the best package deal a guy could ever hope for."

I bite my lip at the sudden wave of emotion. As kids, Matt used to joke about how easily I cried—something I used to punch him anytime he brought it up. Pregnancy and motherhood only made it worse. But I refuse to start blubbering and ruin this special moment.

"So wherever you are, I want to be there, too. I know it's a big ask, but if you'll have me, I want to move to Edmonton with you. If that's where you need to be, that's where I need to be, too."

Well, so much for not blubbering.

He brushes away the tears from my cheek. "Before you freak out, I'd have my own apartment. I won't rush you into anything. I'll find work there. I'll work as a general laborer again if I have to. But none of that matters. The only thing that matters is that I'm with you and Gav."

I give him a wobbly smile. I'm so overcome with emotion, I can't even form words. How could this man possibly doubt his worth? How could anyone not appreciate how completely he loves?

"So, what do you say, Freckles? Are you sick of me yet?" he jokes but there's insecurity in his eyes.

I lean forward, lifting my hands to pull his face closer until we're almost touching. "Matt, I am so completely in love with you."

I hardly finish my sentence before he's scooping me into his arms and sealing his lips to mine. He kisses me with such fervor that I struggle to keep up. I pour myself into the kiss, hoping to prove to him how real my love for him is.

Eventually he pulls away, savoring the moment with small pecks at my lips before leaning his forehead against mine. His eyes are still closed and he sighs deeply. "Thank you."

I cup his face in my hands. "Don't thank me. Loving you is the easiest thing I've ever done. Loving you is like coming home. It's like a sigh of relief. It's safe. It's inevitable." I give his lips a soft peck. "We're inevitable."

He kisses me again, this time slow and full of passion. After a few minutes, I break the kiss, pulling back just far enough that our breath is still entwined.

"I'm not leaving. At least not without a fight," I whisper against his lips. "This is where we belong."

CHAPTER 34

MATT

"You've really outdone yourself this time, Shae. These are beautiful," I tell her as she gives the colorful bouquet a spin for my approval. Today's the big grand opening of the cafe. Avery's been in knots about it all week, so I figured some flowers might help ease some of her nerves and make her smile.

There's no prettier sight than my girl's smile.

They had a soft opening last week and, from my end, everything went great. She told me there had been a few hiccups behind the scenes but I assured her no one noticed. Even so, she's been working her ass off trying to get everything ready for today. I've tried to be supportive and help where I can, but she's determined to do most of it herself. Avery likes to be in control.

Except when she's under me, that is.

I slip Shae some cash and head out the door towards The Book Nook. Even from down the street, I can see there's a small line spilling out the door. I grin. I'm so damn proud of her.

I can't believe how much lighter I feel after the other night. Every time I think about it, I grin like an idiot.

When I planned our date, I didn't intend on showing Avery my work but when I saw the way she reacted to my table, the urge to show her the rest of my designs was too powerful to ignore. I'm not even sure I had fully thought through how much it meant to show her this side of me until we were standing in front of my workbench. It hit me then how I wanted no secrets between us. To be completely and fully myself with her.

If I were to come up with a list of every possible outcome from that night, not even in my wildest dreams would I have imagined it going so perfectly. As if her reaction to my work wasn't enough, the way she shut down my insecurities without being condescending or belittling me meant more than she'll ever know.

I meant every word I said. If she had decided to go back to Edmonton, I would have packed up everything I owned and followed her there in a heartbeat. As much as I hate the city and everything that goes with it, I would've gone with her because now that I have her, I can't imagine not having her by my side.

She's everything.

I cross the street and wave to a few locals in line in front of the cafe's entrance before ducking in through the bookshop's door. Angie had worried that putting two entrances would deter customers from crossing over into the bookshop side and vice versa, but I'm glad she agreed in the end to separate them.

The large opening we created between the two sides allows customers to travel between both shops easily while keeping them separate enough that one doesn't interfere with the other.

Today, both the bookshop and the cafe are packed with customers—locals and tourists alike. I weave my way through the shop, nodding hello to a few people while keeping my eyes peeled for a certain honey-haired woman.

Avery, Angie and Tammy did an amazing job with the cafe. The white walls make the space feel open and bright while the large bay window along the front lets in plenty of natural light. Along the far side are a handful of cozy bistro-style tables with pictures of the bay hanging on the walls. It's perfectly decorated to be welcoming and cheerful.

I finally spot her, scurrying behind the cafe counter. She's boxing an order of what looks like Angie's famous maple cinnamon buns, unaware of my presence.

I love watching her. Whether she's in the bookshop working, playing with Gavin, or kicking my ass in Skee-Ball, I can't keep my eyes off her. She has a way of capturing my attention so that no one else in the room exists.

She looks up and spots me. She beams and it's like a crossbow to the heart. *Man, I love this woman.* God knows what I did to deserve her love, but I'm going to try like hell every day to be worthy of it.

She whispers something to the employee beside her and then rounds the display case toward me. It takes a few minutes as she's stopped multiple times by customers congratulating her. When she finally reaches me, she throws her arms around my neck and squeezes tightly. I smile into her hair, returning the hug before pulling her back enough to plant a quick kiss on her lips.

"Oh my god, Matt. It's been this crazy since before we opened! I got here this morning and we already had a line up out front." Her grin is infectious and she's almost vibrating with excitement. "I know it won't be like this every day, but this is better than we hoped for." She notices the flowers in my hands and, if it's possible, her smile brightens even more. "Are those for me?"

I'll never tire of seeing the look of genuine surprise when I bring her flowers. I vow right there to bring her flowers as often as possible.

I pass her the bouquet, loving the way she marvels at each flower. "Of course. They were for good luck, but I don't think you need it. I guess I'll be taking those back..." I pretend to reach for the arrangement but she swats my hand away.

"No way. These are mine now." She reaches up and kisses me quickly. "Thank you so much. But I have to get back. I don't want any of the staff quitting on their first day."

She turns to go, then stops suddenly. "Oh, I meant to tell you. We've had so many comments on our display case. People have been raving about it all morning. It got me thinking that we should feature some local artists' work in the shop. So then I started thinking about the Dog Days of Summer Festival." She drops her voice to a whisper before continuing. "I think you should put in a booth for your designs. Even if it's only a few pieces, I think it would be a laidback way of debuting your work. Everyone already knows that you create the custom pieces for Bud, so it wouldn't be a total shock."

I hesitate and she quickly backtracks. "It was just an idea. There's no pressure. I thought you might want to show off your work. But if you're not ready for that, I completely understand." She shrugs, suddenly tense. "It was just a thought."

"I'll think about it," I tell her. My head is buzzing but I give her a tight smile and a reassuring squeeze of her hand. "You should really get back. Poor Jackson looks like he's ready to beat that steamer with a bat."

Turning to where Jackson Wells is smacking the side of the machine, Avery's eyes widen and she rushes over to help the teenager before he breaks something.

My head is still whirling as I leave the cafe. I stuff my hands into my jean pockets as I wander down the sidewalk toward my workshop. My initial reaction to her suggestion was a big, fat *hell, no.* I've spent so long hiding this part of me that the idea of putting myself on display like that makes me want to shove my head in a wood-chipper.

I know Avery meant well when she suggested setting up a booth in the festival. I'm sure she has an idea but she doesn't fully understand how hard it was for me to open up to her that way and show her my designs. Sure, I feel lighter and happier having shown them to her. But who's to say I'll feel the same after showing everyone I know?

It's a lot of pressure. Too much pressure.

Before I know what I'm doing, I've passed my workshop and am crossing the street to The Dive. It's too early for it to be open yet, but Rhett's usually in the bar this time of day, checking inventory, booking gigs and whatever else bar owners do. I pull open the door, my eyes taking a second to adjust to the dim lighting. Even with the windows open and the lights on, the bar still seems dark and secluded.

Rhett plans to open the space up by taking down the wall that faces the beach and installing a clear rolling garage door to open onto the patio. That way he can open it up in the summer, giving more space for outdoor entertainment and seating and still have a great view of the bay during the winter.

I'll offer to help him when the time comes. Taylor Construction might be out of his budget, but between Rhett, Luke and I, I'm sure we could get it done ourselves.

"What're you doing here? Isn't today the opening at the cafe?" Rhett calls from somewhere behind the bar. All I can see is the top of his dark blonde head. He's crouched down, screwing around with something under the well so I take a seat on one of the stools above him.

"It is. I just came from there. The place is packed." I can't help the pride in my voice.

Rhett hauls himself to his feet, drying his hands on a rag

he nabs from the counter. "You sound like a proud boyfriend."

He pulls a beer bottle from the fridge below him and tips it toward me in question. I shrug as if to say *why not?* and he places it on a coaster in front of me. He grabs himself a water bottle and we each take a swig.

Rhett's never been much of a drinker. He mostly sticks to Cokes but will have a beer with us every once in a while. I've asked him about it a couple of times but he shrugged me off, never giving a real reason why. After the second time, I never asked again. If he wanted to tell me, he would.

The thing about Rhett is that he's real tight-lipped about his personal life. We've been best friends for over a dozen years and I still only know the bare minimum about his life before he moved to Haven Bay.

Who am I to judge? I'm the last person to criticize someone for wanting to keep part of their lives a secret.

"I am proud. Avery worked her ass off to get the cafe ready and she deserves for it to be a success. She's killing it; first with the bookshop and now the cafe. I'd be crazy not to be cheering her on." The image of her this morning, happy and completely in her element comes to mind. Then another of her in the bookshop, chatting animatedly with a customer about one of the new books that came in. "She's meant for this, man. Every goal, she knocks it out of the park and I'm the lucky bastard that gets the front row seat to her success."

Rhett leans on his forearms over the bar, looking up at me thoughtfully. "It's a good feeling watching the person you care about making their dreams come true," he says in that low, musing tone of his. I used to jokingly call him Dr. Phil in high school whenever he'd use that tone on me.

Then it hits me. Is that how Avery feels about my designs?

Watching Avery work so hard and coming up with new creative ideas to build the business has been inspiring. Soon, it will be hers and I know she has no shortage of ideas for improving the shop. I can't wait to watch her accomplish all of her goals.

Was her suggestion to participate in the festival her way of supporting me to do the same?

The idea putting myself on display for the whole town to analyze and critique scares the shit out of me. But I have to admit, the weight of this secret is starting to exhaust me. Even before Avery's return, it seemed like I was two different people trying to share the same body.

When I think about how much lighter and hopeful I felt after sharing it with Avery, the idea of coming clean with everyone else doesn't seem quite as much like a nail gun to the forehead as it once did.

"You good?" Rhett asks, snapping me out of my thoughts. He doesn't look especially put out by me zoning out on him. He seems more amused than anything. Usually, I'd make a jab back at him but I'm too busy thinking about the festival.

Could I really do it? Am I ready? I'm not sure if I am but, for once, I want to be.

Hoping to distract myself, I sit back and shoot the shit with Rhett for a while before heading back to my apartment. But instead of going back upstairs after letting Ham out to pee, I find myself in the workshop.

I look over at my workbench, my designs scattered along the surface. "What'd you think, Ham? Should I go for it?" I give his head a scratch and he leans into my leg, reveling in the ear rubs I'm absent-mindedly giving him. I stare at the wood pieces for a few more minutes before finally looking down at Ham.

Well, to paraphrase one of the best lines in my favorite cowboy TV show...

"Alright. Fuck it."

I can't help but think I overstepped with Matt the other day. We haven't talked about the festival since then, partly because I'm too chicken to bring it up again.

Should I apologize? Should I try to explain my reasoning? I understand it was really hard for him to show me his work and I don't want him to think I'm pressuring him into something he doesn't want to do.

All I want is for him to be happy and honest with both himself and the people who care about him most. I can tell that keeping this secret is hurting him. He deserves to know how talented he is. He deserves to know that he is loved for every part of who he is and to know that nothing would ever change that.

"Mom, is it still raining out?" Gavin whines from his bedroom. He's been running back and forth from the living room window to his bedroom window, in case the weather has changed from the front yard to the back.

It's the first mutual day off Matt and I have had in almost a week. When Gavin mentioned to Matt that he's never been to Water World, Matt declared that we would have to go on our next day off as, and I quote, "every kid has to experience the wedgie-inducing slides and pee-filled pools of Water World before they hit puberty." Since then, Gavin's been counting down the days until we could go.

But as luck would have it, the day is finally here and it's been raining since before dawn.

My mom and Franny left a few hours ago for their annual girls' weekend in the city with a few of their friends. When she left, she gave Gavin a big hug while he chatted on and on about the water park. Not wanting to crush his excitement, she wished him a fun time and then whispered a sympathetic "good luck" in my ear.

I hoped the rain would slow and we could still go. Unfortunately, instead of slowing, there's now a low rumble of thunder creeping in as the rain pours harder.

Gavin comes skidding to a stop before me. "Mom, did you hear me? Is it still raining?" His face is hopeful and I'm trying to build up the courage to let him down easy when there's a knock at the door.

Gavin rushes to the door with Sushi yipping behind him. He opens the door and Matt and Ham come rushing in from the rain outside. I pass Matt a couple of towels from the bathroom and he dries Ham off with one then himself with the other.

"Hammy! Hi, buddy!" Gavin throws his arms around Ham's neck, kissing his face. "Is Ham coming to the water park, too? Are dogs allowed at Water World?"

Matt looks up at me guiltily from under the towel. He obviously was under the impression that I'd already broken the news about our canceled trip.

I wince then turn to Gavin, bending down so I'm eye level with him. "Gav, we're not going to be able to go to Water World today. It's starting to storm and it's not safe. We'll go another day, okay?"

He looks up at Matt and then back at me. His mouth

twists and tears well up in his eyes. "No, Mom! You said we were going today! We *have* to go! You promised!" His little voice cracks with emotion and my mama heart breaks for him.

I hate to disappoint him, even if it's something I have no control over.

"Gav, buddy, I'm sorry." I reach out to tuck his little body to my chest. "We can go another day—"

"No, Mommy! I want to go TODAY!" The last word comes out as a shriek as he pushes away from me.

Gavin's a good kid, but even good kids aren't immune to tantrums. Which is why when Gavin throws himself to the floor, I'm not completely shocked by the turn of events. He crosses his arms on the floor in front of him, drops his head to his forearms and wails into the floor.

"It's not fair!" he yells, his voice hoarse against the tears that are now rolling freely down his face.

I avoid looking at Matt and lay down beside Gavin on the floor, rubbing his back and talking to him in a calm, subdued voice.

Tantrums are never fun—not for the kids throwing them or for the parents enduring them. But when little people have big emotions, there's only so much room in their bodies to hold them in. When the emotions get to be too much, they explode out in the form of crying, screaming, and body-throwing.

"Why don't we get up and you can go show Ham—" I start to reach for him again but Gavin shoves my hand aside. He lifts his head and tears are pouring down his cheeks now.

"I WANT to go to Water World!" he yells in my face, swinging his arm out to smack me on the arm.

Tantrums are hard and natural, but so are the punishments that follow when they get out of hand.

"Gavin Owen Olsen! I don't care how disappointed you are, you do not hit people. If you can't act nicely, you need to go lay on your bed and take a breather until you can. Now, march, mister." I pull him into a sitting position and point to his bedroom.

The crying and grumbling I expect but the feet stomping and door slamming that follow are totally out of character for him.

I jump to my feet to reprimand him when Matt places a hand on my arm to stop me. I look up as he pulls me to him and wraps me into a tight hug. With one hand, he runs his fingers through my hair, trying to calm me down. I heave a deep sigh, breathing all my frustration out with it and into his chest.

"Bet you didn't expect that when you decided to come over," I try to joke but it falls flat. His fingertips tickle my scalp as he trails them through my hair again.

"Avery, I meant it when I said I love you and Gavin. And you don't only love someone when they're happy and fun. You love them through the hard stuff, the ugly stuff and every-thing in between." His hand pauses at the top of my back. He pulls me back far enough to look at me. "Do you mind if I go talk to him?" he asks and I hesitate. "I know that might sound weird, but I think this warrants a man-to-man talk."

I look up at him but his face is carefully neutral. Well, if he's serious about this, he might as well get used to the "ugly stuff", as he accurately called it.

"Okay. But I'll be outside his room in case you need help. I try not to be too hard on him but he also can't get away with acting like that," I tell him as we walk to Gavin's door.

He nods. "I'll try it my way first and if I miss anything, feel free to jump in and help me." He pauses at the door for my permission and I nod, still a little unsure.

Probably because I've never had to share the disciplining part of parenting before. Mitch's version of discipline was either way too lenient or way too tough. When I tried to explain my parenting style, hoping we could try to meet in the middle, he'd get defensive and stalk off. Eventually, he told me that if I was such a perfect parent, I could do it myself.

Gavin was two years old at the time. I've been doing the majority of the parenting by myself ever since.

It's been hard and it's times like these when I forget that a lot of parents are able to tag out with their partners when they're feeling frustrated or at their wit's end.

To have Matt want to step in and help seems...strange. I'm trying not to be a helicopter mom and see where this goes, but I'm also ready to jump in if things take a turn.

I never know what's going to come out of Gavin's mouth on a good day. Add in the heightened emotions of disappointment and...well. Let's say I'm prepared in case things go south.

I watch Matt softly knock on Gavin's bedroom door then peek his head inside. "Hey, buddy. Is it okay if Ham and I come in for a minute?"

There's a pause and then an unintelligible mumble that Matt takes as agreement. He slips inside the room with Ham behind him but he leaves the door slightly ajar for me to listen in.

I take a couple of steps closer but keep hidden from Gavin's view. The old bed squeaks as Matt lowers himself onto the edge. I can barely make out Gavin's small body lying face down on his Spider-Man pillow.

"I'm sorry we couldn't go to Water World today, kiddo. It sucks, doesn't it?" His voice is low and soothing.

Gavin lifts his head from his pillow. "It sucks BIG time," he declares. His tear-stained face is still pink from crying but he seems to have somewhat calmed down.

The sight makes my chest ache and I slide my back down the wall to lower myself to the floor. Sometimes being the default parent sucks. There's nothing I'd love more than being the fun parent, but when you're a single mom, you don't get that luxury.

"Yeah, I'm disappointed, too. I really wanted to take you and your mom down the water slides. Your mom and I used to race down the slides all the time when we were kids." He drops his voice to a conspiring whisper. "I used to let your mom win so she wouldn't get mad when I kicked her butt."

Gavin's snicker covers up the snort that escapes my throat.

Let me win, my ass. I can count on one hand the number of times Matt beat me down those slides and the look on his face when we reached the bottom was not one of a gracious loser. He used to grumble about my size causing an unfair advantage. It wasn't my fault he was built like a house.

"But you know what sucks more than not being able to go to Water World? How you treated your mom out there," Matt says gently. He's not being accusing or condescending—merely stating a fact. Gavin goes quiet. "I know it's hard sometimes when you get mad or sad and it feels like there's this big monster inside you that wants to be let out."

"Kind of like the Hulk?" Gavin whispers.

I can hear the smile in Matt's voice when he answers. "Yeah, exactly like the Hulk." He grows serious again. "Having those big feelings is okay but it's not okay to take them out on someone else—whether it's your mom, your friends or a pet." He pauses as if lost in thought and I wonder what caused the change until I hear him clear his throat. "'You can be mad but you can't be mean.' That's what my dad always used to tell my siblings and me when we would fight."

I can feel the lump of emotion grow in my throat at the mention of Matt's dad. I remember him saying that exact line over and over again. Matt reminds me a lot of his dad—especially when he's with Gavin. Matt's dad had an endless amount of patience and was never condescending. Even as a young kid, he always talked to us like adults. I thought it was so cool and it made me feel like a grown up.

Exactly like how Matt's talking to Gavin now.

I hold my breath and peer around the doorframe. Gavin seems to be thinking it over while bending over to scratch Ham's head, who's sitting patiently at the side of the bed. I wonder how receptive he'll be to Matt's advice—which I have to admit was pretty damn close to perfect.

"Does that make sense?" Matt asks. Gavin's nuzzling Ham's neck but he looks up at Matt and nods.

"Good. Should we shake hands and head back out to find your mom?" Gavin nods again and sticks his hand out to shake Matt's hand.

I turn my head away from the door and lean back against the wall, letting out a quiet sigh of relief. I'm about to pull myself up when I hear a gasp. I shoot to my feet and am about to go inside when I hear Matt's exaggeratedly appalled tone.

"You call that a handshake? That's not a handshake! Where's the finger guns? Where's the explosions and the knuckles? Oh, kid, we've gotta fix that."

I barely swallow the laugh. Typical Matt.

I leave them to create their elaborate handshake and wander into the kitchen. Now that we'll be staying in, I decide to make Gavin's favorite lunch to cheer him up. Fifteen minutes later, I'm mixing the hot dog chunks into the macaroni and cheese when Gavin comes running from his room with Ham and Sushi chasing after him. He skids to a stop at the kitchen island, bouncing on the balls of his feet.

"Mom! Wait till you see the handshake Matt and I made up!"

He turns at the cough from behind him. Matt gives him a pointed look and Gavin turns back to face me, expression contrite.

"Sorry I was mean to you, Mommy," he says sincerely. He

rounds the island and gives my waist a tight hug and my heart warms.

I put the bowls down and bend to hug him back. "Thanks, Gav. I love you, kiddo."

"Love you, too, Mommy!" He turns and shoots Matt a thumbs up before taking off to run around the living room while the dogs chase after him.

I look over at Matt. He's grinning at the chaos in the living room, then turns to meet my stare. Then, as if I'm not already trying to hold back from , he shoots me a wink. My insides are fighting between melting and bursting into a flame of lust.

Yeah, he's definitely getting laid tonight.

I cross the kitchen to wrap my arms around his waist. He slips one arm over my shoulders and tucks me into his chest. "Thank you," I tell him, hoping I don't look as much like the lovesick teenager as I feel.

"You raised a good kid, Freckles. He's a lot like you."

I smirk up at him. "Good-looking and hilarious?"

"Smartass." He pinches my arm and I laugh. "I meant that he feels things intensely. He's sweet and passionate, which can sometimes get him into trouble; like someone else I know." I pinch him back and he grins. "You did a great job raising him. You should be proud."

I can feel the tears welling in my eyes. Damn him and his sweet words always making me cry. "Thank you."

As a mom, there's nothing better than hearing someone tell you that you're doing a good job. Especially on a day when you feel like you're doing the opposite.

I bite my lip hesitantly. I don't want to ruin the mood but...

"I'm sorry for what I said the other day."

He looks at me quizzically.

"About the festival. I shouldn't have said anything. It

wasn't my place and I completely understand if you want to keep your designs to yourself."

He cuts me off by squeezing me harder and shaking his head.

"Don't be sorry. You were right. I thought about it a lot over the last couple of days and I realized that you're right. I can't keep hiding from everyone. It's exhausting."

I'm a little surprised by his admission. Not by its validity but that he's willing to admit it.

"So even though I'd rather give Dottie a bikini wax than put myself on display like that, I think it's time. No use dipping my toes in; might as well cannonball right in."

I reach up and give him a kiss that lingers. "I'm proud of you," I say against his lips. Eventually, I pull back and turn to grab the bowls of macaroni and cheese. I start to walk away then jump at the sudden slap of Matt's palm against my ass. This time I'm the one to toss a wink at him over my shoulder. Then, because I'm feeling flirty, I put a little extra swing in my hips as I walk into the kitchen. Matt lets out a low whistle and I laugh.

This type of light and simple fun felt so foreign before we started going out but it's easily turning into my new normal. The ironic thing is that during the most stressful time of my life, I've felt the most relaxed and carefree.

I mean, don't get me wrong. I'm nervous to see what Mitch will do next and what our future will look like as a result, but there's a calm that was never there lying idly in the background. It's like even though there's the ever-present stress and anxiety from the divorce, I know there's always this feeling of calm for me to fall back on at the end of the day. It's a sharp contrast from my life in the city, where I was in a constant state of tension, bracing myself for the next inevitable fight. Here, I've finally let myself relax.

I bring the bowls over to the kitchen table while Matt

grabs utensils from one of the drawers. "Sexy *and* she cooks mac and cheese with hotdogs? Damn. If I wasn't already in love with you, that would definitely clinch it." He says it so nonchalantly but my heart still flips at his declaration.

I'm starting to believe that this could actually be something great and that the other shoe I've been waiting to drop might never fall.

To keep myself from diving too deeply into that thought, I call out to Gavin.

He bounces back into the room and plops into his chair, his earlier heartbreak forgotten. "Hey, Matt. Who do you think would win in a fight—Spider-Man or Robin?"

"Well, that depends. Does Robin have any of Batman's gadgets?"

That launches them into a debate on the dexterity of Spider-Man versus the tenacity of Robin and I can't help but think how normal and right this all feels. It doesn't even scare me to think how badly I want all of my days to look like this.

I point my fork between the two of them. "Okay, but the real question is who could do more backflips?"

***

AFTER DINNER, Matt shoos me out of the kitchen, telling Gavin that the person who cooks doesn't clean up. I almost forgot about Franny's most stringent kitchen rule. So I take a glass of wine and my current mystery novel out onto the porch to relax while the boys clean.

After a while, I wander back inside to a spotless kitchen and a chaotic living room. The coffee table has been pushed aside to make room for couch cushions and chairs that are placed strategically in a horseshoe shape. Matt's draping a blanket over the chairs while Gavin's legs poke out from inside the tent-like structure.

"What's going on in here?" I ask, slowly surveying the scene before me. Gavin pops his head out from inside the tent and grins up at me.

"Matt said that the best way to watch a movie is from inside a fort. So we're buildin' a fort!" he exclaims.

A small yip sounds from inside the makeshift fort and I don't have to guess to know where Sushi and Ham are.

Matt finishes securing a blanket and then gestures his arms dramatically at the fort. "Welcome to Fort Olsady!"

I give him a confused look. "Fort Old Lady?"

Gavin bursts into laughter while Matt grins at me. "No, Fort Ols-ady," he says again enunciating each syllable, as if that explains the ridiculous name.

"It's a mix of our names, Mommy! Olsen and Brady!" Gavin proudly explains, pointing at himself and then Matt.

Understanding dawns on me. "Ah. Very clever, Mr. Smarty Pants." I bend down to ruffle his hair. "Looks pretty cozy in here," I tell him inspecting the inside of the fort.

Surprisingly, it does. They've draped the blankets across the chairs so that it opens in the front like a tent. The couch cushions are laid out across the floor inside with blankets and pillows covering them.

"And for the grand finale..." Matt claps his hands against his thighs to the beat of a drumroll. He reaches out to plug something into the outlet behind him and it's then that I notice the Christmas lights that are wrapped around the legs of the chairs and across the entrance of the fort. He flicks the switch of the overhead light until the only light in the room is the twinkling red and green from around the fort.

"I hope you don't mind. I texted your mom and she told me where to find a few things in the basement. She didn't have string lights, so I figured the Christmas lights would have to do." He smiles sheepishly at me.

Jesus, Mary and Joseph.

My heart squeezes. I cross the room and wrap my arms around him. For the second time tonight, I can't help but think how natural and right this all feels.

It feels like home.

Gavin cheers then dives inside the fort onto the cushions. "Mommy! Come inside!" he calls.

Matt kisses my hair and then gives me a little push toward the fort. "You go get settled." He dips his head to call into the fort. "You pick a movie with your mom and I'll be right back with some popcorn."

Gavin pumps a fist and cheers again.

I climb in beside him and we get to work picking out a movie which ends up being (surprise, surprise) Spider-Man.

A few minutes later, Matt climbs in on the other side of Gavin with a bowl of steaming popcorn. I press play on the remote and we lay back on the cushions, digging into the bowl.

An hour or so later, Gavin's barely keeping his eyes open. Ham and Sushi abandoned us long ago to cuddle on the only chair with cushions left on it so it's only the three of us in the fort. I'm laying on my side, arm draped over Gavin's belly. Matt's lying on his back with his forearm propped under his head. Gavin rolls over, his back curling into me. His voice is barely a whisper as his eyes fall closed.

"This was the best day ever."

Then to both of our surprise, he reaches out and wraps his little hand in Matt's. Matt's eyes shoot up to mine. His expression is a mix of shock and awe before it gives way to one of contentment. He smiles then mouths a silent "I love you" to me from over Gavin's sleeping head.

It's the last thing I see before sleep pulls me under, my heart so full it could burst.

CHAPTER 36

MATT

What the hell was I thinking?

It's the first day of the Dog Days of Summer festival and I'm set up with twenty or so other participants in the festival's market. My "booth" turned out to be a plastic folding table that I've lined a dozen or so of my designs on.

I've already sweat through one shirt and I'm halfway through my second. It has nothing to do with the summer heat and everything to do with my nerves. If I thought showing Avery my designs for the first time was nerve-wracking, showing it to the entire town feels like the equivalent of getting a needle jabbed in my eye.

I debated backing out countless times over the past few days. When I mentioned it to Avery, she told me that she wouldn't think any less of me if I decided not to. She told me that everyone gets scared and she understood if it was too much for me. Which sounds like she was being a supportive girlfriend but the side-eye and a smirk told me she was throwing down a challenge. The same way she did when we were kids.

Of course, that meant I had to go through with it. Matt

Brady doesn't back down from a dare. Which, now that I think about it, might've been her intention all along.

She's working at the store today. The festival is one of the shop's most lucrative days of the year, so she had to be there. She was upset that she wouldn't be able to be here with me, but I assured her I would be fine. Honestly, I think I need to do this on my own in case it gets to be too much and I end up bailing. She was hesitant but after I reminded her the shop needed her, she settled by agreeing to meet up after she closed the store and picked up Gavin. That way the three of us could check out the festival together.

Choosing which designs to showcase was just as nerve-wracking. After overanalyzing each piece, I eventually picked a dozen at random and called it a day. I doubted anyone would buy one, let alone twelve anyway.

I was wrong.

It's been three hours and I've sold eight pieces—some to locals but a lot to tourists, too. I'm hoping that means people are buying them because they like them and not just for the novelty of owning a "Matt Brady original" as I overheard my tenth-grade math teacher call them.

Overall, the feedback has been surprisingly positive. For the first half, it was mostly the nosey old buggers of this town who stopped by. I think that was more about fueling the gossip mill than genuine interest. But after a while, the curious onlookers turned into customers. Dottie and Maeve came by and offered to stand in as models for me, only on the condition that they could be nude. "Whittle me like one of your French girls, Matty" were Dottie's exact words.

That comment left me speechless for a solid five minutes. She ended up patting my cheek, telling me to "think it over" while I stood ramrod-still in shock as they walked away. You'd think that after almost thirty years in this town, nothing they'd say could shock me but you'd be wrong.

I finally pull myself together when a woman approaches my booth. It's Krista Jackson, the girl I spilled root beer all over on our first (and only) date when we were fourteen. She's married with a couple of kids now. She still lives in town and is the curator for Bayside Art Gallery.

"Hey, Matt." She smiles and gives me a friendly hug. "I heard through the grapevine that you were selling artwork in the market but I had to see it for myself before I believed it."

"Sure am. Though I'm starting to question my sanity. If I wanted half the town to gawk at me, I could probably have thought of a less painful way—like a pillory."

She laughs and then continues to analyze the remaining designs. At this point, there's only a few left and I'm starting to squirm by the time she turns back to me.

"How long have you been carving?" she asks, her face unreadable.

I figure she probably hates them and is trying to let me down easily with a bit of small talk before telling me some futile advice like to *stick with it!*

"My dad taught me back in high school. I stopped after graduation but picked it back up a few years ago." I wait for the inevitable idle back and forth before she moves on.

Instead, she surprises me by nodding attentively. "Who are you represented by?"

I try not to laugh at the question. "No one. This is my first time selling anything I've made—not including my work for Bud, of course."

Her brows shoot up in surprise. "Why? You're extremely talented, Matt. And I'm not saying that as a friend." She runs her fingers over my design of a wolf, head raised howling into the night. "You can tell that you take extra care in every detail of your designs. The smooth curves, the intricate patterns. You should be selling these or at least displaying them. People pay big money for original pieces like these."

She searches through her purse and pulls out a card, handing it to me. "This is my number at the gallery. Call me and we can set up a time to talk more next week. You've done all the hard work; now let me show it to the world."

With that, she waves and moves onto the next booth but my head is still reeling from her proposition. My designs in a gallery? Being sold to actual art collectors? It's a dream I didn't even know I had until it's now dangling before me like a carrot to a horse.

I know Krista. She wouldn't tell me she believed in my work if she didn't. A smile breaks free and my body is suddenly vibrating with excitement. I absently rub between Ham's ears for something to do with my hands.

I wish Avery was here. She'll be as excited as I am, if not more so. I can picture her throwing herself at me at the news. In fact, I can't wait another hour to see her. I need to feel her in my arms, to tell her everything. Only then will it feel real.

I'm starting to pack up when my mom and Pete come walking over. She stops mid-stride and narrows her eyes at me. Then she stomps over to where I'm standing, hands on her hips.

"Matthew Anthony Brady! Tell me why I have to find out from Tracey Wheeler that you have a booth in the festival for artwork that I knew nothing about." She glares up at me, all five-foot-nothing of her and I swear my balls shrink up inside me.

Nothing compares to an Italian mother's chastising.

I fidget with the cloth on the table while Ham shrinks behind my legs. *Coward.*

"Ah, Ma. I was going to call you this morning but I—" *Chickened out? Came to my senses? Wanted to avoid this very lecture for as long as possible?* "I got busy getting ready and didn't get a chance."

Is lying to your mother a guaranteed ticket to Hell or do you get a pass if she's as scary as Francesca Brady?

"You and I will have words later, mister. Now show me your work."

Feeling thoroughly scolded, I pick up one of the closest pieces and hand it to her.

It's a snow owl, only about six inches tall. It's smaller than the others and was one of my more recent pieces. I was inspired after a trip to Luke's buddy's cabin in the mountains last winter.

Ham and I had been out hiking when a snow owl landed barely fifteen feet away from us. He looked so regal, his amber eyes piercing right through me. He sat there for a while before a noise spooked him but watching him soar away was almost as captivating as watching him up close. As soon as I got back to the cabin, I started sketching. By the end of the weekend, I was itching to get home and start carving him out.

He's easily one of my favorite designs. I don't usually brag but I spent nearly a whole day just on his eyes, trying to capture the same regal stare. But it was worth it.

By the sharp gasp from my mom, I can tell she agrees.

"Matt, this is... stunning doesn't even do it justice. It's breathtaking." She finally tears her gaze away from the owl and looks up at me wide-eyed. "How long have you been doing this? Why didn't you tell me? What other secret talents have you been hiding from me? Are you Banksy?"

I laugh at her rapid-fire questions that are very in character for her. "Dad taught me. I stopped when he got sick. It was too hard doing it without him," I tell her and her face softens.

She takes my hand and squeezes in understanding.

"A few years ago, I did a custom job for Bud and decided to play with the design a bit. The customer seemed to really like it so I tried a bit on my own. Once I started, I couldn't seem to stop." I shrug. "As for why I didn't tell you, I don't know what to say, Ma." I shrug again, at a loss for words.

"I knew you liked to draw but I had no idea it was more than that. I remember you and your dad fiddling around in the shop for hours when you were a kid." She looks back down at the owl. "This seems so... unexpected."

I flinch at her words and, for once, she notices. Her brow furrows and she turns to Pete. "Hon, do you mind going to grab me some of May's fudge? I know she always has a line so one of us should probably go over now or we'll be waiting all day."

One of the best things about Pete is how easy-going he is. He's either used to my mom's odd requests or realizes she's trying to get rid of him. Either way, he nods and kisses her cheek. He reaches out to shake my hand, mumbles "good work" then ambles over to May Polton's booth.

My mom turns back to me and gestures to the picnic table that is a few feet away from my table. Together, we walk over to the semi-private area of the park and sit down.

"Now tell me the real reason why you never told me about your art."

Well, I guess it's now or never.

Taking a shaky breath to gather my courage, I stumble my way through the same explanation I told Avery last week. By the time I finish, my mom's eyes are watery but she doesn't let them spill over when she leans over to hug me. Instead, she takes a deep breath and tells me what I've always suspected but never thought I would hear confirmed by my head-strong mother.

"Matt, when your dad passed away, I was devastated." The corner of her mouth turns up satirically. "What an odd thing to say. Of course I was devastated; my husband had just passed. But it was more than that. I loved your dad so much. He and you kids were my whole world. My mother used to joke that no man could've handled my mood swings quite as well as Jack Brady." She smiles and I can tell she's lost in a memory.

Remembering is always bittersweet, so it's hard for me to watch my mom feel the emotions that I know all too well.

She continues. "When he got sick, I was probably a little naive. The doctors told us that the type of cancer he had was aggressive and had a high rate of recurrence. Even then, I figured we would be in the small percentage that would beat it. I didn't give myself any other option. He would beat this. *We* would beat it." Her voice breaks.

I cover her hand with mine and she smiles gratefully.

She takes a shaky breath before carrying on. "When it was clear he wasn't going to get better, it didn't seem real that it was the end. So when he passed, even though it was a couple of years in the making, I was in shock. The days went by, the funeral came and went and I was merely going through the motions. Then it hit me—he was really gone. A part of me is still ashamed to say that sometimes, late at night when I was alone in our bed, I wished he had taken me with him."

Her words hit me like a runaway train. Even though I had always suspected it, it's a shock to hear how close I had been to losing my mom, too.

"That's when I realized I needed help. I went to the doctor and he started me on antidepressants. I started seeing a therapist once a week and slowly the fog started to lift. Those two things together are what brought me back." She holds my gaze, her expression the most serious I've seen her in a long time. "Believe me when I tell you this: nothing you did or didn't do could have changed that."

Her words wash over me like a tidal wave of emotion. My mind is reeling from our conversation and I need time to process it all.

But most of all, I'm so damn relieved.

Relieved that my mom was able to recognize she needed

help. That she fought so hard to come back to us. That the pressure I put on myself for over a decade has finally been lifted from my shoulders. That all of my secrets are out in the open to the person whose acceptance I crave most.

Whose acceptance I should've never doubted.

We stand and I pull her small frame to me in a tight hug that, if it was anyone else, I might be scared of hurting her, but she holds on just as tightly. This talk has been long overdue and ended up being cathartic for both of us.

"Love you, Ma."

"I love you, too, baby."

My mom runs a finger under each eye to catch the tears that have spilled over. "Well, today was a bit more emotional than I expected. But I think we both needed that." She hugs my arm to her as we walk back to my table. "I'm so proud of you." She kisses my cheeks. "Now I'm going to find my man and get me some fudge. Come by this week and we'll have some cookies and you can tell me more about your art."

With that, she takes off toward the opposite end of the park.

Huh. It's been an...interesting day, that's for sure. Now I definitely can't wait to see Avery later.

My phone buzzes and I pull it from my pocket.

LUKE

Why the hell is Dottie in the diner telling anyone who will listen about your "beautiful wood"?

RHETT

Jesus, Matt. Say it ain't so.

MATT

Are you saying I don't have beautiful wood, Lukey?

LUKE

....

MATT

I'll have you know my wood is goddamn gorgeous. The prettiest wood you'll ever see.

My wood is deeply offended. You better apologize to it right now.

LUKE

....yeah, as a police officer, I'm gonna need you to confirm you're not showing your dick to old ladies now.

MATT

What kind of guy do you think I am?

RHETT

A sick one.

LUKE

You still haven't denied it.

Matt?

Goddamn it. I hate you.

I can't stop thinking about how Matt's doing today. I've texted him a couple of times but we've been so swamped at the shop that I haven't had time to check my phone.

Shortly after we opened, a bus filled with tourists came in and the crowds of customers haven't stopped since. Tammy and I have been running around non-stop. Thankfully, my mom dropped in with Gavin before they went out to the festival, so she jumped on the register while Gavin helped her bag purchases.

But four-year-olds have short attention spans so before long, he decided he had enough and was ready to go. Luckily, Jolie came in and volunteered to take him around the festival.

Since the crowds have started to slow, I decide to let Tammy go, promising to text her if another crowd comes in. I eventually shoo my mom away after she mentions wanting to check out a craft booth before the dog parade.

Finally alone, I check my phone. There's a response that came from Matt half an hour ago.

MATT

Going pretty good. Sold eight pieces so far and got an interesting proposition from Dottie (you can probably guess what about) lol. Hopefully done soon.

AVERY

Yay! *celebrating emoji* That's awesome! I'm so happy for you! *dancing emoji*

But now I'm trying to guess what Dottie said.

Please tell me she made a dirty woodpecker joke.

He doesn't respond right away but the front door bell jingles so I tuck my phone back in my pocket and turn to greet the customer. My smile falls when I see my soon-to-be ex-husband standing before me.

"What're you doing here?" I demand, panic lacing my voice.

Okay, probably not the best way to start our first in-person conversation in months but I'm genuinely shocked to see him. Margot called yesterday to say that my permanent address change had been filed. I knew that Mitch would be notified and likely would try to reach out to me about it. But I hadn't even entertained the thought of him trying to get to me in person.

I can count on one hand the number of times he's been back to Haven Bay since we moved a decade ago. Since Mitch's parents moved to Edmonton the year after we graduated, he decided he no longer had a reason to visit. Whenever I brought up visiting my mom, he always made excuses, like a business meeting he had to prepare for or a social event that would conveniently pop up in his calendar that he couldn't miss.

Eventually, I stopped asking.

My chest twists at the sight of him. His presence already has me on edge. I fight the urge to smooth my hair. He ingrained in me for so long to dress, act and look a certain way, that all it takes is him walking through the door for me to fall back into that toxic mindset.

Just as quickly, the thoughts of inadequacy are replaced with a voice I've missed over the last decade. The voice I thought I had lost so many years ago to this destructive relationship. The voice I let him push aside.

My voice.

My spine straightens. I tip my chin so that I'm looking him straight in the eye as Mitch strides over to me and slaps a piece of paper onto the countertop. I barely suppress the jolt at the noise. I refuse to let him see even a hint of vulnerability.

"What the hell is this, Avery?" he barks.

I look down at the paper but I already know what it says. "Looks like a letter from my lawyer notifying you of my address change. But it's hard to read upside down, so you'll have to tell me if I'm right." I aim for nonchalance but inside I feel anything but.

"I know what it says. What I want to know is what the fuck you think you're doing. You're not moving, Avery. I've let this go on long enough. Pack your shit. You're coming home."

He makes no move toward me but I take a step back anyway. I make sure to keep the counter between us, just in case. He's never been physical with me before but I've also never defied him before.

Until now.

"No."

The simple statement takes a second to register and I can tell the exact moment it does. His expression goes from genuine shock to panic and then contorts into an ugly scowl of contempt. His perfect little world is crumbling before him, the peace I worked so hard to maintain over the years dissipating before his eyes. The woman he worked so hard to bring down and keep hidden away is finally fighting back and he has no idea what to do with that.

Well, tough shit. I'm done hiding.

"What did you say?" His voice is eerily quiet in contrast to the seething rage in his eyes.

It takes all of my control to stay calm but I adjust my stance so that I can reach into my pocket for my cell phone without him noticing. I've only ever seen him this angry once before and it did not end well.

A few years ago, Mitch came home furious after a business deal had ended poorly. It was meant to be an easy acquisition but he lost the account to a competitor, costing his company millions. His father called and berated him for being a "pathetic waste of the family name" before hanging up on him. His father ended up making some calls and reviving the deal but the disappointment and embarrassment in his tone was enough to set Mitch off.

He went on a rampage, destroying anything in his path. He threw lamps, tossed furniture and even took an umbrella to a beautiful antique mirror that was a gift from his mother and had cost over four figures. I tried to calm him down, but nothing I said could take that look out of his eye. So instead, I stood in front of the stairway, blocking his path to the bedrooms while hoping that Gavin would sleep through the noise.

Eventually, he ran out of steam and collapsed onto the couch. I didn't dare approach him, instead standing by in shock, surveying the damage. Our living room was destroyed. Luckily, I had long ago hidden anything of value to me upstairs in case of a break-in.

Little did I know that the real threat was sleeping in my bed next to me.

"I'm not leaving with you, Mitch. My home is here now." I keep my voice steady though my hands are shaking beneath the counter.

Mitch's fingers curl around the edge of the countertop, his knuckles turning white with the force.

The bell above the door jingles. Both of our gazes shoot to the door, where Jolie and Gavin stand, obviously aware of the tension in the room. Gavin stands starkly still, staring wide-eyed at his father. He hasn't seen or asked about Mitch the entire time we've been in Haven Bay. He visibly shrinks and my heart breaks for him while the mama bear inside of me rages.

"Hi, buddy," I say, trying for a cheery tone. "Are you having fun with Jolie at the festival?"

I round the counter to hug him but mostly to put myself between him and Mitch. He nods but his eyes remain warily on his father. I look over at Jolie, trying to reassure her with my eyes but she's too busy glaring at Mitch to notice.

Mitch nods at Gavin. "Son. Come say hi to your dad."

Gavin's eyes shoot to mine, his uncertainty obvious. Then he ducks his head behind my legs, a movement that up until a few months ago was his default. I didn't realize exactly how much Gavin had changed until I saw him revert back to his scared, timid ways.

Oh, yeah. This mama bear is ready to rip something apart. Or should I say someone.

But not in front of my kid.

"Jolie, do you mind taking Gavin out for a bit? I need to talk to his dad for a few minutes."

She starts to protest, still scowling at Mitch but I reach out and squeeze her hand. I need to get rid of Mitch and I don't want to do that with Gavin anywhere nearby.

She seems to understand and takes Gavin's hand in hers to reluctantly leave. "Okay. We'll be right around the corner if you need me." She says it to me but the warning is very clearly directed at Mitch.

Gavin hurries along behind Jolie. He doesn't even bother to glance back at his dad, clearly eager to get away from him.

"So, now you've turned my own kid against me, too?" Mitch snaps.

Before Gavin came in, I was determined. I felt bad about the way things had gone between us. I wanted to work things out so that we all got what was best for us. But after seeing the way Gavin cowered at the sight of his father, the person who is supposed to make him feel safe and calm, any empathy I felt for Mitch evaporated.

Now I'm goddamn furious.

"How dare you? How can you honestly think that the way he is around you has anything to do with me and not how you've treated him his entire life?" I can feel my voice rising and people can probably hear me outside, but I couldn't care less.

You can make me feel tiny and worthless all you want, but no one makes my kid feel that way. Especially not his own father.

He scoffs at my outburst but I continue on.

"How can you possibly think that after chastising, belittling, and then downright ignoring him, he'd come running back to you with open arms? He's four, Mitch; he's not stupid. He knows who shows up for him and who doesn't. And you've never shown up for him a day in his life." I don't know when it happened but I suddenly find myself standing before him, stabbing my finger into his chest to punctuate each word.

By the last stab of my finger, any semblance of composure leaves him. He looks like he's ready to spit steel. "Who the fuck do you think you're talking to, you stupid bitch—"

He's cut off by the harsh bang of the front door against

the wall. I spin to see Matt's broad shape encompassing the doorframe. The look on his face is lethal as he stares down Mitch. I've seen Matt mad before but I've never seen him look the way he does right now. If the look was coming from anyone else, I'd be frightened. But while Matt's temper can be vengeful, he's never careless with it. And he's not looking at me.

"You better watch your fucking mouth when you talk to her, Olsen." Matt's tone is dangerous and low. I feel a shiver go up my spine.

Is it messed up how much that turned me on?

Mitch has the audacity to scoff at Matt before turning back to me. "Seriously? You called your little bestie to come fight your battles for you?"

"I'm not fighting anything for her. She's tough enough to fight them all on her own. I'm only here in case her piece of shit *ex*-husband can't take a hint."

Mitch's body tenses at Matt's use of the word "ex". He whirls back at me, eyes narrowed. "You go ahead and fuck all the guys you want, Avery. Fuck every guy in this town for all I care. But you're not taking my kid away from me," he threatens. "After I'm done destroying you in court, you'll be begging me to take you back. And if you're lucky, I just might."

I level my gaze to his before responding. "I'll never regret being with you because you gave me the love of my life—Gavin. I'll never hate you because to hate you is to hate half of that little boy and he's the best thing in my life. But as long as you continue to treat him the way you do, he's never going to want to be around you. I have no control over that. Only you do." I take a steadying breath. "As for crawling back to you, we're done. I can't blame you for everything that went wrong in our relationship but I won't ever lose myself again. Not to you, not to anyone."

Mitch gives me a long, hard look but I refuse to back

down. After a few moments, he realizes I'm not going to cave and turns to leave. Matt takes one step out of his way but Mitch still has to turn to get past him. He opens the door then stops and spins back to me, ignoring the glare from Matt.

"Enjoy your time in Shitsville, Avery. You might think you're staying here, but we'll see what the judge has to say about that." With that, he slams the door behind him and marches across the street to his BMW. He slides inside then whips his car around and heads toward the highway.

Matt's eyes never leave the car until it turns the corner and disappears. Only then does he tear himself away from the door. He reaches me in two hurried strides.

He pulls me into his chest and I willingly accept his strength. Now that Mitch is gone, my courage is weaning and I can feel the adrenaline leaving my body. I shiver and Matt pulls me tighter against him. We're both not able to speak yet.

Eventually, I look up into his warm eyes, a stark contrast from what they were only moments ago. "Jolie?" I ask and he nods.

"She called me saying you were alone in the shop with Mitch. When I said I was on my way, she told me I had five minutes before she went back in herself to—and I quote— 'feed him his worthless dick'," he says and I laugh.

I brush my lips against his. "Thank you," I say. "Thank you for having my back. But more than that, thank you for giving me the space to handle it myself."

He kisses me back. "Anytime, Freckles. I told you before, I've got you. But you don't need me. You're stronger than you give yourself credit for." He kisses me again, this time lingering.

Eventually, we pull apart.

"Just know, if he comes back here and threatens you again, I'm not going to be able to hold back. I want nothing more than to kick the living shit out of him and wipe that smug look off of his stupid fucking face."

Well, damn. That was kind of hot.

"Are you done for the day then?" he asks. I check my watch and see that it's almost three.

"Yep. I've just got to close up the shop." The cafe already closed at two so it's just the store side that needs sweeping, cleaning up and closing out the register. "I should be ready in about fifteen."

"Sounds good. I'll sweep while you take care of the register. Then let's go find Gavin. All this talk about kicking ass has me craving some cotton candy." He heads toward the back closet whistling a low tune, the tension in his shoulders from earlier long gone.

I should feel surprised by his ability to switch from intense and protective to playful and easy-going, but it's so typical Matt.

I wonder when I'll stop comparing him to Mitch. I know it's not healthy, but I still can't believe the difference between the two men. Seeing the two of them in a room together and how they handle themselves in tough situations makes me even more confident in my decision.

My relationship with Matt might've progressed quickly but there's no doubt in my mind that this relationship is healthier, more stable than my marriage ever was.

My relationship with Mitch was like being on a boat in the middle of a storm—chaotic and unpredictable. Your every step is measured and uncertain. No matter how hard you try to hold steady, a large wave could still knock you overboard at any second, pulling you under.

My love for Matt, though, is like a winding river. It's peaceful, steady and strong. There may be rocky areas or forks that need navigating, but it continues to flow through it all, always coming back to the calm.

"Do you think any broom could be turned into a magic broomstick? Like, could Harry Potter have ridden a Swiffer to victory during the Quidditch finals? Or did he have to have the old-school straw and wood kind?" Matt asks, sweeping his way toward the front of the shop.

Yeah, there's definitely only one Matt.

CHAPTER 38

MATT

It takes us nearly thirty minutes to close up because Avery insists on hearing every detail about my conversations with Krista and my mom. She listens intently as I replay the conversation with my mom and squeezes my hand while wiping away her own tears. She was there through it all, so she knows better than anyone what our family went through.

When I tell her about Krista's interest in my pieces, she nearly knocks me off my feet when she throws herself at me in a hug. Despite my warnings that there have been no official offers made, she's convinced that no one could say no to my designs.

When I pointed out that even if Krista does put them in the gallery, it doesn't mean that anyone will buy my work, Avery scoffed. "Anyone with half a brain cell in their head knows that your work is special. People will take one look at your work and be lining up from miles away to buy them."

With a comment like that, how could I not take her into the back office and show her my appreciation?

After a quickie on her desk, we locked up then dropped Ham off at my apartment to cool down. This summer has been extra warm and I didn't want him to overheat from being outside for too long.

It's a good thing we dropped him off because minutes later, we found Gavin and Jolie near the petting zoo looking at the snakes. To Gavin's delight and my dismay, Jolie had a ball python draped over her shoulders. Jolie reached out, offering to let me hold it. When she took a step toward me, I jumped back, yelping like a little girl and making Avery nearly fall over laughing.

Was it unmanly?

Definitely.

Was the snake plotting my death by staring into my very soul?

Also definitely and there's no one who can tell me otherwise.

As soon as Avery let Gavin hold the python (with the keeper's help, of course), he asked for a pet ball python and hasn't let up since. Thank God Avery's been saying no. I'm not sure I could ever sleep over knowing there's a python in the next room, waiting for me to fall asleep so it could squeeze the life out of me.

We manage to snag one of the only empty picnic tables and are now scarfing down some hotdogs and poutines.

"The zookeeper said that ball pythons are the nicest snakes. He said his snake is twenty years old!" Gavin exclaims through his mouth full of fries.

Great.

"But he said you have to be careful 'cause they like to get out and then they hide under your bed."

Fan-fucking-tastic. Of course they do.

"You already have a pet, Gav, and I don't think Sushi would like to have a snake in the house," Avery says, squirting some ketchup onto Gavin's hotdog before passing it over to him.

More like Sushi wouldn't like being snake food.

"Maybe when you're older you can have a snake at your own house," I tell him.

That seems to excite him. His eyes light up as he babbles on about all the cool things his house will have when he's older, pausing only long enough to chew his dinner.

"Waterslides instead of stairs would be great but you'd be cleaning up water all day. Now a rollercoaster, that's a good way to get around," I explain.

Gavin and I have been debating the best parts of his future house, each idea more extravagant and ridiculous than the last. Every time I suggest something new, he throws his head back giggling and then gives me an even crazier idea.

"Nope, my floors will have holes so the water goes down into the giant pool in the basement." Gavin counters.

Damn, he's got me there. That's an awesome idea.

"Alright, boys, we'd better finish up eating. I heard the dog parade is starting soon and we want to get a good spot to see Gram and Sushi." Avery packs up the garbage onto the tray and carries it over to a trash can while I wipe Gavin's hands down with a napkin.

All clean, we cross the park and head over to Main Street. Most of the booths have been taken down by now, so only the food trucks and drink stands remain.

The dog parade is one of the last events of the day. Brenna Doyle, who runs the dog rescue and sanctuary outside of town, created the event years ago. It starts at the baseball diamonds and ends on the beach at the end of Main Street. The entry fee is a donation to the rescue and awards are given out for different categories such as "Biggest Dog", "Best Matching Costume", and "Oldest Dog".

It's become one of the best parts about the festival and I heard the rescue gets a ton of much-needed donations from non-participants as well.

Ham and I have participated in the parade on more than one occasion. The last time he went as Dorothy (ruby red slippers and all) and I was dressed as Toto. I almost pissed myself laughing before we even made it down the stairs of my apartment. Everyone cracked up and we won "Best Matching Costume" by a landslide. But the look of utter betrayal Ham gave me the entire walk through the parade made me promise him we would take this year off.

Next year, though, we're going as Dr. Evil and Mini Me (complete with bald caps).

Sorry, Ham.

We make our way through the crowds, bobbing and weaving around parade-goers. Many people brought lawn chairs, camping out since early afternoon to get the best seats. Dottie and Maeve are in their usual spots in front of the diner. They spot us and wave us over. We quickly cross the street to join them.

"Hiya, handsome and handsomer," Dottie calls, nodding at me then Gavin. "Why don't you come watch the parade with us? There's no more sitting room but it's not like they'll be throwing candy with all those dogs around." Maeve slides her chair over so there's room on the step of the diner. We squeeze in behind her, careful not to block the entrance.

A few minutes later, Mayor Trenton and Brenna climb onto the stage that's set up in The Dive's parking lot. Rhett plays with the sound system then passes a microphone to Mayor Trenton.

"Good afternoon, everyone! Thank you all for coming to this year's Dog Days of Summer Festival." A round of applause erupts with hoots and whistles. "With your help, this year we've been able to donate $4,325.00 to Doyle's Safe Haven!" Another round of applause erupts as Mayor Trenton passes a ridiculously large cheque over to Brenna then hands her the microphone.

"Thank you so much everyone for the generous dona-tions. We are so thankful for all of your help as we rely heavily on donations to run Doyle's Safe Haven." She continues to explain what the donations are used for but I'm distracted by the hand that brushes against my thigh.

I sneak a peek at Avery, who looks up at me and smiles. As it always does, the sight of her smile causes my heart to squeeze until it nearly bursts out of my chest.

I'll never get tired of that feeling.

Seeing her and Mitch together earlier brought back some uncomfortable feelings that I'm not proud of. The over-whelmingly need to claim her shocked me. Sure, I've been jealous before but this was like jealousy on steroids.

But I knew that if I went into the store on the offensive, trying to fight her battles for her, it would've only made things worse. Not only that, but Avery deserves the chance to say her piece. I meant what I said: she's stronger than she realizes. She always has been.

As I watched her stand up to Mitch, my chest swelled with pride. Despite how much I would've enjoyed pummelling that douchebag into the ground, watching Avery eviscerate him was almost as satisfying as kicking his ass would've been.

Almost.

I wrap her hand in mine then bring her fingers to my lips. She smiles and rolls her eyes at my cheesiness but I can tell she secretly loves it. Which is why I love doing it.

"Now, without further ado, let's bring out our contes-tants. First up, one of our senior dogs from the sanctuary is thirteen year old Lola," Brenna commentates from the stage. A woman with a Doyle's Safe Haven shirt walks a medium-sized beagle with a large pink bow attached to her collar down the street. Lola's tail wags slowly while the smile on her mostly white face earns her applause and encouragement from the crowd.

Gavin climbs onto the step behind me, poking his head out to try to see over the crowd. "Mommy, I can't see Lola," he complains.

Before Avery can answer, I lift him up by the arms and drop him onto my shoulders.

He whoops at the higher vantage point and waves down at his mom. "Look how high up I am, Mommy! I can see all the puppies now!"

"Would you look at that, Maeve. Don't the three of them make the sweetest little family?" Dottie coos.

Avery tenses beside me. She peeks at my face for a reaction. She's done the same thing whenever some festival-goer would comment on us being a family. I can tell she's watching me, waiting for me to freak out from the unintentional (but sometimes intentional) implication.

Each time, I give the same response of thanks and then give Avery's hand a squeeze. There's not much more I can do in front of Gavin, but the second we're alone, I plan to quash any doubt in her mind that I'm not in this for the long haul. I don't know how many times I have to tell her that I'm not going anywhere, but I'll tell her every day until I'm blue in the face if I have to.

"Mommy, look! Here comes Gram and Sushi." Gavin points animatedly toward the street. Sure enough, Angie and Sushi are trotting along down the road. Sushi is aptly dressed as a sushi roll and loving every second of the attention aimed her way.

Before long, the parade ends. We head back to my apartment to pick up Ham then make our way to the beach to find a place to watch the fireworks show. The town likes to have the dog parade early enough that all the skittish animals can make their way home before the fireworks start. Luckily, Ham's been on so many job sites that loud noises don't bother him anymore.

Finding an open space, Avery lays a blanket down that she grabbed from my apartment. We sit and I pull her to me. Her back is pressed against my chest while Gavin sits a few feet away with Ham's head lying lovingly in his lap. I place a kiss on Avery's temple and she cuddles in closer as the fireworks start.

Mitch's appearance earlier shook her up, there's no doubt about that. I did my best to distract her but I know she's probably thinking about it now the same way I am. His threat still looms over us like the rain clouds that are threatening to roll in tonight but we pretend it doesn't exist. Tomorrow will come soon enough, but we'll face that the way we do best.

Together.

CHAPTER 39

MATT

To neither of our surprise, Avery gets a phone call from her lawyer the day after the festival saying that Mitch has officially contested the move. Even though Margot warned her that it was likely, Avery hoped that he would go along with it to save face, time, and money.

Margot asked Avery if she'd be able to come in this afternoon to discuss how they'll proceed. I told her I'd be happy to hang out with Gavin today, which is how he and I ended up at the beach, taking Ham for a walk along the water.

After our fishing debacle, I decided to forego the fishing rods and instead grab a bag of bird feed to throw to the ducks. I figured we could walk along the beach, maybe check out the boardwalk then toss some seed to the ducks. Last time, Gavin loved walking along the edge and watching the ducks dive and bathe themselves.

The bay is still a little choppy from last night's storm. The storm caused quite a bit of damage around town, ripping up a few trees and knocking down a hydro pole. I spent half the morning helping Luke and the other first responders clean up fallen debris, check on those left without electricity and find homes for runaway garbage bins. By mid-morning, the electrical company arrived to repair the pole and the mess throughout town had been mostly straightened out.

I pick up a stick and toss it into the water, watching Ham chase to retrieve it. Gavin laughs as Ham unceremoniously plunges into the bay, looking more like a baby giraffe than a dog. After a few unsuccessful attempts, he finally nabs the stick between his teeth and awkwardly paddles back to shore. He then trots over to Gavin, dropping the stick at his feet. Ham bends, spreading his legs and winding up. I can see the signs of what's to come but I'm not quick enough to move Gavin out of the way in time. Ham shakes, water droplets flying everywhere, effectively showering Gavin and me in the stinky, wet mess.

Gavin erupts into laughter again, doubling over until tears are running down his cheeks. Again, I'm blown away by the difference between the timid kid I met a few months ago to the carefree one today.

After the fireworks, when Gavin was distracted and out of listening distance, Avery told me more about Mitch's appearance and how Gavin walked in and saw him. I didn't want to push her about it before, realizing she needed time to calm down, so I used the festival to distract her. When she finally felt comfortable sharing it with me, I tried my best to hide my emotions when she described both her and Gavin's reactions to seeing Mitch for the first time. It nearly broke me.

And then I wanted to break Mitch.

How could a guy have everything like that and not be on his knees every night thanking the universe for bringing them to him? It blows my mind that he had it all and then threw it away. As if he could ever find better than these two.

Gavin and Avery have filled a space inside me I didn't even know was empty. In a short time, they've become everything to me and now I can't imagine a life without them in it.

"Come on, Gav. Let's go find some ducks to feed before Ham winds up again."

We stroll down the beach, stopping often to admire the stones and shells Gavin finds as we go. I learned pretty quickly that if you're ever going to go to the beach with a kid, it's best to bring along a bag because they will quickly fill their pockets with their beach "treasures". Then they'll fill yours.

About fifteen rocks and shells later, we climb the steps to the boardwalk. It's not nearly as crowded as I expected, so we're able to stop along the edge to check out the ducks without blocking anyone's path. During the tourist season, the boardwalk is usually buzzing with activity as people take advantage of the nice weather to admire the views.

Haven Bay is beautiful. Surrounded by mountains and cottages sprinkled around the horseshoe, the views are some of the best in the area.

Having lived here all my life, I have to admit, I'm guilty of taking the breathtaking sights for granted from time to time. But it's days like today, when the water is calm and the sky is clear enough to see to the tips of the mountains, that I know with every cell in my body that there's no better place to live. It's no wonder a large portion of our economy is based on tourism.

In the summer, we attract outdoorsmen, wine connoisseurs, kayakers and hikers. During the winter, we have a few ski resorts that are a short drive away, making us a great alternative to ski lodges. It's a special town filled with friendly, well-meaning—though often meddlesome—neighbors who would give you the shirt off their backs if they thought it'd keep you from catching a cold. It's a great place to live and a great place to raise a family.

The image of Avery, Gavin and I walking along the board-walk with a stroller flashes through my mind and a feeling of contentment washes over me like the waves below. I bite back a grin at the glimpse into what will hopefully be my future.

"Look, Matt! Ducks!" Gavin calls, pulling me from my thoughts. He scrambles up the last step and darts down the boardwalk until he reaches a section where a family of ducks are swimming below.

"Slow down, Gav," I call, jogging to catch up to him. I reach him just as he's leaning over the edge to get a better look at the birds. "Sit back a bit, buddy. You're too close to the edge. You don't want to fall in."

He plops back onto his bent knees, keeping a safer distance from the edge but never taking his eyes off the ducks. He whirls around. "Can I feed them now? Please?"

I hand him over the bag of seed I brought along and scoop up a handful. I demonstrate how to toss the seed to the ducks so that all the ducks get a taste without him having to get too close to the edge.

"Matt Brady!" someone calls from behind me and I turn to see Lenny Thompson, owner of Thompson Hardware walking over.

"Mr. Thompson. Good to see you. How're they biting today?" I ask, gesturing to the fishing rod and tackle box in his hands.

"Oh, about as well as my great aunt Ida without her dentures in." He nudges my arm with his elbow, chuckling to himself. "But I wanted to come over and say thanks for all your help this morning. That blasted tree would've been a pain in my ass if I didn't have you boys and your chainsaws come out to cut it into pieces."

Lenny was one of the lucky people who had a tree fall on their property last night. Rhett and I went over this morning, knowing Lenny was too old to be handling a chainsaw but would probably try anyway if left on his own. We cut the tree into smaller, more manageable pieces that Luke and the other members of the cleanup crew could wrangle into one of the big trucks later.

Luckily, the tree barely missed his sunroom or the damage would've been a lot worse. As it was, it landed across his front yard, narrowly missing the godawful "abstract" statue that his wife, Trina, loves so much.

The statue is about as tall as my hip and very clearly resembles a vagina with legs coming out the bottom, standing in a Captain Morgan pose. I think the only person in town who doesn't see the resemblance is Trina. Lenny tried to pay me twenty bucks to break it and tell Trina it was from the storm. I almost took him up on it before she came running out to make sure her "beloved Timothy" was okay.

Did I mention this town is strange?

"No problem, Mr. Thompson. Just being neighborly." I keep one eye on Lenny and the other on Gavin, who has inched closer to the edge since I last looked. "Not too close, Gav. Sit back a bit, please." I remind him over my shoulder.

He automatically shuffles backward, then scoops another handful of seed to toss into the water. He and Ham sit staring over the edge, entranced by the ducks who are diving and fighting for the little pellets.

"It's a damn shame about Missy Benson's car, though. Heard that branch smashed up her windshield something awful. Trina said that it was the universe's way of telling her she shouldn't've been 'miscounting' her cards at the Cribbage tournament last week." Lenny gives my arm another nudge and a knowing nod, as if the universe cares about a few extra points in a card game.

I politely listen as he rambles on about the damage from the storm, Missy's damaged windshield and how she's threatening to break her neighbor's window with said branch if they don't trim their trees.

Out of the corner of my eye, I see a blur of movement and

turn just in time to see Gavin tip head first over the edge of the boardwalk. Time slows as I reach out to grab hold of his shirt, pant leg, anything, but all my fingers grab is air as he drops over the edge and into the water below.

I call over my shoulder for Lenny to call Luke before diving into the water after him. Ham leaps to his feet, barking and racing back and forth along the boardwalk but the chaotic noise is muted the second I'm submerged into the bay.

The shock of the cold water hitting my system knocks the air from my lungs. The adrenaline shooting through my veins kicks my heart to an almost painful cadence. I resurface quickly, whipping my head around in search of Gavin.

Does he even know how to swim? Have I ever seen him in the water before?

I rack my brain trying to think if Avery has mentioned anything while I spin in place looking for any sight of him. All thought vanishes when I spot his arms flailing in the air a few feet away from me. He's kicking and thrashing, trying desperately to keep his head above water.

I launch myself toward him.

Please be okay. Please be okay.

The words chant over and over in my head as I race toward him. I shout his name but his head dips beneath the surface of the water. My heart is pounding and I try to force away the panic.

I dive down and grab him under the arms. I shoot to the surface then prop him up so he is flat on his back, head against my chest. I waste no time propelling us toward the rescue ladder that's attached to one of the boardwalk's pillars. Gavin's coughing and crying, the sound both a relief and torture.

I should've never let this happen. I should've never taken my eyes off of him.

Gavin lets out a wail and I tighten my arm that's wrapped

protectively around his waist. "I've got you, buddy. We're almost there, okay? You can do it. Keep taking slow breaths for me."

He heaves a wet breath in and it's like a knife to the gut. *That can't be good, can it?* My mind is racing with all the water safety videos online about the dangers of water getting in kids' lungs and the complications of dry drowning. Even though I'm freaking out, I continue to croak out reassuring words, hoping like hell they're all true.

What if the water had been as rough as it was last night? What if I hadn't looked back when I did? He could've been pulled under and I would've never known.

A few more strokes and I'll be able to grab the ladder. *Hold on, buddy. A little longer and then you'll be safe.*

I finally reach the ladder and use one arm to pull myself up to the first rung.

"Matt!" Someone shouts from above.

I look up and nearly collapse with relief to see Luke a few rungs above me, one arm on the ladder and the other reaching out to us.

"Gav, Luke's going to take you up the ladder, okay?" Gavin whimpers, shaking his head and trying to turn into me but I spin him toward the ladder instead. "I'll be right behind you. You've been so brave, kiddo, I need you to be strong for a little bit longer. Just like Spider-Man. You've got this."

He gives a small nod, uncertain but the trust in his eyes tells me he understands.

A trust you broke.

I force back the angry voice in my head as I lift Gavin up and into Luke's waiting arms. The tightness in my chest eases a small amount as I watch Luke pull him up onto the boardwalk. He's safe.

No thanks to you.

The tightness returns as I heave myself up the ladder and

climb the few steps up before pulling myself over the edge. A towel is thrown over my shoulders but I'm too busy rushing to where Gavin lies to feel its warmth.

Luke has him lying on his side in what I recognize as the recovery position, his wet shirt removed and a large towel draped over his body.

He looks so small and fragile lying there. Without warning, the image of his short arms flailing as he fought against the waves nearly takes me to my knees. I blink and I'm brought back to the boardwalk where he lies. His skin is pale and his eyes are red from crying. The moment he sees me, he tries to scramble up toward me but I rush over to him, holding him in place.

"Hey, hey, slow down. I'm right here, buddy." I grab his tiny hands in mine and force away the panic at how cold they are. "Lie down the way Luke said, okay?" He lays back down, his hands still in mine. "Good job. They want to check you out. Just relax. You're safe now."

His taut muscles finally loosen, seemingly giving in to exhaustion. I continue to hold his hand as the EMTs check him out and again while we relay the events to Luke and his assisting officer. His voice is weak but he answers everything honestly. He admits that he leaned too far over the edge to get a better look at the ducks and lost his footing.

"I'm sorry, Matt," Gavin whispers, his eyes shiny with fresh tears.

"Shh, don't be sorry. I'm happy you're okay." I brush the hair from his face. I resist the urge to pull his tiny body to mine, just to feel his heartbeat against my chest. Anything to convince myself that he's really alive.

Not long after we finish with the officers, Avery comes running from the parking lot. Thankfully, Luke called her while Gavin and I were with the EMTs.

God, you didn't even think to call his mother? What's wrong with you?

She pushes through the crowd, her eyes red and wide with worry. Her head swivels, searching through the chaos for Gavin. Spotting him, she races over to where we are. Since the EMTs cleared him, he's been allowed to sit up and, seeing his mom, he scrambles to his feet. A fresh round of tears break loose as he cries out to her. "Mommy!"

Avery drops before him, pulling him into her lap. He sobs, tucking his head into the safety of her body.

"Shh, baby, I'm here. I love you so much. You're safe," she whispers into his hair, rocking him as her own tears stream down her face.

Guilt overwhelms me and it's all I can do not to lose my head. Luke puts a hand on my shoulder and squeezes. I struggle to swallow past the lump in my throat.

Another image flashes, this time of Gavin's body falling, just out of my reach as he disappears over the edge. I don't even bother trying to shake away the thought. I deserve the gut-wrenching pain of this image filling my mind over and over again. It's my penance for being so careless. For putting this helpless little boy in danger.

"Matt?" Avery's gravelly voice has me rushing to her side. I wrap my arms around them, needing to feel them both safely in my grasp.

"I'm here, Freckles." I squeeze her tightly as they both shake from the force of their tears. I bury my head in her hair as the emotion I've been holding back finally breaks free, pouring silently down my face.

"I'm here."

As it goes in a town this small, when sirens go off, so does the rumor mill. Word spread and when Angie and my mom inevitably heard about the incident, they came straight to the boardwalk to check out every inch of us.

Finally satisfied that we were physically okay, they left but not before my mom made me promise to call her when I got home and again in the morning. Before she left, she hugged me tight and whispered a teary "good job" in my ear.

It takes us another twenty minutes to get to the parking lot, fielding hugs and questions from the growing crowd. Every pat on the back stings, leaving behind a burning sensation that makes me want to crawl out of my skin.

They wouldn't be thanking me if they knew it was all my fault.

The sun starts to fall by the time we finally climb into Avery's car. Exhausted, Gavin's eyes are closing before Avery finishes buckling him into his car seat. She's still shaken up so I insist on driving her home. She slumps into the passenger seat, weary from the traumatic events of the day. Ham jumps into the backseat, snuggling his head into Gavin's lap. He's barely left his side since it happened. I think he feels guilty, too.

But the only person who should be carrying that weight is me.

It's a quick and quiet drive to Angie's. We pull up outside of the house. As I turn off the car, Avery pulls herself forward and gives her head a slight shake. She's been holding herself together for Gavin's sake but I have a feeling once he's tucked into bed tonight, only then will she let herself fall apart.

I let Ham out of the backseat then round the car. Bending to lift Gavin into my arms, I'm careful not to jostle him as I pull him from the car. His sleeping body seems too lifeless. I fight the panic that's sliding up my neck. Its fingers wrap around my throat, squeezing while I struggle to breathe past it. I try to focus on Gavin's steady breathing and his heartbeat that thumps rhythmically against my chest, reassuring myself that he's okay but it does little against the growing panic.

On the front step, I pass him over to Avery and the second he leaves my arms, the grip on my throat loosens. Even in sleep, he clings desperately to her, wrapping his arms around her neck. She starts to open the door and then gives me a hesitant look when I don't follow behind her.

"Are you coming in?" she asks, her voice weak but I shake my head.

As much as I know she needs me tonight, I can't force myself up those stairs. The idea of holding her while she breaks apart over something I caused is too much. Just another way I've disappointed her today.

"Oh." She shifts uncomfortably, only partially from Gavin's weight. "I guess I'll see you tomorrow then?"

"Sure," I answer, though I already know she won't.

I turn before I lose my nerve. Ham and I make the short walk back to my apartment. As soon as the door to my apartment closes, I let the feelings come. I let all of the *what ifs* and images that I know will haunt me surface. Then I let them pull me under, deeper and deeper into the darkness until the only thing I feel is numb.

Because that's what I deserve.

CHAPTER 40

AVERY

I t's been a couple of days since Gavin's accident on the boardwalk and, thankfully, he's back to his normal energetic self.

The first night, I couldn't leave his side—for both of our sakes. After Matt dropped us off, I let Gavin sleep for a bit before waking him. He ate a little dinner while I watched him closely. Eventually, his head started to droop and I carried him to bed. Crawling into his tiny bed beside him, I held him close where he quickly fell into a deep sleep.

Only then did I let the tears fall as I clung to him, needing to feel his heartbeat to reassure myself that the worst hadn't happened. That my baby was alive and safe.

The next morning, we took it easy and lounged around watching movies and playing board games. By mid-afternoon, he was building forts and chasing Sushi around the backyard, the previous day's trauma forgotten—at least temporarily.

The EMTs gave us a list of symptoms to watch for and when to seek medical attention so I've been watching him like a hawk ever since. Luckily, he seems to be doing fine but, to be safe, I made an appointment with the doctor in town.

Now that Gavin is safe and the worries of dry drowning

and other complications are lessened as time goes by, I'm starting to worry about Matt. I haven't seen him since he dropped us off the night of the accident. When he didn't come in after, I figured that he was tired and needed some space to process such a scary event. Everyone kept praising him but I know that it must've been scary for him, too.

I don't blame him for the accident; it could've just as easily happened under my watch as his. But to be a non-parent watching someone else's child fall into danger, I can understand how he might feel responsible.

All things I would've assured him of if he would bother to answer my calls.

It's not that he's been completely incommunicado. He's texted me every few hours checking in on Gavin since he dropped us off—even overnight so I know he hasn't been sleeping. But if I try to talk about anything more than that, invite him over or offer to let him call Gavin, he makes an excuse and then stops answering. I wish I could go to him and make sure he's okay, but Gavin is my priority.

I don't plan on letting him avoid us for long, though.

We're driving through town after Gavin's doctor's appointment where he was given the all-clear. Since most side effects of a near-drowning are usually within the first 24-48 hours, Dr. Katz felt confident that we're safe from any complications. But she told me to call right away if anything changes and even gave me her personal number in case it's after hours.

Another reason to love small towns.

"Mommy?"

"Yeah, buddy?" I look at him through the rearview mirror and see his face is uncharacteristically serious.

"Is Matt mad at me?" he asks, softly.

My chest tightens. "No, baby. Everyone knows it was an accident. Matt's just happy you're okay."

Maybe if he wasn't hiding, he'd be able to tell Gavin that himself.

Gavin swivels in his seat to look out the window as we turn onto our street. "I think he's mad that I didn't listen to him," he whispers. "That's why he doesn't want to see me anymore." He sniffles, his eyes watering.

I pull into my mom's driveway and throw the car in park. I turn in my seat so I'm facing Gavin. "I promise that's not true, Gav. Whatever reason Matt has for not coming over has to do with him, not you. It's not your fault," I tell him, squeezing his leg. He still looks unsure. "I have to go back into town for a bit but why don't you ask Gram if you and Spider-Man can have a snack? I think I saw some cookie dough in the freezer. Maybe you could bake some cookies while I'm gone."

This makes him grin. I help him unbuckle himself so he can scramble out of his car seat and up the steps. Following him inside, I watch from the door as he runs to give my mom a hug on the couch. I call to my mom that I'm going out and will be back soon. Then I climb into my car and throw the car into reverse, jerking the gearshift harder than necessary.

I told Gavin that Matt must have a good reason for why he's been absent. Now I intend to find out what that reason is.

I DON'T BOTHER TEXTING Matt before driving over to his place. It's not like he'd answer if I did anyway. It hits me as I cross the intersection that he could be out on a worksite today. Luckily, I see his truck is parked in its usual spot behind the workshop.

I pull my car in beside his and shove the gear shift into park. I storm over to the workshop's back entrance. Trying the handle, I find it's unlocked so I push my way inside. Immediately, the loud bass of the music blaring through the speakers pulses through me. I walk down the short hallway and round the corner into the shop to find Matt alone at his station. His back is turned to me and I can tell he didn't hear me come in.

Marching over to him, I tap him impatiently on the shoulder with a bit more force than I intended. When he jumps and spins to face me, my anger evaporates. I soften at the sight of his sunken eyes and disheveled hair.

He reaches for his phone on the workbench behind him and taps the screen. The music stops and the room is suddenly too quiet. He tosses his phone back onto the bench and I try to shove aside the images from the last time we were alone in this shop and all the things we did on that same bench.

I let my gaze rack over him. His clothes are wrinkled as if he hasn't changed in days and there's dark circles under his eyes so I suspect he hasn't been sleeping much.

"Where have you been?" I ask softly. I'm feeling less accusatory than when I first arrived but I still need answers.

Gavin deserves answers.

"Working," he states simply, turning back to his workbench.

My frustration builds but I try to give him the benefit of the doubt. Taking a calming breath, I walk around him so he's forced to face me. His eyes are on the workbench where a medium-sized block of wood lays. There are puncture marks and chunks sliced from the wood that look like they were made out of anger.

"Why are you avoiding us?" I try again.

When he continues to avoid eye contact, I step between him and the workbench. Finally, he reluctantly meets my gaze, his expression neutral but his eyes plead with mine.

For absolution or retribution—I'm not sure which.

"How is he?" he asks, voice hoarse with emotion. It reminds me that the accident was hard on him, too.

It definitely doesn't excuse his actions afterwards, but it does make me soften toward him.

I sigh. "He's fine. He's back to his happy, energetic self. He was scared the first night but we talked and he doesn't seem scarred by it. I signed him up for swim lessons at the rec center in a couple of weeks, so we'll see how he does being in the water again." Matt nods and stares down at the chisel he's fiddling with. I cover the tool with my hand and he looks up at me. "He misses you. He thinks you're mad and ignoring him because he didn't listen to you."

Matt curses under his breath and tosses the tool harshly at the wall behind the workbench. He sinks onto the stool behind him. I watch as he drops his head into his hands, tearing at his hair.

"Of course I'm not mad at him. It wasn't his fault," he grumbles, head still in his hands. "It was mine." His voice cracks with emotion.

My heart aches at his confession. How can he think that? He saved Gavin's life. My baby boy is at home, watching Spider-Man and probably eating too many cookies because of Matt. I can't even stomach the thought of what would've happened if things had gone differently. I shake my head, a fresh set of tears brimming my eyes. "No, it wasn't anyone's—"

"You don't get it!" he roars, head snapping up. "It's my fault he fell in. I was distracted and wasn't giving him my full attention. He trusted me to keep him safe and I couldn't even do that right."

I lift my hands to hold his face, refusing to let him hide from me. "Matt, listen to me. Listen." I shake his head gently until his eyes meet mine. "What happened on the boardwalk was an accident. It could've happened when anyone was watching Gavin—even me. The important thing is that he's safe. You're both safe."

Deflated from his previous outburst, he's quiet for a moment. Finally, he responds, his voice low. "He's so small. I keep feeling his limp body in my arms and thinking about what would've happened if I hadn't seen him fall in. If I had been a few seconds later. If I didn't find him in the water when I did..." He doesn't bother trying to cover the emotion in his voice.

I wrap my arms around him and we sit like that for a few minutes until Matt finally lifts his head. His eyes are still red and there's a sadness in them that almost brings me to tears. He stands suddenly and I nearly fall backward, catching myself before I do. Walking to his work station, he leans over the workbench, gripping the edge tightly.

I go to take a step toward him when I hear his hoarse voice. "I can't do this," he mumbles and it's like hitting a brick wall. My steps falter as I freeze in place. The temperature in the room drops and I can feel the heat draining from my body.

"Can't do what?" I ask, too stunned to form a coherent thought.

"I can't do this," he repeats. His back is still turned to me. "As long as you and Gavin are around, I risk losing you. Clearly I'm not capable of keeping Gavin safe. I can't lose another person I love." He turns toward me, his face stoic and his eyes determined. "Not again. I won't survive it."

I stand there for too long staring at him, dumbfounded. "So, that's it? You're done?" I search his eyes for any hint of insincerity but find none.

"I'm sorry. I can't."

Just like that, the heat that was drained from me suddenly floods back through my veins. It boils, raging inside me until it finally combusts.

"Are you fucking kidding me?"

Matt's eyebrows shoot upward at my outburst and I don't blame him. While I could be somewhat of a hot-head as a teenager, years of complaisance have dulled my temper into a meager ember. But Matt's finality stokes it back to life.

"You know, Matt, I'm trying really hard not to lose my shit on you right now because I know you're hurting. You think you're doing the right thing because you're grieving and I get that. I really do." I start to pace, my frustration and annoyance giving me too much energy with nowhere to put it. "I was there when you lost your dad. I was there when your mom was mourning. But your reasoning, while well-meaning, is really fucking stupid."

"Hey, now—"

I stop in front of him and angrily stab a finger into his chest. "No, you've had your say. It's my turn now." I blow out a frustrated breath. "I understand how hard losing your dad was for you. Losing someone is hard. But loving someone means you risk losing them." I begin to pace before him again.

"Every day, my heart walks around in the form of a sweet, hilarious, four year old little boy and every damn day I'm scared for him. For the hurt, sadness, and pain he's inevitably going to endure. I won't always be around to protect him from every bad thing in his life. Even though I could somehow lose him," I choke on that thought but I push through, "I would never, ever wish he wasn't in my life." I stop before him but he merely sits there, watching me with a resigned look on his face.

"Look at my mom. She lives every day to the fullest because she knows that soon, and it'll be sooner than any of us would like, she won't be able to chase Gavin around the yard. Or go on girls' trips in the city. Or lounge on the porch swing, sipping tea and chatting with me. But she does it all, even knowing it's going to end.

"And, yeah, thinking about losing my mom one day makes me want to drop to my knees and cry." I force back the tears that are threatening to fall. "But that doesn't mean I'm going to waste the time I do have with her. I want to spend every second I have with her making memories so when she's gone, I have those memories to look back on when I'm missing her."

I take a breath to steady myself then look him directly in the eye. "Because when you love someone, you're not only loving them through the easy times or the safe times. You love them knowing that your time with them will one day end. You love them because the time you spend loving them is worth more than a million years of living without them. Life without love isn't life. It's messy and unpredictable and scary. But that's life." My face softens before I continue. "Your dad knew that and he'd be heartbroken with what you're doing to yourself right now. Because when you finally pull your head out of your ass, you're going to realize that this," I point between us, "was all you."

I drop my arms in defeat after having said my piece. I walk away then pause, not bothering to turn back to face him. "Oh, and you owe Gavin an apology," I toss over my shoulder. "No matter how this goes for us, he doesn't deserve to be treated like this."

And with that, I march out of the workshop, slamming the door shut behind me. Only when I get to the safety of my car do I let the tears fall. I give myself a second to wallow before I wipe my face, square my shoulders and drive away.

CHAPTER 41

MATT

I'm a fucking idiot.

I've been sitting in the workshop for the last hour, replaying every word from our earlier argument. The more I think about what Avery said, the more I realize how much of a colossal asshat I've been.

Not only to Avery but to Gavin, too. Avery's right; he did nothing to deserve this and he was hurt despite that. After easing him out of his shell and earning his trust, when he needed me most, I buried myself in so much self-doubt and grief that I pushed him away instead.

I fucked up. Big time.

"FUCK!" I yell into the empty workshop, tossing the nearby stool across the room.

Ham lifts his head from his place on his dog bed, unimpressed with my outburst. I swear I can hear his judgment from here.

You deserve it, he says.

"I know, I know. Sorry, buddy." I let out a long breath, easing some of the tension between my shoulders. I walk over to scratch behind Ham's ear then drop to a knee so I'm eye-level with him. "What do you think, Ham? Did I completely fuck this up? Will they forgive me?"

Ham huffs out a breath and I choose to take that as a yes. But how do I fix it?

Avery's had enough men disappoint her and I've just stupidly added myself to the list. She's got a big heart but there's only so many hits a heart can take before it hardens to protect itself. But I refuse to believe this is it for us. Perhaps that's naive of me, but it's all I've got to hold onto right now.

I've watched enough chick flicks with my mom and Avery to know that this is the part where the guy does some big, elaborate gesture to win back his girl. But the idea of leaving Avery and Gavin wondering how much they mean to me long enough to plan and implement a grand gesture makes me sick. I've already worried them enough, they don't deserve it a second longer.

That is if they'll take me back.

They have to.

No, they don't. They don't owe me anything.

But that doesn't mean I won't spend the rest of my life trying to convince them. Because if there was any doubt of where my heart lies, it's long gone after today. It's only been an hour since Avery handed me my ass and I'm already crawling back offering them anything and everything for a second chance. They're it for me. So, no matter how long it takes, I'm going to prove to them that I'm not going to bail again.

Ever.

Decision made, I search frantically around the room for my keys. Finding them on one of the larger shelves near the door, I quickly grab them and head to the parking lot, only stopping to hold the door for Ham.

Normally I'd walk the short distance over to Angie's house, but I've wasted enough time sulking. So we hop in my truck and a minute later, we pull up in front of their house. I climb the steps and knock on the door then shove my hands in my pockets to keep from fidgeting.

I wait, having no idea how this is going to go. I hope Avery will at least hear me out before she slams the door in my face.

But it's not Avery that opens the door; it's Gavin. This is the first time I've seen him since the incident on the board-walk. *The accident,* I correct myself. Because no matter how guilty and responsible I feel for what happened, Avery's right —it was an accident.

"Hey, Gav. How you doing, kiddo?" I crouch in front of him.

I shove the image of his flailing arms out of my head and focus on him standing before me. Thankfully, he looks the same as he did before the accident. But I know first-hand that trauma isn't only on the surface.

"'Kay," he mumbles, staring down at his chubby bare feet.

The carefree kid I've grown to love shrinks back into himself. The same way he did with Mitch.

Fuck. I really messed up.

"Listen, buddy. I'm really sorry that I haven't been around much the last couple days. It's not your fault, it's mine." I lean forward, dropping my voice to a whisper. "Can I tell you a secret?" His curiosity gets the best of him and he leans in slightly, giving me the smallest of nods. "I didn't come around after the accident because I was scared."

Gavin's eyes grow wide. "Really? Why? You're so big. You don't get scared."

I shake my head. "Everyone gets scared. Even big, old guys like me." He giggles at that and I feel the first hint of a smile in days tugging at my lips. "When I saw you fall, I was scared. When I was in the water and trying to reach you, I was scared. Even after we got you out and I knew you were safe, I was still scared."

Gavin's head hangs. "I'm sorry."

I reach out and grip his shoulder. It's the first time I've touched him since that night and feeling him, knowing he's safe, heals something inside me that's been eroding away.

"Don't be sorry. It wasn't anyone's fault, remember? I was scared because I was worried something would happen to you. I was scared I was going to lose you." I swallow hard against the lump in my throat but continue around it. I want Gavin to see that it's okay to be vulnerable no matter your age, gender or size. "Did you know that my dad died when I was younger?"

He nods again. "Miss Franny told me he was sick for a long time 'fore he went to heaven."

I guess to a kid, a couple years is a long time but looking back, it was all too quick. "Yeah, he was. When he died, it was really hard for me. So, when something happened to you, I got scared that I might lose you, too. And that's why I didn't come around after. I was still scared that I'd lose you."

I grip both his hands in mine, squeezing them to reassure both of us that he's okay. "But that's not going to happen. I'm not going to let anything happen to you. Next time, we're going to be more careful. You'll sit back further and I'll make sure you have my full attention. It might be scary to be near the water again at first, but it'll get easier every time. We'll do it together."

Gavin smiles back at me. Then he throws his tiny arms around my neck and squeezes me so tight, it's almost hard to breathe. But this time, I welcome the feeling and instead of panic, I only feel calm.

"Love you, Matt," Gavin mumbles into my shoulder.

The lump in my throat grows as I squeeze him back, taking extra care not to hurt him. "I love you, too, Gavin."

A sniffle from behind Gavin pulls my head up and I see Avery and her mom standing in the entryway, watching us. I offer her a timid smile, still unsure of how she'll react to my presence. Ham jumps onto my shoulder, licking Gavin's face and making him laugh. He pulls away to wrestle with my dog.

"Come on, Gavin. Why don't we go throw the ball out back for Ham and Sushi?" Angie reaches a hand out, guiding him further into the house. She shoots me a wink then mouths a "good luck" behind Avery's shoulder before following Gavin and the dogs toward the backyard.

I slowly stand, careful not to crowd her.

"Hey."

She leans against the doorframe, surveying me. "Hi," she finally manages.

Okay, not a bad start.

"I'm sorry. I'm sorry for bailing when things got hard. I'm sorry for hurting Gavin, even if it was unintentional. It was still a shitty thing to do. I don't know if I'll ever be able to not feel guilty for what happened on the boardwalk but I also realize now that it was an accident." I hazard a step toward her and when she doesn't back away, I take another. "I'm sorry I pushed you both away, that I didn't trust what we have enough."

I take another step until I'm standing inches from her, then reach out and cup her cheek. She leans into my hand and I give myself a mental high-five.

"Most of all, I'm so fucking sorry that I ever made you doubt how I feel about you. How I feel about Gavin. Because you both mean so much to me. You mean everything. And even though one day I might lose you, I don't want to live another day without you. I can't." I brush her soft cheek with my thumb.

"Please forgive me, Freckles."

I hold my breath, waiting while she holds my future in her hands. A slow smile spreads across her face and the heaviness in my chest finally lifts. Then she surges forward and captures my mouth in an enthusiastic kiss and it's all the answer I need.

I drop my hand to her round ass and pull her closer so that every inch of us is touching. Then I dive into her mouth, taking everything she offers and more. I brush my tongue against hers and she moans. It takes all of my control to keep from pushing her against the wall, ripping off our clothes and thrusting into her until there's no doubt in her mind that she's mine.

Always.

Instead I pull back, breaking the kiss. We're both breathless as I rest my forehead against hers. "I'll take that as a yes," I whisper and she laughs. I can't resist kissing her again, softly this time. "Thank you."

Pulling her over to the porch swing, I lean back with her tucked into my side. We sway in silence for a while until the sun starts to dip below the trees. Eventually, she sits up. With a yawn, she stretches her arms above her head, causing her shirt to lift. The soft skin of her stomach teases me and I ache to explore below the waistband of her shorts. I wonder if I can convince her to come home with me tonight.

"I should probably get started making dinner," she sighs. She stands and I immediately miss her warmth. Before she can step away, I grab her hand and spin her back into my lap. She laughs and I'm so damn grateful to be on the receiving end of it.

I crash my mouth against hers and her laugh morphs into a low moan. I trace my finger along the edge of her denim shorts, teasing her like she did me and she arches into my touch.

Painfully aware of our lack of privacy, I pull away. I chuckle at her groan of frustration.

"So, we're good?" I ask, tone somber as I search her eyes.

She gives me a small peck on the lips. "We're good," she assures me. She stands, sauntering to the door and I stand to follow her. "Matt?" she says, peeking around the edge of the door. I lean closer, letting the citrusy scent of her shampoo intoxicate me.

"Yeah, Freckles?"

She shoots me a sweet smile. "If you ever pull that shit on us again, I'll take a scroll saw to your balls and make my own art." She shoots me a wink and disappears into the house while I stand ramrod-still in shock.

Message received.

JOLIE

You owe me a girls' night.

AVERY

Oh yeah? Why's that?

Not that I'm saying no *side-eye emoji*

JOLIE

I happen to remember our last girls' night ending with you and a certain tall, dark and handsome man grinding on the dance floor.

AVERY

We definitely weren't grinding.

JOLIE

Then you ditch me and leave me to deal with Officer Grumpy Pants while you square off with that Dana bitch in the parking lot.

AVERY

Lol I definitely didn't square up with anyone.

JOLIE

Ipso facto, you owe me a girls' night.

AVERY

Even though you're full of shit on half of those details, you're right. I did ditch you.

I'm sorry. I suck.

JOLIE

It's a good thing I'm such an amazing, loving and caring friend with great hair.

I'll forgive you on one condition.

AVERY

I'm not streaking down Main Street with you…

JOLIE

I like where your head's at but no. Make your famous buffalo chicken dip for girls' night-in at my place this weekend.

AVERY

Deal. I'll ask my mom about watching Gav. Saturday good with you?

JOLIE

Perfect. See you then xo

Saturday finally rolls around. I've been looking forward to tonight all week. It's been too long since Jolie and I got together for more than a quick lunch during the day. Between meetings with my lawyer, spending time with Gavin and my mom before school starts in a few weeks and going on dates with Matt, I've been kind of a crappy friend.

Luckily, Jolie is the type of low-maintenance friend who

understands that life's busy and is content to catch up over texts and lunch dates.

Midweek, she texted me to ask if it was okay that she invited Brenna Doyle to girls' night. She and Jolie had met during the Dog Days of Summer Festival and hit it off. Of course I said yes, always eager to make new friends.

As I climb the stairs to Jolie's apartment above her yoga studio, I'm greeted by the sound of Lizzo blaring through her speakers and I laugh to myself. Lizzo is the queen of female empowerment so Jolie must be really leaning into the whole "girls' night" vibe.

I knock and wait until I hear Jolie call out over the music. When she does, I shuffle the tray in my hands to open the door. Stepping inside, I toe off my shoes and then, as I do every time, I take a second to admire Jolie's apartment.

Her walls are painted a soft green that contrast the dark wood floors perfectly. Jolie's family moved around a lot growing up, so you'd think she'd be used to living a minimalist lifestyle. Instead, she's done the opposite and has taken to collecting things. Her apartment has no rhyme or reason to its decorating style. She told me that she merely picks up whatever suits her whether it's a silver Buddha statue, a colorful painting of a dog dressed as Abraham Lincoln or an antique grandfather clock.

If Jolie likes it, it has a place in her apartment.

"I keep telling you to just walk in," she chides me as she puts down her drink to take the tray from my hands. Despite the warm weather, she's dressed in a long sleeve shirt, jogging pants and thick socks.

"Last time I did that, I walked in on you in your underwear doing yoga poses that should not be done in your underwear," I reply dryly.

I follow her into the kitchen where she sets the tray down and hands me a glass. Putting my bag of goodies down on her table, I eagerly accept the pink slushy drink. At my first sip, I moan at how good it tastes. "Mmm, strawberry margaritas. Excellent choice."

She raises her glass to mine in cheers then takes her own sip. "What's a little semi-nude yoga between friends? Don't be such a prude. It's not like I was wearing them in public. *You* came into *my* apartment, remember?"

Like the children we are, I stick my tongue out at her and she blows me a kiss back.

There's another knock on the door and Jolie skips over to answer it. "Brenna! I'm so glad you came." She gives Brenna a quick hug then pulls her into the apartment. "Brenna Doyle, Avery Owens and vice versa," Jolie gestures between us.

She takes the serving tray from Brenna's hands, peeking under the tin foil. "Ooouu, bacon wrapped scallops. You're officially invited to every girls' night from now until forever, Brenna." We watch as she dances her way into the kitchen with the tray in hand.

"I know what you're thinking: she's got a lot of energy. If we could harvest even half of it, we could power the whole town for a year," I joke and Brenna laughs.

"Yeah, but I kind of like it," Brenna replies, smiling.

Jolie returns holding a pink drink in each hand then stops suddenly. "Oh my god, I'm such a dick! I didn't even ask if you drink, Brenna. I'm so sorry. Do you want me to make you a virgin one?" She starts to retreat to the kitchen when Brenna grabs the drink from her hand.

"No, no. Alcohol is good. I'm no boozehound but I love a good drink. Especially a slushy one." She takes a sip of the fruity drink and makes a face. "Oh, boy. I'm glad I don't have any big plans tomorrow. These things are lethal."

Jolie wiggles her hips in celebration. "You go, girl. Have as many as you want. I've got a spare bedroom so feel free to crash here." She scurries back to the kitchen then reappears moments later with trays of food and small plates to set on the coffee table. She drops to the sectional behind her, then grabs a plate from the coffee table.

"Alright, ladies. We've got Avery's buffalo chicken dip and chips, Brenna's bacon wrapped scallops, my jalapeño poppers and, because life is all about balance, chocolate covered strawberries for dessert." She gestures at each dish with her spoon before scooping a spoonful of dip onto her plate then leans back into the couch.

I laugh, dropping onto the couch beside her. "I don't think chocolate covered strawberries count as nutritious, J."

She shrugs. "It's fruit, isn't it? Don't split hairs with me, Owens," she warns, pointing a chip at me. "So, Brenna. Tell me about you. I know we talked a little bit about the sanctuary at the festival but I want to know more. How'd you get into it?" Jolie shovels a chip with buffalo dip piled on top into her mouth.

Brenna sits on the floor next to the coffee table and plucks a jalapeño popper off of the tray. "Well, it's not a very exciting story. In college, I volunteered at an animal shelter near campus. Simple things like cleaning out the kennels, walking the dogs or socializing the cats. I love all animals but dogs hold a special place in my heart."

She takes a bite of her jalapeño popper and chews thoughtfully. "I guess after a while it got to me seeing all of the older dogs or dogs with medical or behavioral issues that would sit in the kennel for months and months without a single application. It broke my heart watching them wait for a family that never came. And when the kennels get too full..."

She shakes her head. "Anyway, my aunt Lynn owned an old dairy farm outside of town that I used to visit when I was a kid. The farm side of it has been shut down for years so it was mostly just a big property with a couple of old barns and some pastures. When she passed away a handful of years ago, she left the farm to me. She never married or had children, so I guess she thought I was the best choice." She shrugs. "I figured I could do something good with it. A lot of red tape, grant writing and elbow grease later and Doyle's Safe Haven was born."

"I love that. How many dogs do you have in your care now?" Jolie asks.

"Sixteen right now. More than half of those are permanent members of the sanctuary but the rest are with the rescue and are waiting for their forever homes. I want to hire more staff so that we can take more in but it's not in the budget right now."

"Wow, sixteen! That's so amazing of you, Brenna," I say. She shakes her head to deny it. "No, really. You're saving those dogs' lives. You're giving them a home. You should be really proud of yourself."

Her face reddens at my praise. She takes another drink so I opt for a subject change. "How're your classes going, J?"

Sensing Brenna's discomfort, Jolie picks up the hint and runs with it. She launches into a story about how she convinced Doug Feldman to come to a class so that he would stop reporting her for noise complaints, only to have Maeve and Dottie decide to help him with his stretching.

"Then, I shit you not, Maeve leans over Doug's back while he's in child's pose and rubs herself onto him, whispering 'Deeper, Doug, deeper,' into his ear. I swear I thought Doug was going to have a coronary right there on the mat." The three of us dissolve into laughter until our bellies are sore and we're wiping tears from our eyes.

"Speaking of rubbing up on each other," Jolie wags her eyebrows suggestively and it brings on a fresh round of giggles from me.

Whew. These drinks are going straight to my head but it feels so good to let loose.

"How're you and Matty doing since the big blow out?"

"Good." I take a sip in an attempt to hide the smile on my face. "Really good."

"Yesss, girl. Get it, get it!" Jolie cheers, pumping her fist while Brenna laughs again.

"Not gonna lie; the Brady genes are top tier. Those men are dangerously hot," Brenna says and we raise our glasses in cheers.

"If only Brother #1 wasn't such an uptight a-hole all the time, it'd amp his hot factor up significantly." Jolie sips her drink while I roll my eyes, having heard it all.

"What's the story with you two?" Brenna asks. "Are you exes?"

"HA! He wishes," Jolie scoffs. "There's no story. He's a pain in my ass both professionally and personally. He wishes he could land such a hot piece of ass like me."

With that, Jolie declares she has to pee and nearly trips running out of the room. Brenna and I exchange smirks.

Luke and Jolie are like fire and gasoline. If they ever got together, it'd be a melding of passion and thrills but also danger and destruction. They would either consume each other completely or they'd combust under the heat.

Either way, neither would be escaping without a few burns.

When Jolie returns, we turn on some awful chick flick that's so corny, it's actually kind of cute. We poke fun at the cheesy lines but all three of us are wiping our eyes by the end when the main characters finally decide to talk like adults and realize that the whole thing was just a miscommunication (surprise, surprise) that could've been solved with one conversation.

Somewhere near the end of the movie, Brenna falls asleep tucked into the corner of the sectional. Jolie gets up and tucks a throw blanket around her, adjusting the pillow under her head.

Having stopped drinking after finishing her second, Jolie reaches for her reusable water bottle and unscrews the lid. Adjusting her position so she's cross-legged, she faces me. "I didn't want to mention anything in front of Brenna but I've been meaning to ask you; how goes everything on the Mitch front?"

I sigh, taking another long drink of my margarita. I already called home to let Gavin and my mom know I'd be spending the night at Jolie's so I'm taking advantage of a night away with snacks, endless alcohol and no responsibilities.

"It's fine. Slow moving but apparently that's to be expected. We finally have our court date set for two weeks from now. Which, of course, has to be the week before school starts." I huff out another breath. "Because the universe seems to have a sense of humor when it comes to my life."

Jolie reaches over and squeezes my knee. "I'm sorry, Ave. That's got to be really hard. It sucks that you're dealing with all of this."

I cover her hand with mine. "Thanks. I keep telling myself we have to go through the shitty stuff to get to the good. So, hopefully that's sooner rather than later. I've had enough of the shitty stuff to last me a lifetime."

"Well, even during the shitty stuff, I've got you, girl. Whenever you need a drink or to belt out some Carrie Underwood song about killing her ex, you know I'll be right there with you."

I lean over and give her a hard hug. "You're the best. I'm so glad I met you."

She hugs me back. "Back at ya, babe." Then she grabs the remote off the coffee table before settling back into the cushion.

"Alright. Enough talk about Mitch the Little Bitch. What's next?" She scrolls through the list of movies on screen. "The movie about the billionaire who falls in love with the baker only for her to find out that he was sent to town to buy her out by his grumpy boss? Or the movie about the single dad who owns a Christmas tree farm and falls in love with his competition?"

I'm so thankful to have a friend like Jolie. She always knows exactly what to say when I need to vent or laugh or punch a hole in the wall. She's the definition of a ride or die friend. She's the friend I'd call if I ever had to hide a body—though she probably would've been the one holding the knife.

For the millionth time, I thank past-Avery for having the guts to leave behind a life she knew wasn't meant to be hers.

"Definitely the billionaire-baker one," I decide. Then I snuggle further into the couch to watch corny movies with my best friend.

CHAPTER 43

MATT

"You're really not going to drop a line?"

I take a long pull of my beer, barely sparing Luke a glance over the end of the bottle.

"Nope."

We're sitting on his boat in the middle of the water. One benefit of living in Haven Bay is that you don't have to go very far from the marina to hit the best fishing spots. The mountains give off the feeling of seclusion but once you pass the bend, the water seems endless.

The view isn't so bad either.

"Great," he grumbles back. "So, you're not fishing because you 'don't want to hurt the fish'." He points an accusing finger at me then shoots a thumb at Rhett. "He's not fishing because he'd rather play his guitar. Why the hell did we come fishing again?"

Rhett sits at the back of the boat, strumming his guitar. His head is bent over, seemingly lost in the song, but I can see the slight smirk on his face.

"Because, brother dear," I drawl, "it's a beautiful day. The sun's shining, the water's calm and we all have the morning off." I relax back into the passenger seat, legs crossed before me.

"Then why'd you tell me we were going fishing?"

I roll my eyes at him. "Lukey boy, every guy knows 'going fishing' is code for drinking beer on a boat."

Luke growls in frustration and it takes all of my control not to burst out laughing. "Are you fucking kidding me?" He jumps to his feet and starts pacing in front of me "Do you know how much work it was to get ready for today? I had to lug all of our fishing gear out of storage. Then I had to buy a new net since you idiots broke my last one trying to catch that 'monster trout' that ended up being a log. Then I had to lug that massive cooler down the hill to put the fish in."

He stops in front of me and bends so we're eye level. He looks like he could spit nails, he's so worked up. His look of pure outrage would probably scare most people, but I think sometimes he forgets that we used to share a room and I know exactly how many nights he spent hiding under the covers at the first crack of thunder.

Don't worry. I remind him every few months.

Hey, someone's gotta keep the town hero humble and, if not his little brother, then who?

"You're telling me I did all that, you *watched* me do all that, knowing that neither of you had any intention of using any of the gear. Is that what you're saying?"

I give him a look of pure innocence. "I just thought you were really committed to the code." Rhett snorts and Luke's head spins to him, shooting him a dark look. But like me, Rhett isn't fazed by Luke's temper.

I can't hold back any longer and I throw my head back laughing.

Luke turns back to me, pointing his "cop finger" at me. "You're paying for my net," he demands.

Rhett catches my eye over Luke's shoulder, pointing his finger and a mocking glare at me in an exceptional Luke impression that has me doubling over again. Luke flops into the driver's seat, grumbling something about being "surrounded by idiots".

Once I've finally pulled myself together, we fall into a comfortable silence. The three of us have been around each other long enough that we don't hold grudges. I mean, Luke could try but he knows I'd bug him mercilessly until he inevitably relented and forgave me.

It's easier all around if he just skips that part.

Besides, I was already planning on paying for his new net. Money well spent to see that look on his face, if you ask me.

"So, how's Avery feeling about the custody hearing this week?" Rhett asks, finally looking up from his guitar.

"She's nervous. I think we both wish it was Thursday already so we could get it over with."

To say Avery's nervous is like saying that the Rocky Mountains are kind of tall. She's been chomping at the bit all week. She's already reorganized the bookshop, baked so many desserts for the cafe that she had to start freezing them and has taken Ham for long walks every day.

It's gotten to the point where when he sees her coming with his leash, he hides under the bed. Poor dog's never done so much exercise in his life.

I've been trying to keep her busy and her mind off the hearing. We've gone on dates, taken Gavin to the arcade and to his swimming lessons together. I even signed us up for a paint and wine night at the rec center that she's been wanting to try. But none of it has been enough to distract either of us from the uncertainty that this week brings.

I'm not naive enough to think that Mitch wouldn't follow through with his threats of contesting the move. But a part of me kind of hoped he'd settle for any of the multiple ammendments Avery's lawyer proposed to their tentative agreement so they could avoid going to court.

No such luck.

"I always knew that Olsen guy was a tool but I didn't think he was this cruel," Luke remarks.

My grip tightens on my beer. "Yeah, you and me both." I take a deep breath and slowly ease my grip. "If he was doing this because he actually wanted custody and wanted to spend time with his kid, then it'd be a different story. But I'm starting to wonder how much of this is about Gavin and how much of it is actually about controlling Avery in the only way he has left."

"You're probably not far off," Rhett says, looking off into the mountains. "Narcissists will use anything or anyone to get what they want—even their own kids."

Luke and I exchange a look. Rhett doesn't talk about his parents much. From what I've gathered from the little tidbits he's mentioned throughout the years, they shipped him off to live with his grandma when he was fourteen and going through his rebellious phase. They claimed he'd become "too much to handle" and, as far as I know, that's the last time he's talked to them.

He never made it seem like that bothered him but he doesn't talk about his past so it's easy to forget that he had a whole life before coming here. Then he makes a comment like that and I wonder what kind of baggage he's been carrying around all these years.

It's usually best to give Rhett space whenever he gets in his head like this.

To change the subject, Luke nudges my foot with his. "How did your meeting with Krista go, Picasso?"

I lean forward and pull two beers from the cooler, offering one to Luke. He's off-duty today so he accepts. I toss Rhett one of his Cokes and he catches it, nodding his thanks. Then he picks up his guitar to lose himself in his music again.

I twist off the cap, tossing it into the cooler. "Good. Better than I expected actually." I take a drink and the cold liquid feels like heaven against the summer heat. "She wants to do an exhibit the first week of September."

Luke sits up straighter and Rhett looks up from his guitar. "Wait, seriously? That's awesome, man," Luke slaps my back.

"Don't forget us when you're famous," Rhett lifts his can in cheers.

"Well, don't go selling my underwear online just yet. She's using it as a trial to see if there's any interest. If there is, then we'll talk about the possibility of a consignment agreement."

When Krista mentioned curating a show for my pieces, I almost laughed. She had to be joking. I mean, to sell a few pieces in a town festival was one thing. But to have an exhibition featuring my work? She couldn't possibly mean me.

But she did. In less than two weeks, my pieces were going to be on display in an honest to God art gallery.

To say my imposter syndrome is in full swing was an understatement.

Luke waves me off. "Oh, stop. I might know jack shit about art but I was in the workshop with Dad, too, and I couldn't whittle a straight line if my life depended on it." He leans forward, his forearms on his knees. "In all seriousness though, you've got talent, man. It was a bit of a shock that you managed to hide it from all of us for so long, but it makes sense. We always thought you were playing with your wood too much, at least now you can make money from it." He smirks.

"Really?" I roll my eyes at his lame joke. "'Playing with my wood' is the joke you're going with?"

"Come on, Luke. It's not his fault it took him this long to learn how to handle his wood," Rhett quips and the two of them dissolve into a fit of giggles, because yes, what these grown-ass men are doing can only be described as giggling.

"Calm down, you hyenas. I handle my wood just fine, thank you very much. Ask Avery," I shoot back at their snickering.

"That poor girl's been stuck with your toothpick so long you've convinced her it's a redwood," Luke cackles, slapping his thigh.

Good, God. Can anyone in my family tell a joke? I hope for my sister's sake she got my comedic skills.

I shoot my brother the finger and the boat rocks as a fresh round of laughter erupts from Rhett. Eventually they pull themselves together, which is a good thing or I might've tossed one of them overboard if they made one more comment about Little Matty.

Yes, my dick is named after me. Who else would he be named after? The Hulk?

Actually, that's a pretty sweet nickname.

"Speaking of Avery, what does she think about the exhibition?" Rhett asks.

I shift uncomfortably. "She doesn't know about it." Luke pauses with his bottle halfway to his lips.

"Why the hell not?"

I blow out an exasperated sigh and list off all of the reasons I've been reciting to myself all week. "The hearing is in a few days and then Gavin's first day of school is right after. I didn't want to add one more thing to her plate." I keep telling myself this and all of my reasons are true. I can't help but wonder, though, if deep down, I'm hiding the exhibition from her because I'm scared it'll fail.

That I'll fail.

I shake my head. Not a thought for today. "Anyway, you should see how excited Gav is for school. He's had his Spider-Man backpack all packed and ready to go for days. He already knows a few kids his age from summer camp that'll be in his class and he makes us ride our bikes past the school almost every night." I smile to myself. "I ordered him these sweet light up Spider-Man shoes. I hope they get here in time. He's gonna love them."

The guys are suspiciously quiet. Luke raises an eyebrow while Rhett gives me a knowing look.

"What?"

"Nothing," Luke shrugs, smiling. "You just surprised me. You sound like quite the family man. I must've missed the wedding."

I smile again but not for the reason he thinks. "Hey, man, if it was up to me, I'd marry that girl tomorrow. And Gavin? He's not some obligation or burden. They're the best package deal. The only reason I haven't gotten down on one knee yet is because I don't want to freak her out. But she's it for me, bro. They're it."

Again, they're quiet before exchanging a look. I'm not overly surprised by their reaction. I've never been serious about a girlfriend before. My longest relationship lasted six months and I never once felt for her anything close to how I feel about Avery.

Looking back, that's probably why she broke up with me. She knew there was no future with us. I felt guilty at the time thinking there was something I could've done or tried to fix whatever went wrong. Then, after a while, I felt guilty for not being more upset about the break up. We were together for a while, shouldn't I have been more upset? Instead, I felt like I failed. One more thing I messed up.

I realize now that I didn't fail. I couldn't give my heart to someone if I didn't have it to begin with. I'm starting to realize that I unknowingly gave my heart to Avery a long time ago. She's always had a part of me with her, whether she knew it or not.

Rhett's the first to break the silence as he stands and walks over to me. He thrusts out a hand to me and gives mine a firm shake. "I'm happy for you, man. You deserve them."

"Thanks, Rhett."

I look over at Luke who's still quiet, just staring at me. I arch a brow at him. Whatever he thinks of me, I can handle it. But if he says one word about Gavin or Avery—

"Good for you, Matt. I won't say it's not weird hearing you talk like that. But it's a good kind of weird." He gives a small smile, looking up into the sky. "It's nice seeing you settle down. Just didn't expect it, I guess." He looks back at me. "Dad would be proud of you, Matty."

Well, shit.

I tip my head back, fighting against the tears that are suddenly blinding my eyes. I'm thankful for the sunglasses covering them. When I think I can finally talk without choking up, I lower my head and stand, pulling Luke into a brief hug. "Thanks, Luke," I whisper.

He nods then pulls away, slapping me on the back.

"Alright, if you ladies are done with your sunbathing, we should head back to shore." Luke turns the key and the engine roars to life. He slides the throttle forward and the boat starts to move. "And if either one of you dipshits think I'm carrying even a single lure off this boat, you can both suck my dick."

Rhett and I laugh but the noise is drowned out by the boat slicing through the water.

I look out, marveling at the view. It really never gets old.

When Luke first suggested going out on the boat, I have to admit I was worried. It was my first time being near the water since the accident. Being with Gavin at his swimming lessons is different than being out on the bay. The pool is controlled and there are lifeguards everywhere. The bay is so wide and seemingly bottomless. I'm not too proud to admit I almost said no.

But then I thought of Gavin, who has been so brave with his swimming lessons. He was a bit nervous at first—understandably so. But after a bit of time, some patience and a lot of prep work outside of the pool, he's swimming circles around his teacher.

If he could conquer his fears and get back in the water at four years old, I sure as hell could get on a boat.

It doesn't take long before the boat slows, reducing our wake as we approach the marina. Luke angles the boat to its designated berth and Rhett and I jump onto the deck to tie it off. True to his word, Luke grabs his sunglasses and keys then jumps onto the deck and struts off to the parking lot.

"Don't forget to lock up, dickheads," he calls sweetly over his shoulder.

I chuckle, shaking my head. "Guess we deserved that one."

"Yeah, probably."

"Worth it."

"Always is," Rhett retorts, the corner of his mouth tilting upward.

We finish tying off the boat then get to work lugging the fishing gear and coolers to my truck. We hoist the last of the gear into the back and Rhett starts to walk toward the bar. I climb into my truck and turn over the engine.

Rhett stops and turns back toward me. "Hey, Matt."

I roll down my window. "Yeah?"

"You should tell Avery about the exhibition."

I pause. "Yeah, I know. I will."

With that, he turns back and continues his climb up the hill, lifting his arm in a wave. Pulling out of the parking lot, I take the drive to Luke's to think about what Rhett said. He's right. I should tell her.

After the hearing. Or maybe after the first day of school.

Yeah, I'll tell her then.

Maybe.

CHAPTER 44

AVERY

The day I've been dreading has arrived. The hearing isn't until this afternoon but I've been up since four this morning. If I'm being honest, I'm not sure I even slept last night. I tossed and turned all night and finally gave up on sleep.

I've imagined, overanalyzed and catastrophisized every possible outcome at least three times over. I've nixed six different outfits and played with my hair so much that it's starting to frizz.

Margot warned us that because Gavin's been with me all summer, the judge may decide that Mitch's visitation starts immediately. I've packed and repacked Gavin's overnight bag in the chance that the judge decides he should stay with his dad tonight.

I tried to point out that I haven't been keeping Gavin from his dad. I would've gladly driven him to the city to see him any time he wanted. But neither Mitch nor Gavin asked for visits, so I assumed they didn't want any.

Regardless, Gavin's things are ready and I've been preparing him for the potential visit all week. I've tried hyping it up to him as a fun weekend with his dad but it hasn't done much for his enthusiasm. He might be young but he remembers what time with his dad is like. He knows his dad doesn't play with him or try to have fun with him or even just spend time with him.

Eventually, I stopped. There's no use trying to convince him of something I'm not even sure I believe myself.

My phone vibrates from my bedside table.

MATT

Get any sleep?

AVERY

Barely a wink.

MATT

I figured. Maybe you can close your eyes on the drive up.

Matt insisted on driving us into the city and I'm grateful. I'm not sure I could focus enough right now to make the drive on my own. My hands are already shaking with nerves and we haven't even left Haven Bay yet.

AVERY

Doubtful but thanks.

I check the time on my phone. 5:23am.

AVERY

Why are you up already?

MATT

Couldn't sleep either.

You up for a sunrise walk along the beach?

I hesitate. I shouldn't. There's too much to do before we

go. Gavin will be up in...well, two hours. I sigh. Screw it. Maybe a walk will get rid of some of this pent-up energy.

AVERY

Meet me at the beach in 15.

I throw on some jogging pants and a long sleeve shirt then tiptoe down the hall, across the kitchen and over to Gavin's room. I nudge the door open a little wider to get a better look inside.

Sushi is snuggled into Gavin's legs, whose arms are wrapped around his stuffed Spider-Man toy. His mouth is splayed open and a soft snore blends with his sound machine on the dresser.

I take a second to memorize the sight. I can't imagine not being able to see him like this every night. Not being there for him if he has a bad dream or if he wakes up sick and needs my help.

For the first time since packing up my car and driving back to Haven Bay, I wonder if I made the right choice in leaving Mitch. Obviously, our marriage was and still is over. But it breaks my heart to think that Gavin and I will be apart for who knows how long at a time, when we've never spent more than a night apart since he was born.

At least if we were living in the same house, I could still be there for him.

I shake my head. Living in that house with Mitch was only half a life. Sure, Gavin and I were together but neither of us were thriving. Neither of us were living to our full potential.

I know deep down that I made the right choice. Gavin is a whole new kid since coming here. He's confident and brave, things I wish I could be. Like him, I'm growing and changing and maybe someday soon, I'll be those things, too.

The court will most likely award Mitch joint custody; they have no reason not to. Though he's not the best father, he's willing to fight for custody, has a stable job, a nice home and no history of abuse. He checks all of the boxes on paper.

I hope for Gavin's sake, he's asking for custody because he actually wants to be a father, not because he's seeking vengeance for our divorce.

Once he's awarded joint custody, the judge will determine the length of each visit after the hearing today to decide where I'll be permitted to live—Haven Bay or Edmonton. No matter where I am, I'm determined to make this work and be as least disruptive for Gavin as possible. If that means moving back to Edmonton, then that's what I'll do.

But I'm never going back to Mitch. I'm confident of that.

I quietly close the door behind me then tiptoe back into the kitchen, scribbling a quick note for my mom in case she gets up while I'm gone. Then I head down the entryway, pull on my old sneakers and unlatch the door.

I stop suddenly and just about jump out of my sneakers when I see a shadow at the base of the steps. Slapping a hand over my chest, I barely keep from letting out a scream that would wake up half the neighborhood.

"Jesus, Mary and Joseph, you scared the shit out of me."

Matt quickly climbs the steps, hands up in surrender. "Sorry, sorry. I didn't want to wake anyone by knocking but you didn't answer my last text." I can tell he's biting back a laugh. "You should've seen your face. Priceless."

I shove his arm and he finally lets loose the laugh he's been holding in. Biting back my own smile, I start down the side-walk. "Come on, funny guy. The sun's going to be up soon."

Together, we walk in a comfortable silence into town then turn toward the beach. Ham trots happily ahead of us, stopping occasionally to sniff a tree or receive a pet from a passerby. When we arrive at the beach, Matt unhooks Ham's leash before tossing a stick into the water for him to chase.

I drop to the sand and Matt follows. We sit with our arms

extended behind us, propping us up as we sit in the cool sand. The sky is starting to awaken, the dark purple of night giving way to the promising pink and blue of daylight. The sun hasn't quite made its way over the mountaintops yet, so there's still a faint bite of cold in the air.

It's beautiful; peaceful. It's exactly what I needed.

I relax into Matt's side. "Thanks for this."

"Any time," he murmurs, then kisses the top of my head. We sit like that for a while, watching Ham tromp through the water, biting at the waves as the sun starts to peek over the mountains.

Matt straightens suddenly. "Hey, do you have a minute? I want to show you something."

I check my watch. Gavin probably won't be awake for a while still. "Sure."

We climb to our feet and Matt whistles for Ham to follow. He clips the leash back on Ham's collar and we walk the short distance to what I've started considering as Matt's workshop. The building might be owned by Taylor Construction, but no one spends as much time or puts as much work into that shop as Matt does.

Bud would be crazy not to put Matt in charge one day. If that's what Matt decides he wants.

Matt unlocks the door and Ham scrambles in ahead of him to flop onto the shop couch where he promptly falls asleep. Closing the door behind us, Matt takes my hand and guides me to his corner of the shop.

I watch his face and the many emotions warring across it. Shyness, excitement, wariness. But the one that seems to shine through the brightest is the unmistakable note of pride.

I'm too distracted by it to notice we've stopped. Matt looks down at me. "Do you remember that night when I first showed you my work?" I nod. "It meant so much to me how you looked at every single piece, taking the time to go over each one with such care and attention—even the pieces that weren't quite finished yet." He squeezes my hand and I can feel the importance of his next words pulsing through the movement.

"There was one piece that you asked about specifically. It wasn't finished, in fact it was just beginning to take shape. At the time, I had an idea of what it was meant to be but it still needed time for its transformation."

He lets go of my hand to move toward his workbench. There's a white sheet covering a figure that's standing about a foot tall. Giving me one last shy smile, he pulls back the sheet.

A gasp escapes my lips as I take in the breathtaking piece before me. It's a phoenix. Its head is raised regally, its wings spread high above its head as if it's rising from the ashes. I take a step closer to examine the soft curves of its wings, the intricate line work of its feathers, and the subtle details in its eyes.

There are so many words and yet not enough to describe how magnificent and majestic this piece is.

"It's yours."

I start to shake my head. "Matt... I..I couldn't..."

"I don't just mean that it's a gift, though it is." He steps around the bench, cupping my face in his hand in the way I love so much. "It was inspired by you. It is you." His thumb strokes my cheek.

"Avery, when you came here, you were scared and alone. I don't blame you for being either of those things. Starting over with nothing is terrifying, let alone with a kid in tow. But you did it because you knew you deserved better. That Gavin deserved better. You were burnt but you weren't destroyed."

I try to swallow past the emotion but my throat is suddenly too tight.

"Then, you started to find yourself. With every new idea for the shop, every lunch with Jolie, every movie night with Gavin and your mom, you built yourself up a little bit more.

You built your life into exactly the one you wanted for you and your son. You smiled more, you laughed more. You rose from the ashes reborn.

"And when someone threatened that new life, you had the courage to fight back. You're still fighting for it and I know you won't stop fighting for it." His hand tightens on my jaw. "Because this life? The one you built from the ashes of your old one? It's yours. And it's worth fighting for."

The tears I've been fighting now steadily flow. God. I've cried more in the past few months than in my entire life. But it's like Matt said: I had to break myself down before I could build myself back up again.

And that's exactly what I did. I'm not the same Avery I was six months ago. I hope I never am. And I hope in six months, I'm different than I am now. I hope I never stop changing, never stop growing into newer and better versions of myself.

Matt's right. This life is worth fighting for. And that's exactly what I intend to do today.

Fight.

I step into his arms, clinging tightly to him, trying to convey all of the emotions I'm feeling and how much this means to me. I'm at a loss for words, but the best I can manage is, "I love you, Matt."

He squeezes me back tightly and I know he understands.

"I love you, too, Freckles."

Hours later, we pull up in front of the courthouse. I turn to face Gavin in the backseat. "Alright, buddy. You're good to hang out with Matt for a few hours while I go to my meeting, right?"

When Margot gave me the hearing date and said that Gavin should be nearby, I asked Matt if he could take Gavin for the day. It was a private hearing, so he wouldn't be allowed inside anyway. But I knew I needed Gavin to be with someone I trusted while I was in the hearing or I'd never be able to focus.

I thought about asking my mom because I didn't want to look like I was flaunting Matt in Mitch's face. But she had a bad couple of days health-wise last week. She's fine now but her doctor wanted her to take it easy for a while.

Gavin bounces happily in his car seat. "Yep! Matt said we can go to the kids' moo-seum and they have a dinosaur there that's as big as a truck!"

Matt laughs from the front seat. "At least that's what the website said. We'll have to check it out for ourselves. Maybe we can convince the dinosaur to stand next to my truck to be sure."

Gavin giggles. "It's not a *real* dinosaur. Dinosaurs are 'stinked, Matt."

"Oh, right. I forgot."

There's another round of giggles from the backseat. I blow Gavin a kiss that he catches and returns.

I grab his from the air. "I'll see you soon, Gav. Love you."

"Love you, Mommy."

I turn back to Matt, my smile vanishing as the worry sinks in. He leans in for a brief but firm kiss, cradling my head in his hands.

"You can do this, Freckles. You're strong and you're brave. You've handed Mitch his ass before and you'll have no problem doing it again." That makes me smile. "No matter what happens in that courtroom, you never have to go back to that old life again. Ever."

I take a deep breath and I nod, the tension in my shoulders lighter than it was a moment ago. He's right. No matter what happens, I'm still going to be me. I'm still going to fight for my life in Haven Bay but even if I lose and I have to live in Edmonton again, I won't be the same woman I was when I lived there before.

I refuse to.

I lean in for another kiss. "Love you," I whisper against his lips. Opening the door, I jump out of the truck. I turn back to lean in through the open window. Matt's angled in his seat toward me, elbow leaning on the top of the steering wheel.

"Okay. I'll see you guys soon. Wish me luck."

"Good luck, Mommy!" Gavin calls excitedly from the back, oblivious to the day's significance.

"Good luck, Freckles," Matt adds, then mouths a "love you" that only I can see. With the image of the two of them together fresh in my head, I spin on my heel and stride toward the courthouse like a soldier going into battle.

Two hours later, Margot and I leave the courthouse and step into the late August heat. I texted Matt quickly after court let out to let him know that Margot and I were having a short meeting and then I'd be ready to be picked up. I can see his black Dodge from the top of the steps but Margot is still talking so I pause to listen.

"So, as of right now, there's nothing else for us to do. I'll be in touch next week but if you have any questions before then, feel free to call." She gives me a pat on the arm, which is more affection than she's ever shown me. Her phone beeps and she quickly excuses herself before taking off down the steps.

I take a deep breath, following her down the steps then head toward the black Dodge like a beacon. Sliding into the front seat, I let my head fall back against the headrest.

"So?" Matt asks.

I turn my head towards him. "The short answer is we can stay in Haven Bay."

A smile spreads across his face and I can feel myself do the same. Don't get me wrong, it's great news and I'm relieved. But with divorce, a victory isn't always a victory. A family still dissolved today. The life Gavin knew before this, no matter how complicated it was, will never be the same again. In some ways, it might be better but I'm still sad for the little boy who will now spend the rest of his life between two homes. We were happy once and I mourn for that little family that will never be whole again.

Like I said, divorce is complicated. Especially with a child.

I look into the backseat but Gavin's busy drawing on his tablet. I turn up the radio and whisper to fill Matt in as much as I can in front of Gavin.

As Margot predicted, Mitch's visitation starts tonight.

Gavin will spend the next three nights with him until I pick him up on Sunday morning. Now that we've determined where Gavin and I will be living while he's with me, our lawyers will discuss custody schedules. If we can agree using our lawyers, we shouldn't need to come back to court again.

I'm not holding my breath on that last part.

After the hearing, Margot and I discussed a schedule I would be comfortable with her presenting to Mitch's lawyer. After some discussion and soul-searching on my end, I decided to ask for majority custody with Mitch having custody on weekends. That way, they're still spending time together but with less traveling. With Mitch's long work hours and Gavin being enrolled in school in Haven Bay, Margot feels this is fair.

But it's not what we think that matters.

"We have an hour to drop Gavin off at Mitch's house," I finish and Matt nods, glancing back at Gavin, who's still doodling away.

"How are you feeling?" Matt asks, reaching a hand across the console to hold my knee.

"Relieved. Sad. Worried. Pretty much every emotion is swirling around my head right now," I answer honestly.

He pulls me into a hug. "I'm sorry you're going through this." I nod into his chest, trying to hold back the tears that threaten to fall. I let him hold me for a few minutes, allowing myself to lean on him until I feel strong again.

"We should probably get going," I mumble, then lift my head, sitting back into my seat. Matt nods then starts the truck. He tips his head at Gavin in the backseat and I sigh, knowing what I have to do.

I turn in my seat to face him. "Hey Gav, remember when Mommy said that you might be having a sleepover at Daddy's house? Well, Daddy said you could stay there for the whole weekend!" I'm trying to keep it light and fun but I'm not sure if Gavin believes it.

His brow furrows. "But I don't want to stay with Daddy."

A piece of my heart breaks for him.

"I know, baby, but your dad wants to spend some time with you. He misses you." *I hope.* "It's only for a few days and you can call me whenever you want, as many times as you want." I reach back and grip his hand. "It's only for the weekend and then I'll come pick you up on Sunday. That's only in three sleeps." I lift my hand up to show him three fingers.

His eyes start to water. "Can you come with me, Mommy?" His voice is small and timid again and another piece of my heart breaks.

"Baby, I wish I could. But I won't be far. If you need anything, I can come and get you in less than an hour. That's like two Spider-Man shows away—"

"Actually, buddy. Your mom and I are going to get a hotel room near your dad's house," Matt cuts in. "That way if you need anything, we're right around the corner, okay?"

Gavin's eyes are still shimmering but he nods. Then he turns out the window, silently crying and it's all I can do not to wrap him up in my arms and take him away from this pain.

It'll get better. It's the first time. It'll get easier every time.

I try telling myself this over and over through the short drive to Mitch's house. Matt's hand is resting reassuringly on my leg. He might not realize it, but his comfort is the only thing holding me together by the seams right now.

We arrive at Mitch's house fifteen minutes later. It's funny how quickly I stopped referring to it as our house. Probably because it never really felt like mine, even when I was living there. The large, ostentatious new build wasn't my idea of a home but to Mitch, the status it brought outweighed the lonely, sterile feeling it left me with each time I walked inside.

I don't even want any of my old stuff back; he could throw it all away for all I care. Nothing in that house means anything to me. I have everything I need now.

I help Gavin out of his car seat, taking extra care while lifting him out of the truck and into my arms. Matt grabs his backpack and stuffed Spider-Man while I cuddle Gavin close, whispering reassurances in his ear.

Mitch opens the large oak door but stays within the frame as we climb the steps to meet him. "Really, Avery? Do you have to baby him all the time? He can walk," Mitch taunts.

I swear I can hear Matt's teeth grinding together from here. Thankfully, he doesn't say anything but shoves the backpack into Mitch's chest then turns back to Gavin.

"Okay, Gav. It's time to go hang out with Daddy." I kneel to the ground to put him on his feet but he's gripping my neck. "It's okay, buddy. It's only for a couple days. I'm sure Daddy has lots of fun things planned for you two to do while you're here." I look pointedly at Mitch over Gavin's shoulder but he just taps his designer shoe impatiently at me.

Gavin looks up at me and I almost burst into tears from the look on his face. I hate this. I hate every second of it. I wish with everything inside me that Mitch gets his shit together and steps up to be the dad he should've always been to Gavin.

Matt kneels beside us and hands Spider-Man over to Gavin, which he immediately hugs tightly to his chest.

"Hey, buddy. I know you're scared and you're gonna miss your mom. We're gonna miss you, too. But just think, when you get home on Sunday, it'll be only two more days until school starts. And then you get to go see all your friends and your new school and meet your new teacher. That's exciting, right?"

Gavin gives a small nod, despite the tears rolling down his face.

Matt leans in closer. "Let me tell you a secret. Your buddy

Spider-Man? He's a little scared to sleep somewhere new." Gavin looks down at his stuffed toy with concern.

"It's true. So, do you think you could be brave for Spider-Man? Remember: it's okay to be scared. But you don't let being scared keep you from doing what has to be done. Right?"

"Right," Gavin's tiny voice has a little more strength to it and I'm so relieved to have Matt with me. I'm a wreck and can barely talk so I'm glad he's stepping in to cover where I'm lacking.

Gavin gives Matt a hug then gives me a long one, too. I hold him close and kiss his head, mentally apologizing for putting him through this. "Be good, Gav. If you need anything, have Daddy call me and I'll answer. No matter what time." I give him another squeeze. "I love you."

"Love you, Mommy. Love you, Matt."

"Love you, too, buddy." Matt ruffles his hair.

I lift my head to see Mitch watching Matt and Gavin together with a barely disguised rage. But there's a little something else in his expression I can't quite decipher but it's gone in a blink. That couldn't have been...jealousy, could it? With Matt and I, sure. But is he actually jealous of Matt and Gavin's relationship?

I hope so. Maybe the jealousy will spark some much needed parental feelings.

"Alright, alright, Brady Bunch. Break it up," Mitch snarks from the step. "Gavin, get inside. The housekeeper will be finished making dinner by now. Say goodbye." Mitch ushers Gavin through the door and closes it before Gavin can say a word.

I can hardly hold myself together long enough to get into the truck before I break into a million pieces. Matt holds me, letting me sob into his arms until there's nothing left inside.

"Baby, I have to let you go for a little bit, only until we get to the hotel. Then you can let it all out and I'll hold you all night, if you want. We can curse Mitch's name or make a voodoo doll of him or order all the room service we can stomach. Whatever you need. But I have to let you go first." He runs his hand over my hair. "Will you be okay if I let you go?"

I nod, turning into the door. I stare out the window of the truck, shrinking into myself. The buildings blur past us as we drive to a nearby hotel.

Soon, Matt parks the truck then runs inside to check-in to our room. Moments later, he returns and guides me inside to the elevator. The hotel is nothing fancy, but it's clean and it's close to Gavin, so I barely spare the room a glance before tucking myself into the closest bed.

Matt plugs our phones into the chargers, turning the volume up high. He helps me undress and pull on his long shirt to sleep in. Then he drops his jeans, turns out the lights and snuggles in behind me. We lie that way for a while, him rubbing his hands gently over my back while I sob into the pillow.

Much later, as I feel myself start to drop into sleep, all I can think about is how I'm the worst mother alive.

CHAPTER 46

MATT

The shrill ring of Avery's phone snaps me out of sleep. I fumble for the light as Avery shoots out of bed. I check the clock on the bedside table. *2:12 am.*

No phone call at this time is ever good.

"Hello? Hello? Gavin?" Avery's eyes are wide and unblinking.

She must have the same thought as me. It took her a while to fall asleep, and when she finally did, she tossed and turned fitfully.

"Mitch? What is it? Is Gavin okay?" She begins pacing as she listens to the voice on the other end.

I pull on my jeans then toss Avery her clothes.

"Okay, we'll be there in ten." She hangs up the phone then tosses me my shirt while rushing to put her clothes on. I grab my keys and we're out the door in less than a minute.

On the way, Avery explains the phone call. Apparently, Gavin had a hard time falling asleep that night. The housekeeper said he finally fell asleep around eleven, so she left shortly after. But a couple hours later, he woke up crying for Avery. When Mitch went in to get him back to sleep, he became hysterical, crying and yelling for his mom. Mitch eventually gave up and called Avery.

My grip on the steering wheel tightens to the point I think I'll leave permanent indents in it. Poor Gavin must be so scared. He's never hysterical, not even during his worst tantrum. Avery is probably burying herself in unnecessary guilt.

"This is not your fault," I tell her but I can tell it barely registers. Her eyes are trained on the road, knee bouncing and ready to jump from the truck the second Mitch's house comes into view. Which she does, barely waiting for the truck to stop before throwing open the door and rushing up the steps to the house.

I follow behind her, once again shaking my head at the pretentious house that I can in no way imagine Avery and Gavin living in. The front door swings open just as Avery reaches it and Gavin flies into her arms. He sobs into her chest, his shoulders shaking with the force of his cries.

"Shh, baby, it's okay. I'm here now. I'm here," she whispers to him.

The scene is too similar to the night of his accident and it makes me want to smash my fist into Mitch's upturned nose. The fact that your son is as equally upset spending a night alone in your house with you as he was the night he almost drowned is beyond inexcusable. Instead, I pull them into my arms. I watch as Mitch's face falls into something that looks suspiciously like regret.

Good. Maybe this will be his wake up call. If not, I'll happily make the call myself. But he won't like what I have to say.

Gavin finally settles enough for Avery to carry him back to the truck. She buckles him into his car seat and climbs into the seat beside him. I shut the door behind them, then against my better judgment, I look back at Mitch. His face is blank, staring through the window where Gavin is sitting. I barely hold back the sneer on my face, before sliding into my truck and driving away.

Back in the hotel room, Avery tucks Gavin into bed with her while I take the spare bed beside them. I watch as Avery strokes the hair from Gavin's now sleeping eyes. She dips her head to kiss his forehead then snuggles in behind him, both of them finally at peace.

I'm not sure what tomorrow will bring because of this but I know one thing for sure. I'll do anything to protect that peace.

And hurt anyone who tries to disrupt it.

AVERY

The next morning, I wake to the smell of bacon and coffee. Rolling over, I see Gavin and Matt sitting at the small patio table on the balcony. Matt's cutting up a pancake on Gavin's plate while Gavin munches away on a bacon strip, dancing in his seat.

It always surprises me how quickly kids bounce back.

For a second, I simply lie there, watching the two of them together. I've said it before and I'll say it again: I could never regret my time with Mitch because it brought me Gavin. But if Gavin has to have a dad like Mitch, I'm also glad he has a man like Matt to show him how a dad should be.

I wouldn't dare say that to Matt though. Not yet anyway. I wouldn't want to scare him away. But as I watch Gavin say something that makes Matt laugh, I can't help but think that it might not scare him at all.

My phone buzzes and I reach for it.

MITCH

Can we talk? In person?

I hesitate, trying to get a read on his tone but I can't. As much as I don't want to have a repeat of the previous night, I know I can't avoid him. He's the father of my child; he'll be in our lives forever, whether I want him to be or not.

AVERY

The park over on Lowen in an hour.

MITCH

Ok.

I go to put my phone down when it vibrates again.

Thanks.

Thanks? That's very... unMitch of him. Now my curiosity is piqued. I finally roll out of bed and slide open the balcony door.

"Mommy!" Gavin runs over to me and gives me a big hug that lasts a little longer than usual. I figure we both need the extra love this morning. "Look! We got breakfast." He points over to the big paper bag with the logo of the cafe around the corner on it.

Gavin and Matt's plates look like they've already been filled then emptied. All that's left are scraps of toast crusts and ketchup. Matt pulls out a third plate and sets it in front of the chair before me. Then he pulls out a container from the bag and places it beside my plate. I'm not sure what it is but it smells amazing. I lower myself into my chair like a dog following its nose.

Gavin and Matt continue their conversation from before I arrived while I scarf down the B.L.T sandwich—my favorite.

Eventually, Gavin goes back into the room to grab a comic book and I take the opportunity to show Matt the texts from Mitch. He looks as perplexed as I feel.

"Maybe last night made him realize he needs to rework his priorities," Matt offers.

"Or maybe he's going to lay into me about taking Gavin back with me last night," I counter.

Or worse. He could use this against me as a reason to take me back to court.

Or maybe he really does just want to talk.

God, I'm so over this emotional roller coaster I've been riding since yesterday. I wish I was back in Haven Bay, sitting on the beach watching Gavin and Matt splash around in the waves while Ham chases a stick into the water.

Matt pulls his chair over to mine then pulls me into his chest so my head rests on his shoulder. "Do you want me with you when you talk to him?" he asks softly.

As much as I want to say yes, I think this is something I need to do on my own. I shake my head. "I'm good."

He kisses my temple. "Yeah, I know you are. But I'll be close by if you change your mind." I nod. I've lost count of the number of times over the past 24 hours I've been thankful for Matt's presence. "We should get going." I nod again, then stand to get Gavin.

Let's get this over with.

THE PLAYGROUND IS PREDICTABLY busy for the last Friday morning before summer vacation ends. All the parents and caregivers are taking advantage of the last little bit of free time with their kids before it's back to the reality of schedules and classrooms.

Somehow, we find a free bench not far from the playground. I finish slathering sunscreen on Gavin when Mitch comes walking up. Matt looks over at me and gives my hand a reassuring squeeze then turns to Gavin.

"Hey Gav, wanna race to the monkey bars?" Gavin nods eagerly then takes off toward the playground with Matt right behind him.

Mitch watches the two of them run off together for a second before turning back to me. "He seems better today," he comments.

"He is," I agree. "What's going on, Mitch? If you're upset that I took him with me last night, you told me to come get him—"

"I'm not," he cuts in.

I snap my mouth closed, waiting for him to explain.

He looks back at the playground. "What's the deal with you and Brady?" For once, there's no malice in his voice, only genuine curiosity.

I'm a little suspicious of the subject change but I decide to answer truthfully. "We're dating."

He's still watching the playground when he asks, "Is it serious?"

I follow his gaze to see Matt holding Gavin by the waist to help him swing himself along the monkey bars and I smile. "Yeah. It is."

Mitch sighs then looks back at me. "So, it's really over then." He says it like a statement but I answer him anyway.

"Yeah. It is," I repeat.

There's a long pause while we sit watching Matt and Gavin play together at the park. They look good together. Like father and son. Or what a father and son should look like together.

"Why are you here, Mitch?" I finally ask.

He sighs again. "My dad wasn't around much when I was a kid. He was always working or entertaining clients at some dinner party or work event. When he was home, he was this looming, daunting figurehead that left my whole family on edge. Nothing was ever good enough for him—our grades, our clothing, our choice of friends. My sister had it a little easier because to him, a woman's job was to marry well then maintain the family home so her husband could be successful. It's what his dad had done so it's what he did. And I guess what I did."

In all the time I've been with Mitch, he rarely talked about his dad in any way other than what could've been dubbed as hero worship. As far as I knew, Mitch has been the apple of his dad's eye from the second he opened his eyes in the hospital room.

Apparently you can be with someone for over a decade and still barely know them.

He looks down at his hands. "I told myself I wasn't going to be like that when I got older. I wouldn't be that kind of husband or father. But once I was in high school, my dad made it known that I'd be working with him after college. From then on, he started paying attention to me and showing me off to his business partners as 'the next CEO of Olsen Financial'. Life was good when he had his spotlight on me."

He looks over at Gavin. "When you got pregnant, I was scared. I didn't know how to be a dad and I was so busy trying to make my own dad proud of me, I didn't have time to learn." He shakes his head. "No, that's not right. I didn't make the time. By the time Gavin was old enough to notice I wasn't around, you two already had this impenetrable bond. Any time I tried to help, you told me it was wrong and it pissed me off."

Though I'm seeing a vulnerable side of Mitch he never let me see before, his words still make me angry. I try to keep my voice calm but it's like chewing nails.

"I didn't say it to piss you off, Mitch. It wasn't like I was criticizing the way you dressed him. I know everyone has their own way of doing things. But when you're putting him in the wrong size diapers or you're trying to feed him foods he can't eat yet, I'm going to correct you. When you have a kid, you have to put your ego aside and realize you're not going to know everything without trying. You have to put the work in because it's not just about you anymore. It's about them."

Mitch's face falls.

I soften my voice. "I'm sorry about your dad. I get it; you didn't have the best role model. But that should've shown you what not to do. Instead you turned into him."

His mouth twists but, surprisingly, he doesn't argue. I think it still surprises him when I stand up to him. It's not something he's used to but I can guarantee it's not going to end any time soon.

"What do you want, Mitch?"

He looks over at Gavin for a minute before hanging his head. "A second chance." I open my mouth to protest but he cuts me off. "With Gavin. I want a second chance with Gavin."

I'm shocked. As much as I wanted that to be why he asked to meet me, I didn't expect it to actually be true.

"When I saw him at the bookstore and he hid from me, it pissed me off. I assumed that you turned him against me, talking shit about me and telling him lies. Then when I saw him with Brady, I got jealous because my own kid liked some other guy better than me. I convinced myself that was your fault, too." He looks up and I can see the sadness in his eyes. "But then last night, I didn't even know what foods he liked. I didn't know he had a favorite toy. I didn't know what time he went to bed. I couldn't even comfort him when he got scared."

I try to feel bad for him but... "Mitch, those are all things you learn by spending time with him. It's not like he was born and I knew all the answers. I had to learn just like you do."

"I didn't have time—"

"You make time," I snap. "If he's important to you, you make time."

He's stunned silent. Instead of answering, he turns back to watch Gavin giggling as he and a little girl about his age bounce up and down on the teeter-totter.

"I called my lawyer this morning and told him I want to revise my custody agreement to day visits only for now. I think Gavin and I need to figure each other out first before we try anything overnight again." He looks back at me. "I'll come to you so you don't have to drive back and forth."

Now it's my turn to be stunned. "Oh. Okay. Well, thanks."

If I could've guessed how today was going to go, this would not have even made the top 100 list.

He stands. "I think I'm going to go. Do you think it'd be okay if I came to visit him soon? Maybe we could find a park to go to." He nods his head in the direction of Matt pushing Gavin on the swings. "That doesn't seem so hard."

"Sure. We've got a great park in Haven Bay that Gavin loves." I pause then decide to throw him a bone. "Why don't you try again Sunday morning? That's when we usually ride bikes to the playground."

"I can't. I have a—" He stops himself then shakes his head. "Never mind. I'll make it work. Sunday it is. Can you text me the address?" I nod and he gives a curt nod back. "I guess I'll go say bye then."

"Mitch," I call after him and he stops. "He's just a kid. All he wants is your attention. Play with him, do things he likes. Don't criticize or belittle him. He'll come around quicker than you think." I drop my voice solemnly. "But make no mistake, if you mess up this second chance, you won't get a third."

He tips his head in understanding then walks over to

Gavin to say goodbye. It's awkward and tense but I don't expect any different. Mitch has a long way to go toward making amends with him but, for Gavin's sake, I hope they can make it work.

But I'll be watching Mitch like a hawk. I won't let him hurt Gavin again. I don't care what the court says.

I watch Mitch leave as I dial Margot's number. When she answers, I fill her in on our conversation. She promises to confirm with Mitch's lawyer that he was telling the truth about the visits and get back to me before Sunday. It's going to take a lot to build my trust back up when it comes to Mitch. For now, this will have to be enough.

I slide my phone back into my pocket then jog over to Matt and Gavin on the playground. I rush toward Gavin, giving him a high push on the swing that makes him giggle and kick his feet excitedly.

"Everything okay?" Matt asks quietly.

I nod. "I'm hoping it will be."

Four days later, I adjust the straps on Gavin's backpack outside of his classroom door. We're on the playground, waiting with the rest of the crowd for school to start. Gavin has already recognized a handful of kids from his summer camp and is itching to get inside. I'm sure that will change as the year goes on but for now, I'm relieved there are no tears in sight.

"Okay, one more picture with Gram," I prompt, gesturing for my mom to step back into the frame as I hold up my phone to take my 300th picture of the day.

"Mommmmy, the teacher's gonna call me soon. No more pictures." Gavin complains but he smiles. He's loving all of the attention.

"Better get used to it, buddy. You've got a lot more first days ahead of you and moms love to take pictures—of everything," Matt teases, slinging his arm around Gavin's shoulders after I finish taking his picture.

"And one day you'll be grateful we did, Matty," my mom jokes back.

"Do you mind if I get a quick one before you go in?" Mitch awkwardly asks. Gavin nods, still a little timid.

They step together and Mitch puts a stiff arm on Gavin's shoulder. Then, as if realizing his mistake, Mitch drops to one knee beside Gavin and circles an arm around his waist. Gavin looks surprised but gives a genuine smile to the camera.

"Thanks." Mitch's tone is still reserved but when I show him the picture, he gives a small smile.

Their relationship is still new, but Mitch actually showed up on Sunday when he said he would, which was a shock in itself. He stayed for a few hours and I hardly recognized him in his shorts and t-shirt (designer, of course). He got down on his knees and played in the sand, then pushed Gavin on the swings. He even took us for ice cream after, as if he wanted to prolong their time together.

I was impressed but it will take a lot more than a few hours of attention before I believe he's serious.

Gavin's teacher blows a whistle to signal that it's time to go in and the kids start to line up beside the door. Luckily, the kindergarteners start a little later on the first day so that the crowds of children from the other grades don't overwhelm them.

Gavin takes turns hugging everyone. When he gets to me, I hug him extra tight. "Have the best day, Gav. I'm so proud of you." I kiss his cheek and squeeze him again. "Love you, bud."

"Love you, Mommy," he says, squeezing me back. Then he hustles over to the line, his backpack bouncing against his little legs as he runs. Just before he disappears into the door, he turns back and waves his whole arm at us. I laugh, waving back wildly.

Once he's inside, the four of us walk over to the parking lot. Mitch excuses himself to head back to the city but not before promising to be back on Saturday morning to see Gavin. He pauses. "Would it be okay if I called him tonight to see how his day was?"

"Of course," I tell him.

He nods quickly then walks to his car and drives away.

"Well, that was surprising," my mom says, watching him drive off. She's never been a big fan of Mitch, for obvious reasons. She's reserving judgment on this new attitude change. But, like the rest of us, she's willing to give him a chance for Gavin's sake.

"You're telling me," I agree.

"I think I'm going to pop in at the shop on my way home. Need anything?" she asks me.

I took the day off of work for Gavin's first day so I could drop him off and pick him up after school. I know I won't be able to pick him up every day when I'm working at the shop, but I wanted to be there after his first day so he could tell me all about it.

I shake my head. "I'm good. Thanks."

She waves as she walks away and I wave back. Matt comes up behind me, wrapping his arms around my shoulders. I lean into his chest and he kisses my temple. "I have a surprise for you," he whispers in my ear and I laugh.

"I don't think a school is the proper place for your kind of surprises," I tease.

He pokes me in the ribs with a finger. "That's not what I meant, smartass." I laugh harder. "Let's go."

He takes my hand and we walk down the sidewalk but instead of stopping at Matt's apartment like I expected, we continue past the workshop and down the hill. We stop in front of Bayside Art Gallery. It's too early for it to be open so I give him a quizzical look.

He surprises me by pulling out a key from inside his pocket and slipping it into the keyhole. The door knob turns easily and he gestures for me to step inside. It's pitch black and I have no idea where I'm going.

"Is this where you murder me and chop me up into a million pieces? Because I have to say, my son's first day of school is a pretty cruel time to do that," I joke but then gasp when the lights flick on overhead.

The gallery is one of Haven Bay's most beloved buildings in the town. It's also one of the oldest. Back in the early 1900's, it was built as the town doctor's house where he would see patients in the front and lived in the back. It was restored back in 1988 and turned into an art gallery. Many of the original wood beams and moldings are still intact.

But that's not what has me gasping. Inside, carefully and artistically displayed are all of Matt's pieces. There's furniture, sculptures, mosaics, bowls—all lovingly and thoughtfully brought to life by Matt's two hands.

"Krista wants to trial my work with an exhibition. She thinks they'll sell well, but she wants to make sure there's enough interest before making it a permanent thing. She said if it does well enough, I'll be able to start selling exclusively with the gallery if I want to." He stares in wonder at the display, as if he still can't believe it's real.

I pull him to me, lifting onto my toes to brush a kiss across his lips. "I am so fucking proud of you, Matt Brady. This is absolutely amazing." He smiles against my lips. "And you're going to sell the shit out of all of your pieces so fast, they'll be begging you for more."

His smile fades as he stares into my eyes and the love I see reflecting back in them wraps me up like a cozy blanket on a rainy day. It's safe, it's warm and I want to live in it forever.

He lowers his head to kiss me again and this time, it's slow and deliberate. Each brush of his tongue has me arching into him, begging for more. As I'm about to find the closest hard surface for him to take me against, Matt pulls back. He's breathing hard as he looks down at me, his eyes almost black with arousal.

He dips his head and his lips graze along the shell of my ear."As much as I want to strip you down and fuck you right here until you're screaming my name and dripping with my cum, I don't think the gallery would take kindly to one of their artists' giving the security guard a private show."

He tips his head to the security camera tucked into the corner of the wall behind us. Heat rushes to my cheeks. I got so carried away, I didn't even notice it.

"You have five minutes to get your sweet ass back to my apartment while I pull myself together and lock up. If I don't find you naked and waiting in my bed, your ass will be red for a week, Freckles."

And with that, he gives my ass a firm slap and points me toward the door.

He doesn't have to ask me twice. My heart leaps with excitement as I close the door behind me and hurry down the street. There's a thrill in seeing your neighbors going about their day, waving and smiling while you rush past them, knowing you're about to get fucked senseless.

I make it back to Matt's apartment with thirty seconds to spare, just long enough for me to race to his room, leaving a trail of my clothes behind me. I consider leaving my panties on to see what he would do but decide against it. I'm way too turned on to play games right now.

Other than the one he's got in mind.

I climb into his bed, unsure if I should pose or lay back against the pillows when I hear the sound of his front door slamming and the lock clicking into place. The loud thunder of his strides causes my belly to clench in anticipation as he stalks into the room. He stops in the doorframe, eyeing me like he's a starving man and I'm his first meal.

My breath comes in shaky pants as I watch him survey my naked body. Suddenly feeling daring, I tilt my hips and drop my legs to either side, spreading myself wide for him. He groans his approval before storming over to me, his long legs eating the distance in two strides. He stops just before me, still fully clothed.

"Touch yourself," he commands, voice low and dangerous.

My eyes never leave his as I slowly trail one hand down my stomach, stopping at the top of my slit. His eyes follow the movement and I watch him swallow hard as I dip my fingers lower, lower until I plunge one finger inside. His low groan makes my heart jump as my blood hums. I no longer feel shy, reveling in his reaction to me.

I feel powerful.

Wanted.

Needed.

I add a second finger and watch as the hands at his sides turn to fists. But still, he makes no move to touch me.

"That feel good, Freckles?" he asks huskily. He loves watching me play with myself and I love seeing his reaction while he does.

I nod, my hooded eyes never leaving his as I plunge deeper inside myself but my fingers are too short for the pressure I desperately need to feel.

"Matt," I moan and he growls in response.

"Yeah, baby?"

"I need to feel you. I need you inside me."

I need him more than my next breath. I'm desperate to feel him and I'm about to beg when, the next thing I know, he's stripping and tossing his clothes then diving onto the bed between my legs.

But it's not his dick he buries inside me a second later but a long, rough finger. My disappointment quickly dissipates as he curves his finger upward, hitting that magic spot that causes me to gasp and writhe beneath him.

He adds another and I moan. "That's it, baby. Ride my

fingers. Show me how bad you want this cock." He picks up speed, thrusting into me harder.

My body arches and I can feel myself getting closer. Deeper, faster he plunges inside me, taking me higher and higher. More. I need more.

"Yes, Matt. More. Please. Oh God, I'm so close."

Then his thumb presses against my clit and it's like a thousand little fires spring to life, lighting me up from the inside. My body goes off like a firecracker—bright, sudden and all-consuming.

It takes a few moments before I come down from my orgasm, my eyes still closed in ecstasy.

"You're so fucking beautiful."

I open my eyes to see Matt watching me in awe. His voice is tender, a sharp contrast between the way he ripped my orgasm from me mere seconds ago. He dips his head to give me an unhurried, consuming kiss. His erection presses firmly against my hip, insistent and eager but he ignores it, taking his time with me.

I kiss him back, holding him against me until every inch of us is pressed together. He feels so good, so safe and so...Matt.

"I love you."

He groans against my lips. "God, Avery, I fucking love you. I love every part of you from your freckles to your toes. I've loved you my entire life and I want to love you every day for the rest of it." He pours himself into the kiss, stealing away any response from me.

He leans back slightly. "Don't worry, I'm not proposing. Even I know it's too soon for that. I just want you to know where my head's at. You're it for me. You're mine and I'm yours. You've always been my girl, even when you didn't know it. Then, now and always."

I can hardly breathe past the emotions swirling around

inside me. He's right, it's too soon. But I can't help but wonder what my answer would be if it was a proposal.

Luckily, Matt saves me from any further thought as he thrusts into me, rocking his hips into mine. It steals my breath as he fills me so wholly and completely. Again and again, he rocks his hips, causing the sweetest pressure against my clit.

Thrust, rock, thrust, rock. The addicting rhythm he sets has me throwing my head back as I hold on for the ride. This time feels different than any other and I know he feels it, too. It's powerful and intense. Every nerve is alive, all seeming to be working towards the same goal.

"Oh, God. Please, yes. Don't stop."

Soon, I'm reduced to a mumbling mess of incoherent sounds and moans while Matt doubles down, lifting my hips to get a better angle.

"God, you feel like heaven. I want you to come all over my cock, baby. Come for me," he groans.

My orgasm catches me off guard as it erupts inside me. This isn't some slow build ending with a smooth slide into ecstasy. This is a shove over the edge, a free fall into the abyss, letting the pleasure swallow me whole.

Throwing my head back as it overtakes me, Matt's breath grows choppy as he grips my hips almost punishingly hard, chasing his own release. He groans, cursing as he spills himself inside me, lost in his own pleasure.

He collapses onto the bed beside me and we lay there, his leg thrown over mine with my arm draped over his chest. We slowly claw our way back to the surface, breathing heavy and limbs limp, our hearts beating wildly. When our breathing finally evens out, I turn to look up at him. He smiles down at me, that adorable lopsided smile I love so much.

Then it hits me.

I almost went my entire life without ever knowing this

kind of love. This selfless, honest kind of love. The kind of love that is as easy as breathing.

That's not to say we won't have to work at it. But it's the kind of love that makes that work worth it.

It's the kind of love that makes all the pain, hurt and uncertainty of the past worth it so you can feel the love you deserve. It feels like safety. Like unwavering support and belonging.

It feels like coming home.

"I swear to God, if I open my eyes and your dick is in my face..." I threaten.

Matt lets out a deep, belly laugh that causes my lips to twitch. He has my eyes covered with a bandana so I'm clutching his arm as he guides me further into the workshop.

"Jesus, Freckles. How can you be so perfect for me?" He guides me another few steps. "A little bit farther and then you can open your eyes."

Since Matt's first exhibition, the response to his work has been astounding. He's been working hard to keep up with the growing interest and his work has been selling almost as fast as he can create it.

Last November, Matt officially signed a consignment agreement with Bayside Art Gallery. That same month, my divorce was finalized. Matt surprised me with a weekend trip to Pete's cabin to celebrate our new lives together.

It's been amazing watching Matt's dreams come true. I couldn't be more proud of him. He's accomplished so much in such a short amount of time, all because he finally let his true self show.

The best part is, I get an up close view to his entire process —from finding the wood to sketching the design to the frustrations of creating and finally, the big reveal of the finished piece. Sometimes, like now, he has a piece he's especially excited about that he doesn't let me see until it's finished.

Those are my favorite because I get to watch his eyes light up and his excitement bleed through as he explains every thought process, every detail while I inspect it for the first time.

This is the first time he's blindfolded me though, so I'm guessing this is a big piece that he can't easily move to hide from me.

He stops me, angling my body then readjusting again until he's satisfied with my stance. I bite back a smile at his obvious nerves. He's been distracted all week, forgetting his phone in odd places and staring into space for long periods of time. This design must be important; I haven't seen him like this since the early days after his exhibition.

"Okay. You can take the blindfold off."

I reach behind my head and untie the bandana, letting it fall into my hands. I blink a few times to adjust my eyes to the low lighting then gasp loudly.

String lights are draped over the wood beams above us and daisies are scattered all over the floor around my feet. Candles of varying sizes and colors are strategically placed on the floor, workbench and window sills. They flicker as a soft melody starts to play through the overhead speakers. I recognize it as the Chris Stapleton song Matt and I danced to that first night at The Dive.

My heart jumps as I realize what's about to happen.

My hands start to shake. I press them together against my lips to try to keep my composure as Matt steps closer. His hands slide down my arms until he holds both of mine in his.

He lets out a shaky breath and it nearly takes mine away knowing he's as nervous as I am.

"Avery, you've been my best friend for as long as I can remember. There's not a single memory I have from when I was a kid that doesn't have you in it. Whether you were getting me into trouble," he arches a brow at me and I let out a watery laugh, "or helping me dig my way out of it, we had the best childhood. Because we had each other." He rubs a thumb over my knuckles, as if needing the touch to gather his courage. "You were there during the best and worst moments of my life. When my dad passed away, I thought I'd never be truly happy again." He looks down at our entwined hands.

"My parents were best friends. They fought, loved and lived for each other. I don't think I realized it, but they were the bar I measured all of my relationships against." He lifts his eyes to mine, a sad smile on his lips. "I'm so fucking glad he met you. He loved you like you were his own daughter." He chuckles. "He knew I loved you before I did. He would've been rubbing our relationship in my face if he was still here."

My eyes start to water at the mention of Jack. He was the dad I never had and I loved him more than I can describe. I miss him. I wish he could see how Matt turned out. I know he'd be puffing his chest with pride knowing everything he's accomplished.

Matt clears his throat and continues. "Before you came back into my life, I thought I was happy. I had my job, my family and my goofy dog. What else could I want?" He smiles up at me. "But then I opened the bookshop door to find your pretty smile and adorable freckles and knew the truth—I wasn't happy. All that time, I'd been waiting. Waiting for you. Waiting for Gavin."

The tears are rolling down my face now but I've never felt so happy. My heart feels like it's ready to burst and all I can do is stare into the eyes of the man I love. I don't want to breathe, I don't want to blink and risk missing a single second of this moment.

"You made me work for it," he quips and I smile, "but I'm so glad you did. You deserve everything, Freckles. You deserve the world. In fact, you should demand it." His eyes search mine. "You are so fucking strong, Avery. You're the strongest person I know. You tore down the life you had and built up one worthy of you. And I'm so proud that I'm the man you chose to let into that life."

He swipes a tear away with his thumb. "Avery, you showed me how brave it is to be vulnerable. You showed me that love isn't conditional and I don't have to earn love from those who matter most. You're the first person to love me for all of me. I don't think you'll ever know how much that means to me."

He drops my hand to reach behind him and pull something from his back pocket. He lifts his hands, keeping what's inside covered. "You and Gavin are the best things in my life. My world starts and ends with you two." He lifts his right hand and in the palm of his hand is a small wood box. There's a quote engraved on the top of the lid.

It's always been you.

I've never felt a feeling as strong, as overwhelming, as bone-deep, as the elation I feel at this moment. Then, as if he's determined to prove me wrong, he opens the lid to reveal a stunning, vintage solitaire ring. The oval diamond glistens in the glowing lights in the dim room.

"It's my mother's ring." Matt's husky voice is thick with emotion. My hand shoots to my lips to stifle my gasp. "It was always meant to be yours. She agrees." He picks the ring out of its place in the box, holding my left hand to his chest. "You've had me wrapped around your finger since we were kids. You've owned my heart in a way no one else has. It's always been you. You're mine and I'll always be yours." He lifts the ring so I can see the inside, where it's been engraved. "Then, now and always." I read the line as he repeats it.

He slowly lowers to one knee, taking my hand with him. The ring he holds in his other hand shakes and we both laugh. "Gavin and I practiced this part so many times, you'd think I'd be a pro by now. I guess the nerves don't help my grip."

I grab his hand with my free one. "Matt—"

He squeezes my hand and I stop. "Freckles, let me do this. The right way." Gazing up into my eyes, I see all of the love I feel reflected back in his. "Avery, will you do me the honor of making me your husband? Make us a family—you, me and Gavin. Be my best friend. Be my light. Be mine." He smiles up at me with that lop-sided grin I love. "Then, now and always."

He barely finishes his sentence before I'm screaming out a "yes!" and throwing myself into his arms. Laughing, Matt somehow manages to hold onto the ring and when I lean back, he slips it onto my finger. Raising it to his lips, he presses the sweetest kiss over it.

"I love you so damn much, Freckles."

I drag his mouth to mine, putting all of myself into the kiss. A long moment later, he pulls back and rests his forehead against mine. A calm washes over my whole body. It leaves me feeling light as if I could float away at any moment.

"I love you, Matt. You're right; I'm yours and you're mine. You've filled a space in my heart I didn't think would ever be whole. I'm so grateful for everything before this because it brought me back to you." I lean in to brush another kiss against his lips.

"It brought me home."

EVENTUALLY, we pull away from each other long enough to go pick Gavin up from my mom's house. Strapping him into the truck, we make our way into town for Matt's baseball game.

We decided to keep the engagement just between us for a little longer. With the way news travels in this town, our whole wedding would be planned by Dottie and Maeve before the third inning.

Knowing how loose a five-year-old's lips can be, we figured it was best to tell Gavin after Matt's baseball game tonight. Matt didn't want him to spill the beans early, so he didn't tell Gavin when he was proposing, only that he was.

Until then, the ring is tucked away safely back in Matt's apartment.

After making a quick stop at the gas station for snacks, Matt swings the truck into a parking space beside the diamonds. Gavin hops out, running to where Luke and Franny are standing by the dugout. I round the truck to find Matt waiting for me. He holds out his hand and I accept it. We walk hand-in-hand toward where the rest of the team is warming up.

"What do you think about a spring wedding?" Matt says, his thumb running over my knuckles. "Seems like a good omen; spring being the season of new beginnings and all that." He smiles down at me, his warm eyes bright and hopeful. I can't keep the smile from spreading across my face.

"Spring sounds perfect."

Sometimes, I still can't believe this is my life. Two years ago, I was in a toxic relationship that felt more like a prison than a marriage. No one should be treated like they're inferior —especially not by the one person who's meant to treat them best.

It's taken a while, but I've forgiven Mitch. He's been working hard to change and be there for Gavin in all the ways he should've been before. Gavin went for his first overnight visit a month ago and, according to him, they had a blast together. He said Mitch even cooked them dinner that night —macaroni and hotdogs. Mitch's talking about moving closer to Haven Bay so that he can be around more often.

Last summer, if you told me Mitch would willingly move back to this area, I would've thought you were crazier than this town.

But it seems everything is working out the way it was meant to.

I have an amazing son who is blowing his teachers away with how smart and kind he is. He's made a ton of friends and is coming further and further out of his shell every day.

I have my mom who is healthy and thriving in the early stages of her retirement. There are still some papers to sign before we can transfer the store over to me, but she's stepped back from the business already and is enjoying life. She even went out on a date last weekend. She wouldn't tell me much about him but they're going out again tomorrow night so I'm assuming it went well.

Then there's Matt.

My best friend for as long as I can remember. The boy that starred in every single memory from my childhood is now the man I'll spend the rest of my life making new ones with. He's stepped into our family like he was made for it–which I'm starting to wonder if he was. Gavin adores him. My mom already treated him like a son, she'll be ecstatic when it's official. Even Sushi is smitten. And soon, I'll be walking down the aisle toward him and our life together.

Did I mention I couldn't be happier?

Matt's steps slow as we get to the dugout. Is it just me or is everyone looking at me funny? I'm about to turn to ask Matt if he knows what's going on when I notice the scoreboard in the outfield light up.

Big orange letters appear on the old screen, the words "WILL YOU MARRY ME, AVERY?" scrolling across. I turn to a grinning Matt beside me, my brow furrowed in confusion. He leans toward me and whispers "just go with it" in my ear before dropping to one knee in the grass beside me.

"Avery Owens, I've loved you since before I knew what love was. You and Gavin are my entire life. I love our little family and I want nothing more than to grow that family with you. I want to love you today and every day after." He pulls the wooden box that was supposed to be hidden in his apartment from his pocket. "Will you marry me?"

For the second time tonight, my eyes tear up and I let out a shaky "yes" before cheers and applause erupt from around us. Matt stands, slipping the ring on my left hand before pulling me to him. I lean over to whisper in his ear. "Want to tell me what that was?" I laugh. "Didn't you already propose to me once tonight?"

"The first one was for us," he answers, smiling softly. "That one was for him." He tilts his head toward Gavin, who's jumping eagerly up and down with our moms. "This was his idea. He told me his mom deserved the best proposal ever."

Damn it. Here comes the waterworks again.

Gavin gives Luke a high-five before running over to us, wrapping his arms around our legs. "Mommy! Were you surprised? The whole town is here! Even my teacher's here!" He stops. "Why're you crying, Mommy? What's wrong?"

I bend to scoop him up, ignoring the strain that comes from lifting his growing body to mine. "Nothing at all, buddy. I'm just so happy, I can't keep it all inside."

He instantly wraps one arm around my neck and the other around Matt's, squeezing hard.

The cheers start up again and I laugh, looking out into the crowd. Some people are holding up handwritten signs, with sayings like "She said yes!" and "Shit just got real!" scrawled on them. The Avery from a year ago would've been embarrassed by the attention but I can't help but laugh.

This frickin' town.

Matt's right; the proposal from earlier was perfect and just for us. But this proposal is every bit as special because I get to share it with the people I love most. Looking out at all of the faces on the field, I know one thing for sure.

I'm home.

ACKNOWLEDGMENTS

First, I want to give a big THANK YOU to you for taking a chance on this indie author's debut novel. I hope you loved Avery, Matt and the rest of the Haven Bay crew as much as I do!

Next, I want to thank my husband for encouraging me to pursue this lifelong dream of mine. It means the world to me that you believe in me and I am forever grateful for your support.

To Danika, words cannot describe how much your friendship means to me. I wouldn't have written a word of this book if it wasn't for you. You've talked me off the ledge more times than I can count and kept me from spiralling (or tried to) when I was ready to scrap the whole thing. This story is as much yours as it is mine and I can't thank you enough for all you've done to make this book what it is today. There are no other words than simply: thank you, thank you, thank you.

Finally, to StorySpark, I appreciate everything you've done to make this book great. Thank you for putting up with my endless questions and long (sometimes ridiculously so) meetings because I just couldn't make a decision. I'm grateful to have you all on my team.

www.ingramcontent.com/pod-product-compliance
Lightning Source LLC
Chambersburg PA
CBHW030924120726

47906CB00002B/473